# Maralinga

## Judy Nunn

pic

PIATKUS

First published in Australia and New Zealand in 2009
by Random House Australia Pty Ltd
First published in Great Britain as a paperback original in 2011 by Piatkus

A CIP catalogue record for this book
is available from the British Library.

ISBN 978-0-7499-5495-6

Typeset in Caslon by M Rules
Printed and bound in Great Britain by
Clays Ltd, St Ives plc

Papers used by Piatkus are natural, renewable and
recyclable products sourced from well-managed forests and certified
in accordance with the rules of the Forest Stewardship Council.

**Mixed Sources**
Product group from well-managed
forests and other controlled sources
www.fsc.org  Cert no. SGS-COC-004081
© 1996 Forest Stewardship Council

Piatkus
An imprint of
Little, Brown Book Group
100 Victoria Embankment
London EC4Y 0DY

An Hachette UK Company
www.hachette.co.uk

www.piatkus.co.uk

*To Justine*

# Author's Note

The Indigenous names and regions used in this book are those used in the *Encyclopaedia of Aboriginal Australia* (D. Horton, general editor) published in 1984 by Aboriginal Studies Press for the Australian Institute of Aboriginal and Torres Strait Islander Studies.

I have made this choice for the purposes of uniformity. During the period in which this book is set, many of the words would have differed as Indigenous names have altered in their spelling and pronunciation over the years. The use of this relatively recent reference provides some form of consistency. For dramatic purposes, I have occasionally employed anglicised terminology when referring to smaller Indigenous groups such as 'kin' and 'clan'.

In researching the subject of Maralinga, I have encountered many contradictory reports in both the literature I've studied and the material I've accessed on the internet. While weaving the facts through my fictional story I have aimed for a general consensus of opinion, but there are so many variables I've come to the conclusion that no-one really knows the full truth, and probably never will.

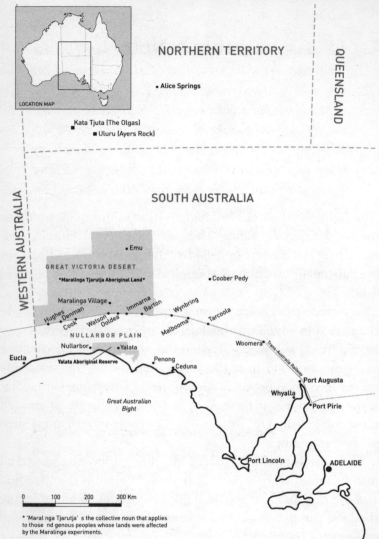

LOCATION MAP

NORTHERN TERRITORY

QUEENSLAND

• Alice Springs

Kata Tjuta (The Olgas)
■ Uluru (Ayers Rock)

WESTERN AUSTRALIA

SOUTH AUSTRALIA

• Emu

GREAT VICTORIA DESERT

•Maralinga Tjarutja Aboriginal Land•

• Coober Pedy

Maralinga Village •

Hughes    Denman    Immarna    Barton    Wynbring
    Cook    Watson  Ooldea                      Tarcoola
NULLARBOR PLAIN              Malbooma

Nullarbor •        • Yalata              Woomera •   Trans-Australia Railway

Eucla •          Yalata Aboriginal Reserve

                        Penong •
                        • Ceduna

Great Australian
Bight                                    Port Augusta

                                    Whyalla
                                        •Port Pirie

                        • Port Lincoln           ADELAIDE

0    100    200    300 Km

* 'Maral nga Tjarutja' s the collective noun that applies
to those nd genous peoples whose lands were affected
by the Maralinga experiments.

*His name is Amitu, and he is a Kokatha man from the southern desert of the Ancient Land. He stands alone, the sole of his right foot resting against his left knee, the spear in his right hand providing perfect balance. He is waiting. He has been waiting like this since dawn, but he feels no fatigue; he is a strong man. The father of two sturdy young boys, he is an excellent hunter and highly respected amongst his clan. But he is far from his clan now. They are many days' walk to the south.*

*In a dream, Amitu has been summoned by the Rainbow Serpent to the site of sacred boulders. He has been travelling northward for ten days, following one of the many Tjurkurpa tracks that lead to Kata Tjuta and Uluru, and he is now in Pitjantjatjara country, less than one day's walk from the mother rock of all people. Yet the spirits do not wish him to travel any farther. It is here, beside this waterhole, that he knows he must wait.*

*The day lacks even a scintilla of breeze. The land is an unruffled carpet of red, and the leaves of the desert willow droop motionless over the near-dry bed of the waterhole. The sun is high in the sky, the heat at its zenith and all is breathlessly still. No bird flies overhead, no insect stirs the dust, no animal rustles the nearby spinifex grass.*

*The land is waiting, Amitu thinks. The spirits are close. He can feel their presence, and he has slowed his breathing to a minimum, blanketing his mind of thought in order to receive them. He is in a trance-like state, but even so he cannot quell his sense of fear. What if the spirits are mamu? Deep in his heart, he believes that the Rainbow Serpent would not summon him to his destruction, for he has committed no wrong that would warrant the visitation of devil spirits upon him. But still the fear is there.*

*He can see them now, coming from the west across the rolling plains of sand, dark shadows dancing in the shimmering heat haze. Nearer they come. Nearer and nearer until his entire vision is filled with their dancing forms. They are chanting as they surround him, and their voices are the sound of the land itself, the echo of all things living. Like flickering tongues of fire they envelop his body, and the song they sing envelops his mind. Amitu is being consumed. But he is no longer afraid. He is joyful. These spirit beings are not mamu. These are good spirit beings who wish him well.*

> Ho! Amitu, you are patient
> Waiting silent with your songs
> We are of the Dreaming being
> Come to sing you a new song
> Dance before you, dance around you
> Hear us sing this dancing song
> Dance inside us, dance within us
> Amitu, learn this dancing song
>
> Amitu, learn this song of warning
> Teach your children this new song
> Ho! Amitu, teach Anangu
> Teach them all this fateful song.

*Amitu gives himself up to the spirit beings. He joins in their corroboree, dancing and singing until evening descends, and then on and on throughout the night. He repeats the song he is taught. It is the Song of the Seven Stars, the spirit beings tell him. He does not understand the song's meaning, but he does not question its import- ance. Over and over he sings the words, until he knows every single one by heart.*

*Throughout the whole of the next day Amitu dances and sings. Then, as the sun sets, he falls unconscious, and the spirit beings come to him in a dream. He sees them staring at his inert body where it lies in the dust, and he watches as they gather about him. One by one, they kneel at his side, and he listens as they complete their prophecy in song.*

*In Amitu's dream, the spirit beings foretell of a series of cataclysmic events that will befall the land and his people far in the future. It will be a time when men with white skin inhabit the world of the Kokatha, and that of the Pitjantjatjara, and of the Yankuntjatjara, and of many others who roam the Ancient Land.*

*Seven stars will be born, the spirit beings tell Amitu; seven births, and each birth will rival the others in fer- ocity. There will be a flash of light so powerful that any who look directly at it will lose their sight, and as each star rushes into the sky, a cloud of birth dust will follow, killing all those it touches.*

*The spirit beings foretell that the earth will become cursed, a barren place where no creatures will survive. For these stars, they say, are mamu. These newly born mamu will wield great power, and will bring about the death of many of Amitu's people. The unborn children of Amitu's people, too, will die, all victims of the birth dust. And the land itself will become mamu country.*

*Amitu awakes alone, and cries for his people. He reaches out his arms, pleading with the spirit beings to intercede with the Great Serpent and save his people. All is silent. He weeps, and the desert dust drinks his tears.*

*Then a breeze stirs the leaves of the willow. The spinifex grass rustles and, carried on the wind, he hears the voices of the spirit beings:*

*The song, Amitu. Teach your children the Song of the Seven Stars. You have learnt the words of this dancing song well. One who cannot be humbled and cannot be cursed will shake the dust from the land. A child of your people must sing this song, Amitu. Only then will the mamu release their hold.*

# BOOK I

# Chapter One

Elizabeth couldn't understand her father's passion for oleanders.

Alfred Hoffmann had shifted from London to the leafy county of Surrey, where all forms of glorious flowering shrubs thrived, and yet in the impressive conservatory at the rear of his house he'd chosen to grow nothing but oleanders. A veritable forest of them, in all shapes and sizes. Some remained gangly bushes while others towered to a height of eighteen feet, their leathery leaves sweeping the arched dome of the conservatory. Their pink and white blossoms were not unattractive, but the overall impression was one of unruliness. They were cumbersome plants, there was no denying it, and very much at odds with the surrounding countryside.

The entire situation was bewildering to Elizabeth. For as long as she could remember, her father had been a businessman, and a highly successful businessman at that. If, in his semi-retirement, he'd developed an interest in horticulture, which itself was surprising, why was he limiting himself to just one species? And why a species as mundane as the oleander, considered by some to be little more than a noxious weed – perhaps even poisonous, if she were to believe her colleague at *The Aldershot Courier-Mail*.

'Don't go chewing on the leaves, Elizabeth,' Walter had warned her during an afternoon tea-break, 'you'll end up as sick as a dog.' When she'd laughed, he'd assured her he wasn't joking.

'Why on earth did Daddy choose oleanders?' she finally asked her mother.

'I've no idea.' Marjorie Hoffmann had accepted her husband's idiosyncratic behaviour without question, as she always did. 'Perhaps it's his love of travel.' Noting her daughter's mystified expression, she drifted a typically vague hand through the air as if she were conducting a heavenly choir. 'I mean they're so . . . *Mediterranean*, aren't they?'

Mother and daughter were very alike in appearance. Above average height and regal of bearing, both had dark eyes and auburn hair offset by the fairest of complexions, creating an overall effect that was striking. They were the sort of women people referred to as handsome. In character, however, they could not have differed more greatly. Elizabeth was already wondering why she'd bothered asking her mother about the oleanders. She should have known better.

'They're all over the place in Europe,' Marjorie blithely continued, 'particularly in Italy and Greece. I'd rather he'd chosen olive trees myself – symbolism and beauty combined. I would have enjoyed painting olive trees.' Marjorie's skill with watercolours was considerable; her landscapes adorned the walls of many a boutique gallery in London. 'But there you are, that's Alfred.'

With an impatient shake of her head, Elizabeth gave up on her mother and made the enquiry directly of her father, whose response, although less vague than his wife's, was ultimately just as unfathomable.

'I admire the oleander,' he said after she'd cornered him in the conservatory where he sat with a glass of claret. 'So hardy. Such a passion for life. It's heat and drought resistant, you know, can survive anywhere.' He appeared most gratified by her interest. 'Versatile too. Is it a shrub or is it a tree?' Stroking his trim grey beard thoughtfully, he gazed up at the tallest of the plants. 'As you can see, Elizabeth, it can be either. All dependent upon the way it's pruned. Don't you find such adaptability marvellous?'

Elizabeth didn't, and she didn't see how her father could either. 'Somebody told me it's poisonous,' she said in her customary blunt fashion, 'but that's not true, surely.'

'Oh yes, quite true. The whole plant's highly toxic. Leaves, branches, bark – the sap in particular. Ingestion can produce gastrointestinal and cardiac effects, which, I believe, can be fatal – to children anyway, and most certainly to animals.'

'Ah, so *that's* it.'

All had suddenly become clear. Elizabeth's grin was triumphant. Her father's chain of pharmaceutical outlets, over which he still presided as chairman, made him first and foremost a businessman, but didn't alter the fact that he had started out a humble, and highly dedicated, chemist. It was only natural that such a man would be interested in the chemical properties of a potentially lethal plant.

'That's what?'

'The oleanders. You're making a study of their chemistry.'

'No, no.' Her father was dismissive. 'I doubt whether the toxic properties of the oleander could ever serve any medical or pharmaceutical purpose.' As he returned her smile, however, there was a gleam in his eye. 'But you're right, their poison does add to their fascination. It's yet another tool in their survival kit, you see. The oleander poisons those who might harm it –

extraordinarily tenacious, wouldn't you agree?' His question appeared rhetorical. 'But then tenacity is the key to survival,' he said. 'I think I'll have another glass of claret.' It was plain he considered he'd answered her question in full. 'Will you join me, Elizabeth?'

She shook her head. 'No, thanks, Daddy.' And, left alone with the oleanders, she heaved a sigh, none the wiser.

Elizabeth Hoffmann was an eminently practical young woman. At times she despaired of her parents' eccentricity, but she loved them for it too, knowing it was their eccentricity that had afforded her the life opportunities she so valued. For Alfred and Marjorie Hoffmann, eschewing the conventional attitudes of the day and firmly believing in equal rights for women, had offered their daughter every educational advantage and encouraged her in the pursuit of the career she so obviously yearned for. Now, at the age of twenty-three, when most of her contemporaries from Ralston Girls School were settling down to have babies, Elizabeth, having graduated with a BA from St Hugh's College, Oxford, majoring in History and Literature, had been working as a journalist with *The Aldershot Courier-Mail* for a whole eighteen months.

'We're very proud of you, Elizabeth,' her father had said when she'd been offered the position fresh out of Oxford.

'*The Courier-Mail*'s just the start, Daddy,' she'd answered. 'I'll give it two years in Aldershot, then I'll be back here in London working for *The Times*. I intend to be their first female feature writer.'

'Of course you do, my dear.'

A year later, when her parents had shifted from their grand townhouse in Belgravia to the rambling cottage in Surrey, Elizabeth had been deeply concerned. The property her father had bought was barely five miles from the township of Aldershot in nearby Hampshire, where she lived in a humble boarding house several blocks from the offices of *The Courier-Mail*. She'd been appalled at the thought that her mother and father might have made such a drastic change to their lifestyle simply in order to be near her.

'Good heavens above, no,' Marjorie had replied when her daughter tentatively raised the question. 'What would be the point? You'll be back in London soon with *The Times*, won't you? Two years, you said. No, no, I'm in need of rural surrounds – I've run out of trees in London.' She'd laughed distractedly. 'I must have painted every single tree and every single bush in every park in Westminster. Besides, your father very much wanted a country place with a conservatory. For some unknown reason he's decided to start a garden.'

Elizabeth had hugged her mother fondly, marvelling, as she did, at her parents' constant ability to surprise.

Over the ensuing months, she'd visited the cottage in Surrey on a regular basis, watching the oleanders grow until she could bear it no longer. But her question had resulted in no answer and the oleanders had remained an unfathomable mystery – until the day she brought Daniel home to meet her parents.

Elizabeth herself met Daniel Gardiner in the spring of 1954, two months before her twenty-fourth birthday. The occasion was a military event, which was hardly surprising in Aldershot. The township was not known as the 'home of the British army' for nothing.

What a splendid sight, Elizabeth thought as she stood with the other journalists and photographers in the area specially allocated to the press, right beside the main entrance to Princes Gardens. The military never failed to put on a good show, and she never tired of the spectacle, but today was particularly impressive.

Down the entire length of High Street the parade was in full swing, brass bands strutting their stuff with all the pomp and ceremony only the army could offer. Military police on motorcycles preceded tanks, armoured vehicles, transport trucks and cars of every description. Troops marched with perfect precision, regimental colours and battle honours held high. Infantry, artillery, tank, parachute – on and on they came, a sea of men, the thousands of spectators cramming the pavements cheering each unit as it passed. The citizens of Aldershot were out in force this fine spring morning, along with hundreds of others from nearby towns. This was a day of historical significance for the entire area.

Upon command, the colours and escorts peeled away in turn from the grand parade to enter the broad, grassy square of Princes Gardens, where they took up their allotted positions flanking the brand new fountain that sat in the centre.

The fountain, simple and unadorned, was to be presented as a gift from the military to the township, commemorating the centenary of the British army's association with Aldershot. Indeed, the fountain's location, Princes Gardens, was the exact spot where the Royal Engineers had camped during the time of the Crimean War while planning the permanent military base to be established with Aldershot as its centre. In the decades following the base's establishment, the extraordinary growth of Aldershot from a small village to a thriving Victorian town had been a direct result of its relationship with the army. Now, 100 years on, the fountain was to become the proud symbol of a fine and happy marriage between borough and military.

Elizabeth carefully scrutinised the regimental banners as they passed, scribbling the details of each in her notepad. She was unsure how much of the data she would use in her article, but her research, always meticulous, was of particular importance today. Today's story would be the best she had ever written, for she intended to send a copy of it to *The Times* as an example of her work – along with her application for employment.

A twinge of guilt accompanied the prospect of deserting her current employer should her application meet with success. *The Courier-Mail* had offered her many opportunities she would never have experienced elsewhere. But then she and Henry Wilmot, the editor, had shared an unspoken understanding from the outset.

'You're very talented, Elizabeth,' he'd said bluntly, as if it were an accusation.

'Thank you, sir.'

'And, I suspect, very ambitious.'

She'd remained silent.

'Sign of a good journalist, ambition.' Again, despite the apparent compliment, his tone had been strangely accusatory. 'Ah well, I suppose if you're determined to put your talent to good use, we at *The Courier-Mail* had best take advantage of the fact.' And instead of assigning her to social events befitting a female, as he would normally have done, Henry Wilmot had offered Elizabeth her very first feature story. 'Just a trial, you understand. I don't promise to print it.'

But he *had* printed it.

'What's your middle name?' he'd asked when she'd presented him with the piece.

'Jane. Why?'

'E. J. Hoffmann,' he'd said with a brisk nod. 'Has a nice ring. We'll publish you as E. J. Hoffmann until I feel readers are ready to accept the fact you're a woman.' Then he'd added, 'Or until we part company, whichever comes first.' It was plain he anticipated the latter.

Henry Wilmot genuinely admired Elizabeth, both for her talent and for her audacity in assuming she could compete in the male-dominated arena of the press. But her femininity would be her downfall, he'd thought, particularly in a town like Aldershot. God almighty, they'd all be after her. She'd no doubt resist the obvious young studs bent on sexual conquest – she was smart. But she was also handsome, and a young woman of breeding – perfect officer's wife material. She'd be in love in six months, probably married within twelve, and then children would claim her and goodbye career. Such was the natural scheme of things.

Now, eighteen months later, Henry thought differently. Elizabeth Hoffmann appeared impervious to the attentions of even the most eligible young officers whose family connections saw them hurtling through the ranks destined for distinguished military careers. Apparently she had no wish to be married. How very, very odd, he thought. He was pleased to have retained her services longer than expected, but was prepared for her departure nonetheless. If Elizabeth's ambition outranked the natural desire for a husband and children, then her days with his provincial newspaper were surely numbered. In his heart of hearts, Henry Wilmot wished her luck.

The last of the colour sergeants and escorts had taken up their position around the fountain. The formal ceremony was about to commence.

'I'm off to the other side of the park,' Walter muttered. 'I'll get a better angle on the official party from there.'

Walter was *The Courier-Mail*'s principal photographer and invariably accompanied Elizabeth on her assignments. The two had become close friends.

She nodded. 'Make sure you get plenty of shots of the fountain.'

'What a good idea,' he said mockingly. She'd told him at least a dozen times to photograph the fountain from every possible angle. 'Just as well you reminded me – might have slipped my mind otherwise.' Then he winked, gave her the thumbs up and disappeared.

Elizabeth had already completed the historical aspect of her feature article, and made few notes during the official speeches, which offered nothing new. She was keen for the formal ceremony to be over so she could mingle with the crowd. What she needed now was the human element.

She glanced around at the other journalists, most from nearby towns or neighbouring counties – they often bumped into each other at local events. Pete Hearson of *The Farnham Gazette* was scribbling away furiously in shorthand, taking down every single word of the mayor's tedious speech, but it was the pouchy, middle-aged man beside Pete who was the focus of Elizabeth's attention. He'd stopped making notes and appeared as bored by the mayor as she was. This was the journalist who'd come down from London, or so Walter had told her.

'You're sure?' she'd whispered.

'Absolutely. Look at him, for God's sake. Can't you just smell Fleet Street?'

She could. While the county journalists, respecting the occasion, had worn suits, the pouchy man from London was in a none-too-clean, open-necked shirt with a sports jacket that had seen far better days. Did he consider this provincial event beneath him, she wondered, or was his crumpled exterior a conscious and calculated statement intended to impress? Elizabeth suspected it was a little of both.

'Which paper is he from?'

'*The Times*, I think.'

'Really?'

'Yep, pretty sure.'

'Ah.' She'd kept a special eye on the pouchy man from that moment on.

Now, as the official proceedings came to a close, she was surprised to see him pocket his notebook. Surely he wasn't going to leave it at that, she thought. What about the all-important human element, essential to any good feature article? But sure enough, as the band struck up and the troops marched back into High Street, leaving the park free for the festivities that would follow, the pouchy man glanced at his watch and started elbowing his way through the crowd.

He's heading for the railway station, she thought. He's on his way back to London. Good, she told herself; better than good, in fact – excellent. The editor of *The Times* would surely be impressed by her article after the dry report submitted by his own journalist. She prayed that Walter had his facts right and that the pouchy man really was from *The Times*.

Within only minutes, it seemed, Princes Gardens had transformed into a fairground. The tantalising smell of frying onions permeated the air, and one of the army bands, now stationed near the fountain, was playing 'C'est Magnifique', the popular number from Cole Porter's new musical *Can-Can*. Several portable booths, which had stood deserted on the periphery of the park during the proceedings, had suddenly come alive. One was selling soft drinks and ice-creams; another, pork pies and pasties; and at another an enterprising middle-aged man with a Hawaiian shirt and a wife frantically tending a hotplate of onions was doling out American hot dogs and hamburgers. Elizabeth interviewed him. He was a Hampshireman, he said, born and bred in Portsmouth.

'If it hadn' been for the Yanks, I wouldn' be servin' this sort of grub now, would I?' he said, indicating the queue and the fact that his booth was doing a far brisker trade than the others. 'I owe those Yankee Doodle Dandies, 'n that's the truth.'

Elizabeth scribbled his words down verbatim. Of course, hot dogs and hamburgers had taken over the world, but it was interesting to note that the American forces had been stationed around Portsmouth and Southampton prior to the D-day landings. The whole of the area had been of huge military significance throughout the war, and the army's presence continued to have a profound effect on all local communities. 'Yankee Doodle' and the success of his hamburger booth seemed historical proof of the fact.

There was even a London hawker's cart selling jellied eels and pickled periwinkles, which may have appeared surprising but wasn't really. Colin the Cockney, in his traditional 'pearly king' outfit, wheeled his cart off the London train at country railway stations all over England, visiting any town and any occasion he considered worthwhile.

'Oh, yeah,' he replied in response to Elizabeth's query about the day's significance. 'This is the most highly significant of days, no doubt about it. I wouldn't miss a day like this for quids. The home of the British army! Makes you downright proud, dun'it?'

Elizabeth strongly suspected that Colin never went anywhere unless there was a personal quid in it for him, but she didn't intend to come from that angle. Colin the Cockney was a symbol. Together with his signature suit of pearly buttons, his hawker's cart, his jellied eels and pickled periwinkles, Colin gave the day a very special stamp of approval.

A young couple had just purchased a small waxed paper cup of Colin's jellied eels, and the girl's nose was screwed up in dubious anticipation as she contemplated the shapeless grey object her boyfriend proffered on the end of a toothpick. She'd never eaten a jellied eel before.

'Do you mind if we take a photograph?' Elizabeth asked.

As she'd roamed amongst the crowd conducting her interviews, Elizabeth had made sure Walter stayed religiously by her side, clicking away at every opportunity. It was the standard tack they adopted. Walter was essential for Elizabeth's credibility. Many people refused to take female journalists seriously, and his presence was proof she was a bona fide member of the press.

The young couple with the jellied eels were certainly impressed. The girl stopped pulling a face, fluffed up her hair and posed, mouth open and ready to engulf the eel.

'Would you mind, Colin?'

Elizabeth beckoned the Cockney into the shot and he happily joined the young couple. The presence of the press was attracting attention to his cart, and a picture in the local rag was always good for business. Indeed, Colin had appeared in any number of provincial newspapers and was quite a recognisable figure on the county fair circuit.

'Ooh, it's tough, isn't it?' the young girl said several photographs later when Elizabeth encouraged her to actually eat the eel.

'What's it taste like?' her boyfriend asked.

'Nothing really.' She chewed harder. 'It's like eating rubber . . . ergh.' She looked around for somewhere to spit, but with the photographer nearby decided to swallow instead, nearly gagging as she did so.

Colin rapidly returned to his cart and his customers, wishing the girl would bugger off. It's a bleedin' eel, he thought, what did the daft cow expect?

Elizabeth ushered the couple to one side. 'So how did you feel about the ceremony?' she asked.

'Well, it's who we really are, isn't it?' The young man, like his girlfriend, was eager to make an impression and he said all the things he thought the reporter might want to hear. 'A grand military history . . . proud to be British . . .'

Elizabeth jotted down several quotes, which she thought would look apt beside a picture of the couple with the Cockney and his jellied eels, but it was time to move on. She'd explored the civilians' reaction to the day, now she needed the military point of view. Twenty minutes later, she realised just what an uphill battle she was facing. The hundreds upon hundreds of soldiers now mingling with the crowd seemed to belong to two categories only.

'Ah yes, good show, wasn't it,' said the major, and the colonel, and the others of senior rank whom she approached. They posed happily enough for Walter, but the moment she attempted to interview them their manner became patronising and dismissive. 'Yes, yes, very good show indeed. Excellent turnout all round.' Then, one by one, they proceeded to ignore her. Elizabeth came to the conclusion that they found her confronting. They felt threatened to be seen publicly taking a female member of the press seriously, she decided, and she rather pitied them their insecurity.

The other category treated her just as frivolously and, in Elizabeth's opinion, was even more irritating.

'An interview? Of course. Shall we go somewhere a bit more private?' The leer was unmistakable. One brash young corporal even gave Walter a comradely wink and a jerk of the head that said *get lost*, intimating they both knew this was too good an opportunity for any red-blooded male to resist. Walter, always protective, and a little in love with Elizabeth although he'd

15

never let her know it, wanted to attack the man. But he didn't. They'd encountered insulting behaviour before and Elizabeth preferred to handle things her own way. Her methods invariably proved successful, so Walter left it to her.

This time, however, Elizabeth was at a loss. She'd become confident interviewing men on a one-to-one basis. Her fierce intelligence quickly convinced those who would patronise her that she was not their intellectual inferior, and her wit was an instant dampener to the Casanovas who assumed she was easy game. But she had never been assigned a job interviewing men en masse in an area where they were obviously conscious of how they were being perceived by other men. She scribbled down several observations. It was a very interesting topic for a future article, she thought, albeit highly controversial and therefore probably unpublishable.

'Excuse me. May I be of assistance?' The voice, with a slight Midlands accent, was pleasing in tone, and the manner respect-ful.

Elizabeth looked up from her notepad. The two pips on the young man's shoulder informed her that his rank was that of lieutenant. But for how long, she wondered. He couldn't be more than twenty. Pleasant-looking, fair-haired, little more than a boy really; she'd bet her last shilling he was fresh out of military school.

'Of assistance in what way precisely?' she asked, her voice clipped, her message clear. The younger, the brasher, she'd found. No doubt several of his army chums were nearby, nudging and winking.

'Well, you're press, aren't you?' The young man darted a glance at Walter. 'And you're interviewing people . . .' Or *trying* to, he thought. He'd been watching Elizabeth for quite some time and felt sorry for the way she'd been fobbed off or leered at. It didn't seem fair to him. 'I'm happy for you to interview me if you like.' She was scrutinising him so closely, he felt a little uncomfortable. 'That is, if it'd be any help,' he finished lamely.

'It would be a *great* help, Lieutenant, thank you very much.' Elizabeth, recognising he was sincere, smiled warmly and offered her hand. 'I'm Elizabeth Hoffmann from *The Courier-Mail*, and this is Walter Barnes.'

'Daniel Gardiner, how do you do.' By golly, she was a looker, he thought.

They shook hands all round.

'Shall we have a cup of tea?' Elizabeth led the way over to the trestle tables and urns, where army wives were selling tin mugs of tea and shortbread biscuits for threepence, proceeds to go to the Widows and Orphans Fund.

'No, no,' she insisted as they got to the end of the queue and Daniel dug in his pocket for change, '*The Courier-Mail* takes care of all incidentals.'

Daniel looked at Walter. It didn't seem at all right that a woman should pay, but Walter just shrugged and nodded. He was eager to get his mug of tea and take off. Elizabeth didn't need him for the moment, and there was a wealth of photographs yet to be taken. *The Courier-Mail* intended to accompany Elizabeth's feature story with a pictorial souvenir lift-out section devoted entirely to Aldershot's military centennial celebrations.

'So tell me about yourself, Lieutenant,' Elizabeth said when Walter had gone and they'd settled themselves in the only two spare canvas chairs at the far end of one of the trestle tables. 'How long have you been stationed in Aldershot?'

'Only a few months,' he replied. 'I graduated from Sandhurst just last year.'

'Ah.' She gave a nod and smiled, inwardly congratulating herself. 'I thought so.'

'It shows that much, does it?'

'Well, yes, it does rather. You're very young.'

'Twenty's not that young. Not when it comes to a war.' There was no belligerence in his tone, but he was quite firmly correcting her. 'Men much younger than me have died for this country.'

'Oh.' Elizabeth felt instantly contrite. 'Oh God, how awful of me.' She'd just treated him in the very same manner she herself so detested. 'I didn't mean to patronise. I'm sorry, Lieutenant.'

'You didn't patronise, and you don't need to be sorry, and the name's Daniel.' He grinned, eager to put her at her ease. 'No offence taken, I assure you. But if you really want to make amends . . .' He looked at her hopefully. 'Do I get to call you Elizabeth?'

She laughed. His boyishness was disarming and she was thankful to be so easily forgiven. 'Elizabeth it is.' Then her manner briskly reverted to that of interviewer. 'So, Daniel, you're with what unit?' she asked, pencil poised over notepad.

'I'm actually with the Royal Army Service Corps. Transport.'

She noted it down. 'And you were posted here to Aldershot direct from the Academy?'

'That's right. How about you?'

'I beg your pardon?' She looked up.

'Are you from Aldershot?' She didn't look like a country girl, he thought.

'No. I'm from London.'

'Oh. Right.' Well, that made more sense. 'So why'd you pick Aldershot?' He was genuinely intrigued. 'I mean, Aldershot of all places – seems strange to me.'

'Why don't *I* ask the questions,' she said firmly, but not unkindly. He didn't appear to be flirting, indeed she found him most pleasant, but wiser to keep things on track, she thought.

'Sorry.' He shrugged apologetically. 'It's just that I've never met a female reporter before, and it's really interesting. I wondered why you chose Aldershot, that's all.'

'I didn't. Aldershot chose me.' There was something so ingenuous about young Daniel Gardiner that Elizabeth felt a sudden obligation to give an honest answer. 'The editor of *The Courier-Mail* is a brave, modern-thinking man who believes in allowing a woman journalist a chance.' She recalled the steady stream of rejections she'd received from the other provincial editors to whom she'd sent applications – over fifty in all. 'Believe me, there are many who don't.'

'Oh, I see.'

Daniel did. From the candour of her response, and the flash of rebellion in her eyes, Daniel saw a great deal. Elizabeth Hoffmann was not only good-looking, she was intelligent and tenacious and downright fascinating. He put his mug on the table and leaned forward on his elbows, keen to discover more. 'What made you want to become a journalist, Elizabeth?'

But the boyish enthusiasm didn't work a second time. In his eagerness, he'd just overstepped the mark.

'Let's get on with the interview, shall we?'

The brief glimpse Elizabeth had allowed was over. The shutters were down and it was back to business.

'Yes, of course. Sorry.'

He sat up, straight-backed and duly chastised, but already wondering what possible tack he could take that might afford him another glimpse. He wanted to get to know Elizabeth Hoffmann.

'Tell me how you felt about today's ceremony, Daniel. How did it affect you personally?'

'In what way?'

'In every way. You're a young man embarking on a military

career, and here you are in Aldershot, the very home of the British army, celebrating 100 years of military tradition. Surely the symbolism of today must have had a tremendous impact upon you.'

As her eyes locked onto his, seeking to make a connection, Daniel knew exactly the tack to take. The way to get to know Elizabeth Hoffmann was to appeal to her intellect. And the way to appeal to her intellect was to give her the best possible interview – one that would, hopefully, surprise her.

'Symbolism's fine when you're dealing with the past,' he said, 'but you need to consider the future. It's all very well to celebrate the *last* 100 years, but what about the *next*?' Good, he thought, that had got her attention. 'Wars don't go away, you know.'

It was the catchphrase repeatedly trotted out by his superiors in the officers' mess, and it had exactly the desired effect. This was clearly not the response she had expected and he could tell she was interested.

'Go on,' Elizabeth said.

'The government has developed a dangerous sense of postwar complacency,' Daniel continued, in an excellent imitation of his superior officers. 'The assumption appears to be that the army is nothing more than a peacekeeping force in Europe, when in fact our troops are still serving in highly volatile areas – Palestine, Korea, Singapore ... Anything could happen. It's most unwise of the British government to cut back on military funding to the degree that it has.'

Elizabeth didn't interject, she had no desire to stop the flow. Here was a whole new viewpoint to add to her feature. Post-war unrest in the military – an excellent angle, she thought. Contemporary, and also a touch controversial, particularly given the fact that she was reporting from Aldershot, the very home of the British army. She looked up intermittently from her notepad to nod encouragement.

'In my opinion, it's all because of the Cold War,' Daniel went on. Gratified by her attention, he stopped imitating his superiors and warmed to his own personal theme. 'The government's concentrating its resources on the race for nuclear power, and you can hardly blame them. They can't rely on America to the extent they'd hoped – the Yanks are keeping their secrets very much to themselves. So if Britain wants to compete with Russia and France in the nuclear stakes – which, of course, she does – then she has to fork out hugely on scientific research. Which is exactly what the government is doing,' he concluded, reverting to the imitation of his superiors, 'and, might I add, to the severe detriment of its own armed forces.'

Elizabeth flipped over another page of her notepad and hastily scribbled the last sentence. The speed with which he'd voiced his argument had tested her shorthand skills, but she'd got it all down.

'Well, Daniel,' she said finally, leaning back to survey him with new-found respect, 'for one who's been in the army a relatively short time, you've certainly formed strong opinions.'

'Not altogether original ones,' he admitted. 'Not in regard to the government cutbacks anyway.'

'Oh?'

'It's all they talk about in the officers' mess.'

Elizabeth found his admission astonishing. 'So you were actually quoting your superior officers?'

'I certainly was, word for word.' He grinned conspiratorially. 'You wanted the opinion of the top brass, didn't you? Well, now you've got it. Just don't reveal me as the source.'

He was so refreshingly candid that she couldn't help but laugh. 'I won't. I promise. I'll keep it to "the general feeling amongst many senior-ranking officers . . ." How does that sound?'

'Spot on.'

She jotted down a reminder, then again looked up. 'Why are the Americans so unwilling to share their nuclear secrets with Britain?' she asked. 'We're allies, after all.'

'Oh, no, we're not. Not any more.'

She looked a query.

'The war's over,' he said. 'The Americans lead the field in the nuclear race, and they're not about to share that power with anyone, including their "best buddy" Britain. And, of course, with the Russians breathing down their necks they're paranoid about security. They might view us as a friendly nation, but they're not game to place their trust in us.'

'Is this "the general feeling amongst senior-ranking officers"?' She raised an eyebrow teasingly.

But this time Daniel's response was not frivolous. 'I wouldn't know,' he said. 'Topics like nuclear power and the Cold War aren't bandied about so openly by the brass. It's a pretty logical assumption though, don't you think?' She was silent – he didn't seem to expect a reply. 'We younger chaps talk about that sort of stuff a lot. After all, it's a new kind of war we're going to be facing, isn't it?'

'Yes,' she said thoughtfully. 'Yes, I suppose it is.'

Lieutenant Daniel Gardiner made a strong impression upon Elizabeth that day. So much so that she allowed a friendship to develop, which was surprising. With the exception of Walter, Elizabeth had avoided friendships with young men – they invited far too much complication. But as time passed and Daniel did not overstep the mark, she could find no reason to deny herself the pleasure of his company. He was fun and his

22

conversation was interesting. Indeed, she could talk to him the way she could to no-one else. Daniel was understanding, sympathetic in a way others were not to the obstacles a woman encountered in a bid for a career. Elizabeth enjoyed having him in her life. It was like having a younger brother, she thought.

As for Daniel . . . he was smitten. He'd wanted to meet Elizabeth from the moment he'd laid eyes on her during the march down High Street. There she'd been, the sole female amongst the covey of press gathered by the entrance to the park, so conspicuous that surely the eyes of every single soldier on parade must have flickered distractedly in her direction. What young man would *not* wish to make the acquaintance of such a woman? It had not, however, been his plan to fall head over heels in love. Nor had he been seeking a wife. On the contrary: marriage had been the farthest thing from his mind. But all that had changed now. Daniel, young, passionate and idealistic, had met the perfect woman. He was determined to make Elizabeth Hoffmann his wife.

From the outset, he was aware he must tread with care. Elizabeth had her sights set on a career, and he admired her for it. Should she agree to marry him, he would not stand in her way, but he knew that any premature attempt at courtship would most certainly frighten her off. He also knew that Elizabeth had allowed no other man into her life, and his ego told him that she found him attractive, although she wouldn't admit it. He must be patient, he decided. Frustrating though it was, he must say and do nothing until he could sense his feelings were reciprocated.

'Just listen to this: *Dear Miss Hoffmann* . . .' Elizabeth's tone was cynical as she read the letter out loud. It had been a whole seven weeks since she'd posted her application to *The Times*, and the response she'd finally received was decidedly lacklustre.

'I suppose it's what I should have expected,' she'd said when Daniel had joined her in the corner of the little teashop in Victoria Road not far from the post office. It was a regular meeting place of theirs when he was on weekend leave.

She read on. '*With regard to your application for employment, we regret to advise that* The Times *currently has no suitable position vacant.* 'Note the royal "we",' she said, glancing up from the letter with a moue of disgust. 'And just look at that.' She jabbed a finger at the name on the bottom of the page. 'L. P. Ogden, Dep. Ed. It's not even from the editor.'

Daniel gave her a look of sympathy. She was so bitterly disappointed he felt sorry for her, but he couldn't help a guilty sense of relief at the thought that she wasn't about to charge off to London and a whole new life.

'*We return herewith the feature article "One Hundred Years of Marriage: Aldershot and the British Army", which you were kind enough to forward to us,*' Elizabeth continued. '*While we are impressed with the quality of the piece, we must point out that this is not the style we would require from a lady journalist should such a position become available in those sections of* The Times *that are favoured by our female readers.*'

She thumped the letter down on the table, rattling her cup and saucer. 'How insulting is that! They're saying don't bother applying ever again! They're offended that the article was written by a woman!'

'It's a bit of a compliment in a way, don't you think?'

'A compliment?' She looked at him in blank amazement. 'How on earth could a comment like that be conceived as a compliment?'

'They said they were impressed by the quality of the piece –

that must mean something.' Daniel was doing his very best to mollify her. 'Golly, Elizabeth, if they hadn't known you were a woman, they might well have offered you a job.'

'Oh.' Elizabeth's tirade came to an abrupt halt. 'You're right. They might have, mightn't they?'

'Bound to, I'd say.'

'Good heavens above.' She smiled. 'I hadn't thought of that.'

'Do you mind if I order my tea now?' He was pleased that his attempt at mollification had met with such success.

But it wasn't until a week later, and exactly two months from the day they'd met, that Daniel's major breakthrough occurred.

'Want to come to the Hippodrome next Saturday?' he asked casually as they sat near the teashop's open doors, which afforded the slightest of breezes on what was a surprisingly hot midsummer day. 'An army chum of mine can't use a couple of tickets he bought – pity to waste them.'

He'd purchased the tickets himself that very morning in the hope of escalating their relationship. It was all part of his plan.

'Oh, I'm sorry –'

Elizabeth didn't appear to find his offer suspect, but the answer was obviously about to be 'no', so he dived in with an enthusiastic sales pitch.

'It's the new revue that's on tour, the one the critics have been raving about. We'd get to see it before it opens in the West End. Brilliant stuff, they say.'

'I know all about the revue, Danny,' she said with a smile. 'I work for a newspaper, remember?'

'So why don't you want to come?'

'I do want to come. I'd love to. But I can't.'

'Why not?'

'Because I've promised I'll have dinner with my parents next Saturday.'

25

'You could make that the following weekend, couldn't you?' He knew she saw her parents regularly, but her visits didn't appear to follow any pattern.

'Not really.'

'Why not?'

'Because next Saturday's my birthday, that's why not. Now stop badgering.'

'Your birthday? That's even better. We'll go to the Hippodrome for your birthday, what do you say?'

'I say *no*, Danny. I am *not* going to the Hippodrome, I am going to have dinner with my parents. I haven't seen them for a whole three weeks, and I promised.'

'Oh,' he said sulkily, 'what a pity. I'd have liked to be with you on your birthday.'

She smiled, aware that his childlike petulance was aimed to amuse. 'Well, you can't, can you,' she said briskly. 'Not unless you swap a West End revue for dinner with Mummy and Daddy, and I hardly think –'

'What a good idea.' Manna from heaven, he thought. This was a definite step in the right direction. 'I'll come to dinner. I'd like to meet your parents.'

'Don't be ridiculous. What about the Hippodrome?'

'My friend can give the tickets to someone else. Don't worry, they won't go to waste.'

How on earth had *that* happened, Elizabeth wondered, but she didn't question his motives. It was typical of Danny's impetuosity. And also of his immaturity, she thought, both of which could be rather endearing. She rang her parents and told them there'd be an extra guest for dinner.

'She's bringing a *young man* with her,' Marjorie announced.

Alfred looked up from his journal to where his wife stood

framed in the doorway of his study. He had long ceased to be
startled by her sudden appearances.

'Who is?'

'Your daughter.'

'She's bringing a young man where?'

'Here. To dinner. Next Saturday.'

'Good God, is she really?' 'Yes.' 'How extraordinary. Why?'
'I'm not sure. Perhaps because it's her birthday.' 'Ah.'

# Chapter Two

'Happy birthday to you, happy birthday to you . . .'
Marjorie's entrance was spectacular, Alfred having dimmed the dining room lights to add to the drama of the moment. In her outstretched arms she held a tray upon which sat a gigantic chocolate cake complete with twenty-four blazing candles and the words *Happy Birthday Elizabeth* starkly etched in white on its black-brown icing.

'*Happy birthday, dear Elizabeth, happy birthday to you . . .*'

Alfred joined his wife in song as she placed the cake ceremoniously on the table, and both of them encouraged Daniel to sing along.

Elizabeth refused to cringe, although she flashed a wry glance in Daniel's direction. She'd warned him her parents were eccentric, even a little odd. This was so typical, she thought. Sometimes they forgot her birthday altogether – they'd done so on occasion even when she was a child, which she'd found devastating at the time – then, when they did remember, they went to ridiculous lengths, possibly to assuage the guilt of previous years. Tonight was a perfect example. Candles belonged on the cakes of ten-year-olds, Elizabeth thought, and the cake itself was utterly impractical. Obscenely large, it would have fed thirty hungry people and, furthermore, it was chocolate. Her father was allergic to chocolate.

Daniel found Elizabeth's *I told you so* glance confusing. He could sense nothing at all odd about her parents. Throughout the dinner, he'd recognised that her mother was perhaps a little vague, but that hardly constituted odd, and her father seemed a most reasonable and intelligent man. When the conversation had touched briefly on politics, Alfred Hoffmann's criticism of Winston Churchill as a peacetime prime minister had indeed differed radically from Daniel's own father's views, but then his father was of the old military school, Daniel had reminded himself. There were, after all, many who were critical of Churchill's leadership these days, and their opinions were hardly a sign of eccentricity. As for the birthday cake . . . to Daniel, it epitomised normality. It was a reminder of the many birthday cakes his mother had baked for him and his younger brother over the years.

'*For she's a jolly good fellow* . . .' He sang along heartily and joined in the three hoorahs which followed Marjorie's 'hip hips', and also the loud cheer as Elizabeth obediently blew out the candles with one breath.

Marjorie carved the cake into portions, serving a huge wedge for Daniel and smaller slices for herself and Elizabeth. Alfred's dessert plate remained conspicuously empty.

'Do start, Daniel,' she urged as she noted the young man's hesitancy. 'Alfred won't be having cake – he's allergic to chocolate.'

'Right.' Daniel wondered, as he picked up his fork, why she'd chosen to make a chocolate cake given her husband's allergy. 'By golly, Mrs Hoffmann,' he said after he'd taken the first mouthful, 'this is truly magnificent.'

Daniel would have complimented Elizabeth's mother had the cake been virtually inedible, so determined was he to make a favourable impression, but he was genuine in his praise. And he was, after all, somewhat of a connoisseur. His mother prided herself, and justifiably so, on her baking skills. Prudence Gardiner's sponges were fluffy, her fruit cakes full-bodied and her scones as light as a feather.

'Yes, it is rather good, isn't it,' Marjorie agreed.

'It's more than good. It's even better than my mum's, and that's saying something, I can tell you. She's a wonderful cook, but you've outdone her tonight.'

'Good heavens above, I didn't *make* it,' she laughed.

'Oh.' Daniel was momentarily stumped. Surely all mothers made cakes.

'I don't bake. I've never baked. But there's a lovely little shop I've discovered in Reigate where they make things exactly to order.'

'So why chocolate when Daddy's allergic?' Elizabeth asked bluntly.

'Because chocolate cakes are synonymous with birthdays,' Marjorie replied, as if the question were one only a simpleton would ask. 'Isn't that right, Daniel?' She flashed a smile to include their guest, who fortunately wasn't required to answer. 'Probably because the wording stands out so wonderfully well, don't you think?' She gestured to the starkly white *Happy Birthday Elizabeth*, of which the *eth* was now missing. 'A lemon sponge wouldn't offer the same impact, would it?'

'Mummy doesn't cook,' Elizabeth said. She intended no insult to her mother, but the conversation was taking a ridiculous turn and Daniel was looking bemused, so she thought it best to explain the situation, which actually made a great deal of sense. 'She doesn't like to cook, and she believes that people shouldn't be forced to do things they don't wish to do unless absolutely necessary.'

Marjorie ignored her daughter. 'The truth is, Daniel, I have no skill in the kitchen.' The humility of her statement and the charm with which it was delivered plainly signalled there was nothing more to be said.

But Elizabeth wasn't about to drop the subject. 'Only because you've never tried! And you've never tried because you don't *want* to.'

How she wished her mother would stand up for her principles! Marjorie Hoffmann was an intelligent woman who, in Elizabeth's opinion, should proudly acknowledge her refusal to conform.

Alfred drained the last of the claret from his glass and watched with interest. These days, mother and daughter rarely clashed. There had been times, he recalled, during Elizabeth's adolescence, when Marjorie, who always preferred to avoid confrontation, had been forced to take a stand. 'Some of us don't wish to make statements, dear,' Marjorie had finally said in response to her daughter's continuous badgering. 'Some of us are, perhaps, a statement in ourselves.' The argument had infuriated the adolescent Elizabeth, who had considered it not only irresponsible but tantamount to a betrayal. She clearly believed that in not speaking out, her mother was shirking her duty as a modern woman. Alfred had noted, however, that somewhere along the track the argument's irrefutability had hit home. Maddening as Elizabeth found her mother at times, it was evident she'd developed a healthy respect for Marjorie's unorthodox approach to life. In any event, she'd stopped nagging.

That is until tonight, Alfred thought. Tonight, for some strange reason, his daughter seemed to have reverted to adolescence.

31

'You have no skill in the kitchen, Mummy, because you don't *wish* to.' Elizabeth continued, dog-like, to gnaw at the subject. 'For goodness sake, you refuse to even boil an egg. You absolutely *loathe* the kitchen, why won't you admit it?'

'She's right, Daniel.' Marjorie acquiesced with sudden good grace and a faintly theatrical sigh of resignation. 'The joys of cooking are lost on me, I fear.' She smiled benignly at her daughter. 'Although even Elizabeth would admit I do make a fine cup of tea.'

'But the meal . . .' Daniel looked from one to the other, confusion gaining the upper hand. A perfectly prepared chicken and mushroom casserole could surely not have been purchased at the bakery in Reigate.

'Elizabeth's father,' Marjorie admitted. 'Alfred loves to cook.'

'Oh yes, indeed.' Alfred nodded emphatically. 'Soups, stews and casseroles for the most part. I like to mix things; the transformation process is most fulfilling. It's the alchemist in me, of course. Can I tempt you to another glass of wine, Daniel? I have an excellent Bordeaux to hand.'

'Um . . .' Daniel was caught out by the question and the need to respond. Things had turned swiftly bizarre and he was thinking that perhaps Elizabeth was right after all, and her parents were odd.

'I intend to have another myself.' Alfred rose eagerly from his chair.

'Well, yes, thank you, sir.'

'Excellent.'

Marjorie stood also. 'Cup of tea, Elizabeth?' she asked.

'Lovely. Danny and I'll clear the table.'

'Thank you, dear.'

Daniel was surprised. Elizabeth's antagonism towards her mother had disappeared as quickly as it had manifested itself.

And when her parents had left the dining room, she made no further comment, so he simply followed her lead and started clearing the table.

'Well, well, well, who would have dreamt it possible,' Marjorie said, placing the kettle on the stove.

Alfred carefully drew the cork from the bottle of Bordeaux, pleased that Daniel had agreed to another glass. He would have felt a little indulgent opening a second bottle just for himself, and he did so enjoy his clarets.

'Who would have dreamt what possible, my dear?'

'Elizabeth. She's in love.'

'Good God, why on earth would you think that?'

'Put it down to female intuition if you wish, but I'm quite sure I'm right.' Marjorie took the teapot from the cupboard. 'She wants him to know us, Alfred,' she said, then quickly corrected herself. 'No, that's not quite right – she wants him to know *me*. You've always passed with flying colours, my darling. You are your daughter's hero.'

'Is that why she was on the attack?'

'Oh, yes. She wants him to respect me, which I find rather sweet, but the fact is, Alfred, she wants to *share* us with this young man. She wants him to know us the way *she* knows us. Normally Elizabeth couldn't give tuppence whether people like us or not – and why should she? But this particular young man's opinion is important to her, which, to my mind, means she's in love.'

'How extraordinary. I would have thought it the other way round myself. I would have thought *he* was in love with *her*.'

'Well, of course he is, that goes without saying.' Marjorie busied herself setting things out on the tea tray. 'She's not aware of it, of course.'

'Not aware of what? That *she's* in love with *him*, or that *he's* in love with *her*?'

'Both. Blinkered vision, it's so typical of Elizabeth.'

'Dear me.' Alfred didn't doubt his wife for one moment; Marjorie was most perceptive about things of importance. Her vagueness sprang principally from a lack of interest in the minutiae of everyday life, which Alfred found perfectly understandable. 'But this could play havoc with her plans for a career.'

'Yes, indeed.'

'Do you think he's serious?'

'He appears to be, but then he's so very young. Who can tell?'

'Oh dear, dear me,' Alfred said anxiously.

'There's no point in worrying, my darling. After all, there's nothing we can do, is there?' Marjorie obviously expected no response as she blithely continued. 'If Elizabeth refuses to acknowledge her feelings to herself, she's hardly going to acknowledge them to us,' she said as she filled the milk jug and placed it on the tray. 'And if you were to question Daniel's intentions, you'd only humiliate her dreadfully. She'd never forgive you for that.'

The kitchen door opened just as Marjorie picked up the tea tray. 'No, no, things will sort themselves out one way or another. Now where shall we have our tea and our wine?' she asked loudly as Elizabeth and Daniel entered with the dishes.

'The conservatory.' Alfred's answer was instantaneous. 'I haven't yet shown Daniel my oleanders.'

'The conservatory it is then.'

As they crossed paths at the door, Marjorie issued instructions to Elizabeth. 'Just rinse the dishes and stack them in the sink, dear, they can wait until morning. I'll come back for the teapot, the water hasn't quite boiled yet.'

Alfred, bottle in hand, held the door open for his wife. 'Leave the dishes to Elizabeth, Daniel. We need two fresh glasses, on the double.'

'Yes, sir,' Daniel said as Alfred and Marjorie disappeared.

'The oleanders.' Elizabeth smiled. 'I think it means he likes you.' She pointed at the cupboard above his head. 'Wine glasses up there.'

'Right.'

Daniel left the kitchen, thinking how appalled his mother would be at the thought of unwashed dishes remaining stacked overnight.

'So, Daniel, what do you think of my oleanders?' Alfred asked several minutes later when he'd poured the wine and they were seated at the table, Marjorie having returned to the kitchen for the tea.

'Most impressive, sir.'

Daniel looked about at the unkempt mass of bushes and trees that filled every inch of the conservatory. They were impressive in sheer volume alone, but their limbs were gawky, their foliage tough, and even their pink and white flowers, pretty though they were, seemed to belong somewhere else.

'Unusual, aren't they?'

'Yes.' Daniel agreed with enthusiasm – he'd gathered from Elizabeth's comment that the oleanders were something special. 'Very unusual indeed.'

'Only here, in an English conservatory.' Alfred's smile was wry. 'They're as common as muck throughout the whole of the Mediterranean and the Middle East – the damn things grow like weeds.'

'Oh.' Daniel felt self-conscious and a little uncomfortable. He hoped Elizabeth's father hadn't been trying to catch him out. 'I wouldn't know, sir,' he answered. 'I haven't travelled much.'

'Ah well,' Alfred laughed, 'I've no doubt that'll be rectified soon enough.' He hadn't been trying to catch the boy out at all, but he liked the honest simplicity of his reply. 'Join the army and see the world, eh?' He raised his glass.

'Yes, sir, I certainly hope so.' Daniel responded to the toast.

Alfred took a hefty mouthful of wine, and there was a moment's silence while he savoured the aftertaste. He swirled the contents of his glass, studying the colour and 'legs' of the Bordeaux. 'Wonderful thing, travel,' he said finally, and once again he contemplated his oleanders. 'My wife thinks I keep them because they're evocative of my travels and she's quite right, but that's not the principal reason for my attachment.'

After a moment's confusion, Daniel realised they were back to the oleanders.

'They're an ancient plant species, Daniel, from the Old World. True survivors, and great travellers . . .'

Marjorie and Elizabeth arrived with the teapot and a small dish of shortbread. They sat in silence, and Marjorie began to pour. Daniel's gaze flickered longingly to the pot. He was un-accustomed to red wine and would vastly have preferred a cup of tea.

'Hardy, tenacious, a remarkable plant with a passion for life . . .' Alfred, having ignored the women's arrival, had barely drawn breath.

Daniel tore his eyes from the teapot, hoping his momentary lapse had gone unnoticed.

'The oleander is a wanderer, Daniel. A wanderer that settles wherever it can find a home . . .'

As his eyes met Alfred Hoffmann's, Daniel found that he could not look away

'It adapts to its environment even under the harshest of con-ditions. Little wonder I find it such an interesting species, wouldn't you agree?'

Goodness, Elizabeth thought, Danny was certainly copping

the full brunt of her father's obsession. She tried to signal a look to him, but couldn't seem to catch his attention.

What was Elizabeth's father trying to say, Daniel wondered. He seemed to be seeking something – an answer, perhaps. But an answer to what? What was the question?

'Would you like to know the true reason for my interest in oleanders, Daniel?'

Daniel nodded wordlessly, sensing he was about to receive either the question or the answer, or possibly both.

'I identify with them. The oleanders are a reminder of who I am.'

Marjorie stared at her husband over the rim of her teacup, suddenly realising his intention. How very clever of you, Alfred, she thought.

Elizabeth stared at her father in a state of complete mystification. What on earth was he talking about?

'The oleanders remind me, Daniel, that I am a Jew.'

Alfred Hoffmann, searched the young man's eyes for a sign. Would he see the involuntary flicker of alarm? Was the boy anti-Semitic? If he were, it wouldn't have bothered Alfred one bit. But if Elizabeth was about to relinquish her hard-earned career and follow the conventional path of marriage and family, then Alfred needed to know she had chosen the right man. And if by chance she'd chosen the *wrong* man, then it was his intention to scare the boy off before it was too late. Alfred's declaration was both a challenge and a test.

'Really, sir?' Daniel held his gaze. 'I didn't know that.'

The boy's reaction was one of surprise, certainly, but there was no flicker of alarm. Far from it. The flicker Alfred saw in the boy's eyes was strangely akin to elation.

'Elizabeth never told me.' Daniel flashed a smile at Elizabeth, trying to sound normal, but barely able to disguise his joy. He was being put to the test! Alfred Hoffmann clearly believed that he, Daniel Gardiner, held a place in his daughter's affections! A quick glance at Elizabeth's mother told Daniel that she felt the same way, and knew exactly what was going on. The only one who appeared unaware was Elizabeth herself. She was studying her father, not with suspicion but utter bewilderment.

Child-like in his excitement, Daniel pushed her for a response. 'Why didn't you tell me, Elizabeth?' he asked, willing her to look at him. But she didn't.

'Why would I?' Elizabeth continued to stare at her father. 'Daddy never tells anyone himself. He doesn't even consider himself Jewish.'

'Exactly, my dear, that's why I need the oleanders to remind me.' Alfred turned once again to Daniel. He was pleased that the boy had passed the test – he liked him. 'I am descended from a long line of Anglicised Sephardic Jews, Daniel,' he explained, 'but I'm afraid I'm a very poor example of my tribe. I could, perhaps, lay the blame at the feet of my father and grandfather, but I prefer not to. The decision was one of my own making.'

Good heavens, Marjorie thought. Alfred was serious. Surely he didn't have regrets.

'My father and grandfather turned their backs on Judaism,' Alfred continued, 'both of them marrying Gentiles and bringing their children up outside the faith. One would have assumed that by the third generation, the passion for a Jewish identity might have burnt itself out, but as a young man there was a time when I was interested in rekindling the flame. I decided, however, to take the easier path and follow the example of my father and grandfather.'

Alfred looked at his wife and smiled reassuringly, knowing just what she was thinking, and remembering how strongly she'd urged him to allow her to convert. Dear, fearless Marjorie who would willingly have severed all ties with her staunchly Protestant parents in order to please him.

'I have had no regrets,' he said, 'no regrets at all.' He continued to address himself to Daniel, but his words were intended for his wife, as she well knew. 'In fact, I would feel a fraud if I attempted to embrace the Jewish faith now. But at this later stage in my life, I like to remind myself of where I once came from. And who I believe, deep down, I really am.'

Marjorie Hoffmann leaned across the table and took her husband's hand, squeezing it briefly. The look of tenderness shared between the two did not go unnoticed by Elizabeth and Daniel.

It was Marjorie herself who broke the moment. 'Well, well, I do believe,' she remarked to her daughter, 'that the mystery of the oleanders has finally been solved.'

'Yes,' Elizabeth replied with a smile. 'I do believe it has.'

'May I top you up, my darling?' Marjorie reached for the wine bottle.

'Please.' Alfred felt quite euphoric. His aim had been simply to put his daughter's potential suitor to the test, but he'd unburdened himself in the process. He'd never intended to share the intensely personal secret of his oleanders, but now that he had, he was glad. He'd found the exercise strangely cathartic.

As she poured the wine, Marjorie noticed Daniel's barely touched glass. 'I think Daniel might prefer a cup of tea,' she said.

Daniel left barely half an hour later. Thanks and farewells were exchanged at the front door, and Elizabeth walked with him down the front path to where the army Land Rover was parked by the dirt track that led to the main road. Daniel and his several fellow lieutenants who were in charge of the battalion's motor pool had a simple arrangement – whoever was on duty signed out a vehicle to whoever wasn't. The regulation warning they issued had become a running joke. 'Naturally, no non-military person will be transported in this vehicle . . .' 'Naturally,' came the response, and winks were exchanged.

'I've had a grand evening,' he said as they arrived beside the Land Rover. He'd driven Elizabeth out from Aldershot, but she was staying the night with her parents, as she always did. Her father would drop her at Reigate railway station the following day.

'So have I,' she replied. 'Birthdays don't mean much to me as a rule, but tonight's been special.'

'That's good.'

For Daniel the evening had been far more than special. Elizabeth's parents had raised his hopes in the most spectacular fashion. They'd not only confirmed his secret belief that she cared for him more than she would admit, but he was convinced that in so doing they had signalled their blessing. Daniel felt part of a glorious conspiracy.

'I wonder why he chose tonight,' Elizabeth continued thoughtfully.

'Who? What?'

'Daddy. I've been nagging him for ages about the oleanders, and he's never mentioned their symbolism. Why would he decide to talk about the Jewish connection tonight of all nights? And to you, of all people?'

Daniel smiled to himself. For such a highly intelligent woman, Elizabeth could be quite obtuse at times. 'Perhaps he needed to tell a stranger.'

'Yes.' She nodded. 'Yes, I think you're right.' Of course, she thought, that would make sense. 'In fact, I'm sure you're right.'

She laughed lightly. 'And my goodness, he certainly enjoyed telling you, didn't he? It was rather like a confession, I thought.'

Daniel nodded, but he wasn't concentrating. His eyes had strayed to her lips and he was wondering whether he dared kiss her.

'I'm glad you were here, Danny,' she said. 'I'm really glad. Thank you for coming.'

As she pecked him affectionately on the cheek, he realised she was about to go.

'I like your parents,' he said, stopping her in her tracks.

'They liked you too, I could tell.'

'They're extraordinary people,' he said, 'truly extraordinary.' Now? he asked himself. Was now the right moment?

Elizabeth gave a sudden hoot of laughter. He was studying her as if she were some sort of alien species – he'd obviously found her parents far more than extraordinary. 'Well, I did tell you they were odd.'

'Yes, they're odd,' he agreed. 'But they're admirably odd.' Her laughter warned him to be careful. She was so unsuspecting that perhaps it would be wiser to signal his feelings rather than shock her. 'They're just the sort of admirably odd people who would produce a daughter like you,' he said. And he kissed her.

He didn't take her in his arms the way he would have liked, but at least he kissed her. He didn't kiss her in the way he would have liked either, but at least it was on the lips. It was the sort of safe kiss that affectionate family members might share. But they were not affectionate family members, were they? The message was loud and clear, he thought. The next move would be up to her.

'Goodnight, Elizabeth.'

Elizabeth watched the Land Rover take off down the track.

How strange, she thought, Danny had never kissed her on the lips before. He was young and impetuous and no doubt inspired by the warm reception he'd received from her parents, but it wasn't the sort of thing to be encouraged. She wondered whether she should say something.

But as she walked back to the house, she chastised herself. His gesture had been one of brotherly affection, nothing more. It would be very silly of her to over-dramatise the episode and threaten the perfect balance of their friendship.

The following weekend, Daniel was rostered on as duty officer at the barracks, and, unable to bear the thought of waiting nearly a whole fortnight to see Elizabeth, he telephoned her mid-week at *The Courier-Mail*.

'Want to come to the Hippodrome on Friday?' he asked. The invitation was offered casually enough, but this time he didn't lie about having been given tickets by a friend. He didn't think it necessary. She would surely have recognised the subtle shift in their relationship after Saturday night's kiss. He listened intently for any giveaway nuance.

'I can't,' came the brisk reply down the line. 'Sorry.'

His heart sank. This was not at all the outcome he'd anticipated. He'd obviously offended her.

'I won't be back from London in time,' she said. 'I'm going up on Thursday and staying overnight. I have an appointment Friday afternoon.'

He breathed a sigh of relief. She sounded more businesslike than angry. Thank God for that, he thought. 'What sort of appointment?'

'Oh, Danny, the most wonderful thing's happened. Well, it hasn't happened *yet*, but it *could*. I won't know until Friday.' No longer businesslike, the words were tumbling out in her excitement. 'Wish me luck,' she said breathlessly. 'I'm going to need it.'

'For what? What on earth's going on?'

'I'm not saying. It's a secret and I'm not saying another word. But think of me at three o'clock on Friday, and keep your fingers firmly crossed.'

'Three o'clock, right you are.' A thought occurred. 'Why are you going up Thursday? Why not take the Friday morning train?'

'I have a fitting with a tailor in Mayfair on Thursday, and I need to learn, very quickly, how to smoke a cigar. I'll telephone you when I get back. Bye.'

The line went dead and Daniel hung up the receiver. He didn't ponder the mystery of Elizabeth's trip to London. All he could think about was Saturday night's kiss and the fact that it had made no impact whatsoever.

# Chapter Three

There was a tap on the door of Lionel Brock's office.

'Enter,' he called in full baritone. He was a heavily built man with a voice to match.

The door opened, but only slightly, as pretty little Mabel Tomley popped her head through.

'Your three o'clock appointment is here, Mr Brock . . .'

'Show him in then, dear.'

Lionel glanced down at the open file on his desk, pushed back his chair and levered himself to his feet. He would have preferred her to have informed him of his three o'clock appointment via the telephone's intercommunication system as he'd instructed, but young Mabel was new to the job and still learning the ropes, so he decided to let it go for now.

Mabel cast a hesitant glance over her shoulder.

'Show him in, show him in,' Lionel said with a slightly impatient wave of his hand.

'Well, that's just it, sir . . .Um . . .'

'Um, what?' The girl was becoming annoying.

'*Him* . . .' Mabel's big baby-blue eyes were saucer-like. 'I thought I'd better warn you, Mr Brock. You see he's not actually –'

'That's quite enough of that, Mabel,' Lionel said sharply. 'I'll be the judge of character around here. Now do as you're told and show the man in, there's a good girl.'

Mabel's barely perceptible shrug could have been one of subservience, but as the door swung open and she stood to one side, the baby-blue eyes said, *Right you are, see if I care.* Mabel was much feistier than most people realised.

A young man stepped into the open doorway. A very self-assured young man, Lionel thought. Legs astride, one hand on hip, the stance could even be construed as arrogant. Lionel looked him up and down. First appearances were of the utmost importance in Lionel Brock's book. Elegant chap, he thought, very dapper, well-cut pinstriped suit, dove-grey fedora of top quality, but very, very young, little more than a youth. Lionel was rather surprised – this was not the middle-aged rustic journalist he'd been expecting.

Then, to his amazement, the young man saluted him with a lighted cigar, raised it to his lips and took a leisurely drag. The cheeky devil, Lionel thought. But he couldn't help admiring the impudence of the performance, recognising, as he did, that he was being played at his own game. His advice to budding journalists about the importance of first impressions had been widely broadcast, and it was a well-known fact that he himself was a cigar smoker. The lad had done his homework and was making a statement in putting on such a show. Well, good for you, boy, Lionel thought.

'Mr Hoffmann,' he said as he circled his desk, hand outstretched.

The young man exhaled a perfect plume of cigar smoke and strode boldly forward to receive the handshake.

'Yes, sir. E. J. Hoffmann at your service.'

The voice and the hand made their impact simultaneously.

The voice Lionel heard was not that of a man, and, although the clasp of the hand in his was firm and manly enough, the slenderness of the fingers and the texture of the skin were most certainly not.

Lionel pulled his hand away as though he feared contagion, and his eyes darted to the doorway where his young secretary stood watching.

Mabel gave another tiny shrug which could have been apologetic, but which really said, *See? I tried to warn you.* Then she raised an obediently secretarial eyebrow seeking instructions.

'Thank you, Mabel,' he said. 'That will be all.'

'Yes, Mr Brock.'

Mabel glanced at E. J. Hoffmann as she closed the door. God, she wished she had guts like that.

Lionel returned to his desk, seeking a safe distance and a barrier between them. He was confronted and angered by the deception, but, above all, he felt foolish, humiliated even. He needed to buy time.

'So you're a woman, my dear,' he said with an over-hearty chuckle, wishing he could turn the whole thing into a joke and pretend he'd known all along. 'Very clever, I must say, very clever indeed. Had me fooled for a minute, I must say.'

'Pity I couldn't have fooled you a bit longer – we might have been able to have an intelligent conversation.' Elizabeth followed him to the desk, aware of his embarrassment, knowing she might well be pushing too hard, but having taken the extreme steps she had, what did she have to lose? 'Because that's all I ask, Mr Brock – the same conversation you would have had with the writer of that article,' she waved her cigar at the open file on his desk, 'had that writer been a man.'

In the eyes that met his from beneath the brim of the fedora, Lionel could see no mockery, no sense of triumph at his humiliation. All he could see was the intense desire to make contact. He looked down at the open file and the newspaper article that sat there.

'"One Hundred Years of Marriage: Aldershot and the British Army." It's a very good piece.'

'It's also the reason you were interested in meeting E. J. Hoffmann, isn't that right?'

'Yes, that's right,' Lionel admitted. 'The originality of the journalist's style intrigued me.' His tone was cynical. 'Perhaps I now know why, Miss Hoffmann. Or is it Mrs?'

'Elizabeth will do.'

'Would you like to sit down?' The offer was made with reluctance; he was aware he had little option.

'Thank you.'

They both sat, and Lionel selected a half corona from the ornately carved cigar box on his desk. He clipped the end and lit up, then struck another match and offered it to her. 'You've gone out,' he said. She appeared not to have noticed.

'Thank you.' Elizabeth took short, rapid puffs, the way the man in the elite Bond Street cigar store had shown her. She didn't care if Lionel Brock was testing her, which he no doubt was, she was prepared to smoke the whole putrid thing and another five if necessary.

'Can we talk, Mr Brock?' she said, leaning back and staring unflinchingly at him through the veil of smoke. 'Can we forget I'm a woman and talk business, man to man?'

That would be difficult, he thought. Close to, despite the masculinity of the body language, the androgynous youth had taken on a distinctly female form.

'We can try,' he said.

'Firstly, I have a reference from an old friend of yours.'

Elizabeth took a folded sheet of paper from the inner breast pocket of her suit and handed it to him.

'Henry Wilmot.' As Lionel's eyes flicked to the name at the bottom of the page, he smiled involuntarily. 'Of course, I'd forgotten it was Aldershot he'd disappeared to – well, that explains a lot.'

It certainly did, he thought as he read the reference. It explained why Elizabeth Hoffmann had been given the opportunity to work as a feature journalist in the first place. Henry was a renegade who believed in doing things differently and in giving underdogs a chance.

'He speaks very highly of you,' he said, looking up from the page.

'As I would expect – we've had an excellent working relationship for nearly two years.'

What was it about her manner, he wondered. She was not arrogant, nor was she boastful. Nor, he was quite sure, did she intend any disparagement of his old colleague and rival. But such assurance in a woman was most unsettling. Lionel found himself instantly on the defensive.

'I trust you are aware, Miss Hoffmann,' he said stiffly, hoping it was 'Miss'; she hadn't clarified her title, and he couldn't bring himself to say 'Elizabeth', 'that Henry Wilmot is one of the best newspaper men in the business.'

'Yes, I'm aware of that. He says the same thing about you, by the way.'

Lionel sat back, savouring his corona and studying her closely through the cigar's lazy smoke, but he could detect no insincerity. It had just been a statement.

'I can see why the two of you would get on,' he commented dryly. 'Henry didn't believe in playing games either.'

'I know. He still doesn't. That's why he decided to opt out for the country, he told me. He got sick of having to play the games.'

'Did he indeed?'

Well, it was an honest admission, Lionel thought, albeit somewhat of an understatement. Henry Wilmot had detested the internal politics of big city newspapers. He'd flouted the rules and offended right, left and centre. Which was just as well, Lionel thought with a wry smile. Had Henry played the necessary games, as he himself had, it might well have been Henry Wilmot who was now features editor of *The Guardian*.

'I presume Henry is responsible for all this?' He gestured at the hat and the suit.

'Indirectly, yes. He told me how important first impressions are to you.'

'The idea was your own then?'

She nodded.

'And the cigar?'

'That was his. When I told him what I was going to do, he thought you might find it an amusing touch.'

Lionel laughed, and for the first time since she'd appeared in his office, he started to relax. 'So much for the two of you not believing in games,' he said.

Elizabeth smiled pleasantly. 'But it's not really a game, is it, Mr Brock? You and I are talking in a very different way than we would be if I'd arrived as Elizabeth J. Hoffmann.' Good God, he wouldn't have agreed to see her at all if he'd known she was a woman, she thought, but she didn't say so, aware that he found her quite confronting enough as it was.

Damn her hide, Lionel thought, but he couldn't argue the fact. She was, after all, right.

Over the next hour, as Lionel Brock continued to relax, he found it progressively easier to talk to Elizabeth J. Hoffmann.

Perhaps it was the pinstriped suit and the fedora, or perhaps it was Elizabeth J. Hoffmann herself, but he talked to her the way he'd never talked to a woman before. Indeed, it was rather like talking to a man.

Elizabeth didn't telephone Daniel until the following Monday, aware that he was on duty over the entire weekend, and when she did speak to him, she refused to say one word about her business in London.

'Not over the phone,' she said, 'it's far too exciting. I'll see you in the teashop, usual time, and I'll tell you absolutely everything.' She laughed. 'Oh, Danny, you won't *believe* what I did!'

Come Saturday, true to her word, she not only told him everything that had happened, she acted it out from her first entrance in the doorway of Lionel Brock's office to the final man-to-man handshake upon her departure. And Daniel, watching in silence, aware that the several other customers in the teashop were enjoying the show, wondered how she could have thought he wouldn't believe what she'd done. To his mind, it was so very Elizabeth.

'And you know what I'm most proud of?' she said in triumphant conclusion.

He shook his head.

'I smoked every inch of that hideous cigar!'

Daniel joined in her laughter. He had mixed feelings about the possible outcome of her trip to the city, but for now he wasn't thinking of where he fitted in. He was happy because Elizabeth was happy. He was excited for her and proud of her and so in love with her that he wanted to shout it out.

'God, I wish I'd seen you,' he said.

'You will. I've kept the suit and the fedora, and I shall present E. J. Hoffmann to you in person.'

'Complete with cigar?'

'Oh yes, definitely with cigar. You're entitled to the full performance – it was your idea, after all.'

He was mystified.

'Don't you remember, Danny? When *The Times* turned me down sight unseen? I read you the letter, we were sitting right over there.' She pointed to the table tucked in the far corner. 'And you said if they hadn't known I was a woman, they might well have offered me a job.'

He remembered the day clearly – he'd been trying to cheer her up. How ironic, he thought, if this should prove to be all his own doing. But he smiled jokingly. 'Are you really telling me that the whole ludicrous idea of your going to an interview in London dressed as a man and smoking a cigar was *mine*?'

'No,' she admitted, 'the cigar was Henry Wilmot's. But as for the rest of it, yes, you're entirely to blame, and I can't tell you how grateful I am.'

She was radiant in her excitement, and he thought that she'd never looked more beautiful.

'Isn't it strange, Danny,' she said, suddenly thoughtful, 'that until you gave me the idea, it never once occurred to me to keep my identity a secret?'

'No, I don't find that strange at all,' he replied. 'You're not accustomed to lying.'

'But I didn't lie. Not once.'

His look was sceptical.

'I didn't, I swear. Admittedly, I didn't say I was a woman when I sent the Aldershot article to *The Guardian*, but then I didn't say I was a man either. And when they replied telling me to phone for an interview and I made an appointment for E. J. Hoffmann, I didn't say I was Hoffmann, it's true, but then I didn't say I wasn't. I didn't lie and they didn't enquire.'

It was their automatic *assumption* that made everything so easy.'

Daniel studied her knowingly. He recognised the passionate gleam in her eyes. Elizabeth was out to make a point.

'They'd *assumed* the application for employment had come from a man,' she continued, 'and they *assumed* when I telephoned that I was that man's secretary. At least, I assume that's what they assumed,' she added in all seriousness, feeling she should be fair, 'but I know I'm right. Now I ask you honestly, doesn't that say something?'

'Yes. It says you're cunning, devious and manipulative.'

'For goodness sake, Danny, I'm talking about the male attitude to women in the workplace and –'

'Of course you are, and your tea's stone cold. Shall I order another pot?' He'd drunk two cups while hers had remained untouched.

'I'm raving on, aren't I?'

'Not yet, but you're about to,' he said agreeably. 'And I'd rather hear the outcome of the interview if that's all right with you. Shall I order more tea?'

'No, thanks.' Elizabeth was not in the least offended. She adored having a friend like Danny who knew her so well and always spoke his mind. 'I'd much prefer a walk.'

'Good.' He stood and offered her his arm. 'So would I.'

The late summer sun was warm and the day inviting as they turned into High Street, automatically heading for Princes Gardens.

'So what happens now?' Daniel asked, trying to sound nonchalant. 'I presume they're going to offer you a job?'

'They already have.'

'Oh.'

'Well, more or less. Lionel has to run everything by the

editor-in-chief, but he says that's really only a matter of courtesy.'

'Lionel. First names already – I'm impressed.' Daniel was desperately reminding himself that London was only thirty miles away, and that this wasn't exactly the end of the world, although he was starting to feel it might be.

'Yes, I was impressed myself, but he was quite insistent. *All my feature writers call me Lionel, my dear.*' Her impersonation was amusing. '*I see no reason why E. J. Hoffmann should be an exception.*'

They'd arrived at the gardens, but they progressed no further as Daniel came to an abrupt halt.

'*Feature* writer? You didn't tell me that.'

'Of course not. I was leaving the best bit till last.'

'Elizabeth, that's incredible.' He was genuinely amazed. 'It must be, surely. I mean, how many women feature writers would there *be* at *The Guardian*?'

'None. Well, none working under their own names anyway. Perhaps there are other E. J. Hoffmanns lurking behind closed doors – how could one possibly know?' She laughed lightly. 'From now on, I shall be highly suspicious of any newspaper article featuring the journalist's initials.'

'Really? Do you think that's true?'

'No, Danny, I don't think it's true at all.' She was no longer joking but in deadly earnest. 'I think I'm being offered the chance of a lifetime, perhaps even the opportunity to create history.'

His look was curious, although he didn't doubt her for a moment. In his opinion Elizabeth was capable of anything.

'My articles will appear under the name E. J. Hoffmann,' she explained, 'but once I've proved myself, I intend to fight tooth and nail for my own by-line. I want to be recognised as the first woman feature writer in the history of *The Guardian*.' She smiled as she once again took his arm. 'In the meantime, of course, I shall have to report a whole lot of rubbish. Come on, let's sit down.'

They entered the gardens and headed for one of the wooden benches that bordered the broad, grassy square.

'What do you mean rubbish?' he asked. 'E. J. Hoffmann doesn't write rubbish.'

'That's the catch. I don't know how often they'll let me be E. J. Hoffmann. Lionel's given his personal guarantee that he'll assign me features, but I'm not sure how regularly. In the meantime I'll be a nameless staff writer who covers matters of interest to women.' She grimaced. 'Everything from fashion parades and hair trends to family nutrition, childcare and kitchen appliances – in other words, everything that either bores me witless or upon which I'm totally unqualified to report.'

They sat on a bench, and as Daniel gazed at the fountain in the centre of the square, he recalled the army's centennial celebrations and the day they'd first met. He'd known from that very first day that he loved her. Just as he'd known that he wanted to marry her. Now was obviously the time to tell her, he thought, before she walked out of his life. But how should he go about it?

'Lionel says it'll do me good working as a staff writer,' Elizabeth continued, unaware that she'd momentarily lost her audience. 'He says that I'll learn a lot covering such a broad spectrum, and I grant he may have a point, but I'm not so sure about the other aspect of his reasoning.' She launched into a further impersonation. '*Serving as a lady writer will establish credibility with your colleagues, my dear.*'

Jolted from his thoughts, Daniel stopped gazing at the fountain and gave her his full attention.

'Lady writer,' Elizabeth added with a moue of distaste. 'I

don't know why, but I find the term demeaning. They never refer to male journalists as "gentleman writers", do they? Anyway, Lionel's intimation is that in getting to know my fellow journalists as a "lady writer", I'll be somehow protected from the harsh masculinity of their world. But of course we both know what he's really saying.'

'And that is?'

'He's sounding me out. He's buying time while he assesses my value as a journalist and also my stamina in the marketplace. I appreciate his concern, unnecessary though it is. Poor Lionel's wondering if I'll be able to handle the slings and arrows that may come my way, or whether the pressure will be too much for me.'

'Little does he know.' Daniel's tone was droll, but the irony of his response was lost on Elizabeth.

'Exactly,' she replied briskly. 'I've said I'll give it a year, after which we'll review the situation. Strictly between you and me, that's when I'll demand my own by-line, but I think it's a pretty reasonable arrangement, don't you?'

He couldn't help but laugh. For someone who was being offered the chance of a lifetime, Elizabeth seemed insistent upon calling the shots.

'Very, I'd say.' And now for the crucial question . . . 'When do you start?'

'Surprisingly enough, in a fortnight.'

He felt a sudden sense of panic. Two weeks! So soon!

'That is, presuming Lionel gets the go-ahead from the editor-in-chief. But the timing is so wonderfully coincidental, Danny. Do you know, they were actually thinking of advertising for a female staff writer.'

Daniel wasn't listening. Surely, he thought, she'd be required to give at least a month's notice to *The Courier-Mail*.

55

'Apparently they were employing a woman journalist on a freelance basis,' Elizabeth rattled on, 'but she's given up work to have a baby, and they've been considering employing a female writer full-time. Isn't that the most incredible good luck?'

'Incredible, yes. A fortnight, you say? But what about *The Courier-Mail*?'

'Oh, Henry's been marvellous, he'd let me go tomorrow if necessary. I think he's rather proud of the fact that he was the one to launch my career. He's certainly the reason Lionel Brock's taking me on. He'll miss me, he says, but –'

'So will I.'

Elizabeth stopped mid-stream. Danny looked quite bereft, she thought – how sweet. 'I'll miss you too,' she said. And suddenly she realised how very much she would. She'd never had a friend like Danny. 'I'll miss you a lot.'

'Will you, Elizabeth?'

'Of course.' She was touched by his obvious concern. 'But we'll still see each other, this isn't goodbye.' She smiled fondly. 'Heavens above, you're part of my life, Danny, you're the best friend I've ever had.'

That was all he needed. 'Then marry me,' he said.

A stunned silence followed, and he regretted having blurted the words out so clumsily as he watched her astonishment become suspicion.

'Are you making fun of me?' she asked.

'Of course I'm not.' He spoke lightly, careful not to alarm her with any outburst of passion. 'But surely the best friend you've ever had would be a good choice for a husband, don't you think?'

'If this is a joke, I'm afraid I'm missing the point.'

'Why would I be joking?'

'I have just announced the career opportunity of a lifetime and you suggest *marriage*?' Elizabeth gave a snort of derision. 'It's either a joke or it's some sort of statement about a woman's place being in the home and her life's purpose marriage, in which case it's an insult. Either way, it's not particularly funny.'

'But I wouldn't expect you to stay at home,' he protested in earnest. 'I'm proud of your achievements. I would never wish to change one thing about you, Elizabeth, and that includes your commitment to a career.'

She stared at him, speechless, as the realisation that he was serious finally registered.

'Your career is who you are,' he continued, 'I know that. Why should I want to change the very person I fell in love with?'

In love? Elizabeth couldn't believe what she was hearing. In love!

'But . . . you're so . . . young!' She couldn't think of anything else to say; she was flabbergasted. 'You're so very young. I mean . . . surely you must see that this . . . this . . .' She fumbled foolishly for the right words; she seemed incapable of expressing herself intelligently. 'This . . . *feeling* you have is just some sort of . . . *infatuation* . . .'

His proposal had hardly met with the reception he might have wished, but Daniel laughed nonetheless. 'I'm not a teenager, Elizabeth,' he said. Then he added good-humouredly, 'You're patronising me the way you did when we first met – it's not frightfully flattering, I must say.'

Yes, she remembered how she'd patronised him that day. And she remembered how he'd come back with the perfect response. *Men younger than me have died for this country*, he'd said. She'd been impressed. Everything about him had impressed her that day, which was why she'd allowed their friendship to develop. And now he was spoiling it all.

'But you're like a little brother to me,' she began.

'No I'm not,' he snapped. 'Don't demean our relationship.' He fought to curb his exasperation. 'I'm not your little brother, Elizabeth,' he said as patiently as he could. 'I've never been your little brother, and you know it.'

'Yes, yes, I'm sorry.' She was flustered; she hadn't intended to sound so insulting. 'Of course you're not, you're far, far more. You're my best friend ... you're my one true confidant ... Please, Danny ...' Her eyes implored him. 'Can't we leave things that way?'

'Of course we can. We can be best friends and true confidants for the rest of our lives. What better basis could there be for a marriage?'

No, she thought, no, you can't change the rules like this. Why was he ruining everything?

Daniel was sure he could sense her faltering, and he took her hand in both of his. 'Marry me, Elizabeth,' he said, dropping flamboyantly to one knee. 'Marry me. I'm the perfect husband for you. You won't regret it, I promise.'

'Oh, for goodness sake, get up,' she hissed, common sense prevailing. It was time to put a stop to the charade, he was being childish. 'You've no idea what you're saying, you're acting on impulse. This is a load of romantic nonsense and I won't listen to another word.'

He released her hand and sat obediently on the bench.

'Pity,' he shrugged, 'I rather liked the romantic approach myself. But as for the rest, I can assure you, you're wrong. I'm not acting on impulse and I know exactly what I'm saying. I've been in love with you from the day we first met.'

For the second time in only minutes, she was rendered speechless.

'Come on now,' he chided, 'you must have sensed it.'

She shook her head. 'Why would I have sensed it?' she asked, her voice a disbelieving whisper. 'You never said a word.'

He thought how very vulnerable she looked. 'I didn't dare. I was worried that I might frighten you off.'

'We've always been honest with each other, we've never had secrets.'

'I know, and I'm sorry. But be reasonable, Elizabeth, if I'd told you I was in love with you, what would you have done?' She made no reply. 'I doubt I would have seen you for the dust.' He smiled. 'We had to get to know each other first.'

'I see.' She nodded slowly, and when she finally spoke her tone was measured. 'So everything has been a lie, right from the start.'

Only then did Daniel realise his mistake. What he'd per-ceived as vulnerability was anger. And it was growing by the second.

'I had presumed,' she continued coldly, 'that our friendship was based on trust and some form of mutual respect.'

'It was. Of course it was.'

'Oh, no, it wasn't. Not as far as you were concerned, not for one minute.' She was steadily working herself into a fury. 'It was based upon deceit.'

'Oh, for God's sake, Elizabeth.' Daniel's patience ran out as exasperation got the better of him. 'I'm a man, you're a woman, it's natural! Men are not the enemy! Why must you feel so *threatened*?'

He was surprised by the instantaneous effect of his words. She was clearly taken aback.

'I'm not a threat,' he said firmly, 'I'm an ally. I believe in you and I believe in your career. I love you, and what's more I think you love me. Not to the same degree, of course, but be honest with yourself . . .' He willed her to look at him, and she did, meeting his gaze squarely. 'You do love me just a little, admit it.'

'Of course I do.'

There was an irritable and patronising edge to her reply, which strangely pleased him. She was on the defensive, he thought. She didn't like being cornered.

'I love you as a friend,' she said with a haughty nonchalance.

'Then I rest my case. What better basis could there be for a marriage?'

'I said as a *friend*! I love you as a *friend*!'

'So marriage should be based upon enmity, should it?' He could see that his smugness annoyed her further, but he didn't care. Sensing victory in his grasp, Daniel was elated. 'I'm not the only one who thinks we should marry, you know. I have your parents' approval.'

'I beg your pardon?'

'Your mother and father were sending signals loud and clear the night of your birthday party.'

'It wasn't a *party*, it was a *dinner*. And what exactly were the signals?'

'Well, all that stuff about the oleanders for starters.'

'And what *stuff* about the oleanders would that be?'

Daniel, in his youthful exuberance, failed to read the warning signs. 'All that symbolic stuff – it was a test to see how I felt about your father being Jewish.'

'I think the analogy went a little deeper than that,' she said coolly. 'I think my father was sharing something intensely personal that night.'

'Of course he was! But why did he choose that night of all nights? And why did he choose to tell me of all people? You asked that yourself, don't you remember?'

Elizabeth said nothing. Of course she remembered. And of course, she realised, with a sudden rush of anger – of course he was right.

Daniel misguidedly read approval in her silence and, considering himself well and truly on the home stretch, made his final, irrevocable mistake.

'Your mother knew what was going on all along,' he said. 'In fact, I got the distinct impression she approved.'

'Of you?'

He was halted just a little by the bark of her question. 'Of *us*,' he said. 'I got the impression your mother and father both approved –'

'Of *us*.'

'Yes.' Daniel faltered. Things seemed to have taken a turn for the worse.

'You passed the test then?'

'It would appear so, yes.' Something was definitely wrong.

'Well, bully for you.'

'What is it, Elizabeth? Why are you angry?'

Elizabeth was far more than angry. She was hurt and humiliated by the thought that her parents and Danny had been in collusion that night. She felt stupid for not having recognised the signs. Her father's admission about the oleanders had touched her deeply, and she'd considered it a personal and precious gift that he'd chosen her birthday, of all nights, to share his secret. How gallingly stupid of her, she thought.

'I'm delighted,' she said caustically as she rose from the bench, 'that you and my parents have come to such an amicable decision regarding my future. What on earth would I do without you all?'

Daniel also stood. 'Good God, Elizabeth, it wasn't exactly a conspiracy, they were only –'

'It certainly sounds that way to me.'

'Don't you think you're overreacting just a little?' he said. 'You're not normally one for paranoia.'

'I'm not normally one to be dictated to either. Nor am I one to be easily influenced by the opinions of others. It does not impress me in the least that you have the approval of my parents, Danny. The answer to your ridiculous proposition is a definite no.'

She stormed off without another word, and he was left wondering what had happened. How had things got so out of hand? What had he said that was so terribly wrong?

The following week was a miserable one for Daniel. He didn't call Elizabeth for fear of annoying her further, and decided to leave any contact until shortly before her departure. Perhaps when he rang to say goodbye she might have cooled down. Perhaps he might sense a change in her feelings. He desperately hoped so.

The weekend came and went, and then, on the Monday . . .

'Call for you, Lieutenant.'

He'd just walked into the guardroom, and the duty sergeant handed him the receiver before discreetly disappearing into the transport office.

'Hello,' he said as he sat at the desk, 'Lieutenant Gardiner here.'

Elizabeth's voice came down the line. 'It's me. I'm sorry,' she said stiffly. 'I realise that I overreacted and that I owe you an apology.'

'That's all right. I'm sorry I gave you such a shock. I didn't mean –'

'Don't apologise, Danny. Please. That's my job.'

'Right. Apology accepted then.' He wanted to say, *So where to from here*, but didn't dare, she sounded so brittle. 'When do you leave?' he asked.

'On Friday.'

'Oh. So soon.'

'Yes. Daddy's driving me up to London. An associate of his has a real estate business and he's going to show us some flats in South Kensington.'

*Will I see you before you go?* he wanted to ask, but he didn't because he knew he'd sound desperate. 'That's good,' he said.

'I feel ridiculously mollycoddled, but Daddy's insistent that he won't be satisfied until he sees me properly settled, so I've had to give in.'

'Well, you'd be insane not to take advantage of his contacts, Elizabeth, and surely it's a father's prerogative to look after his daughter.'

'Yes, yes, I know, and I'm grateful.'

There was a moment's awkward pause as they both realised the small talk had run out.

'I don't want to lose your friendship, Danny,' she said.

'You don't have to.' He felt weary and suddenly defeated. *I don't want to be friends with the woman I love!* he felt like yelling. *I want to be friends with my* wife*!* 'We'll always be friends, Elizabeth,' he said instead.

'That's good. I'm glad.' Another pause. 'I'll let you know where I am and we'll keep in touch then?'

'Yes, absolutely.'

'Bye, Danny.'

'Bye, Elizabeth.'

Several months later, Daniel was posted to Frankfurt to serve with the occupying forces for six months. When he rang Elizabeth in London to tell her the news, there was another brief and awkward farewell over the phone. Then, shortly before Christmas, he departed, thankful to leave Aldershot.

*Yarina crouches in the red dust, motionless, the child beside her, a boy barely three years of age, equally still, equally silent. Aware of his mother's unspoken signal, he clutches tightly to her hand, and the two become one with the landscape, melding into the shadows of the mallee scrub. In the gathering dusk, they are all but invisible to the approaching strangers.*

*As the truck slowly passes, Yarina hears the voices of the two white men through its open cabin windows, but she does not understand what they are saying. She does not speak the white man's language.*

*She watches as the truck pulls up barely a hundred yards from her, and watches as the men alight and take equipment from its tray.*

*Her eyes flicker beyond the truck to where she sees her husband, Ngama. He has been hunting, and the fat ramia he has caught for their dinner is slung over one shoulder. He stands frozen amongst a clump of mulga trees, the only movement being a droplet of the goanna's blood that slowly winds its way down his bare chest. Ngama has not bothered to hide from the strangers, but like Yarina he too has become a part of the landscape. It is easy to remain invisible to the white man, they have found.*

*Yarina squeezes her little boy's hand. He is a healthy, boisterous child, unaccustomed to staying still for any length of time. But her warning is not necessary. The boy* has seen white men only once before in his short life, and even then from a distance. Instinctively, he fears them.

From their separate vantage points, Yarina and Ngama continue to watch as the men attach something to the fence of wire. They have heard of this fence of wire, which encompasses a part of the desert plains to the south, and they are confused. They are Arrernte people from the centre. They are unaccustomed to fences on their own lands. Why have the white men done this, Yarina wonders.

It is the question on the lips of many. Why do the white men intrude upon our land, ask those of the Pitjantjatjara and Yankuntjatjara and Kokatha. The Luritja, Arrernte and Antakarinja people, who traverse the area, ask the same question. Why do the white men wish to keep us from our tracks? Why do they deny us access to our sacred sites and our waterholes? This is a puzzle to many people. What could the white men want in the desert country that is so foreign to them? There is nothing for the white man here, they say.

Yarina and her tiny son remain motionless for the fifteen minutes it takes the men to attach the sign and move on. Then, as the truck disappears and the desert dust settles, Yarina joins her husband. Together they examine the strange symbols on the notice that now hangs from the fence. But they do not understand its meaning.

# Chapter Four

'Maralinga,' Harold announced. 'They're calling it Maralinga – means "fields of thunder" in some sort of native lingo, I believe.' He gave a hoot of delighted laughter. 'Rather apt for a nuclear bomb test site, what?'

'It's certainly colourful,' his wife agreed. 'Who came up with the idea?'

'The Australian chief defence scientist, so I'm told, a chappie by the name of Butement. Never met the fellow myself, but then I haven't bumped into any of the Australian contingent as yet.'

Harold took a sip of the second cup of tea his wife had just poured him and, discovering it not warm enough for his liking, decided to ring for a fresh pot. He rose from his cosy armchair beside the open fireplace and crossed to the French windows. 'Bound to meet up with them shortly, of course, now that I'm officially on board,' he said, giving the bell sash two brisk tugs. 'I shall be going down there any tick of the clock, I imagine.'

He looked out at the serenity of the landscape, where the elm tree cradled its burden of snow in the comfortable crooks of its giant limbs, and the white-laced hedgerow wound its elegant way down the slope that led to the brook. He did so love winter. The romantic in him particularly loved a white Christmas, and, the cold snap having well and truly set in, this Christmas of 1954 held every promise of being white.

'Probably just in time for a stinking hot desert Christmas,' he added, 'blast my luck.'

'How does the Australian public feel about this Maralinga business?' Lavinia asked.

'I don't think they know.'

'Really? How extraordinary. One would assume such drastic action would lead to immensely strong public opinion. What a strange breed they must be.'

'No, no, my love, you misunderstand. The majority of them don't know what's going *on*. Well, not yet anyway. Their government's keeping the news pretty much to itself – at least until the site's established, and even then they'll let the populace know only the barest minimum. In fact, if we have our way, the Australians will know only what we tell them they can know.'

'Dear me,' Lavinia tut-tutted. 'And they'll accept that, will they? The *British* public wouldn't take kindly to being so ill-informed.'

She stopped abruptly. A light tap on the door was a precursor to the maid's appearance, and she knew better than to discuss her husband's business in front of the servants. Indeed, Lavinia felt privileged that Harold, in his position as deputy director of MI6, should see fit to share so much of his work with her. She was aware there was material that he did not offer up for discussion, and she never posed a query without his encouragement, but she enjoyed the degree of trust he placed in her. It meant that she could share at least a proportion of the huge burden of responsibility his job entailed. And that, in Lavinia's opinion, was a wife's bounden duty.

'We need a fresh pot,' Harold called to the maid from his position by the windows.

'Yes, m'lord.' The girl bobbed a curtsy and, leaving the double doors open, crossed to the large circular coffee table and picked up the tray.

'And perhaps one or two of Freda's scones?' Lavinia directed the question at her husband rather than the maid.

'Oh, by jove, yes,' Harold readily agreed.

'Jam and clotted cream, please, Bessie.'

'Very good, m'lady.' Another bob, and Bessie left, placing the heavy silver tray briefly on the hall table outside as she pulled the drawing room doors closed behind her.

Lavinia waited several seconds before continuing. 'So it's to our advantage that the Australians are so gullible.'

'Dear me, yes.' Harold returned to his armchair beside the fire. 'And we have their prime minister well and truly in our pocket,' he said as he sat opposite her. 'Several years back, when Menzies agreed to our nuclear weapon testing off the coast of Western Australia, he didn't even inform his own cabinet.'

'Oh, don't be ridiculous, Harold, that can't be true.'

'But it is, my love – heard it directly from the Old Man himself.' Harold had just returned to his country estate in Sussex following his London meeting with Prime Minister Churchill. 'Winston told me that in 1950 Attlee sent a top-secret personal request to Menzies regarding the use of the Monte Bello Islands,' he explained, in response to his wife's obvious disbelief. 'Menzies agreed immediately in principle to the nuclear testing, and, according to Winston, there's never been any record whatsoever of the man having consulted a single one of his cabinet colleagues on the matter.'

'Goodness gracious.' The impeccable arch of Lavinia Dartleigh's brow furrowed ever so slightly. 'Isn't that somewhat irregular?'

Harold laughed. He adored his wife's talent for understatement. Lavinia was the quintessential upper-class Englishwoman. Still beautiful in her early forties, she was the epitome of elegance, highly intelligent and at all times unruffled. Harold valued her greatly. She was the perfect wife for a man in his position.

'Yes, my love, it is somewhat irregular.'

Harold Rodin Dartleigh, KCMG, KCVO, 6th Baron Somerston, was typical of many born to a life of privilege. He was arrogant and insensitive and took the services of others for granted. But, unlike a number of his contemporaries from equally advantaged backgrounds, he was not lazy and he was not a wastrel. Nor was he stupid. As a young man, Harold had distinguished himself in History and Philosophy at Cambridge University's Trinity College, after which he had embraced a highly successful diplomatic career, serving in under-secretary positions in the British embassies of Beirut, Istanbul, Tokyo and Prague.

Upon the outbreak of war in 1939, Harold's father, William, 5th Baron Somerston, had been so horrified at the thought of losing his only son and heir that, through his many connections, he'd had the twenty-nine year old appointed special government envoy to Washington. The move had not dismayed Harold, who had had no deep desire to join the fray – not through any form of fear or cowardice on his part, but solely due to ambition. Death on a distant battlefield was not the destiny young Harold had in mind.

Having seen out the war in relative comfort, Harold had returned to England to care for his ailing father and, upon William's death in 1946, had taken his seat in the House of

Lords. Given his wealth of diplomatic experience, the Secret Intelligence Service had soon beckoned and he'd jumped at the chance, quickly advancing through the ranks to become deputy director of MI6.

To Harold's extreme satisfaction, his achievements had been recognised in the highest of circles. In 1949 he had been awarded Knight Commander of the Order of St Michael and St George (KCMG) by King George VI for his work in the diplomatic service, and he had recently, early in this very year of 1954, been made Knight Commander Royal Victoria Order (KCVO) by Elizabeth II for service to the Queen and other members of the Royal family.

Forty-five years of age, just over six feet tall, and with a fit body but for a slight thickening of the girth, Harold was a distinguished-looking man. A good head of hair turning steel grey matched eyes of a similar colour, and his features were chiselled, patrician. But there was no denying a coldness about Harold.

A coldness that some, in their self-admitted envy, dismissed as the arrogance of the privileged, and that others, perhaps of more generous nature and mostly numbering amongst his colleagues, maintained went with the job. The deputy director of MI6 *had* to be aloof, they said. And Harold was fun when you got to know him. He was frightfully clever, frightfully witty and an excellent dining companion. All of which was correct, so long as Harold was in the right mood.

Lord Dartleigh did have some genuinely staunch defenders, particularly amongst the high-ranking clergy, and the women with whom he mingled – mainly his colleagues' wives, whose standing in society gave them a power of their own. They found it most admirable that never a breath of scandal could be laid at his doorstep. A family man with two grown children, Harold was faithful to a woman whom he clearly adored. The clergy applauded the exemplary marriage of so public a figure, and the women found his openly demonstrative devotion to his wife romantic, even enviable. Indeed, so enviable that several of the wives who indulged in the odd dalliance to match those of their husbands regretted the fact that Harold Dartleigh was unavailable.

And then there were the others – those who lived in fear of Harold. Some feared him instinctively upon first meeting, and for some the fear grew over time, but the results were the same. He unnerved them.

There was one element, however, upon which all were bound to agree. Harold Dartleigh was not a man to be crossed – by friend or by foe.

'You mentioned the desert,' Lavinia prompted. 'I presume one's not to know precisely which desert, or where?' She only ever raised queries when the way had been paved for her, and in this case it had. She found the subject of Maralinga most interesting.

'Quite right, my love, all very hush-hush, mum's the word.'

'Naturally. My guess is, nevertheless, South Australia. Wasn't that the location of Emu Field?' she asked innocently.

Harold chortled. He did so delight in his wife's intelligence. 'How the deuce did you know about Emu Field?'

'I saw a brief report in the cinema last year.' Lavinia's reply was a mixture of apology and criticism. 'In a Pathé Pictorial, I'm afraid. Hardly hush-hush.'

'Ah. Well . . .' Harold's smile faded. 'Maralinga will most certainly be hush-hush, at least for as long as we can keep such a place a secret. Once we start detonating, of course, the whole world will know, but by then we'll have the site thoroughly secure and be able to monitor how much information we feed to the press. It's one thing for the Monte Bello and Emu sites to be made public, but we're talking about the establishment of a permanent nuclear testing ground, my love. All the more reason for MI6 to be running the show, and that's exactly what I told Churchill. Our department should have been brought in right from the start.'

Harold enjoyed having a wife in whom he could confide, and was aware of how highly Lavinia valued his trust, but there was an added advantage to their shared confidences about which he was thoroughly objective. Their mutual trust was an invaluable element to the success of their marriage and, therefore, to their public image. Being confidants consolidated them as a team, not only to each other but to the world at large. And appearances were, after all, essential for a man in his position.

'Winston and I are in agreement that it's a bit of a worry giving the boffins free rein,' he continued. 'They can be a sloppy bunch at the best of times. Scientists care about nothing but the results of their experiments, which leaves the gates wide open for breaches of security.'

'But the military will be running Maralinga, surely.'

'The day-to-day operations, yes, but William Penney's been put in charge of the tests – and all things relative to them – which is a bit of a worry, in my opinion. The fellow's a physicist, for God's sake.'

'He's also one of the world's leading authorities on nuclear weapons and he's been in charge of the British nuclear program for years.'

'Well done, my love.' Slinging one leg languidly over the other, Harold lolled back in his armchair and gave her a round of applause. 'Pathé Pictorial?' he queried.

'No. *The Times*.' Lavina smiled, unfazed by her husband's blatant mockery. 'And it's *Sir* William now, by the way – he was knighted three years ago.'

'Ah yes, so he was, it had slipped my mind.' It hadn't at all – a further mockery. 'Poor old Penney,' Harold sighed, 'he's going to hate my guts more than ever when he hears I'm running the show.'

'Why more than ever?'

'He didn't much like me at Cambridge, I'm afraid, and he won't take kindly to this turn of events. In fact my personal involvement in the Maralinga project will be thoroughly irksome to him.'

Lavinia was faintly surprised. She'd known the two had attended Trinity College at the same time, but Harold had never mentioned any antipathy.

'But the fellow will just have to put up with me, I'm afraid. MI6's presence in Australia is essential. The last thing we need is another Fuchs episode.'

Harold was referring to the highly publicised conviction of the British physicist Klaus Fuchs four years previously. A German-born British citizen, Fuchs had been a key figure in the atomic bomb developmental program devised by the Americans during the war and early post-war years. The Manhattan Project, as the program was codenamed, had been largely dependent upon American resources and personnel, but a number of British scientists had been involved, and the shocking discovery that one of the most high-ranking amongst them had been a Soviet spy for years had reverberated around the world.

'One can hardly blame the Americans for closing shop on us,' Harold said. Then, dropping the flippant façade, he leaned forward, steel-grey eyes gleaming with the familiar intensity that his colleagues at times found disturbing. 'We cannot afford to be slack in the nuclear stakes, Lavinia. There's a Cold War in progress and the Russians have proved their ability to infiltrate the most seemingly inaccessible –'

Another tap at the door announced the maid's imminent arrival.

'I do hope you won't be called away for Christmas, dear . . .'

The drawing room doors opened and Bessie appeared.

'. . . Catherine and Nigel will both be home this year,' Lavina smoothly continued as the girl bobbed back into the hall for the tray she'd placed on the table. 'It would be such a pity to miss out on the full family affair.'

'Nigel? Really?' As always, Lavinia's transition to the banal had been seamless, but Harold was taken aback by the news of his son. 'Nigel's coming home for Christmas?'

'Yes, he telephoned this morning, while you were in London.'

'Good heavens above, why didn't you tell me?'

'There seemed so many other things to talk about, didn't there?' Lavinia's attention remained focused upon the maid as Bessie carefully placed the tray on the coffee table between them. 'He's very much looking forward to being home.'

'Well, I shall certainly tell the department that I'm unavailable until after the festive season,' Harold said, rubbing his hands together in pleasurable anticipation, perhaps of his son's arrival or perhaps of his afternoon tea – it was difficult to tell which as he eyed the dish of scones. 'I very much look forward to his being home too. They are *warmed*, aren't they?' he asked.

'Yes, m'lord.' Bessie nodded as she set out the Spode fine bone china side plates, together with the linen napkins and silver cake knives. 'Freda's had them in a hot oven for a good five –'

'Excellent, excellent. So when does he get here?'

'In a fortnight – just three days before Christmas.'

'What fun. How jolly.'

Harold enjoyed his son's company; they had a great deal in

common. Twenty-four-year-old Nigel, having emulated his father, had joined the diplomatic corps and was currently an attaché at the British embassy in Rome.

'And I told you, didn't I,' Lavinia continued, 'that Catherine will be arriving Saturday week?'

'Yes, you did mention it, I recall.'

The news wasn't of equal interest. Harold didn't really understand his daughter, and wasn't sure if he cared to. Catherine was nineteen, studying art in Paris and had turned into quite the bohemian. He'd threatened to cut off her allowance the previous year if she didn't enrol in university, or at least attend the Swiss finishing school he'd offered, but her mother had taken the girl's side in the argument. 'She's very headstrong, my dear, and she'll go to Paris in any event, so it might as well be with our support – God knows what she'll get up to otherwise. Just for the two years of her art course, Harold. And she *is* very talented, you must admit.' Harold had reluctantly acquiesced, but he'd been annoyed that Catherine had not followed her brother's example and conformed to the image expected of one of her station in life. Her behaviour did not at all befit the daughter of a man in his position.

'I'll pour, thank you, Bessie,' Lavinia said.

'Very good, m'lady.' Bessie bobbed and left, closing the doors behind her.

Silence reigned briefly while Lavina poured the tea and Harold attacked the scones. After slicing one down the middle, he smothered both halves with jam and then piled on the clotted cream.

'My God, that woman's worth her weight in gold,' he said as he devoured the first half. Freda was undoubtedly the best cook they'd ever had.

'You said Maralinga is to be a *permanent* testing ground,'

Lavinia remarked, passing him his tea. 'How long do you antici-
pate being there yourself?'

'Oh, I'll come and go somewhat, I would think.' Harold put
down the cup and saucer, tea untouched, his scone taking priority as he embarked on the second half. 'I plan to have an office
permanently based there and a cipher clerk on site to send me
regular reports, but I'll front up for the detonations. The first
series of tests won't take place until around September next
year; they have to finish building the place first.' He shovelled
the remains of the scone into his mouth and reached for another.
'Aren't you having any of these?'

'I ate a late lunch.'

'Ah, right.' He piled more jam onto his side plate. 'I'll be off
on a recce trip shortly, of course – have a look at the site and
check out the Australian scientific representatives. Although I
have dossiers on all three and they're not only harmless, they're
ideal.' He gave a snort of laughter as he scooped up a spoonful
of cream. 'Two of them are actually *British* – accepted positions
in Australia after the war – perfect choices to liaise with the
Australian government. Penney's done a damn good job there,
have to give him that much.'

Harold paused long enough to demolish another half a scone,
then, dabbing his mouth with his napkin, continued. 'I'll be
gone a good several weeks, I'd think, given the travel there and
back, and I need to get the full layout of the place. I must say,
the prospect intrigues me. Do you know they're building a
ruddy great township in the middle of the desert? It's quite
extraordinary. The airstrip's a mile and a half long! Imagine that.
Right out there in the middle of nowhere. Quite, quite extraordinary.'

He contemplated the remaining half-scone that sat on his
plate and decided against it, picking up his cup and saucer

instead. 'They'll want me to leave pretty soon, I should imagine, but I'll stave off any plans until the new year so I can catch up with Nigel.' Then he hastily added, 'Catherine too, of course – don't want to miss out on the family Christmas, what?'

He could tell from the look in his wife's eyes that she was on the verge of beseeching him, yet again, to disguise his blatant favouritism in the presence of the children, but Harold couldn't be bothered talking about Catherine. He had far more important and exciting things on his mind.

'I have a plan up my sleeve which I don't intend to share with the boffins,' he said, 'nor with the armed forces. In fact, just to be on the safe side, I shan't even inform my own officer who's to be stationed there.' He leaned back in his armchair, cup and saucer cradled against his chest. 'There will be a covert MI6 operative salted amongst them,' he announced with a smug smile. Then, little finger delicately extended, he lifted the cup to his lips and sipped. Harold always drank tea in the daintiest manner.

'I'm having one of my top undercover men seconded to Maralinga,' he said, and toyed briefly with the notion of telling her who – she knew Gideon Melbray from their embassy days in Washington. But he decided against it. *No names, no pack drill* must remain the order of the day. Pity, he thought, he'd have enjoyed her reaction. Lavinia had liked Gideon a great deal, he remembered, she'd found him a most attractive fellow. But then, everyone did. People were drawn to Gideon's beauty and tended to trust him – which, of course, made him such a valuable covert operative.

'By jove,' he said with a gleeful grin, 'wouldn't old Penney be just livid if he knew he had an MI6 spy in his midst.'

'I have to say I'm not happy about this, Harold. I'm not happy about this at all.'

Three days later, having been informed by the Prime Minister's Office of MI6's involvement, Sir William Penney appeared bordering on livid, which was unusual for a man of his normally affable disposition.

'Just a precautionary measure, old chap. You mustn't take it personally.'

Aware of the perverse pleasure Harold Dartleigh was finding in his one-upmanship, Penney wondered exactly how else he was supposed to take it. 'I have headed Britain's nuclear weapons program since 1947,' he began testily. 'My leadership skills have never been questioned –'

'And they're not being questioned now.' Harold was quick to appease, although he felt superior – Penney was such a typical boffin in his opinion. Good God, even the look of the man – small in stature, lanky straight hair, horn-rimmed glasses . . . It was a source of wonder how he'd ever achieved leadership in the first place, Harold thought. 'No-one's undermining your authority, William. We're just keeping an overall eye on things for security purposes. Can't be too careful after the Fuchs affair, can we?'

The comment only added insult to injury as far as Penney was concerned. 'There's been not the slightest hint of any breach of security throughout the tests I've conducted.'

'Well . . .' Harold looked just a little dubious. 'A whisper did reach our ears that Operation Hurricane came close to being compromised.'

'How?' William Penney was understandably appalled. Having received a knighthood from Queen Elizabeth II for heading the successful detonation of Britain's first nuclear device in the Monte Bello Islands, he was outraged that Dartleigh should cast a shadow over the momentous event. 'How and by whom, exactly, was Operation Hurricane *compromised*?'

'Oh, come, come, William, *you* of *all* people can't expect me to answer such a question.' Harold managed to flatter and patronise at the same time, a skill he'd perfected over the years. '*Need to know*, old man.' He smiled and tapped his nose with his forefinger in true conspiratorial fashion. '*Need to know*.'

The adage was one Sir William Penney himself regularly used, and the practice was one he intended to adopt at Maralinga, where everyone, scientists and armed forces alike, would work strictly on a need-to-know-only basis. It was clear that Harold Dartleigh intended to annoy him, Penney thought. He maintained a dignified silence.

Harold decided it was time to back off. 'Nothing to worry about, William, I can assure you. A minor leak – safely discovered and contained.' There had been no breach of security at all at Monte Bello, but Harold had felt the need to establish himself in the pecking order. 'Just as I can assure you,' he continued, 'that MI6 will in no way influence the chain of command at Maralinga.' He smiled jovially. 'Good heavens above, I won't even be there half the time.'

'I trust you will communicate that in the briefing,' Penney said stiffly. 'Shall we go in? I believe they're ready for us.'

William Penney had reluctantly invited Harold Dartleigh to a heads of departments meeting at Aldermaston in Berkshire. Roughly twenty miles northwest of Aldershot, RAF Aldermaston, an abandoned World War II airfield, had for several years been the selected home for Britain's nuclear weapons program.

'After you, William.' Harold stepped courteously aside, giving a quick nod as he did so to Ned Hanson, his assisting officer, who had been waiting by the main doors discreetly out of earshot. 'After you.'

Ned joined them, and the three entered the briefing room,

where around twenty men were seated waiting. Scientists and engineers from every area of expertise, they headed the various departments of Sir William Penney's research team.

Harold and Ned Hanson sat in the vacant chairs that had been reserved for them down the front, while William Penney marched directly to the table facing the assembly, behind which, on the wall, was a projection screen. He did not introduce Harold Dartleigh, nor did he make any formal address to the gathering, having greeted his team earlier and chatted with each man personally, well before the arrival of the MI6 representatives.

'Let's get straight down to business, shall we,' he said, signalling to his young assistant who was standing by the slide projector at the rear of the room.

Shades were drawn over the windows, the room dimmed, and a large map of Australia appeared on the screen. Picking up the slender wooden baton that served as an indicator, William Penney proceeded to give an account of the testing ground, its location and the reasons for its choice.

The Maralinga site, he explained, was approximately 250 miles north-west of the coastal township of Ceduna, and roughly 600 miles from Adelaide, the capital city of South Australia. A remote region where the Great Victoria Desert met the Nullarbor Plain, it was barren, uninhabited and the perfect choice for nuclear weapon testing. The desert terrain was flat with little scrub cover, but sandhills to the south formed a natural barrier, which was ideal for security purposes. His glance at Harold Dartleigh was a reminder that security was always uppermost in his mind.

Harold read the meaning in the glance and smiled pleasantly.

Penney called for the next slide, and a plan of the site appeared on the screen. He talked his team through its layout: the landing strip and airport, the experimental areas and laboratories, and the village designed to accommodate, during peak requirements, up to 3000 men.

Contrary to Harold's scathing opinion, William Penney excelled in command, and the team members present, most of whom had worked with him on previous projects and held him in high regard, listened respectfully as he continued.

Further slides were projected and, over images depicting a vast and desolate landscape, Penney explained the harsh conditions under which they would all live – the searing heat of the days and the unexpected chill of the desert nights. He summed up with good humour, however. 'Most of the time it'll be as hot as Hades,' he said, 'but the army is building a swimming pool, so all is not lost.'

There were chuckles amongst the men, and, as Penney placed the baton on the table signalling the end of his talk, there was a smattering of applause, which he acknowledged but quickly stemmed, holding up his hands for silence.

'I have received notification from the Prime Minister's Office that MI6 is taking a particularly strong interest in the Maralinga project. As everyone here is aware, security has been a foremost issue in all our past work, and will continue to be so at Maralinga. I am sure, therefore, that you will all join me in welcoming aboard Harold Lord Dartleigh, who, as most of you will know, is the deputy director of MI6.'

The abrupt, and very pointed, introduction did not in the least bother Harold who rose from his chair offering his hand.

'Thank you, Sir William,' he said.

As they shook, Harold gained a smug satisfaction from the image they presented. No-one could fail to notice that the peer of the realm stood a good half a head taller than the bespectacled little scientist.

Gesturing that the floor was now Harold's, William Penney

retired to a nearby chair, and Harold initiated a token round of applause, which to some might have seemed just a fraction patronising.

'One might well ask what possible advantage MI6 has to offer in the light of Sir William's impeccable leadership over the years,' he said with a smile, which, if intended to be self-deprecating, didn't work, but then he didn't really intend it to. 'And the answer is very little, because very little is necessary. Our presence at Maralinga will simply be an added precaution, given the precarious and uncertain times in which we live.'

He beckoned to his assisting officer, and Ned, a burly, pleasant-looking man in his early thirties, joined him.

'I'd like to introduce Ned Hanson of MI6's Defence Signals Branch who will be permanently stationed at Maralinga.' Dropping the charm, Harold got down briskly to the business of the day. 'I'd be most grateful if you'd extend Ned every courtesy and assist him with any enquiries he may have on my behalf. Your help will be of inestimable value, and most appreciated, believe me. I shall, of course, be down there myself from time to time, but for the most part,' he clapped Ned heartily on the shoulder, 'Ned's your man.'

Business over, the charm once again emerged. 'Our presence will be very low key,' he said, 'more secretarial than anything really. None of that cloak-and-dagger stuff, I can assure you – in fact you'll hardly notice we're there.' He gave a personable grin and gazed around the room, establishing eye contact with as many as he could. 'I look forward to working with you all very much, and I thank you for your attention.'

Harold was pleased. The tone of his address had impressed the men, he could tell – as well it should. The situation had called for diplomacy, and his balance between the authoritative and the informal had been perfect.

'Thank you, Sir William,' he said, relinquishing the floor with gracious aplomb. 'I appreciate this opportunity to chat to the team.' He returned to his seat, the implication being *you may carry on.*

As Sir William Penney rose to conclude the briefing, he thought how very little Harold Dartleigh had changed. The man was as arrogant, detestable and self-opinionated as he had been at Cambridge. They didn't need him at Maralinga. The whole team had been working like a well-oiled machine for years – on every level, including that of security. And now, when all their hard work had paid off and they were to be awarded the supreme opportunity of a permanent nuclear testing site, MI6 was stepping in. They didn't need MI6, he thought. And certainly not in the form of Harold Dartleigh.

The King's Rooms, in the heart of London, not far from Soho Square, was a highly exclusive gentlemen's club. Rumoured to have been one of King George IV's favourite haunts, with bawdy bars and backrooms and accommodation upstairs for whatever resulted from the evening's activities, its architecture and its history were colourful. The former tavern had been converted to a club for gentlemen in the early Edwardian era, when adventurous entrepreneurs had simultaneously acquired the adjoining property and linked the two to create an opulent health spa, complete with black and white marble-tiled steam rooms and mineral baths. Now, nearly fifty years on, the King's Rooms, with its historic bathhouse, plush lounges, fine dining and service par excellence, was a renowned oasis for gentlemen of the upper classes. Here the idle rich and the elite of the professional world could mingle freely, unbothered by the common herd.

For Harold Dartleigh, the King's Rooms was a home away from home.

'I shall be staying at the club tonight,' he said to his wife as he prepared to leave for London.

'Very well, dear. You haven't forgotten that Catherine's arriving tomorrow, have you?'

'Of course not.' He had. 'I shall be home in time for dinner, I promise.'

He picked up his briefcase, and his wife followed him into the main hall where Wilson, the butler, was waiting beside the front doors.

'Excellent.' Lavinia's smile was just a little forced. He'd forgotten all about his daughter's arrival, she thought. He wouldn't have forgotten if it had been Nigel. 'She's so looking forward to seeing you.'

Lavinia very much doubted whether Catherine was looking forward to seeing her father at all – the friction between them was not one-sided – but she considered it her duty to offer the pretence of their daughter's affection.

Harold donned the hat and scarf Wilson offered, but not the overcoat, choosing to carry it instead – it would be warm in the car.

The butler swung open the doors, and Harold and Lavinia, arms linked about each other's waists like young lovers, walked outside into the main courtyard and the crisp cold of the morning.

'Take care, my darling,' she said, kissing him tenderly on the lips as she always did.

'I shall, my love.' He returned the kiss with equal tenderness, feeling the faintest sense of arousal as he recalled their lovemaking the previous night.

'I'll miss you,' she whispered, and they exchanged a smile, both aware of what the other was thinking.

'I'll miss you too.' He kissed her again before crossing the gravelled courtyard to where the Bentley was waiting, the chauffeur standing to attention beside the rear passenger door.

The engine turned over, Harold settled himself and, as the car slowly pulled away, gazed through the window at his wife. Captured in the clear frosty light, with the ivy-clad stone walls of the house a perfect background, she looked so beautifully English. Lavinia was still such an attractive woman, he thought. How very lucky he was.

Harold made love to his wife on a regular basis. With the exception of those times when he was called away from home, he made a point of having sexual intercourse once a week, sometimes twice if business did not necessitate his staying in the city for a night or so. He considered sex beneficial on all levels. Good sexual relations lent vitality to his marriage, ensured his wife's contentment, and enhanced their public image as a couple. Besides, he very much enjoyed it.

The steam baths and pools of the King's Rooms were deserted, as was customary in the mid-afternoon. But this was Friday. In an hour or so they would be crowded with prominent businessmen, barristers, politicians and the odd judge, all winding down after a long week's work, some buying time before embarking upon a weekend of family duties they might have preferred to ignore.

Harold, towel around his waist, skin a glistening mix of sweat and water, sat alone on one of the marble benches in the main steam room, the mist all-enveloping and the silence absolute but for the steady drip-drip of condensation. The steam rooms of the Edwardian bathhouse had been beautifully preserved. A large arch led from the main room to several smaller rooms, all linked with arches, and the floors throughout were impressively tiled in black and white marble. The ceramic wall tiles also being black and white, the overall effect was surreal, a misty, maze-like, all-consuming chessboard.

Having checked out the steam rooms and finding them deserted, Harold now sat facing the main door, awaiting the arrival of his guest. He loved having the place to himself. He'd deliberately arrived a good twenty minutes early in the hope there'd be no-one here. He hoped no-one would arrive during his planned meeting too – he enjoyed talking business in the steam rooms. No matter though – if the place got crowded, they could easily adjourn to one of the private lounges.

To Harold, the King's Rooms was far more than a home away from home; it was a highly valued place of business where confidences could be exchanged free of potential eavesdroppers and gossipmongers. At the King's Rooms an English gentleman's privacy was respected, which, in Harold's line of business, was eminently desirable.

The door opened and a towel-clad figure stood silhouetted against the light. Even through the veil of steam, Harold couldn't fail to recognise the body. Few were as finely honed as Gideon Melbray.

'Hello, Gideon,' he said.

'I take it that's you, Harold?' Gideon closed the door and made his way towards the voice.

'Of course it is, man. Good to see you.'

Harold shook the younger man's hand, and Gideon sat, peering about, his eyes adjusting to the gloom.

'Got the place to ourselves, have we?'

'We have.'

'That's lucky.'

'Not really. The baths are generally deserted around this time of day.'

'Ah.' Gideon nodded. 'Right.' He wouldn't know himself –

he wasn't a member of the King's Rooms, visiting the club only on the rare occasions Harold summoned him. Usually they met in one of the lounges.

'I left word at the front door,' Harold said. 'I presume you had no trouble getting in?'

'Good God, no, far from it. Mention your name and it's *open sesame* around here. The head doorman treated me like I was royalty.'

'Glad to hear it.' Harold smiled, pleased by the remark. But then he'd always found Gideon's admiration pleasing. Anyone would. It was flattering to be admired by an Adonis.

Gideon Melbray was indeed a handsome man. Gifted with a charm he knew how to use and with golden-haired looks that belied his thirty-five years, Gideon somehow managed to maintain the essence of youth. He and Harold had met at the British embassy in Washington just prior to the end of the war, when Gideon, a newly-arrived attaché, had replaced Harold's previous assistant.

Gideon had been instantly in awe of the worldly Harold Dartleigh, heir to a peerage and the epitome of sophistication. Harold, in turn, had been flattered by the young man's unashamed admiration, and had happily become his mentor, inviting him into his home and therefore his life.

Lavinia, too, had taken Gideon under her wing. She'd introduced him to Washington's elite, who, impressed by his beauty, had welcomed him into their midst. Gideon's beauty, however, had not been his principal calling card. Any friend of the Dartleighs would have been acceptable. The acknowledged doyens of Washington society, along with the crustiest of old-money families, had embraced Harold and Lavinia from the outset. An English title always had been, and always would be, the perfect entrée to the capital city of the free world.

At the end of the war, when the Dartleighs had returned to England, they had relinquished all personal ties with Gideon, despite the fact that he too had returned to his mother country. Lavinia would have liked to have kept in touch, but Harold had deliberately allowed the relationship to peter out, deeming it wise for professional reasons, which he did not share with his wife.

In accepting his position with MI6, the first person Harold had recruited had been Gideon Melbray. Gideon, with his looks and charm, had a talent for insinuating himself into the lives of others, an asset Harold had recognised as invaluable in a covert operative. His judgement had proved correct and Gideon, while ostensibly serving in the diplomatic corps, had become one of MI6's most valued undercover agents. It was no longer possible for the two of them to socialise openly as they had in Washington.

'How's Lavinia?' Gideon sprawled indolently on the bench, his back against the wall, his legs spread wide, surrendering himself to the sensuality of the heat. 'I haven't seen her since the French embassy ball, and that was months ago.'

Whenever he bumped into Lavinia, as he did on occasions – London could be a very small place for those who mingled in certain circles – Gideon took great care to observe the rules. He always had an excuse at the ready when an invitation was extended, but he regretted the necessity. He missed Lavinia. He'd been immensely fond of her during their Washington days.

'I thought she was looking splendid,' he said. 'Quite the most beautiful woman there in fact –'

'Lavinia's very well, thank you,' Harold interrupted, brusquely dispensing with the niceties – they were not here to talk about his wife. 'Let's get on with things, shall we,' and he proceeded to give a succinct account of Sir William Penney's briefing at Aldermaston the previous week.

Accustomed to Harold's manner and unfazed by his rudeness, Gideon raked the damp hair from his face, sat forward, elbows on his knees, and listened attentively.

'The boffins will close ranks on us,' Harold said in conclusion. 'Penney's highly protective, and his team works on a strictly need-to-know basis – they'll play safe and report only on their specific areas of expertise. Not one of them will dare offer an inside observation or opinion, which means we'll be left well and truly in the dark.' Annoyance flashed in his steely eyes. 'It's ludicrous allowing boffins to run the show, it's not their place. I intend to know everything and to be one step ahead the whole time, which is where you come in.'

'What about your man from Defence Signals Branch, Ned what's-his-name?'

'Hanson – he's a plodder. Non-assertive, strictly clerk material, which is why I chose him. He'll do his job, mind his own business, and everyone will feel safe with him.' Wiping the sweat from his face with a hand towel, Harold allowed himself a small smile of satisfaction. 'Ned will be our perfect frontman. He'll plod along unwittingly, the face of MI6, while you will gain people's trust and gather what you can.'

'And my cover?'

'You'll be working with the Department of Supply. I'll have you transferred for training in the next couple of months, and when you've served time there, you'll be seconded to Maralinga as senior requisitions officer. As SRO you'll have freedom of access to most areas, but if you run into any difficulties, you'll contact me and I'll arrange the necessary clearance.'

'Sounds like the perfect set-up.'

'Yes, it does rather, doesn't it?'

They shared a smile, and Harold stood. 'Ready for a cold plunge?'

'I'm game if you are.'

Outside, the modernised pools, shower bays and benches, which retained the black and white tiled motif of the original steam baths, remained deserted, but business was clearly about to pick up. From the nearby change rooms came the sound of male voices and the slam of locker doors.

Gideon followed Harold's example. He dumped his towel in one of the wicker laundry baskets and, as Harold submerged himself naked in one of the two cold plunge pools, he took a deep breath and threw himself into the other.

'Bloody, bloody freezing,' he said breathlessly as he scrambled out and accepted the fresh towel Harold handed him. 'Bloody, bloody freezing and bloody, bloody stupid – I don't know why you do that!'

Harold laughed, and led the way to the large heated spa pool at the far end of the complex. They lolled in the shallow warmth of the water, watching as a number of towel-clad men in various shapes and sizes emerged from the change rooms.

'Good timing,' Gideon said.

'Yes.' Harold glanced at the clock on the wall. 'The first bunch usually arrives around four.' Then he noticed Gideon's eyes were focused upon the one man in the group with a well-built body. 'No funny business, Gideon,' he muttered, 'not around here. I won't have it.'

Gideon's gaze lingered a second or so longer, then, as the man disappeared into the steam rooms, he turned to Harold wide-eyed. 'I meant good timing because we had the place to ourselves,' he said.

'Of course you did.'

Harold scowled a warning, which Gideon met boldly, in a way no others would dare.

'Where's your sense of humour, Harold?' he said, finally breaking the moment with a rakish grin. 'A little joke, that's all. No harm intended.'

'You may need to watch your particular brand of humour at Maralinga.'

'Oh, really? And why's that?'

'It might not be appreciated by hundreds of men captive in the middle of the desert,' Harold said dryly. 'You might just find yourself in a spot of bother.'

Gideon laughed. 'I would have thought, given the circumstances, I might just find myself somewhat in demand.'

'You know exactly what I mean, damn you,' Harold growled. 'You could draw unwanted attention to yourself and put us in jeopardy.'

'I have never put us in jeopardy.' Gideon dropped the flippant manner. He too was annoyed now. 'And I can assure you that, in the line of duty, my attentions have never once been *unwanted*.'

'All right, all right.' Harold held up his hands in uncharacteristic surrender. 'I take your point.' He did. There was no denying the fact that Gideon's powers of seduction were unparalleled. Men and women succumbed equally to his charms and Gideon himself was quite happy to serve both. A true hedonist, he found pleasure in all forms of sex, and gave pleasure in return. The information he'd garnered from his willing conquests had proved invaluable over the years.

'You're good at your job,' Harold said with rare magnanimity, 'I'll admit that. I'm just telling you to practise a little caution, that's all.'

'Of course I will.' Gideon was placated in an instant. Praise from Harold was scarce and he valued it highly. 'I'll be one of the boys, I promise.' He grinned suggestively. 'But you just never know, do you, what some boys might get up to out there in the desert?'

Harold couldn't resist a snort of laughter. Gideon was incorrigible.

It had been that very incorrigibility that Harold had found so attractive upon first meeting. Along with Gideon's beauty, of course – Harold had always admired beauty. The brief affair they'd had in Washington had been the only time he'd succumbed to a sexual relationship with a man. Apart from an experimental episode at Cambridge, but then everyone succumbed to the odd university crush. Harold had no regrets at all about the affair. In fact, these days he considered his actions to have been very much in the line of duty. Through his personal influence and, indeed, his inspiration, Gideon now served a far greater purpose than that of a mere clerk in the diplomatic corps. Their mutual infatuation had, in Harold's firm opinion, been most advantageous.

'I'm done,' he said, climbing out of the spa and grabbing his towel.

Gideon continued to loll. 'Are we going back into the steam room?' he asked.

'I'm not. You can. Feel free to stay as long as you like.'

'Oh.' Gideon was clearly disappointed. 'I was hoping we might have a quiet bite of dinner somewhere.'

'Impossible, I'm afraid, I'm dining with colleagues.'

It was true, but even if it were not, Harold would have lied. Self-discipline was far easier to put into practice, he'd found, if one kept well away from temptation.

'Treat the club as your own,' he said. 'I've arranged for all expenses to go on my account and the masseurs here are excellent.'

Beauty was to be admired from a distance, Harold thought as he crossed to the shower bays. Some things were simply not possible for a man in his position.

# Chapter Five

Elizabeth returned to Aldershot at the end of 1955, in order to spend the festive season with her parents. On her arrival, three days before Christmas, she rang Daniel at the barracks, half-expecting he wouldn't be there. But he was.

'I thought you might be having Christmas with your family,' she said. His parents lived in Cheshire, in the industrial township of Crewe, where, he'd told her, his father worked part-time at the Rolls-Royce factory.

'Yes, I'll be heading home,' he said, 'but not until Christmas Eve.'

'I don't suppose you have any time off tomorrow then?'

'I do indeed.' He tried his hardest to sound nonchalant. 'The entire day, in fact – my night roster finishes at precisely 0600 hours.'

'How about afternoon tea then? That is, if you're not too tired.'

The bluntness of the offer surprised Daniel. He hadn't seen Elizabeth for well over a year – in fact not since that day in the park. They'd telephoned each other on a semi-regular basis since his return, but after the general recounting of his experiences in

Frankfurt, their brief conversations had become stilted and self-conscious. She spoke little about her work, which he'd found most unlike her. 'Just keeping in touch,' she'd say. Then, several weeks later when *he'd* ring *her*: 'Just thought I'd check how you're going,' he'd say. The calls had continued in a similar vein over the months following his return. Always, they were 'just checking', or 'just keeping in touch'. London was only a brief train trip away, but neither had suggested they meet, both unsure whether the other would be interested.

'I'd love to have afternoon tea,' Daniel said. 'Four o'clock? Usual place?'

There was the briefest of pauses before Elizabeth answered. 'Could we meet in the park first?'

'It'll be freezing,' he warned.

'I know. It'll also be deserted. We can walk to the teashop after we've had a chat. Would you mind awfully?'

'Not at all. I'll wear a scarf.' Daniel hung up the receiver, intrigued, and impatient for tomorrow.

The day was as chilly as the weather reports had forecast, but not too uncomfortably so. There was no biting wind, just the still, hushed breathlessness signalling snow was on the way. Daniel arrived at Princes Gardens a good five minutes early, well rugged up in his three-quarter navy coat and the thick woollen scarf his mother had knitted him the previous Christmas. He walked briskly through the main entrance, hands in his pockets, wishing he'd remembered his gloves, but enjoying the air's crisp bite.

The park was deserted, just as Elizabeth had predicted. The threat of an impending snowfall and the dullness of the after-noon, which was already descending into early dusk, was an uninviting combination. Daniel didn't seek out a park bench. Deciding it was warmer to keep moving, he proceeded to do several laps of the fountain while he kept an eye on the main entrance to the gardens.

He'd just completed his third lap, chasing his own busy puffs of steam, and was about to start on a fourth, when he noticed the young man. He hadn't seen him arrive, which was not particularly surprising, there were other entrances to the park, but now, having noticed him, he was intrigued. The young man was dressed in a khaki trench coat, belted at the waist and with the collar turned up. The trousers beneath the coat were pinstriped, and on his head was a grey fedora worn at a jaunty angle. The overall appearance was dapper, but it was the arrogance of his pose and his stillness that attracted Daniel's attention. One highly polished shoe planted on a park bench, the young man was leaning forward, elbow on knee, other hand on hip, his gaze fixed resolutely ahead.

What on earth was he staring at, Daniel wondered, looking around to see if someone else had appeared. No-one had. The park remained deserted, and, as he turned back, he realised that it was he upon whom the young man was so focused. He averted his eyes and started on another lap of the fountain. It was most disconcerting to be studied so intently. He wished Elizabeth would hurry up.

Having completed the lap, his eyes once again flickered to the young man, who he noticed was now lighting a cigar, an action that in no way detracted from the gaze, which remained as unwavering as a bird of prey's upon its quarry. Daniel felt more than disconcerted, he felt decidedly embarrassed. The signal was loud and clear. The young man was a homosexual.

He was about to embark upon another lap, but halted as, to his horror, he saw the young man remove his foot from the bench and start slowly sauntering towards him. Daniel was in a quandary. What on earth should he do? He could hardly take off on another lap, it would look like running away; obviously he had to confront the chap. How very unpleasant.

A step closer. Then another step. And then another, this time accompanied by a leisurely drag on the cigar. Bold, Daniel thought, unable to decipher the face behind the billowing mix of smoke and steam. Foolish too. The man appeared little more than a youth and was not heavily built – he wouldn't stand a chance in a fight. This sort of audacity would get his head kicked in at the barracks.

A step closer, then another step, and the youth suddenly looked familiar. Oh my God, Daniel thought. It couldn't be, surely.

'Elizabeth?'

She stopped just one pace from him. 'I promised I'd introduce you to E. J. Hoffmann in person,' she said. 'Well, here he is.'

'Good God, I don't believe it.'

'Had you fooled, didn't I?' There was mischief in her eyes, and she smiled, cheekily, irresistibly.

'You certainly did.'

Daniel was spellbound. This was the stuff of fantasy. Having dropped her act, Elizabeth's male attire only served to emphasise her femininity, and he had an insane desire to crush her to him and kiss her with all the passion he could muster, the way actors did in American films. He resisted the urge.

'An excellent performance, my congratulations,' he said light-heartedly but with genuine admiration. 'In fact you won't believe it . . .' He wondered whether he should tell her. 'I actually thought . . .'

She laughed as he hesitated. She knew exactly what he'd been thinking. She'd seen the horror in his face.

'I actually thought you were about to proposition me,' he said.

'I was.' She stopped laughing and took that one step closer. 'I am.'

Their bodies were almost touching, their mouths barely inches apart, the steam of their breath mingling momentarily before spiralling into the still, chill air. Daniel remained spellbound but confused, and more than a little tormented by a vestige of hope. She was joking, of course. Wasn't she? She couldn't be serious. Could she?

'I've missed you, Danny.'

It was Elizabeth who initiated the kiss and, gentle though it was, there was no mistaking its intention. This was no sisterly kiss but the most tender of caresses.

For Daniel, fantasy had suddenly become reality. But far from fighting off an insane desire, he simply succumbed to the love he'd felt from the very first day of their meeting, and, as he embraced her, Elizabeth willingly surrendered.

Any onlooker, although shocked to the core by the sight, would have assumed the two men were lovers, and in one sense they would have been right. Daniel and Elizabeth *were* lovers – in thought if not in deed – for their kiss was a declaration, and, upon parting, they smiled their unspoken acknowledgement.

'Just as well you're in mufti.' Elizabeth broke the moment, striking a pose and twirling her cigar, Groucho Marx style. 'If you were in uniform you'd be court-martialled for this.'

'I probably still could be. Let's get rid of the hat. Oh my God,' he pretended horror as he took off the fedora, 'you've cut your hair.'

'Trying to be one of the boys,' she said apologetically, 'although it hasn't altogether worked with the chaps at *The Guardian*. They just make fun of me.'

'I'm not surprised.' Of course it wouldn't work, he thought.

The stylish bob was no doubt androgynous from a distance, but close to it formed a perfect frame for the womanliness of her face. 'May I?' he asked, taking the cigar from her.

'Be my guest.'

He inspected it closely. 'Cuban,' he said, nodding his approval, 'only the best,' and he took a deep drag.

'I didn't know you liked cigars.'

'I don't all that much. This is by way of self-protection.' His face disappeared briefly in a cloudy haze. 'It'll be more fun if I don't feel like I'm kissing my colonel – all the top brass smoke cigars, trying to emulate Churchill.'

He drew her to him and they kissed again, sharing the warmth of their mouths and the muskiness of the tobacco. The cigar itself fell forgotten to the frosty grass where it glowed in persistent defiance of the odds. But the kiss continued, Daniel and Elizabeth oblivious to everything about them, and when they finally parted, the cigar had lost its battle and lay a soggy twig at their feet.

'My God,' Daniel said unnecessarily, 'it's snowing.'

They looked about the park, where, in the stillness, gently spiralling snowflakes disappeared like magic upon contact with the ground. The silence was absolute. The moment seemed timeless and somehow specially theirs.

In wordless unison, Elizabeth jammed on her fedora, Daniel pulled his scarf up around his ears, and together they set off at a brisk pace out of the park and into High Street. By the time they arrived at the teashop, the snowfall had become steady. Stepping inside the front door to the small alcove entrance, they took off their coats – and their scarf and fedora – and gave them a brief shake before hanging them on the coat rack alongside the accoutrements of the other patrons.

Daniel noted that beneath the trench coat, Elizabeth was not wearing a man's suit. The pinstriped trousers were men's certainly, but she'd accompanied them with a white high-necked shirt and a grey cashmere sweater – all in all a sporty image, which had become highly fashionable of late.

'I chose the Katie Hepburn look just for you,' she whispered with a rebellious glance in the direction of the half-dozen or so customers seated at the far end of the teashop near the small open fire. 'I don't give a damn what anyone else thinks.'

'I prefer the trench coat myself. Very Bogart.'

'My father will be delighted to hear it.'

He raised an eyebrow at the non sequitur.

'I borrowed the trench coat from Daddy,' she explained. 'We're around the same size, surprisingly enough – he says it's because he's shrunk with age.'

'He doesn't know *why* you borrowed it, surely.'

'Oh yes, he does. He thought it was an excellent idea. He said if I *must* make a statement, you're the right man to make it to. We'd like to sit by the window, please.' The middle-aged waitress who'd arrived had been about to lead them to a table near the fire. 'Oh.' Elizabeth turned apologetically to Daniel, aware that she may have sounded bossy. 'Sorry, I didn't mean . . .'

'We'd like to be by the window, thanks,' Daniel said. 'We want to look at the snow.'

The woman nodded uninterestedly, showed them to one of the front tables, and hovered nearby as they settled themselves.

'I've no idea why Daddy thought I was making a statement when it was simply a joke,' Elizabeth continued, 'but you obviously have his seal of approval, which is nice.'

Daniel hid his smile behind a menu. Did she really think that declaring her feelings in the form of E. J. Hoffmann was *not* a statement? 'Are we doing cake?' he asked.

'Oh yes, the works, wouldn't you say?'

'I would. A pot of Darjeeling for two and we'll select from the cake trolley, thanks,' he said to the woman, who scribbled down the order and left without a word.

'She's new,' Elizabeth said disapprovingly, watching her go. 'What on earth happened to young Sally?'

'I don't know. I haven't been here for quite some time.'

He hadn't been to the teashop since that day in the park, he remembered. He hadn't consciously boycotted the place, there'd simply been no reason – afternoon tea had lost its attraction.

'Gosh, it's coming down,' Elizabeth said. 'Just look at that.'

They gazed out at the barely visible street, where vehicles had slowed to a crawl and where, here and there, a pedestrian scurried for cover. The snow was falling heavily now, gathering on the awnings of shops and on the roofs of parked cars. The town was slowly turning white.

They continued to gaze for several minutes, comfortable in the cosiness of the teashop and each other's company. Then, simultaneously, they turned to one another, as if sensing now was the time to talk. There was a moment's pause, Daniel giving Elizabeth first option, but for once she didn't take up the offer.

'Why the change of heart?' he asked. He was curious, naturally, although, strangely enough, the reason itself didn't seem to matter. Nothing mattered. Nothing in the world was of any importance apart from the fact that Elizabeth loved him. Daniel was in a state of utter bliss.

'I realised you were right on both counts.'

'And which particular counts would those be?'

'I *have* viewed men as the enemy, and I *do* love you.'

'Ah. Well, I'm glad we cleared that up.' He grinned, and was about to say something else, but the waitress interrupted.

'Darjeeling for two,' she said, placing the tray on the table.

While Daniel watched the woman set out the tea things, Elizabeth studied him thoughtfully. Did he realise how deeply he'd shocked her that day? She doubted it. He probably didn't even remember what he'd said. *Men are not the enemy! Why must you feel so threatened?* The accusation had been only one of a series of shocks that day, but it had affected her like a slap in the face. She'd reacted defensively at the time, but over the ensuing months she'd pondered his words. And the more she'd missed him, the more she'd realised that he was right. She'd pitted herself against men from the moment she'd entered university, and she'd been doing battle with them ever since. In her blinkered view, all men had become a threat – to the point where she'd even blinded herself to the man she loved, the man who just happened to be her dearest friend.

The waitress, having announced that the cake trolley would be along shortly, left with her tea tray tucked under her arm. As Daniel returned his attention to Elizabeth, he caught her studying him.

'What is it?' he asked.

'I missed you.'

'So you said in the park. I'm glad.'

'No. I'm talking about my change of heart. You asked why, and that's the reason. One can only miss a person so much before one realises one loves them.' No further explanation was needed, she thought – good heavens, he knew her better than she knew herself. 'I've probably always loved you, Danny. I've just refused to admit it – even to myself.'

The magnitude of her admission both surprised and impressed him, but in his euphoria he couldn't help pushing her that little bit further. The opportunity was too good to resist.

'So let's get married straightaway, shall we? Next week, what do you say?'

'Oh.' She looked suddenly panic-stricken. 'Oh . . .'

He laughed. 'I'm sorry, I didn't mean it. I won't rush you, Elizabeth, I promise. I'll wait for as long as you want. A *year* if you like, *two* years!' His smile disappeared, he was serious now. 'But you will marry me, won't you?'

'Yes.' Her answer was instant. 'Yes, I will.'

'Good, that's settled. The tea's getting cold.' Picking up the milk jug, he poured a small dash of milk into her cup – she liked her tea strong. 'Now come on,' he said, 'I want to hear all about *The Guardian*. You never talk about your work over the phone.'

Elizabeth automatically picked up the teapot and started to pour – they'd always worked as a team. 'Oh my God, where do I begin?' she said. 'Things were even tougher than I'd expected, I was thrown to the wolves right from the start. But I've decided it was probably the best thing that could have happened, Danny. I've learned such a lot . . .'

Daniel smiled to himself – she was off and running.

'. . . You see, in some ways I'd had it easy, with my parents' support and a forward-thinking employer like Henry Wilmot. Even battling the system, I'd always known that the people who mattered took me seriously. Well, I can tell you here and now, nobody at *The Guardian* did.' She plonked down the teapot and the thud as it hit the table was like an exclamation mark.

'What about Lionel Brock?'

'Oh, I'm not talking about him,' she said dismissively. 'I'm talking about the staff reporters, every single one of them, down to a man!'

'Of course. Sorry.' Better to just let her go, Daniel decided.

'They didn't even notice me. . .'

*Like hell they didn't.*

'. . . except for wolf-whistles under their breath whenever I walked past.'

*Precisely.*

'That's why I cut my hair.'

'Did it stop the wolf-whistles?'

'Not really.'

*Well, it wouldn't.* He nodded sympathetically.

'Lionel wasn't much help. He couldn't give me a feature for months – orders from above – and what was he expected to do anyway? It's simply the way of the world.' Elizabeth pulled a face and sipped at her tea as if to rid herself of a sour taste. 'I don't know which was worse – pretending an interest in the mindless fashion parades and flower shows I was expected to report on, or putting up with the infantile behaviour of my colleagues.'

Daniel wasn't sure whether she meant to be amusing or not, but he couldn't help laughing anyway.

'What's so funny?'

'I can't see you putting up with your colleagues' "infantile behaviour" for long. I bet the poor sods copped some flak.'

'Yes, one or two of them did,' she admitted, recalling Buzz Barker.

Barry 'Buzz' Barker, a popular sports columnist known to be 'a bit of a lad', had certainly copped some flak from Elizabeth. She'd been suffering the unwelcome attentions of her colleagues in silence for some time when, on this particular day, she'd seen the wink Buzz had shared with a couple of his chums just before he'd 'accidentally' collided with her. On groping about to recover his balance, he'd managed to grasp a healthy handful of her left breast and she'd belted him as hard as she could across the face, right there in the middle of the crowded newsroom. The action hadn't endeared her to Buzz, who'd insisted he'd tripped, nor to his chums who'd egged him on, and thereafter they'd attempted to spread the word to all who would listen that Elizabeth Hoffmann was a stitched-up cow with tickets on herself. But Elizabeth had successfully drawn attention to her predicament, and in so doing had gained the respect of a number of the others who realised they too may have overstepped the mark, albeit inadvertently and not in quite such spectacular fashion.

'They leave me alone these days,' she said. 'And now that my features are published they've changed their tune altogether. It was a whole six months before E. J. Hoffmann appeared in print,' she added dryly, 'but when he did, they all got one hell of a shock. They couldn't believe it was me at first, and they weren't prepared to ask. Just whispers in corridors, which I ignored. Then Lionel let it be known that the public was not to be informed of E. J. Hoffmann's true identity. So there I was, suddenly on an equal footing.'

She sipped her tea. 'Strange,' she said, 'how quickly we became friends once they respected my work.' With the exception of Buzz Barker, she thought. But then Buzz had been publicly humiliated – and by a woman! For that, he would never forgive her.

Elizabeth was halted by the arrival of the cake trolley, and the next several minutes were devoted to a plethora of choices, including the many varieties of cheesecake for which the teashop was renowned. Ignoring the sponges, trifles, meringues and chocolate puddings, they selected variations of the house specialty.

'I don't suppose you've seen any of them, by the way?' Her tone was casual as she toyed with her choice of lemon cream.

'Seen any of what?' he asked, concentrating on his baked vanilla. He knew very well she was referring to her articles in

*The Guardian*, and that she was pretending indifference while waiting with bated breath.

'My features. The last one was a piece on Churchill. It came out the first week in December.'

He popped a hefty forkful of cheesecake into his mouth and looked up from his plate vaguely, as if trying to recollect.

Elizabeth disguised her disappointment with a careless shrug. 'Well, naturally you wouldn't have seen it, why on earth should you? I brought a copy along – it's in the trench coat . . .' She stood. 'Won't be a minute . . .'

'Don't bother. I've read it.' A pause as she froze. 'Of course I saw the article, Elizabeth. How could I *not* see it? I scour *The Guardian* on a daily basis.'

'Do you really?'

He nodded. She sat. Another pause, and Elizabeth found herself literally holding her breath. His approval was of immense importance to her.

'So come on, tell me,' she said after several agonising seconds, 'what did you think?'

'I thought it was brilliant. Bloody brilliant. In my opinion, quite the best thing you've written yet.'

'Honestly?'

'Honestly.' She was clearly waiting for him to go on and he was happy to oblige. 'It was a controversial piece, as I'm sure you meant it to be,' he said, 'and I'll bet a lot of staunch Churchill fans were offended. But I thought your argument about a "man *of* his time, *for* his time" was really well-balanced.'

'Oh, good,' she said with a huge sigh of relief. 'I was a bit concerned that . . . well, you know . . . that being military, you might disapprove of the negative aspect.'

'Why would I? And even if I did, I'd still admire the article, it was really well-written.' He raised his teacup in a toast. 'I'm proud of you, Elizabeth.'

'I'm glad.' She raised her own cup. 'I can't think of anything I'd rather hear you say.'

They clinked and drank to each other, and she dived back into her cheesecake.

'The piece certainly aroused some comment here amongst the top brass,' he added casually.

She halted, cake fork mid-air. 'You mean they *saw* it?'

'I left the odd open copy lying around in the officers' mess. I thought you might be interested in the reaction of the old brigade.'

She was. 'And . . .?'

'There was a lot of very strong feeling, as you can imagine. The members of the old brigade don't like being told that Churchill's had his day.'

'They'd like it a lot less if they knew they were being told by a woman.'

'My word, yes, that *would* cause a stir.' Daniel laughed at the thought. 'Mayhem, in fact.' He pushed aside his dessert plate with its half-finished cake and started pouring himself another cup of tea. 'No wonder your colleagues at *The Guardian* are so respectful these days.'

'But why did they feel the need to be *dis*respectful in the first place?'

'Ah.' She'd stumped him. She'd also misunderstood him. 'I'm sure they didn't *mean* to be disrespectful, Elizabeth.'

'I know.' Damn, she thought, she hadn't meant to sound so combative. The words had just sprung out in response to his rather glib comment. But now that they had, she couldn't back down altogether. 'You're going to tell me they were just *doing what comes naturally*, right?'

'Right. They're men, you're a good-looking woman – of course they'd admire you.'

'I don't want them to admire *me*, I want them to admire my *work*.'

'And they do. You said so yourself. They changed their tune when your features appeared – they respect your work now, that's what you said.'

'Yes,' she agreed, 'yes, I said that, and yes, they do. But I needed E. J. Hoffmann to prove my worth, didn't I? Without him I was nothing.'

Elizabeth stopped herself. Argument was futile. Danny existed in the exclusively male domain of the military. For all his support and encouragement and pride in her, he had no idea what it was like for a woman in the workplace. Indeed, how could he?

'The day will come,' she announced with more than a touch of theatricality to lighten the moment, 'when the name Elizabeth Hoffmann will stand on its own.' She drained the last of her tea. '*The Guardian*'s brought out the fight in me, Danny.'

'God forbid,' he said, and he poured her another cup.

They stayed at the teashop for a further hour, and were the last to leave. They would have stayed longer, but the teashop closed at six o'clock.

It was no longer snowing, and the street lamps shone mistily through the gloom of early evening as he walked her to the railway station. She'd insisted upon the train, maintaining his offer of signing out an army vehicle and driving her home was altogether too complicated.

'It'd take ages,' she said, 'and Daddy's expecting me to ring when I arrive at Reigate – that's our usual arrangement. Please, Danny, I'd much rather get the train. We'll see each other after Christmas.'

The previously deserted streets were swarming with an exodus of people who'd sought shelter from the snowstorm, and when they arrived at the station, the platform was more crowded than usual. Amongst the regular commuters were those determined to beat the rush of the following day, Christmas Eve, when the hordes would be heading out of town. There was nowhere to sit, the benches were all taken, but they had no desire to sit anyway. Instead, they snuggled together in a corner by the stairs, the fedora Elizabeth clasped crushed and forgotten between them. They snuggled close, not because they needed to, and not because they were cold, but because they wanted to.

They'd discussed their plans fully, deciding not to announce their imminent engagement to their parents over Christmas. 'We'll wait a month or so before making it official,' Daniel had said, wary of rushing her. 'There's plenty of time.'

'I need time to digest it all myself,' she'd replied. 'I'm about to become a *fiancée*!' Her expression had been comical as if the word were faintly obscene. 'I never thought I'd live to see the day.'

There seemed no more to discuss, and they were silent in their cosy corner by the stairs. Only five minutes until the next train, Daniel thought. He wished it were hours. He wished he weren't leaving in the morning. He wished he could stay here, right here, just like this.

She lifted her face to him and they kissed, oblivious to the bustle of those jostling for position on the ever-increasingly crowded platform.

Any minute now, Daniel thought, any minute now the train would arrive.

'What if I stayed tomorrow,' he whispered.

'Oh, Danny, you couldn't do that. Imagine how disappointed

your parents would be. Besides, you told me how much you always love your family Christmases.'

Yes, he always had, but the family Christmas had paled into insignificance after today's events. 'Of course, you're right,' he said. She was. It would break his mother's heart if he didn't turn up. 'Just got a bit carried away, that's all.'

He could hear the distant clack of the train. They both could. Reluctantly, they broke from their embrace.

'Oh, dear me, look.' Elizabeth held up the crushed fedora. 'It may never be the same.'

'Does it matter? You won't need it again.'

'Perhaps not the hat,' she said with a rueful smile, 'but I doubt I'll lose E. J. Hoffmann that easily.'

They could see the train now, slowing on its approach.

'I'm glad you came home for Christmas, Elizabeth.'

The words resonated for a moment as a brief image of childhood Christmases flashed before Elizabeth's eyes – a series of nameless restaurants and faceless people. She'd always felt just a little self-conscious admitting to her schoolfriends that she'd had Christmas dinner in a restaurant. Any minor embarrassment had been outweighed, however, by her superior knowledge, from a very early age, that Father Christmas did not exist – it had seemed to Elizabeth quite a fair exchange.

'Christmas doesn't mean much in the Hoffmann household,' she said.

The train's engine pulled into the platform and, as the carriages snaked past, the crowd edged forward, eyes following each door, trying to pick which one would stop nearest, like the lucky draw on the slowing spin of a chocolate wheel.

'Christmas isn't why I came home, Danny.'

The train stopped. Doors slammed open. 'All aboard,' the guard called.

She kissed him, and with a squeeze of the hand was gone, swept away amongst a sea of commuters. All he could make out was an auburn bob and the upturned collar of a trench coat.

Moments later, the doors slammed shut and the guard's whistle sounded. He waved to the train as it pulled away from the platform. Just in case she could see him.

# Chapter Six

Two months later, towards the end of February, Daniel and Elizabeth told their respective parents of their engagement. Alfred and Marjorie Hoffmann were not in the least surprised and both were delighted. Kenneth and Prudence Gardiner were completely taken aback and both had their reservations. Daniel was bemused by their reaction. He'd thought that he'd well and truly signalled his intentions during the Christmas break, when, it had seemed, he'd talked of nothing but Elizabeth, to the point where his younger brother, Billy, had accused him of being besotted. 'I most certainly am,' Daniel had readily agreed.

'I thought she was just a girlfriend,' his father said bluntly. 'You're far too young to get married.'

'I'm twenty-two – exactly the same age you were when you married Mum. And we're not going to get married for at least a year anyway. Elizabeth needs to establish her career.'

'You said she's Jewish . . .' Prudence got straight to the point.

'I said that her father is. I don't think Elizabeth –'

'You know that the children of Jewish women must be

brought up in the Jewish faith, don't you? You are *aware* of that fact.' Prudence was clearly of the opinion that he wasn't.

'I really don't think it'll be a problem, Mum.' As his parents exchanged a dubious glance and, as he sensed his mother about to continue, Daniel held up his hand signalling no more discussion. 'Let's just wait until you've met her, all right?'

'No offence intended, son,' his father said. 'Your mother and I only have your best interests at heart.'

'I know, Dad. I know.'

Daniel couldn't help feeling disappointed by the lukewarm reception of his news, but deep down he was not surprised. It wasn't that his parents were anti-Semitic, but rather they were wary of those who were 'different'. Both from staunch Protestant families, they'd grown up in the same country town, been childhood sweethearts, and were products of their own closeted upbringings. Daniel was aware of all that. When his father talked about the war, as Kenneth did vociferously, his heartfelt slogan was *live and let live* – 'Bloody Hitler's why we fought this war, and he's why we won! Right over wrong! Live and let live!' – but in his private life, Kenneth Gardiner did not happily embrace change, and nor did his wife. Preferring to follow their own well-worn path, and preferring others maintain theirs, *live and let live* really meant *to each his own*.

'My parents are very conservative, Elizabeth.' During the train trip to Crewe for their planned long weekend, Daniel felt it necessary to caution her.

'So you've said – several times.'

'No, I mean *very* conservative. Very set in their ways.' He wanted to warn her that she may find them narrow-minded, but he loved his parents and felt disloyal in his criticism.

'Oh.' She was a little surprised. 'Do I take that as a warning? Am I to be on my best behaviour?'

'Good God, no,' he said, and laughed. 'Don't you temper your behaviour for a minute, I want you to be as outrageous as you wish.'

'Excellent. I'll take it as a dare then.' Her smile assured him that she would do no such thing, but there was a challenge in her voice as she asked, 'So what have you told them about me?'

'Everything. Well, no, not quite everything,' he corrected himself. 'I haven't told them about E. J. Hoffmann.'

'I should hope not.'

Elizabeth suppressed a smile as she caught Daniel's look across the table. *I did warn you*, his eyes said, but at the same time they told her to respond in her own way. *Go for it, Elizabeth*, he was saying, and he even gave her the slightest nod of encouragement.

She returned her attention to his father.

'. . . Traitorous talk in my opinion – traitorous talk from those with short memories.' Kenneth, a large man in his forties with a well-built body that made the ungainly limp of his right leg just that bit more shocking, was currently mid-tirade. 'Winnie led our boys to victory and saved this country – there are some who are too quick to forget that these days . . .'

Kenneth himself had brought up the subject, referring to a recent article in *The Manchester Guardian* about a possible general swing in popular opinion. It seemed that many, particularly amongst the younger set, favoured the current foreign secretary, Sir Anthony Eden, over Prime Minister Churchill as leader of the Conservative Party.

'Dad reads most of the major newspapers,' Daniel had remarked meaningfully to Elizabeth, 'including *The Times* and *The Guardian*.'

Daniel seemed determined to stir her into action, but she remained unmoved.

'Where do these journalists get their statistics from anyway?' Kenneth continued. 'The average man in the street supports Churchill. At least the average man from around these parts does, I can assure you.'

The small coterie of Kenneth Gardiner's friends who met at the pub on a Friday night being like-minded war veterans, it was doubtful their opinions would have been representative of the average local, but Kenneth was sincere in his belief that they were.

'Who's for more beef?' As her husband drew breath, Prudence seized the moment and rose to her feet. She was a pleasant, tidy woman, her matronly figure neatly compacted in place thanks to the corsetry she wore at all times. 'Dan?' she queried, carving fork poised over the platter of sliced meat.

'Thanks, Mum.' Daniel slid his plate across the table.

'Help yourself to gravy and pudding. And Ken, dear . . .' Turning to her husband she continued in the same motherly tone, 'Do eat up. You've hardly touched your food and it's getting cold.'

To Elizabeth's complete amazement, Kenneth Gardiner did just as he was told. He ceased his tirade and, like a large, obedient child, applied himself diligently to his dinner.

'Excellent as always, Mother,' he said after several mouthfuls, and he beamed at his son. 'There aren't many who can serve up a baked dinner like your mother, eh?'

Daniel nodded and helped himself to another perfectly puffed Yorkshire pudding.

Elizabeth was intrigued. The compliment was obviously a mealtime ritual, but it seemed out of character for a man like Kenneth Gardiner. As the meal progressed, however, and as the state of play became apparent, she realised Kenneth Gardiner was not the martinet she'd assumed him to be upon first meeting. Like many of his generation, he was set in his views, which to Elizabeth's mind rendered some areas of discussion pointless, but he seemed a nice enough man who genuinely appreciated his hard-working wife.

How clearly defined the roles of the two were, she thought. Kenneth obviously deferred to his wife in all matters domestic, and Prudence, who appeared a non-subservient and highly capable woman, acknowledged her husband as the undisputed head of the house. Elizabeth was bemused by her own reaction to a patriarchal system she'd expected to find irksome. There was something surprisingly comfortable about the Gardiners. They worked well as a team.

As she made her observations, Elizabeth was unaware she herself was being observed. Daniel found the degree of fascination with which his fiancée was studying his parents amusing. Perhaps for the very first time, he thought, Elizabeth was witnessing life as lived by the masses. Perhaps in their own marriage they might find the perfect balance – somewhere between his parents' conformity and the eccentricity of hers. Not that it mattered. Whatever the outcome, Daniel couldn't wait to marry Elizabeth. His weekend leave visits to London had become an increasingly tantalising taste of the life he so longed to share with her.

Each fortnight for the past two months, Daniel had booked into a bed-and-breakfast lodging in South Kensington, just several blocks from Sumner Place, where Elizabeth rented a cheaply converted basement flat in a once-grand terrace house. They spent their days together exploring London from the tops of double-decker buses or walking tirelessly through the parks and along the Thames embankment, Elizabeth taking great pleasure in showing him the London she knew so well.

A visit to the theatre had become the regular outing on a Saturday, and one night, having returned to her flat from the

West End and having shared their customary pot of tea in the kitchen, Elizabeth had protested when he'd risen to go.

'It's ridiculous, honestly,' she'd said. 'It's late and you're tired, why don't you stay?'

The look he'd given her had been one of mock outrage, and she'd laughed.

'I'm not propositioning you,' she'd said. 'We can make up a perfectly comfortable bed on the sofa.'

But he'd refused the offer. She was known to the other tenants in the building, he'd said, word would get around amongst her neighbours, she'd be compromised.

Elizabeth's response to such a remark would normally have been 'Damn the neighbours, who cares what they think?' But on this occasion she'd made no such retaliation. Instead, she'd kissed him, very lovingly, and with just a hint of her own sense of longing.

'Goodnight, Danny.'

'Goodnight, Elizabeth.' Oh God, how he'd wanted to stay. But not on the sofa, and they'd both known that.

They planned to marry in the late spring. Elizabeth was sure that by then *The Guardian* would accept her work on a freelance basis, enabling her to write her feature articles from wherever her husband was stationed.

'Well, they may not accept *my* features the way I'd hoped,' she'd wryly admitted, 'but they'll accept E. J. Hoffmann's – he's become very popular. And if they insist upon my staying in London and slogging it out as a staff reporter, I shall resign and sell E. J. Hoffmann's work elsewhere.'

Now, as Daniel watched her watching his parents, he realised how assiduously he was counting the days. Two months down, he thought, another two to go.

\*

117

'I believe you're a journalist, dear.' Prudence decided it was time the conversation was directed towards their guest. Elizabeth had politely refused the offer of a second helping, the men were both happily tended to, and Kenneth was no longer intent upon ranting from his soapbox. But then he'd just been showing off, Prudence thought, the way all men did in the presence of a pretty girl. And this one was more than pretty, she was downright handsome. 'How very modern and adventurous of you to have a career,' she said admiringly.

Prudence approved of the new trend that allowed young women a degree of life experience prior to marriage. It couldn't help but strengthen their character before household duties and motherhood claimed them.

'And journalism seems such a very bold choice,' she added. 'I must say, I'm lost in admiration.'

'What do you write about?' Kenneth asked with a bluntness that could have sounded aggressive, although this was not his intention; he was merely bewildered. To Kenneth, a woman journalist was a contradiction in terms.

Elizabeth refused to look at Daniel as she answered. 'Fashion parades and flower shows for the most part.'

'How thrilling.' Prudence was hugely impressed. 'Fancy being paid to go to fashion parades and flower shows – you must be the envy of every young woman you know.'

'Yes, I suppose I must be.' Elizabeth smiled. 'I've never really thought about it like that, but you're probably right.'

'Of course I am.' Prudence laughed. 'Dear me, if I were a young woman I'd be green with envy. What a wonderful career you've chosen, Elizabeth. You must be very proud of your achievements. Don't you agree, Ken?'

'Yes. Oh yes, yes, I do.' Kenneth's response was gruff and a little too pat, but he made the concession willingly enough, he and Prudence having talked about the situation. Kenneth Gardiner did not at all approve of young women having careers. 'Not if they want to get married,' he'd said. 'They can't have it both ways – it's demeaning to men.'

'It's *temporary*, Ken, that's what it is. She'll give up her career when she gets married.'

'Dan obviously doesn't think so. It seems to me like he does-n't even *want* her to.'

'Oh, she will, dear, of course she will. Every woman does – especially when the babies come.'

'Even so,' Kenneth had pursued the broader argument, 'a woman journalist isn't right in the first place. That's a man's job. She's taking a man's bread and butter, depriving a man's family of his wage. She wouldn't like having it done to her now, would she?'

Prudence had agreed in principle – indeed, she'd found her-self unable to refute the argument – and they'd quickly called a truce, as they always did. She'd convinced her husband to draw a veil over their future daughter-in-law's career, given its very temporary nature, and Kenneth had agreed that it was their duty to welcome their son's fiancée into the household.

Prudence was glad now that Elizabeth had proved so per-sonable and so distractingly good-looking, but she decided not to push too hard. Her husband had graciously acknowledged the girl's career, which was all that was necessary, so she changed the subject.

'What a pity Billy couldn't be here. You'd so like Billy, would-n't she, Dan?'

'She certainly would,' Daniel agreed. 'Damn shame they've landed him with weekend manoeuvres, but that's typically Sandhurst.'

Billy, two years Daniel's junior, was in his second year at mili-tary college. 'We're following in Dad's footsteps, I suppose,'

Daniel had told Elizabeth, 'but we made our own decisions. It's what we both wanted.'

'I feel I know Billy already,' Elizabeth replied, 'Daniel's talked about him such a lot. You're quite a military family, Mr Gardiner.'

'We certainly are,' Kenneth said proudly. 'Just a pity I had to cop it so early. I would have continued to serve if they'd given me half a chance, but they don't when you've got a shattered hip.'

He made no attempt to disguise his resentment, but Elizabeth was not surprised. Daniel had warned her.

'Dad was invalided out after Dunkirk,' he'd said. 'He wanted to stay on and make a career of the army, but he had to go back to being a clerk like his old man. He's pretty bitter about that.'

'No matter . . .' Kenneth, not wishing to seem self-indulgent, dismissed his mood with a shake of the head. 'There are many who copped a great deal worse. Besides, I did the right thing. I was prepared to lay down my life for my country; a man can do no more than that.'

The brief six months' active service Kenneth Gardiner had experienced, together with the intense military training preceding his duty in France, had been the highlight of his life. At least that was the way he remembered it. The learning of new skills, the comradeship, the knowledge that they'd all served a great purpose had now, fourteen years down the track, obliterated even the mind-numbing fear and carnage that had been Dunkirk. These days, the camaraderie of his fellow veterans on a Friday night elevated him from the rut of his existence and distracted him from the sense of uselessness that at times threatened to engulf him. The constant pain in his hip had worsened as arthritis had set in, and his workload had been reduced to three days a week by a company that valued his long-term commitment. He was grateful, but it didn't stop him feeling bitter. Much as he told himself his incapacity was noble proof of his service, it angered him to be a cripple at forty-four. Kenneth's greatest delight now lay in the knowledge that his boys would lead the military life he'd always yearned for.

'There's no greater honour than to serve your country,' he announced to the table in general, 'no greater honour on this earth. And that's what I've instilled in my sons, Elizabeth.'

The grin he flashed her was one of sheer joy, and in its very boyishness Elizabeth suddenly saw Daniel. She hadn't noticed the likeness between the two until that moment.

'I'm proud,' Kenneth said, 'so very, very proud that they chose such a path.'

But did they, Elizabeth asked herself as she stared back at him in a wonderment of incredulity. Were they given any *choice*? The man was a zealot; they'd been brainwashed, surely. As she glanced at Daniel, she realised her face must have been readable. Unable to contain himself, he let out a hoot of laughter.

'No, we weren't brainwashed,' he said, and Elizabeth didn't know where to look. 'At least, if we were I wasn't aware of it.'

'Brainwashed?' Kenneth was confused. 'Who said you were brainwashed?'

'No-one, Dad. You're pontificating a bit, that's all.'

'Oh. Am I?' He looked to his wife, and Prudence gave the gentlest of nods. 'Well, well, fancy that.' Kenneth smiled, caught out but unembarrassed. 'I tend to get a bit carried away at times, don't I?' He eased himself carefully from his chair, trying to disguise the pain as his frozen muscles screamed. 'A superb meal as always, Mother,' he said.

Then – once again to Elizabeth's amazement – he started clearing the dishes from the table. The action itself was surprising enough, but so too was the fact that neither his wife nor his son intervened. The man seemed extremely unsteady on his feet.

'Let me help, Mr Gardiner.' She sprang up and was about to take the plates from him, but he protested.

'No, no, leave me,' he said sharply, and she backed off.

In a matter of seconds he'd regained his balance and, as he turned to her, his tone softened. 'You can lend a hand if you wish, my dear, but I like to do my bit. It keeps me on the move, you see. I can't sit still for too long.'

'I'll get the dessert,' Prudence said. 'You bring the meat platter, Dan, it's heavy.'

Elizabeth didn't notice the look between mother and son as they rose from the table. Kenneth Gardiner never admitted to his limitations in front of strangers – it seemed his future daughter-in-law had made a favourable impression.

'What are we having?' Daniel asked. 'Apple crumble or jelly trifle?' His mother always prepared one of his favourites when he came home for the weekend.

'You have a choice,' Prudence answered, 'I made both.' And, gathering up the gravy boat and the bowl with its few remaining Brussels sprouts, she disappeared to the kitchen.

'She spoils those boys rotten,' Kenneth said to Elizabeth. 'Just as well the army's taking them in hand. They'd be fat as butter if they stayed here.'

Gideon Melbray gazed through the aircraft's window at the cloudless blue sky, and then down at the even bluer ocean below where not a speck of land was in sight. The whole world seemed blue. They'd left Indonesia, having refuelled at Djakarta, and were now on the penultimate leg of their arduous journey to the other side of the world. Next stop Darwin, the northern gateway to Australia.

Gideon had boarded the Hastings Mark IV at Lyneham RAF Base on February 20 and had now been travelling for almost a week. The four-engine aircraft, specifically designed for long-range transport, could carry up to fifty troops with full kit at a flying speed of 250 miles per hour, but on this trip there was little equipment and only twenty on board. Amongst the soldiers of various ranks, both officers and enlisted men, all from different regiments, the mood had been relaxed. They were not en route to a combat zone – the officers were on relief duty assignments and the enlisted men were additions to a general workforce – and from the outset a spirit of anticipation had prevailed. Gideon, the only man in mufti, had enjoyed the odd looks from the soldiers who'd wondered at the mystery of him.

'Department of Supply.' He'd been quick to engage in conversation and had readily offered the information. 'I'm taking over the post of senior requisitions officer. You chaps will be seeing quite a bit of me, I should think.'

'What a handy chap to know,' a young captain had remarked with a wink to the others. It was a response generally acknowledged, and Gideon had rapidly become 'one of the boys'.

He'd very much enjoyed the company of the soldiers and the mode of military transport. As diplomatic staff, he was accustomed to travelling on civilian aircraft and he'd found the change of atmosphere and camaraderie exhilarating. Even the draughty discomfort of the unpressurised cabin and the tasteless packaged meals acquired at their various stops along the way had failed to daunt his enthusiasm. He'd liked being surrounded by rowdy masculinity and the smell of sweat. But then he'd always liked 'roughing it'.

The whole trip had been something of an experience, he now thought as he stared mindlessly out the window, particularly the enforced overnight stop in Istanbul. He glanced about the cabin. Some of the men were quietly chatting, others having a nap – they'd be landing in Darwin soon. The soldiers were a nice enough bunch, but he'd ascertained very early on that they were conservative to a man – he could sense no kindred spirit amongst them. It rather titillated him now to imagine their reaction if they knew what had taken place during the Istanbul stopover.

After take-off, the Hasting's intended destination had been the British RAF base on the island of Cyprus in the Mediterranean, the first of several planned refuelling stops, but bad weather had forced a diversion. The pilot had landed the aircraft in Istanbul instead, where it had been grounded for twenty-four hours while a replacement engine cowling had been located and fitted.

Unlike the military personnel with whom he was travelling, Gideon had been free to choose accommodation to his personal liking and he'd immediately booked himself into the luxurious Hotel Istanbul. No stranger to the city, having at one time spent six weeks on temporary duty at the British embassy there, he'd whiled away the afternoon reacquainting himself with its breathtaking beauty.

He'd forgotten just what a seductive city it was, he'd thought as he'd mingled with the tourists in Eminonu, the heart of the ancient town, where the Topkapi Sarayi and the Hagia Sophia and the Blue Mosque stood in a row, as if competing for awards in sheer magnificence. From one of the six towering minarets of the Blue Mosque a muezzin was calling the faithful to prayer, and he remembered how very stirring he'd found the relentless chants of the muezzins throughout the day. Stirring, sensual, visceral even, they'd aroused him in a way that was certainly not their intention.

Upon his return to the hotel, he'd showered and gone to the lounge for a pre-dinner Scotch, noticing immediately the attractive blonde seated near the main doors sipping a martini. He'd considered making an approach, but had decided against it. She was not only attractive, she was patently rich. Attractive, rich blondes did not travel alone. She was waiting for her husband, he'd decided, or perhaps her lover, but either way, a man many years her senior – he'd put his money on it. He'd seated himself at a table near the bar and paid her no further attention.

'Do you mind if I join you?'

Only minutes later, there she was, standing beside him, martini in hand.

He rose. 'I'd be honoured,' he said. 'Please,' and he gestured to the large leather armchair opposite his own.

'My husband is keeping me waiting, as usual,' she said with a mixture of apology and embarrassment. 'I do so hate being in hotel lounges on my own.' She sat. 'I'm Caroline Hardinge. How do you do.'

They shook hands. 'Gideon Melbray,' he said, and sat.

'I heard you ordering your Scotch. You're English, of course.'

'Yes. You too?' It was a joke.

'Dear me, yes, can't you tell?'

'I can rather.' And they shared a laugh.

'This is my first time in Istanbul. Marcus has been here before, many years ago, with his first wife, but this is my very first visit. Isn't it the most divine place? Have you been here before yourself?'

'Briefly, yes.'

'We caught a taxi into the old part of town and then walked for hours all afternoon. I'm sure that's why Marcus is taking so long now. He said he'd only be five minutes, but he's probably soaking in a hot bath. It really is naughty of him.'

She seemed happy to conduct her own monologue and, for politeness's sake, Gideon more or less listened, although he knew it wasn't necessary – eye contact was quite sufficient. She was out to seduce him, and he wondered why. An upper-class English callgirl in Istanbul? Hardly. Her elderly, impotent husband asleep in their suite upstairs was a far more likely scenario, he thought, and he bought her another martini. Then Marcus arrived.

Gideon congratulated himself on his initial deduction. Marcus, in his fifties, was indeed a good twenty years older than his wife. He was not, however, elderly, nor did he appear the impotent type. In fact Gideon found him stylish and rather good-looking,

'Oh, darling, at last,' Caroline said with an attractive pout. 'You've been frightfully rude. This is Gideon Melbray, my knight in shining armour. Gideon, this is my husband, Sir Marcus Hardinge.'

'Sir Marcus.' Not a flicker showed on Gideon's face as he offered his hand, but old habits died hard – a title still impressed him.

'Marcus, old man, please,' Hardinge said as they shook. 'Thanks so much for looking after Caroline, most appreciated. I'd be in such trouble if you hadn't. Will you join us for dinner?'

This was a game, Gideon realised, a game which had suddenly become far more interesting than the simple bedding of Caroline Hardinge.

'I'd be delighted.'

They had another drink and, as they rose from their chairs to adjourn to the dining room, Gideon offered his arm to Caroline.

'Lady Hardinge?'

She smiled and, slipping her hand into the crook of his elbow, shared a look with her husband. A look not lost on Gideon; a look that said they were pleased with their find. Well, so was he. A ménage à trois? If so, what fun.

But as it eventuated, a ménage à trois was not the intention. Following dinner, when they adjourned to the Hardinges' suite, it turned out Marcus wanted no more than to watch his wife copulate with another man. Gideon was happy to oblige. It seemed the poor fellow was impotent after all, and the superb dinner and wine they'd shared certainly deserved a return of favours. Besides, he enjoyed being watched – almost as much as he enjoyed observing the watcher – and he manoeuvred Caroline into the perfect position where he could see Marcus in the mirror.

As Caroline's body started to heave, he focused on the mirror. Marcus's arousal at the sight of his wife's pleasure was obvious and Gideon willed their eyes to meet so they could share the eroticism of the moment, but Marcus's gaze remained focused on the act itself.

Gideon slowed his thrusts to a minimum, then stopped altogether and remained motionless, waiting for Caroline to get the message. She was altogether too receptive – she'd orgasm any minute and they'd only just started. Not that it mattered, she was the sort who'd orgasm all night, but the woman had no natural rhythm, no self-control. She was sexually indulgent.

When he sensed she'd calmed down a little, he withdrew, turning her over onto her knees to take her from behind, and, glancing once again in the mirror, he recognised the truth. Marcus was not aroused by the sight of his wife in sexual congress. Marcus was aroused by the sight of a man rutting. Marcus Hardinge was not impotent at all. He was homosexual.

Gideon stood, a naked Adonis with a glistening erection, and smiled as he held out his hand. 'Come and join us, Marcus,' he said.

Marcus did. Never before, in all the years of his voyeurism, had he taken part in the action. But such an offer from such a man was irresistible.

The following morning, Gideon breakfasted in his suite – he would be departing the hotel before the dining room opened – and, as he sipped his tea, he wondered briefly about the Hardinges' reaction to the events of the previous evening. Would Caroline thank him for revealing her husband's homo-sexuality? He'd sensed, very strongly, that she'd been unaware of Marcus's sexual preferences. And what of Marcus himself? Gideon suspected Marcus Hardinge kept his dark secret for those tormented nights when he was driven to a bar where male prostitutes plied their trade. Caroline was, after all, his second wife. He'd probably pretended to a voyeuristic fetish through-out both marriages in order to keep his wife satisfied while simultaneously fulfilling his masturbatory needs.

One would never know, Gideon had thought as he'd gone downstairs to his pre-ordered taxi. And ultimately, of course, one would never care. There were far bigger adventures in store. He would shortly be on a 2500-mile flight over the Zagros Mountains of Iran, to Karachi. How very exciting, he'd thought. Pakistan, then Indonesia, then Australia.

But he had to admit, the dalliance in Istanbul had been an unexpected and highly pleasurable experience.

# Chapter Seven

Under Prudence's regime, the Gardiner household appeared to revolve entirely around mealtimes, and, after a massive hot breakfast the following morning, Elizabeth was thankful when Daniel said they wouldn't be home for lunch.

'Dad's lending me the Wolseley and we're going for a drive,' he told his mother.

'Of course, dear. I'll keep the cottage pie for dinner.'

They drove along the Nantwich Road then up the hill of Edleston Road and into the township, where Daniel parked his father's cherished 1935 Wolseley. Any scratch on the vehicle and there would have been hell to pay, but Kenneth trusted his older son. Daniel had an affinity with cars. Billy was another matter altogether. Young Billy never scored a loan of the Wolseley.

Away from the surrounding industrial areas, the town centre of Crewe, dominated by its ornate stone market hall and clock tower, was attractive.

'I'm very fond of this place,' Daniel said, as they strolled down the main street hand in hand, rugged up against the cold. 'I grew up around here and so did my parents. Dad's father was from Chester. He was a clerk with the railways, and Dad would have been too, but when Rolls-Royce built its factory here in the thirties, he changed his mind and went to work for them instead. He's always been passionate about cars. Bit of an irony really, because with the threat of war the factory went straight into aircraft engine construction – they didn't produce a single car until 1946. By that time, of course, Dad had resigned from the company to join the army, gone to war and got shot up, and then come back to exactly where he'd left off. He'd done the full circle before the first Rolls or Bentley was ever wheeled out of the factory.'

Their stroll had brought them to the park and Daniel halted momentarily, feeling the need for clarification.

'I do feel sorry for him, Elizabeth, and perhaps that's influenced me in some way. But I don't feel sorry enough to live his dream without wanting that dream myself. Billy's the same. Honestly. We've talked about it. We both really want a career in the army.'

'I'm glad, Danny.' Whether or not his father's fixation was the indirect cause for his choice was none of her business, Elizabeth thought, so long as he was happy. She squeezed his hand. 'I'm really glad.'

'Me too,' he said. Then, with an all-encompassing gesture at their surrounds, he changed the subject. 'So here we are, Queens Park, the town's pride and joy.'

Elizabeth gazed about at the huge, sprawling park where supple willow trees kissed the greenest of grass and garden beds exploded with early spring blossom.

'I didn't know Crewe was so pretty,' she said. 'I don't mean to be insulting, but I've always thought of the place as a giant railway junction.'

'A lot of people do. I'm sure half the travellers who change

130

trains at Crewe don't even know there's a thriving market town barely a mile away.' He grabbed her hand again and she was forced to keep up with him as he strode purposefully back in the direction of the car. 'Come on, let's go for a drive.'

For the next several hours, they drove through the lush Cheshire countryside, taking detours down narrow tracks, exploring picturesque villages, stopping for a beer at a cosy wayside pub, and, by the time they arrived home, Elizabeth found she was more than ready for Prudence's cottage pie, which, not surprisingly, turned out to be a masterpiece.

Then, suddenly, it was Monday afternoon and they were sitting side by side the non-stop express to London. The long weekend seemed to have sped by as fast as the landscape that now hurtled past.

'I like your parents, Danny,' Elizabeth said as they both gazed out the window.

'I hoped you might. Yours and mine, chalk and cheese, eh?'

'Yes.' She turned to him with a smile.

'They like you too, I can tell.'

'Yes, they do. For the moment.'

'Oh?'

'I don't think they'll like me all that much when they realise my career isn't a hobby.'

'I was expecting you to set them straight on that actually.'

'Yes, you were, weren't you? You kept egging me on. Why?'

'You're a genuine maverick, Elizabeth.' Daniel's tone remained light, but they both knew the conversation was taking a serious turn. 'I thought you might want to make your own statement about a woman's right to a career. I was all ready to back you up.'

'But if you expected me to make a statement, don't you think you should have given your parents some sort of warning?'

'Nope. I mentioned your career when I was home for Christmas, but I could tell they didn't really understand. I didn't want to feed them any preconceived ideas before they met you.'

'You've given this a lot of thought, haven't you?'

'Yes, I have. And I think we should tell them our plans before we get married – we should keep everything out in the open. But if we're going to shock them, as we obviously are, it's better to do it together, as a team, don't you agree?'

'I do.' Elizabeth's look was one of profound respect. Flaunting social convention had been part of her upbringing, but Daniel? From such a conservative background, Daniel's stand showed great strength of character in Elizabeth's eyes. 'You're a maverick yourself, Danny,' she said.

'Hardly,' he scoffed.

'You are. You're a true rebel, in your own way.'

He beamed with pleasure. Whether or not he believed her was incidental. Such a remark from Elizabeth was a vast compliment. 'Well, who knows? Perhaps you're right.'

'So I suppose the next step will be to tell your parents about E. J. Hoffmann,' she said. 'That'll certainly shock them.'

'Yes, it will, but they'll get over it. We'll just have to pick the right time.'

She stared at him, wide-eyed with disbelief. Was he joking? He had to be. He was, and simultaneously they laughed. There would never be a right time to tell Kenneth Gardiner about E. J. Hoffmann.

From his window seat aboard the Hastings, Gideon Melbray gazed down at the earth below: a vast expanse of ochre-red splashed with mysterious and dramatic swirls of white. He found the sight mesmerising. From 20,000 feet, the desert and its salt pans resembled a never-ending primitive artwork, bold, stark and highly effective in its simplicity.

Not exactly welcoming though. Hardly the place one would want to live, he thought, recalling Harold Dartleigh's parting words: 'You'll find it rather a change from Mother England, old chap.'

They'd left Darwin hours ago and yet the desert of this vast land continued to unfold relentlessly and unchangingly beneath them. There had been thrilling moments in the flight nonetheless, when the pilot had dropped to 3000 feet to give them a closer look at the landscape. They'd flown low over the cracked, raw red of the MacDonnell Ranges, where, from the air, the dried bed of the Todd River appeared a raging torrent, and where, tucked into the primitive landscape, the township of Alice Springs stood as a tribute to human survival. A hundred and fifty miles further south, the pilot had dipped low again to give them a look at the giant monolith of Ayers Rock, which eerily marked the very centre of the island continent. Every man aboard had been in awe of the sight.

And now they were dropping altitude once more – this time in preparation for landing.

They flew lower, and lower, and still Gideon could see nothing but desert. And then, suddenly, they were circling a massive bitumen airstrip. It had appeared out of nowhere and sat in the middle of nowhere, like a huge grey scar. Running due north–south, it had to be at least a mile and a half long. Leading off to the east was an impressive parking apron, around a quarter of a mile in length, where a number of aircraft were assembled, and to the side of the apron was a small, prefabricated building, which obviously served as an airport. On the other side of the airport was a sea of tents, and a mile or so away Gideon could make out a town. An orderly town with streets and blocks of barracks set out in rows.

There was the clunking sound of landing apparatus being

activated – the Hastings was a noisy aircraft – and not long afterwards, wheels hit bitumen and brake engines screamed.

Gideon Melbray had arrived at Maralinga.

The decision to confront Daniel's parents paled into insignificance when, one month after the visit to Crewe, a far more
important issue presented itself.

Daniel rang Elizabeth at *The Guardian* with the news.

'I've been offered a posting.'

She accepted the announcement calmly. They'd been led to
believe that another overseas posting wasn't likely to come
through for some time, but Daniel had warned her anything
could happen, and she'd been prepared for the possibility.

'When do they want you to leave?' she asked.

'In one month – the end of April! You wouldn't believe it,
would you!'

The wedding was planned for early May – no wonder he
sounded tense. But he shouldn't, she thought. The date could
easily be moved forward. 'And where are they sending you?'

'Australia.'

'Oh, my goodness.'

That part was a definite shock, she had to admit as images of
gum trees and kangaroos flashed through her mind. Australia
was so appallingly remote! Still, she told herself, 'par avion'
made the world a small place. Even given delays, articles sent
by air would surely reach *The Guardian* in a fortnight or so.

'Oh well,' she said flippantly, eager to put him at his ease, 'I
suppose I'll just have to buy a summer wardrobe with an outback theme. That shouldn't be too difficult.'

'Things aren't that simple, Elizabeth. I can't say any more on
the phone, it's all pretty hush-hush. But there are big decisions
to be made. We need to talk. I'll see you next weekend.'

Elizabeth hung up, mystified. There was no established British army base in Australia. Australia had its own army. And if Daniel were being sent to the embassy as a military attaché why would such a posting be 'hush-hush'? She decided to pay a visit to Reginald Dempster, the foreign correspondence editor. She and Reg had become good chums now that he'd accepted the fact she was engaged to be married and therefore unavailable.

'Maralinga.'

She confronted Daniel with her knowledge as soon as they'd kissed at the front door. Her arms were still about him and her mouth still invitingly inches from his, but he was too astonished to home in for a second kiss as he would normally have done.

'The army wants to send you to a place called Maralinga,' she said. 'The nuclear testing ground the government is establishing in South Australia – am I right?'

'Good God, Elizabeth, how could you know that? Maralinga's top secret.'

'Not to the elite of the British press corps, my darling,' she replied smugly. Then, taking him by the hand, she led the way through to the kitchen, where, as usual, the kettle on the stove was starting to whistle and the teacups and saucers were neatly set out on the table. 'Oh, there's an embargo all right,' she said, 'and *in the interest of national security* the top guns of the press have been sworn to secrecy.' Relinquishing his hand, she rescued the kettle. 'According to my source, the government's terrified the Russians will find out, and no-one's to print a word – well, not until they start exploding their bombs anyway. After that he says it'll be open slather.'

Daniel sat at the table feeling overwhelmed.

'In the meantime,' Elizabeth continued as she prepared the tea, 'the press is being kept very much in the dark. Particularly about the location, so my source tells me.'

'I should certainly hope so,' he replied, finally able to get a word in. 'We weren't even told of the location ourselves in the advance briefing – a desert region in South Australia is all they said. It'd be a year's posting, taking over from chaps who've already done their twelve months – and I got the feeling that if we agree to go, we still won't find out where we are until we actually get there.'

'So what exactly *were* you told in the advance briefing?' she asked, bringing the teapot with her and joining him at the table.

'Not much. Warnings mostly, about the harsh conditions and the remoteness of the place – testing our mettle, I presume – then they told us to go home and discuss it with our families, bearing in mind the Official Secrets Act and the need for discretion, which,' he added with a touch of irony, 'in my fiancée's case doesn't seem to apply.'

'Oh, I'm sorry,' she said, shamefaced as she realised how completely she'd taken over. 'That was insensitive of me, wasn't it? I didn't intend to steal your thunder, my darling, I just couldn't resist –'

'That's what it means, by the way.'

'What?' She halted, puzzled.

'Maralinga. It means *fields of thunder* in some sort of native dialect. A piece of information your source apparently didn't have to hand,' he said with the triumphant ring of one-upmanship.

'I really am sorry. I was showing off. I know I sounded arrogant –'

'No, you didn't, you just sounded like you. And there's no need to grovel, I'm not remotely cross.'

'Oh, that's good, I am glad.' She commenced her customary ritual of teapot turning – always three times, and always slowly. 'I thought you seemed a bit snappy.'

'I didn't mean to be.' He stared down at the revolving pot. 'I'm just . . .' He struggled to express himself. 'I suppose I'm just . . . distracted, that's all.'

'Why?'

Dragging his eyes from the teapot, he stared at her as if she was mad for asking, but Elizabeth refused to be deterred. To her, everything appeared extremely straightforward.

'You want this posting, don't you, Danny?'

'Yes.'

His response was somewhat lacking in conviction, she thought, and she waited for him to continue, but he didn't.

'You told me on the phone there were big decisions to be made and that we needed to talk,' she prompted.

'There's a promotion involved,' he said. Then it all tumbled out. 'I'd come back a captain – that's the carrot they're dangling. That and very good money in the form of allowances. God, Elizabeth, do you know how long I'd have to serve under normal circumstances to achieve captain's rank?'

'So why the agony of indecision?' she said briskly. 'It's all perfectly simple. You accept the posting, I resign from *The Guardian*, we put the wedding forward a fortnight, then we pack our bags and we're off to Maralinga. I can post my articles from there by airmail, it's simple –'

'There are no married quarters at Maralinga.' Daniel interrupted before she could go any further. 'In fact, there's no accommodation at all for females. Women aren't allowed anywhere near the place.'

'Oh.' She was instantly deflated. Of course, she thought, how very stupid of her. Maralinga was no ordinary military base.

'Your source didn't tell you that, I take it.' There was no edge of one-upmanship this time – he found her endearingly vulnerable when her ego was punctured.

'No,' she admitted, 'but then my source wasn't aware of any personal interest on my part. He assumed my queries were those of a fellow journalist.'

'Well then, you can see our dilemma, can't you? Things aren't really simple at all.'

'But they are, Danny. Or rather, they can be.' In her determination to solve the problem, Elizabeth was once more on the attack. 'I'll get a place in the nearest city and work from there, and we'll meet whenever you can arrange any leave, just the way we do now. Except we'll be married,' she added meaningfully. 'If we can't actually *live* together, then at least when we *do* see each other it will be as man and wife.'

'Oh, Elizabeth . . .' His laughter was unexpected. 'Oh dear, dear Elizabeth, how I do love you.' As he dragged his chair close to hers, there was the rasping sound of wood on cheap linoleum. 'For such an intelligent woman you really do have a talent for closing your eyes to reality,' he said, and, taking her face in his hands, he kissed her.

'Why? What did I say that was so very stupid?'

'Troops stationed at Maralinga won't be popping into town on weekend leave, dearest. They'll be marooned in the middle of a desert hundreds of miles from anywhere.'

'I didn't say *weekend* leave, don't be so patronising.' Elizabeth refused to admit to stupidity twice in the space of only minutes. 'Even if the nearest town *is* a hundred miles away,' she said archly – and she couldn't envisage it being any further, he was surely exaggerating – 'then I've no doubt the army would grant an officer leave on compassionate grounds, just *once or twice* in an entire *year*, to visit his wife. That would be all I would ask.'

'Why should the army do that?' Daniel stopped teasing. 'We're talking about a top-secret military site, Elizabeth. The army wants its men isolated from prying eyes and ears. The army would have no wish to encourage fraternisation, even amongst wives and families. That's why we're being offered huge allowances and promotions. Soldiers need incentives for a job like this.'

'I see.' Elizabeth's entire defence crumbled. She felt more than stupid, she felt mortified. How could she have been so self-absorbed? She'd given no consideration to his personal predicament; she'd been too busy showing off the knowledge she'd gained through her press connections. No doubt the incentives on offer included danger money, she thought, but even his safety hadn't occurred to her, had it? She was so ashamed of herself she didn't know how to apologise.

'Well then,' she said forlornly, looking down at her fingers and fidgeting with her engagement ring, 'we'll send smoke signals, shall we?'

'Nope.' He took her hands in his, forcing her to look at him. He could see she felt guilty, but there was no need. 'We won't be able to send smoke signals because you won't be coming to Australia.'

'Of course I will –'

'Why? What would be the point? We wouldn't be able to see each other, and you'd be giving up a splendid career for no purpose. You're much better off staying in London.'

'Don't be ridiculous. Even if we can't live together, I would want to be near my husband.'

'But that's just it. I wouldn't be your husband. I think we should postpone the marriage until after my return.'

She was speechless with shock, and he hastily continued before she could recover.

'It's the sensible way to go about things, Elizabeth. When I get back, we'll be in the perfect position to marry. I'll have my captain's rank and my captain's salary and no doubt a huge amount of accrued savings. Well, of course I will,' he said jok-ingly, 'what can one spend money on in the middle of a desert?' She made no response. 'You can see the wisdom of such a plan, can't you?' he urged. 'This would set us up in our married life, we could even buy a house.'

'Yes, I can see the wisdom of such a plan,' she replied, although from the tone of her voice he found it difficult to gauge her mood. 'I can also see that you've made up your mind. You've made up your mind about everything, haven't you?'

'I'm afraid I have rather . . .'

'Then I don't understand your agony of indecision.'

'Those were your words, my darling, not mine. I said I was distracted. I've been distracted all week, battling my own dis-appointment, wondering how on earth to tell you. And I'm sorry, I'm so sorry . . .'

'Don't apologise, Danny, whatever you do.' The vehemence with which she interrupted surprised him. 'This is a huge step in your military career – naturally the decision must be yours, and naturally I'll abide by whatever that decision is. But surely.' She paused, and in her bewilderment was the tiniest element of hurt. 'Surely you'd like us to marry before you leave?'

Of course he would. He would like nothing more in the world. 'No,' he said firmly. 'No, that wouldn't be fair to you.'

'Why?' Then the alarming thought struck her. 'It's because of the danger, isn't it? You're worried that something might happen to you.'

'Good heavens, no, I'm hardly going into a war zone.' He smiled, but there was an element of truth in what she said. The work at Maralinga would be dangerous, and accidents did happen – what if she were left a widow? The thought had occurred. But something else governed Daniel's decision, some-thing less definable, a matter of principle.

'Then why?' she persisted. 'Why don't you want to get married?'

She was plainly not about to give up, and he was forced to respond. 'Because it wouldn't be right, that's why.'

'I can't for the life of me see what would be so very wrong.'

'It would *feel* wrong,' he said. 'It would feel wrong to *me*, Elizabeth. It would feel very, very wrong to marry you and then, barely weeks later, to leave you alone for a whole year. It would feel as if I'd taken advantage of you.'

He knew how old-fashioned he must have sounded, particularly to someone as modern as Elizabeth. He waited for her to make fun of him. He wouldn't have minded if she had. But she didn't laugh.

'The tea's cold, and it's nearly lunchtime,' she said. Then she kissed him and sprang to her feet. 'Shall we go to the pub?'

'What an excellent idea.'

Daniel could not have known that, at that very moment, Elizabeth had made a momentous decision of her own.

# BOOK II

*From the shadows cast by the grove of stunted eucalypts, Mimitja watches in silence, her sleeping baby clasped to her breast, her other arm encircling her five-year-old daughter. The child presses so tightly against her mother she is like an extension of Mimitja's body. Mimitja hopes the baby will not wake, for if he does, he will alert the white men.*

*The truck approaches. The two men are scanning the desert through its open cabin windows, and Mimitja hears their voices clearly. She has not spoken English for many years, but she knows the white man's language. She understands every word they are saying.*

*'I saw her – a woman with a child. And she was carrying something. It might have been a baby.'*

*'Your eyes can play tricks on you out here in the desert, mate. You'll get used to it.'*

*'But I saw her, I swear I did!'*

*'I'm not saying you didn't, they're around the place all right. But you won't see her again. Not unless she wants you to.'*

*The truck passes close by the grove of mallee trees where Mimitja stands. She remains motionless until it is well out of sight and even the dust raised by its passing has settled. The only danger of detection, she knows, lies in movement, for the white man is blind. Stillness confuses him – he sees nothing in the land's shadows.*

*Satisfied that the danger has passed, she releases her*

*hold on her daughter and the two go about their business of gathering firewood. Mimitja's husband is hunting for their evening meal, but she has no concern for his safety. He does not share her innate fear of the white man, but for her sake he will not allow his presence to be detected.*

*Mimitja's memories of the Hermannsburg Mission are vivid – even those from the times when she thought she'd been happy. She still recalls how she enjoyed her lessons at the mission school and how she liked to sing hymns during the church services on Sundays. But the pleasant memories have long been outweighed by the sound of her mother's wailing and the screams of her sisters on that fearful day ten years ago. She remembers returning from the waterhole to the reserve, hearing the sound, running towards the humpy where she lived with her parents only to see her two little sisters being forced into the car by the man from the government. She still hears the voice of the missionary, the man whom, above all, they had trusted, as he holds her mother back.*

*'It's for their own good, Lila! It's for their own good!'*

*Then she sees the look in her mother's eyes and she hears the desperate scream. 'Run, Mimitja! Run! Run!'*

*She had done her mother's bidding. She had been fourteen years old, strong and healthy, and she had run as she'd never run before.*

*Mimitja has her own children now, and her mother's ordeal has taken on a new meaning. As a mother herself, she dares not risk the loss of her babies.*

*She knows that the men in the truck are not government men. Nor are they missionary men, but she has*

146

*heard of these trucks that patrol these lands. And she has heard what it is these men do. They do not steal children. They offer lollies to people and they make friends with them, and then they put whole families into their trucks and they take them away. She does not know where they take them, and she has no wish to find out. But always they say the same words. 'It is for your own good,' they say.*

*The white men are not to be trusted.*

# Chapter Eight

Daniel had very quickly discovered that 'the middle of nowhere', as people were wont to describe the desert area of Maralinga, was in fact overwhelmingly beautiful. He was astonished by the depth of his reaction, which was totally unexpected. It wasn't that the information imparted during the briefing sessions at Aldershot had been incorrect – much of the terrain was indeed 'flat with little scrub cover', and there were indeed 'sandhills to the south of the village' – but nothing could have prepared him for the sheer magnitude of the desert, nor for its primitive and ever-changing splendour.

As an officer with the transport corps, one of his first major duties had been to acquaint himself with the surrounding area, particularly the route to Watson. Access to rail being essential for the delivery of supplies, the proximity of the Trans-Australian Railway line had been a major factor in the choice of location for the township, and Watson, the nearest siding, was roughly thirty miles south of Maralinga.

A young private called Toby had accompanied Daniel on his reconnaissance trip, a pleasant lad from Manchester, very talkative and all of nineteen. But then Daniel had noted the majority of non-ranking British soldiers were very young, some even seventeen.

They'd left in the early morning, Daniel taking the wheel of the Land Rover himself, keen to adjust to the desert driving conditions as quickly as possible. The military's well-laid and well-used road to Watson had proved no hardship, but after they'd passed the railway siding with its fettlers' camp, they'd driven a further seventy miles along roughly cleared desert tracks, Toby directing the way, to the main coastal road, which led to Ceduna – a further 150 miles or so to the east, Toby had said. Time to turn back, Daniel had decided, and he'd allowed Toby to take the wheel on the return trip.

During the drive south, Daniel had been aware of the dramatic landscape, but the task of driving and Toby's chatter had been a distraction. Now, with the late autumn breeze fanning his face through the open window, the immensity and power of the desert had overwhelmed him. Beside him, talkative Toby, sensing his awe, had remained mercifully silent.

They drove through vast saltbush plains that stretched for miles – squat, round little bushes forming bubbling seas that shimmered from silver to grey-green and back again, dependent upon the continuously changing light. At the capricious whim of passing clouds, shadows would brush the land, giving a constant sense of movement, as if the very earth itself was breathing, and, in the far-off distance, the silhouettes of mallee trees circled the mottled mass like stunted sentries. Then, past the saltbush and the mallee scrub, they were suddenly surrounded by the leafless, treeless, barren grey stubble of a frightening and lifeless landscape; and a little farther again, the salt pan, flat and stark, a parched white patch set against an orange earth. But, as they approached Maralinga, the greatest surprise was yet to come, for just beyond these apparent wastelands lay the Ooldea

Range. Here, at the south-eastern border of the Nullarbor Plain, the earth was vibrant with colour – undulating sandhills of vivid ochre-red, vegetation no longer silver-grey but startlingly green. Here, the landscape took on a raucously coastal appearance, which was in keeping with its history. The place was a palaeontologist's paradise. Here, fossilised shells and marine life abounded, as a reminder of a time when the sea had covered the Nullarbor.

Over the ensuing weeks, as Daniel had settled into life at Maralinga, the ever-changing face of the desert had remained a source of fascination. But today his eyes had been opened to another aspect altogether. An aspect which, upon his arrival, he hadn't even known existed – the people who belonged to this land. During the briefings at Aldershot, he and his fellow officers had been told the desert area of Maralinga was uninhabited. No mention had been made of the local Aboriginal population.

'Sometimes they're curious and want to say hello,' Pete Mitchell told him. 'And sometimes, if they've heard about us, they'll come up to the truck and ask for lollies. But if they're scared, you won't see them. Or if you do catch a glimpse, like you did today, they'll vanish,' he snapped his fingers, 'just like that. Here one minute, gone the next. They're experts in the art of invisibility.'

'That must make your job difficult.'

'Too right it does, mate. It makes my job a bloody farce.'

Lounging in a corner of the officers' recreation mess, cold beers in hand, Daniel had brought up the subject of the woman he was convinced he'd seen through the truck's window that very afternoon. The image of the woman and her child remained vivid in his mind.

It was the first time he'd accompanied Pete Mitchell on his

patrol, and he'd been flattered to be asked, knowing it was an invitation Pete didn't offer freely. But in the month Daniel had been at Maralinga, the two had formed a friendship of sorts. They'd had to – they shared a donga. The dongas were the two-man rooms in the orderly rows of prefabricated aluminium barracks set out in blocks and dissected by the grid system of streets that formed the basic structure of the Maralinga town-ship. Each of the barracks, with lavatories and showers at the far end, housed a dozen men, and it was generally considered a good idea to get on with the person whose donga you shared. Pete Mitchell, a wiry, sun-leathered man of forty with perman-ent facial stubble that saw a razor once a week just before a beard threatened, had made the fact abundantly clear to Daniel upon their first meeting.

'I wasn't too happy to hear I was copping another Pom,' he'd said. 'The bloke before you was a real whinger and I was hoping for an Aussie. Unrealistic of me, I know – this is a British estab-lishment and we're hugely outnumbered. Still, you seem like a nice enough young fella, so welcome to Maralinga.'

The none-too-subtle hint had not fallen on deaf ears, and the two had got along from that moment. Daniel was only too eager to learn, and Pete Mitchell had opinions he was willing to air to those few he liked, of whom young Dan Gardiner appeared to be one.

Daniel had found Pete Mitchell an interesting but strangely contradictory character right from the start. Even his name had come as a surprise.

'My real name's Petraeus,' he'd said. 'My mother was a Boer – Petraeus was her maiden name.' Pete's father had been killed at the Somme, and he and his four siblings had been raised by their mother on a small property near Tea Tree Well, about 100 miles north-west of Alice Springs. 'She was a teacher in the Transvaal,' he'd said – 'raised on a farm herself and as tough as they come.'

The surprise of his name was only one in the series of contradictions that was Petraeus Mitchell. The second was his academic background. It turned out Pete, the quintessential 'outback bloke', was a highly qualified anthropologist.

'Ironic when you think about it,' he'd said with a snort of self-derision. 'My big chance came via a university scholarship from the AFA.' In response to Daniel's querying look, he'd added, 'The Aborigines' Friends' Association – founded by a group of bored, wealthy socialites for the most part, but it does serve a purpose.' Then he'd given one of his rare barks of laughter. 'Some *friend* I've proved to be, eh? Here I am all these years later doing the government's dirty work. I'm the Lolly Man who kicks the poor bastards off their land.'

Although Pete's official title as head of the patrol team was that of Aboriginal liaison officer, he was commonly known as the Lolly Man. He accepted both the joke and the title – the lollies had, after all, been his idea. 'Ah, well,' he'd said with a philosophical shrug, 'I get paid big money and it's better than slogging it out in the army, so who's complaining?'

Pete Mitchell's anthropology degree had seen him commissioned into the Australian army as a lieutenant in 1942, and he'd worked with the PNG natives as a coast watcher in New Guinea for three long years. Following the war, his academic background and fine military record had made him the perfect candidate for a government position, and the name Petraeus Mitchell had quickly become well-known in federal government circles. Petraeus Mitchell was the perfect 'fix it' man for all forms of Aboriginal problems. No-one knew exactly how or why, but he seemed to understand the blacks – he could cut corners and get the results others couldn't. Now, with the

Maralinga project underway, Petraeus Mitchell was invaluable. Indeed, given the added attraction of his military background, there was no man in the country more qualified for the job. He could even be accommodated in the army barracks. The civilian quarters were mainly reserved for the scientists and administrators on site, and for the high-ranking boffins and government officials who would fly in for the detonations.

Pete had been quick to take up the offer.

'The bastards pay me a bloody fortune,' he'd said to Daniel. 'And, let's face it, *somebody* has to be the Lolly Man. It might as well be me – at least I speak a bit of the locals' lingo, which shows just a *little* respect, I reckon.'

And that was the biggest contradiction of all, Daniel now thought as he took another swig of his beer. Pete *did* care. It was obvious that, deep down, Pete cared a great deal. The degree of the man's frustration hadn't been apparent until today, but since they'd come back from the afternoon patrol, he'd really opened up.

'The whole attitude to the Aboriginal situation at Maralinga's been a farce from the start,' Pete continued as he dragged on his freshly lit Craven A. 'It's a farce that they put up warning signs in English – we're dealing with people living in a primitive state, for Christ's sake! It's a farce when an idiot Pommie brigadier says if the natives have a complaint, they can *take it up with the government* – the Aboriginal population doesn't even have the vote in this country! It's a farce that Butement, the key liaison between the British organisers and the Australian backup team, warns us about *placing the affairs of a handful of natives above those of the British Commonwealth of Nations*! His very words! God almighty, the man's our spokesman, he's supposed to be protecting this country! And that means the people in it. Except, of course, to him the blacks aren't people, are they?'

153

Pete downed the rest of his beer in one hit, aware that he'd allowed himself to get a bit carried away, which wasn't like him.

'Ah, what the hell, there's bugger all a bloke can do,' he said, wiping his mouth with the back of his hand. 'But Walter's right – we might as well declare war on the poor bastards.'

'Who's Walter?'

'My chief patrol officer, Walter McDougall – he lets the situation get to him a bit . . .'

He's not the only one, Daniel thought.

'. . . I tell him not to. "Just obey the job instructions, mate," I say. "Send the trucks out, locate the Aboriginal people in the region, communicate with them and tell them to move on. Even offer transport if they want it, you can't do more than that." But, of course, as you saw today, locating them isn't easy. That's what worries Walter. What happens when the bombs go off? What do we do about the blackfellas then?'

The question seemed rhetorical, but surely, Daniel thought, *surely* there must be some form of answer to such a dire predicament.

'What *do* you do, Pete?'

'You pray, mate. That's what you do.'

Pete stubbed out his cigarette and stood, calling a halt to the conversation – he'd had enough for now. He liked young Dan, but he sensed the kid was an idealist, and conversations with idealists could be tiring. 'My round,' he said, and he walked off to the bar where a line of privates from the catering corps stood stiffly in attendance with bottles on trays. White-jacketed and bow-tied, they looked like penguins, he thought. God, the army was a joke. As a senior government official, Pete had an open invitation to the officers' mess, but he preferred the hoi polloi of the beer garden himself.

Daniel was aware of Pete Mitchell's signals, which were

eminently readable, and he had no intention of plaguing the man with further questions, but there was much he yearned to know. How did Pete come to speak the black man's language? This was surely not something taught at university. Why did he pretend not to care when it was obvious that he did? To Daniel, Petraeus Mitchell seemed as mysterious and contradictory as the land itself.

*Dearest Elizabeth,*
*This is the strangest place, a place of such contradictions. These early days of winter are as hot as any summer's day at home, yet the nights can be bitterly cold. The desert itself is both terrifying and serene, both ugly and beautiful – far more variable than one could ever have imagined – but even the most barren area's immensely overpowering . . .*

Daniel wrote regularly to Elizabeth, always keeping his topics general, avoiding any specific description of the township or the site, knowing that the army would censor all mail. Possibly even incoming letters, he'd warned her before he'd left. They'd been told from the outset that security was paramount at Maralinga.

*My darling, you will never guess the first thing I saw when I got off the plane, he'd written the very evening he'd arrived. The pathway leading up to the small airfield terminal where we were checked through immigration is lined with oleanders! Isn't that extraordinary? The army has landscaped the airport entrance to make us feel at home upon arrival, and apparently the oleander is one of the few flowering Mediterranean plants that will survive in this place. I must say, it worked for me – I felt very welcomed indeed. The trees weren't in blossom as it's*

*nearing winter, but they were the same rangy, leathery plants as*
*those in your father's conservatory, rows and rows of them,*
*and I recalled that first night when he gave me a lecture on the*
*tenacity of the oleander. Do you remember? He was testing me.*
*He knew that I loved you. And I do, Elizabeth. More than you*
*could possibly imagine. Let me know that all is well, for if*
*anything should happen I will be on the first plane home.*

Daniel anxiously awaited word from Elizabeth. Even as he
relived their last weekend together, over and over, savouring
every moment, he worried that there may have been repercussions.

'You're *cooking dinner?*' He'd been amazed when she'd
informed him so over the phone. For as long as he'd known her,
Elizabeth had displayed no interest whatsoever in the culinary
arts. He'd resigned himself, a little regretfully it was true, to the
fact that his married life would not include the high-quality
home-cooked meals his mother had provided for as long as he
could remember. Elizabeth had insisted. This was to be his last
trip to London before leaving for Australia and she wanted to
prove her commitment to the wifely duty of becoming a fine
cook. She'd bought a cookbook, she said, and she was making
a lamb casserole.

He'd arrived as instructed on the dot of seven, to a faint
though distinct smell of burning, but made no comment as she
ushered him into the sitting room where the dining table in the
corner was set for dinner, complete with candles, as yet unlit.
She was looking particularly attractive, her auburn hair and dark
eyes offset by the starkness of the simple white halter-neck
dress she wore.

'I bought a claret, which the chap in the shop assures me is
a rather nice one,' he said, offering her the bottle in its brown

paper bag. Apart from beer, liberally dosed with lemonade, Elizabeth's only other preference in alcohol was an occasional glass of fine red wine, a taste she'd inherited from her father.

'Lovely,' she said, 'we'll have it with the lamb. But let's start on that first,' and she gestured to the unopened bottle of champagne sitting in its ice bucket on the coffee table beside the sofa.

'My goodness, we are going posh, aren't we. I didn't even know you owned an ice bucket.'

'I didn't until this morning. I bought it at Selfridges, along with the casserole dish.'

She disappeared through the door to the kitchen, returning only moments later with a tray of hors d'oeuvres and two champagne flutes.

'All courtesy of Selfridges,' she said, placing the tray and the glasses on the coffee table and sitting beside him. 'I've been on a shopping spree.'

He opened the champagne. 'To your first lamb casserole,' he toasted.

'To us, and to the future, and to the hope that by the time you return I'll be able to cook like your mother.'

They drank their way through most of the champagne and ate the hors d'oeuvres, talking non-stop as they always did, and then Elizabeth left to serve the meal. She refused his offer of help.

'No, you stay here and light the candles,' she said. 'Matches on the table. And there's a corkscrew in the cabinet – you can open the claret while you're at it.'

He did as he was told and, when she returned, the candles were flickering, the wine was opened and he was about to pour the second glass. But on looking up, he was surprised to see her in her dressing gown.

She struck a humorously hapless pose at the kitchen door. 'Well, that's one lesson I've learnt,' she said. 'One must never wear white when one cooks.'

He'd laughed. He'd actually laughed. Daniel could hear himself now. 'That's what Mum says – she always wears an apron.' Recalling the moment, he couldn't believe his naivety, but he had suspected absolutely nothing.

'Let's have the overhead light off for atmosphere,' she suggested, 'just the corner lamp and the candles. Then I can make an entrance.'

He obliged and the lighting dimmed. But he was puzzled when she remained stationary, silhouetted in the spill of light from the kitchen.

'Do you need some help?' he asked.

'No thanks. This part I can handle on my own.'

Stepping away from the kitchen door into the candlelight's glow, she untied the sash at her waist and let the dressing gown drop to the floor. She wore a bright red chemise of the sheerest silk, the gossamer fabric caressing her flesh, outlining her naked body's every contour.

'Which do you want first, Danny? Dinner or me?'

He'd been unable to take his eyes off her. In the silence that followed, his shock had been palpable as he'd stared at her body in a mixture of admiration and disbelief that may well have looked comical.

She stood her ground. 'I strongly suggest me. The dinner's a disaster.'

Still he said nothing. He was dumbfounded, incapable of speech.

She continued to play her role with bravado, tracing a flirtatious path with her fingers over the chemise. 'I know what you're thinking,' she said, 'Selfridges, this morning, but it's not, it's Harrods. And I bought it nearly a fortnight ago, on the Monday after you told me about Maralinga.'

It was only then Daniel recognised the insecurity beneath the façade. He'd heard the faint giveaway tremor in her voice and, suddenly, he saw the fear in her eyes, the fear that perhaps she had lost his respect. But she had misinterpreted his silence. He'd been overwhelmed by the magnitude of her action, which he'd rightfully judged to be a measure of her love. He was aware of the courage it must have taken for her to offer herself in such a way. There were no words to express what he felt, but Elizabeth, as usual, had made everything easy.

'You've always looked beautiful in red.'

The instant he said it, he saw the fear and insecurity vanish. And as she slowly walked towards him, he was reminded of that day in the park. This was a fantasy men only dreamed of.

He'd stayed the night, and they'd made love again the following morning, an easier, gentler experience than the first time, when he'd worried that he may have hurt her.

'Nonsense,' she'd said briskly. 'It's called losing one's virginity, and it's meant to be painful.'

There were times when Elizabeth was brutally non-romantic.

Their lovemaking in the morning had been a different matter altogether. Tenderly, gently, they'd explored one other, giving pleasure and accepting pleasure, pledging themselves with their bodies until they felt they'd truly become one.

Afterwards, as she lay with her head snuggled into his shoulder, Daniel ran his fingertips over her skin, marvelling at the satiny touch of her. He was overcome with love, but this change in their circumstances had brought with it complications.

'We'll get married early Monday morning before I leave for Aldershot,' he said.

'No, we won't,' she replied.

'Come to Aldershot with me then. We'll get married there – I don't take off until Wednesday.'

'No, we'll say goodbye this weekend just as we planned.'

'But, Elizabeth . . .'

She propped herself on one elbow. 'It was not my intention to blackmail you into marriage.'

He sat bolt upright, aghast. 'Who said anything about *blackmail*?'

She laughed at his horror, then continued in her practical manner. 'You've made all the decisions, my darling, and I've respected every single one of them. But this was a decision I believe was rightfully mine to make. I love you, Danny, and I wanted to be a wife to you in the true sense before you left. I have no desire to change the rules.'

And that had been that. She'd steadfastly refused to marry him. He'd brought up the subject of possible 'repercussions', but she'd dismissed pregnancy as highly unlikely. She'd done her homework, she said, and, according to the rhythm method, this was the safest time in her cycle. The threat of conception was negligible.

She'd sounded very practical and very knowledgeable, but he'd worried nonetheless.

A full six weeks passed before Daniel heard from Elizabeth, or indeed until he received mail of any description. No doubt letters were delayed in transit, he told himself. Mail bound for Maralinga would be held in keeping somewhere until the next flight was due to leave. Or perhaps they were held up right here, he thought, at the post office just down the road from his barracks. Did the army *really* vet incoming correspondence? Who could be sure?

He finally received five letters all at once, four from Elizabeth and one from his family, and he looked for any signs of interference, but could see none. Perhaps he was being paranoid. He read Elizabeth's letters sequentially. The final one was dated three weeks after he'd left, and she'd just received the first of his own letters.

*Danny, my darling, How wonderful to hear about the oleanders. I rang Daddy with the news and he said he could just see them thriving in noble splendour out there in the middle of the desert. He thinks the army is most astute in making such a choice.*

*Of course I remember that first night when he tested you, my darling. How could I forget? I was the only one who didn't know I was in love with you.*

She carried on in a light-hearted vein, and it was only at the end of the letter he received the news he'd been awaiting so anxiously: *By the way, I'm not pregnant, so there's no need to come rushing home . . .*

Had she forgotten his warning about the possibility of mail censorship, or did she simply not care about prying eyes? Daniel strongly suspected the latter. He even held the vaguest suspicion that her boldness might be deliberately aimed at those prying eyes. He couldn't query her on the subject, however, because outgoing mail was most definitely screened.

It was July, two months before the first in the series of tests codenamed Operation Buffalo was scheduled to take place, and Maralinga was in a general state of limbo. The township and its amenities were now completed and all stood in readiness for the influx of visitors. Thirty miles away, work on the test site continued. Construction of the ninety-foot steel tower from which the bomb would be suspended was underway, as was the construction of the two camera observation towers at Roadside, the firing area ten miles from the blast, but the erection of these was the work of specialist teams. Back at the township, with the waiting game upon them and little to be done, the men's lifestyle was relatively easy, although, in true military tradition the army maintained its disciplines. In the small ceremonial parade square situated in the centre of the village, the ritual raising and lowering of the Union Jack and the Australian flag was observed, and soldiers of various regiments were seen on a daily basis marching around the peripheral roads of the township, the barks of their sergeants assaulting the silence of the surrounding desert. In passing the swimming pool, they invariably met with some comment.

'Pick it up, lads,' the men would shout to the passing brigade as they lounged on the broad, concrete steps that led up to the pool, which was above ground level. 'You can do better than that.' And one of them might even down his bathing costume to flash his backside at the men marching past, knowing full well that in a few days' time it would be him being drilled by his sergeant and suffering a man's bare behind flashed at him from the concrete steps of the pool.

The Olympic-size swimming pool, complete with a low springboard and a proper 'ten-footer' where the bold could show off their skills, had already become of prime recreational importance. It sat invitingly alongside the volleyball court and the tennis court, and, over the blistering summer months down the track, would prove a positive lifesaver. The supply of water was, surprisingly enough, not a problem. During the building of the township, water had been trucked from Watson, but since the army had sunk bores there was a plentiful supply for all purposes, freshwater for the village itself being stored in a massive steel water tower that dominated the landscape.

Sporting facilities abounded at Maralinga, and also at the tent city adjoining the nearby airfield, where a golf course had been incongruously laid out on the red dusty plain and where the bitumen airstrip served as the world's largest cricket pitch. This city of tents, wooden-floored and connected by boardwalks, with mess rooms and canteens of timber-framed corrugated iron, was home to the air force. All other troops and civilian personnel were housed at the Maralinga township, which accommodated 550 permanent residents, with facilities to cater for up to 3000 during peak times, as was anticipated during the forthcoming tests.

In a bid to alleviate the boredom and frustration of men denied ready access to leave, the military keenly encouraged competitive sport, and the venue of greatest significance was undoubtedly the oval. Complete with grandstand, and with the proud title 'Durance Oval' erected in huge letters over the metal-framed archway of its entrance, the oval stood as a magnificent example of man's impertinence against so primitive a backdrop. There were times when it hosted events of gladiatorial proportion, for here the British played soccer, the Australians Aussie rules football, and rugby union matches were fiercely contested by all.

Ample provision had also been made for leisure activities, with separate dining and recreation messes for officers and NCOs, a canteen and beer garden for other ranks, and a cinema that screened the ever-popular Ealing comedies from back home or the latest of Hollywood's offerings.

Maralinga was by now a fully functioning town, with administrative offices, a hospital, a post office, a fire station and a chapel. There were repair garages, workshops, laboratories, and even an army barber's shop and bakery. Together with the rows of barracks, all of these tidily arranged and, for the most part, prefabricated buildings were neatly dissected by she-oak-lined streets bearing comfortingly familiar names. For the British there was London Road, Oxford Street, Cardiff Road and Belfast Street, and for the Australians there was Perth Road, Canberra Road, Sydney Road, Melbourne Street and Adelaide Crescent. There was even an Ottawa Street for the Canadian engineers of the radiation detection teams.

For all its community appearance, however, and for all the army's provision of recreational facilities, there was a social aspect missing in Maralinga. The open camaraderie normally shared by men marooned in a remote army base was somehow lacking. Even before the tests had started, it was evident that Maralinga was a secret military state within a state. One and a half miles east of the village was the highly restricted and heavily guarded area where visitors, having gained prior permission, entered under military police escort. Here were the laboratories where the plutonium was stored and the bombs constructed. Although the average serviceman had no involvement in this exclusive domain of the scientists, he was affected by the surrounding secrecy and, above all, by the need-to-know policy adopted and strictly observed at Maralinga. Each man worked in his designated field, and mateship was not encouraged between those qualified in different areas of expertise or working in different locations. Even during normal social discourse, conversation about one's duties was officially frowned upon.

Which was probably why the swimming pool and the football oval were so popular, Daniel had decided. They were places where men could simply be men. It was also why he enjoyed the company of Pete Mitchell. Pete might not give much away about himself, but, when in the mood, he talked quite freely about his job, albeit at times with an intense irritation that Daniel found understandable.

This evening, however, Pete's irritation was at a minimum. He was affable and in the mood for a chat.

'What the stupid buggers around here fail to understand,' Pete said, halting for a second to take a swig of his beer, 'is that this land we're sitting on is a veritable highway to the desert Aborigine.' He plonked his glass back on the table and wiped the foam from the stubble of his upper lip in a gesture Daniel had come to recognise as characteristic.

They were once again in the officers' recreation mess. The place was more crowded than usual, further teams of experts having arrived for the first in the series of tests, which was scheduled to take place in only a few weeks. Things were becoming busy all round in the central block of the township, where the buildings housed the social amenities. Men wandered out into the dusty square, cigars and glasses in hand, from the special VIP dining room reserved for the upper echelons of the visiting hierarchy while, on the other side of the common kitchen that served all, soldiers flocked from the canteen into the beer garden, ignoring the chill air, to smoke and drink and socialise. The general ennui that had pervaded Maralinga was being replaced by a sense of anticipation.

'You see, when this site was surveyed,' Pete continued, oblivious to the burgeoning crowd around him, 'the large permanent water base at Ooldea was a major consideration. But the boffins and the military don't seem able to credit a 40,000-year-old race with similar intelligence. When you apply a bit of common sense, it's pretty understandable that a permanent water source to the south would be the ultimate destination for a desert people leading a nomadic lifestyle, wouldn't you say?'

Daniel nodded. They were only halfway through their first beer and yet Pete was waxing loquacious the way he did when he had quite a few under his belt. He'd probably downed a hefty amount of the whisky he kept back at the donga before meeting up at the mess, Daniel thought. Pete regularly drove into Ceduna to top up his supply. He was a heavy drinker, Daniel had discovered.

'The Ooldea soak's an important gathering place. They come from all over – from the east and the west as well as the north.' Pete gave an airy wave of his hand. 'Even the Arrernte from the central ranges up my way – they all head for Ooldea. The Ooldea soak's more than a watering hole; it's a focal point for trade, and for ceremonial events and general socialising. They've been heading for Ooldea from the beginning of time. Christ, that's why Daisy Bates set up her camp there.'

'Daisy Bates?'

'Yeah.' Pete paused, his expression enigmatic as he waited for a reaction. But there was none. 'A remarkable woman, pretty famous – I'm surprised you haven't heard of her.'

Daniel looked duly chastened, but Pete shrugged forgivingly. Hell, the kid was a Pom, he could hardly be expected to know about Daisy Bates. Christ, the majority of Australians didn't bloody well know about Daisy Bates, why should the kid? Pete knew that he was getting a bit pissed, but he didn't care. He enjoyed imparting his knowledge to young Dan. Young Dan was one of the very few who appeared remotely interested in the Aboriginal situation.

'She was Irish by birth, Daisy Bates. I met her once, in Adelaide just before the war, at a lecture she was giving to promote her book. She was well into her seventies by then, but still a pretty formidable figure. Handsome woman. Tall and regal and very Victorian, with a little hat and metal-framed glasses. Difficult to imagine her out there in the desert living with the blackfellas, but that's what she did. Back in 1919 she pitched her tent near Wynbring Siding, east of Ooldea, set herself up as a sort of one-woman welfare centre and stayed there for a whole sixteen years.'

'So she was a missionary?' Daniel asked. He was fascinated.

'Christ, no – just the opposite. She didn't want to convert the Aborigine, she wanted to protect him from the white man's influence that she believed was destroying him. She devoted her life to the Aboriginal people, recording their language and culture, tending to the sick and looking after their babies. Her work's been recognised by the government and she's respected in anthropological circles, but it was always the people themselves she cared about.'

Pete paused long enough to take a healthy swig from his glass before continuing. 'The stories about her are bloody amazing. When livestock was taken from the rail cars and butchered by the siding to supply the fettlers' camps along the line, Daisy Bates would be standing by with her wheelbarrow – primly attired, as she always was. She'd collect the sheep heads and offal and cart the whole lot away to her tent, where she'd feed the Aboriginal families who'd flocked to be near her.' He skolled the remains of his beer. 'Like I said, a remarkable woman!'

Daniel waited expectantly for the next instalment, but it appeared there wasn't to be one.

'My round,' Pete said.

'What happened to her?' Daniel jumped in quickly before Pete could rise from the table.

'She died in her nineties, just a few years ago.'

Any number of questions were gathering in Daniel's brain, but, knowing the call for beer took precedence, he was prepared to bide his time.

'Hello, Pete, Dan. There's a shortage of tables. Do you mind if we join you?'

Looking up at the handsome face of Gideon Melbray, Daniel realised that the moment had passed. The subject of Daisy Bates would not be revisited over the next round. She'd been one of those brief glimpses into the Aboriginal world that Pete shared with him and no-one else, because, as he said, 'No-one else is interested.'

'G'day, Gideon,' Pete said as he stood. 'G'day, Nick, haven't seen you around for a while,' and he offered his hand to the man with Gideon, a tall Australian of around forty whose uniform displayed the rank of colonel. 'The bigwigs running you ragged, are they?'

'Yeah, sort of.' Nick's smile was wry as they shook. 'Canberra for a fortnight,' he said. 'It's good to be back amongst real people.'

Pete returned the smile. He and Nick were aware of each other's background and shared the knowledge that they'd both served in delicately diplomatic areas. Pete knew only too well the political tightrope Nick Stratton would be expected to negotiate over the coming months. Pleasing two masters was never easy, but fielding the press into the bargain? He wouldn't have Nick's job for quids.

'I'm grabbing a beer for me and Dan – I take it you blokes are all right?' Gideon and Nick held up their glasses, which were virtually full. 'Pull up a pew then, I'll be back in a tick.'

As Pete walked off to the bar, he couldn't help thinking that if anyone was capable of handling such a job it would certainly have to be Nick. Strange that he liked the bloke as much as he did – Nick was such a product of the military, but there was something admirable about him. Perhaps it was the fact that in doing his job, he wouldn't sell others down the river, Pete thought with a familiar sense of bitterness. Something he hadn't been able to achieve himself.

'Have you two met?' Gideon asked, and Daniel rose from the table.

'Not in the official sense,' Nick said pleasantly as he offered his hand, 'although I think we've swum a simultaneous lap or two of the pool.'

'Colonel Nick Stratton, Lieutenant Dan Gardiner.' Gideon made the introduction.

'How do you do, sir,' Daniel said as they shook.

Nick briefly considered suggesting that over a beer in the mess, the young man might call him Nick, but he decided against it. The lieutenant was, after all, British and the British were sticklers for protocol. Dan Gardiner might well find such a suggestion confronting.

'Pleased to meet you, Lieutenant.'

Gideon and Nick pulled up a couple of chairs.

'Dan's with the transport corps, we work together a lot,' Gideon said chattily to Nick as they sat. Then to Daniel, 'Nick's our official go-between.' In response to Daniel's understandably blank look, he added, 'Liaison officer between the British and Australian defence organisations. And he's soon to become Maralinga's conduit to the world!' Gideon ensured the delivery had a suitably dramatic ring.

'Give it a break, Gideon.'

Nick's warning look was wasted on Gideon, who made a regular point of flaunting the need-to-know rule, which he openly stated did not apply to him.

'I'm hardly revealing top-secret information,' he said reasonably. 'You're the press liaison officer as well – good God, you'll soon be the voice of Maralinga. The eyes and ears of the world will be –'

'Fair enough, you've made your point. I'd just prefer it if you got your facts right, that's all.'

Nick's tone, although not disagreeable, sent a clear signal. Gideon was amusing and, like most, Nick enjoyed the man's company – indeed, he considered the likes of Gideon valuable to the social fabric of Maralinga. The cloak-and-dagger policy the British had adopted was not only un-Australian, it was unproductive in Nick's opinion. So long as there was no threat to security, surely mateship should be encouraged amongst men stranded in so remote an outpost. But there were times when Gideon's garrulousness jarred and Nick found him just a little bit grating.

'Well, if you'd tell me the facts, then I'd be able to get them right, wouldn't I,' Gideon replied with a grin. 'But of course that would be breaching the need-to-know rule.' He backed off, albeit cheekily. He always knew exactly how far he could push, and Nick was the last person he would wish to offend.

Gideon had a crush on Nick, he had to admit, but then he'd always been drawn to the rugged type. And Nick Stratton was certainly rugged. Dark-haired and strong-boned, there was a bit of the Gregory Peck about him, Gideon thought. Perhaps in another time and another place . . .? But no, he'd only end up with a broken jaw. Ah well, there were plenty more fish in the sea.

'So who's going to win the match tomorrow?' he asked, and, with a wink to Daniel, he added, 'I'd put us at two to one.'

When Pete returned with the beers only minutes later, Gideon was running a book on the following day's rugby match.

'Are you in, Pete?' he asked, marking down the bets in the notebook he always carried, as Dan and Nick placed their money on the table.

'What are the odds?'

'Two to one the British, and three to one the Australians.'

'I'm in,' Pete said, digging a fiver out of his pocket.

Gideon had wasted no time in ingratiating himself through-out Maralinga. Everyone knew him, he was well-liked by most, and even those of his countrymen who found his behaviour at times inappropriate respected his talents. For Gideon had sub-stituted his calling card of good looks with a sporting prowess that was of great significance in such a man's world. Admittedly, he'd been forced to concede defeat to the Australians in the swimming pool, but he was Britain's star soccer player, one of their most valuable rugby team members, and on the athletics track he'd proved himself second to none.

Gideon Melbray had also successfully infiltrated every area of Maralinga, including the heavily restricted zone to which he had a regular pass. He hadn't needed Harold Dartleigh's influence to gain access – necessity had sufficed. He was, after all, senior requi-sitions officer, and everyone needed supplies, including the scientists in their laboratories. Those very men who had been instructed by Sir William Penney to answer to none other but him, and to allow no intimidation whatsoever by Lord Dartleigh, did not suspect for one minute that they were regularly wel-coming a covert MI6 agent into their midst. Gideon's was the perfect cover. Just as Gideon himself was the perfect personality.

'Only three weeks to go! I must say, I'm frightfully excited about the whole thing.' It was an hour and several rounds later, the mess was more crowded than ever and Gideon had to pitch his voice above the noise. 'I mean, it's thrilling, let's face it – a nuclear explosion before our very eyes! Well, that would be silly, wouldn't it,' he corrected himself, 'if we keep our eyes open we'll be blinded, but you know what I mean. How many men can say they've seen an atomic bomb go off and lived to tell the tale? I for one can't wait!' He raised his glass in a personal toast to the powers that made such things possible, then downed the rest of his beer.

Daniel glanced at Nick Stratton. Gideon's behaviour was overly flamboyant and very much out of place in the officers' mess, surely the colonel agreed. The colonel plainly did. But as Nick's eyes met his, Daniel saw in them a truth that he instantly recognised. Let's be honest, Nick's eyes said, he's only voicing the feelings of us all.

# Chapter Nine

The de Havilland Heron made a perfect landing, slowed to a near standstill, then taxied towards the apron, guided into its position by the ground crew. The huge parking area adjacent to the runway boasted an extraordinary collection of aircraft. There were the sturdy Hastings transport planes, the Herons and Doves reserved for the VIPs, the Shackletons used for weather reports, sundry Dakotas and Vulcans, and the Canberra bombers, especially rigged for air-sampling tests after each of the nuclear detonations. With just one week to go before the first test in the Buffalo series, Maralinga's airfield presented a remarkable sight.

Daniel wished yet again that he could paint the extraordinary picture of Maralinga in his letters to Elizabeth. He longed to share everything with her. Oh well, he thought with a wry smile as he looked at the profusion of scarlet and pink and white blossom that formed a welcoming pathway to the terminal, at least there were the oleanders. In the early spring, the desert oleanders were proving even more colourful than their English counterparts. Alfred Hoffmann would be most impressed, he thought, as he returned his gaze to the Heron from which Harold Dartleigh was alighting.

Five minutes later, he introduced himself.

'Lord Dartleigh, how do you do, sir. I'm Lieutenant Gardiner. I've been assigned to drive you to your accommodation in Maralinga.'

'Oh, good show.' Harold gave the young first lieutenant a cursory glance, then looked around as if expecting something more of a welcoming committee.

Daniel was quick to respond with his colonel's instructions. 'Sir William Penney wishes to convey his apologies, sir. He said he would have liked to have been here to greet you personally, but –'

'Good heavens above, lad, Sir William has better things to do with his time. Besides, this is hardly my first visit – no need to stand on ceremony, what?'

Harold perceived a distinct message in William Penney's absence. On the two previous occasions he'd visited Maralinga – during the early days of the township's construction, and then for the first in the series of minor tests – Penney had personally greeted him upon arrival. Now that they were about to embark upon the major detonations, Sir William was clearly stating he was in total charge and that the deputy director of MI6 was present in the capacity of observer only. Harold refused to take offence. If a personal snub was intended, he didn't give a damn, and he had his own methods of gaining the covert form of control he wished anyway. Gideon would have been very busy over these past months.

'Gardiner, was it?' he asked as they set off for the township, Daniel having loaded his two bags into the back of the Land Rover.

'That's correct, sir.'

'First name?'

'Daniel, sir.'

'Goodo, Dan.' On such occasions Harold liked to present a casual and friendly front. 'Marvellous day, what, hardly a breath of breeze – let's hope the weather conditions remain the same next week, eh?'

'Yes, indeed, sir.'

'Mind you, one can never tell what's going on up there.' He squinted as he raised his eyes to the mild scattering of clouds high in an otherwise clear, blue sky. 'Could be wind conditions we know nothing about. The final decision will rest in the hands of a few. We'll be at the mercy of the meteorologists, no doubt.'

'No doubt we will, sir.'

As they approached the village, Harold instructed Daniel to drop him off at headquarters, where his office was permanently maintained by his cipher clerk. The buildings allocated for VIP accommodation were close to HQ in any event, and he had no need to freshen up. 'Only flown in from Adelaide, after all,' he said to the young lieutenant. 'Hardly the long haul.'

Having travelled to Australia in the relative comfort of a Qantas Airways flight, Harold had whiled away several days in Adelaide, timing his arrival at Maralinga to coincide with the final briefings before the test took place. He saw no point in hanging around in the middle of a desert any longer than was absolutely necessary, although he'd come to the personal conclusion that Adelaide wasn't really all that much better.

'Thank you, Dan,' he said as he picked up the two bags Daniel had lifted from the Land Rover, 'most obliged.'

'My pleasure, sir.'

But Harold Dartleigh had turned his back and was already striding towards the doors of HQ, his mind on other things. He would pretend interest in the boringly predictable reports that had been submitted to Ned Hanson, he thought, and then he'd send Ned off to lunch. A private meeting with Gideon was bound to prove far more interesting.

It did.

'I've managed something of a coup,' Gideon said boastfully as he lounged in one of the wicker chairs opposite Harold's desk. The second lunchtime shift being underway, there were fewer men in the building than normal and it was unlikely he'd been observed entering Harold's office. Not that it would have mattered particularly – Gideon was observed everywhere about the village.

Harold made no reply, waiting for him to go on. He found the arrogance of Gideon's body language annoying, but when Gideon showed off in such a manner, there was usually a good reason, so he turned a blind eye.

'I've wired the telephones of five key scientists –'

'Heavens above, have you really?' The body language was instantly forgiven.

'Including Sir William Penney's.'

Harold guffawed. 'Good God, wouldn't he have a fit if he knew!' The thought pleased Harold immensely. 'Well done, I must say. How the hell did you manage it?'

'Their egos made it easy,' Gideon said with a careless shrug, although he was very much enjoying himself – he did so love impressing Harold. 'They wanted instant access to each other without having to go through the switchboard, so I provided them with personal interconnecting phones. Lovely bright red ones – they liked that touch. The sixth of the set is in my office at the storage depot – I can tap into each and every one of them whenever my pilot light flashes.'

'Excellent work,' Harold said approvingly. 'Good man.'

'I must say, for the most part, they're a frightfully boring lot.' While basking in Harold's praise, Gideon continued to pretend nonchalance. 'Half the time I can't understand a word they say. But there is one chap I believe you'll find very interesting.'

Harold could tell from the gleam in his eye that Gideon had made some sort of breakthrough. 'Go on.'

'Dr Melvyn Crowley, head pathologist and a megalomaniac of sizeable proportion,' Gideon announced with a ring of triumph. 'Crowley sees Maralinga as the perfect grounds for experimentation on all levels. The use of human guinea pigs is already planned to a certain extent, but he thinks, in the name of science, full advantage should be taken of Maralinga's isolation and the opportunity it offers. Given our precarious times, all ends justify the means, according to Crowley.'

'You learned this from your telephone tap?' Harold was most surprised.

'Not exactly, although the disagreements he has with Penney speak for themselves – they both seek the same ends, but Penney's reluctant to push things to the absolute extreme like Crowley. No, I learned it more from the horse's mouth so to speak.' Gideon's eyebrows arched suggestively. 'Melvyn's frustrated in his work. He seeks an outlet through which to express himself and, as you know, I've always been an excellent listener . . .'

'Good God, man, I told you there was to be no funny business here,' Harold said with a flash of annoyance. 'Those were my orders –'

'And I've obeyed them to the letter.' Gideon held his hands up in a gesture of innocence. 'I've done my job, nothing more. I encouraged the man to talk and he did.' His smile was satyrlike. 'I can hardly be blamed if Melvyn Crowley is smitten.'

Harold's annoyance abated as quickly as it had ignited. There was no denying Gideon was good – one of the best. But of course he'd recognised him as a natural right from the start – it was why he'd recruited him. Harold Dartleigh was as proud of his own talents as he was of his protégé's.

'So tell me why I'd find Melvyn Crowley so very interesting,' he said.

Having made his impact, Gideon dropped the indolent manner and leaned forward, eager to communicate.

'Crowley desperately wants the freedom to make decisions he believes others are too scared to make. He says that all of the scientists want to use every experimental opportunity Maralinga has to offer, but that the upper echelons amongst them are frightened of the public outcry should word get out.'

'So Crowley would welcome approval from a higher source. Excellent,' Harold said with a smug chuckle.

'And on being granted that approval,' Gideon continued, 'he would most certainly provide you with all the detail Penney wishes to keep to himself. The guarded reports that come in via Ned Hanson could be thrown out the window.'

'Excellent, Gideon, excellent. I shall pay Melvyn Crowley a visit and assure him he has the full approval and protection of MI6. After all, the experiments conducted at Maralinga are for the good of Britain – Dr Crowley is doing his country a great service.'

'He certainly is,' Gideon agreed, and they shared the self-congratulatory smile of a job well done by a first-rate team.

Harold's social chat with Daniel in the drive from the airport proved ominously correct. After months of meticulous planning and with all in place for the initial Buffalo test, codenamed One Tree, the final decision rested in the hands of the meteorologists, and their predictions were not favourable. To avoid contaminating Maralinga village and Watson railway station to the south, steady winds were necessary to carry the cloud in an easterly, northerly or westerly direction for at least twenty-four hours. According to the meteorologists' reports, however, the wind patterns over the test range continued to fluctuate and, as each day passed and yet another test firing was aborted, the strain of being on constant standby started to take its toll. Servicemen who'd been living with the promise of action became restless. They craved excitement, and if a scuffle broke out in the beer garden, the protagonists were urged to turn it into a fight for the amusement of others as men sought ways to alleviate the irritation and boredom of repeated disappointment.

Tempers were fraying amongst the scientists too, who felt thwarted and frustrated by the continuous postponements. None more so than Sir William Penney.

'It's sheer political procrastination, Colonel,' he complained in private to Nick Stratton after the sixth aborted firing. 'The safety committee has overreacted to a ridiculous degree.'

The Atomic Weapons Tests Safety Committee (AWTSC) had advised against the latest firing in the belief there was a chance that fallout carried east might be brought down by the rainfalls that had been forecast over Adelaide and Melbourne. Sir William vehemently disagreed. In his opinion, the amount of contamination, should such an incident have occurred, would have been negligible.

'Radioactive counts in the rainwater have been magnified out of all proportion by political troublemakers,' he continued. 'The committee must be made to recognise this, and Menzies must be approached and warned that this form of interference is counter-productive.'

Nick listened attentively as Penney vented his spleen, but he said nothing. There was nothing he *could* say. He agreed wholeheartedly with AWTSC's findings. In fact, during his previous day's meeting with the committee's three founding members, he'd openly supported their decision, which was most unlike him. His job was not to lend opinion, but to report and to liaise, which called for a great deal of diplomacy, and at times restraint. On this particular occasion, however, he'd been unable to resist voicing his agreement. He'd considered this the first decision the committee had made that actually had Australia's interests at heart.

Colonel Nick Stratton's job was not an easy one. As the Australian Defence Department's liaison officer to the British Ministry of Defence and the Atomic Weapons Research Establishment, headed by Sir William Penney, his principal ally should have been AWTSC. The committee's founding members were Ernest Titterton, professor of nuclear physics at the Australian National University, Alan Butement, chief scientist in the Australian Commonwealth Department of Supply, and Leslie Martin, whose career as professor of physics at Melbourne University and scientific adviser to the Defence Department combined both academic and civil duties. All three were eminent scientists with a wealth of experience in defence-oriented ventures, and the appointment of each to the Maralinga project had been approved by both British and Australian governments. There was, however, an imbalance. Of the three, Martin was the only Australian born and bred. Titterton and Butement were both British, both had accepted post-war positions in Australia, and their scientific experience had been principally gained while working on top-secret British and American allied defence projects. To Nick, it was patently obvious that these men's loyalties lay with the mother country. He was further aware that Leslie Martin was kept on the outer to a certain degree and, at times, denied access to data that had been supplied to his colleagues.

Nick Stratton was possibly one of the few Australians who

knew that his country's perceived representation in the scientific aspect of Maralinga was a sham. But he was also one of the few who knew the reasons why. The situation was a delicate one, and dictated primarily by Anglo-American relations.

Following the war, the United States government had decided that the safest way to thwart atomic proliferation was to keep the relevant technology in American hands. The British, denied the support of their former ally, had therefore turned to Australia to provide atomic test facilities, but in so doing they had found themselves in an awkward situation. They hoped, through their atomic experimentation, to revive Anglo-American relations, but if they were to involve the Australians on a scientific level, they would risk contravening the American non-proliferation policy. The situation was further aggravated by the United States' innate distrust of Australian security measures.

Ernest Titterton and Alan Butement had provided the perfect solution. They were ideally qualified to represent the host country, but neither was actually Australian. Furthermore, both men were highly respected in American scientific circles, having contributed significantly to joint wartime atomic projects. America wholeheartedly approved the choice.

As a salve to Australia, Britain had invited Leslie Martin to join the team, albeit reluctantly, and, in the early days, as an observer only. The eminent nuclear physicist Mark Oliphant, however, Australia's foremost authority on atomic energy, had been deliberately, and insultingly, excluded. The Americans considered Oliphant and his outspoken views a security risk.

Nick recognised the fragile issues at stake. Indeed, he had to. It was his job to recognise every aspect and to play the game accordingly. The British were toeing the line for fear of offending the Americans, and the Australians were bending over backwards to appease Mother England. Australia needed Britain, just as Britain needed America, and he was in the middle, fielding on all sides. He would shortly be fielding the Australian press too. Following the One Tree detonation, he would be the public relations voice of Maralinga and, as such, virtual spokesperson for all parties.

Nick Stratton's job was a challenge at the best of times and, though he had no wish to be back in the front-line, he did occasionally think that fighting in the jungles of New Guinea and on the battlefields of Korea had been a great deal simpler.

'I'm relying upon you, Colonel.' Sir William Penney's diatribe had come to an end. 'It's not in your charter, I realise, and perhaps it's even a little unethical of me to suggest it, but surely you can bring some influence to bear on the safety committee. They need to be made aware that these unnecessary delays really cannot be tolerated.'

Nick recalled the look he'd exchanged with Leslie Martin during yesterday's meeting, as Titterton and Butement had hummed and hawed about whether or not the firing should be aborted.

'I agree with Leslie,' he'd heard himself say, to the astonishment of those present, not least of all himself. 'It's not worth the risk.'

The burly Australian had given him a none-too-subtle wink, while Titterton, with slender fingers, had patted down his perfectly parted hair and Butement had polished his spectacles yet again. The two had not liked him at all for voicing his opinion, but they'd liked even less the thought that he might voice it elsewhere. Nick, in speaking out, had swung the balance.

'Of course, Sir William,' he now said. 'I shall attempt to bring to bear whatever small degree of influence I may have on the committee, I can assure you of that.'

'Thank you, Colonel. The sooner we get on with things, the better for all concerned.'

For once, Harold Dartleigh was in agreement with William Penney. He wished they would just get on with the job and blow up the damned bomb. But he was keeping well out of the political debate, which was hardly his area, and anyway it bored him. His meeting with Melvyn Crowley had been far more to his liking, and ultimately more constructive.

Even without Gideon's description, Melvyn Crowley had been exactly as Harold had imagined him – colourless. Short, balding, physically under-developed and with glasses, he was a typical boffin in Harold's opinion. But there was something else about the man that Harold found eminently familiar: the manic gleam in his eyes, which even the thick lenses of his spectacles could not disguise. Crowley was the sort who would have been bullied at school, and now, given a little power, liked to make others pay for it. Harold knew the type well. Every man who'd been to a British public school did.

Dr Melvyn Crowley, of the renowned Birmingham medical research team, headed the principal pathology unit, which was located in the decontamination and radiobiological zone, one and a half miles east of the village. Access to the DC/RB area, as it was known, was highly restricted, and those visitors who had gained prior permission entered under military police escort, for here was where the plutonium was stored and the bombs constructed. Here, too, were the experimental laboratories, and also the decontamination units, a series of white vans linked to each other, where those showing high radiation readings would be forced through a process of vigorous cleansing.

Harold had needed no special pass to enter the DC/RB area, but he'd nevertheless been personally escorted to Crowley's laboratory by a member of the military police – 'for his own safety'

183

he'd been told. It appeared even the deputy director of MI6 was not free to wander at leisure around the secret heart of Maralinga.

Harold had emphasised to Crowley the casual nature of his visit – 'just wanted to say a brief hello to you chaps who are doing such a sterling job,' he'd said. Then he'd shared a cup of tea with the scientist, noting the way Crowley's eyes lingered on the young assistant who delivered the tray – another symptom Harold recognised from public school days. He'd be willing to bet Crowley didn't acknowledge his homosexuality – the man wouldn't have had the guts – but there was no doubt Crowley lived with a chronic lust, possibly alleviated by the occasional male prostitute when time and place permitted. Little wonder, Harold had thought, that Gideon had made such inroads.

As they'd drunk their tea, Harold, in his insidious way, had encouraged Melvyn Crowley to talk freely.

'I imagine these delays must be particularly frustrating for a man of your talents, Dr Crowley. You must be positively champing at the bit.'

'Oh, indeed, Lord Dartleigh, indeed I am!'

'These damn safety issues are too restricting all round, in my opinion. Pity we can't hurry things along a bit, what?'

'Oh, I'm sure we'll be able to pick up the pace after the first firing,' Crowley had said a little guardedly. 'There's a natural tendency to be over-cautious at the start of a series.'

'The over-cautious don't win the race though, do they, Melvyn?' Harold had noted the immediate impact as he'd cut to the chase. 'Caution is hardly the keyword in a global battle for nuclear supremacy. Britain needs to use every advantage she has to hand, wouldn't you agree?'

Well, there'd been no looking back after that. Gideon had been spot on, Harold thought – it didn't take much to crank

Crowley up. But Gideon was wrong in one respect. Crowley wasn't your run-of-the-mill, blinkered megalomaniac. Crowley was actually a smart thinker.

'We choose middle-ranking officers with career ambitions and encourage in them ideas of heroic proportions, Harold, that's the secret.' Melvyn had quickly embraced the suggestion that as like-minded, forward-thinking men, he and the deputy director of MI6, a peer of the realm no less, should address each other on a first-name basis.

'These officers would be placed well beyond the safety zone,' he eagerly continued, 'perhaps just a mile or so from ground zero, where they would observe the detonation, after which they would return to their regiments as visible proof that there is life for the conventional soldier following a nuclear attack. They would be heroes to their regiments, Harold.' Melvyn's eyes flickered with the light of the true zealot. 'And their honourable service to the cause would see their careers skyrocket. What greater incentive could a serviceman have?'

He mopped his expansive forehead with his handkerchief. The heat generally did not agree with him, although here, in the cool of his laboratory, it was excitement that was promoting his tendency to sweat. Melvyn had never had such an auspicious nor attentive audience.

'And, of course, in the process,' he concluded, 'we would get the test results we're after.'

'Perhaps.' Harold's agreement was dubious. 'Presuming there are any of them left to tell the tale.'

'Either way, we would have our test results, wouldn't we?' Melvyn's thin lips curled into the slyest of smiles.

Harold gave a boisterous bark of laughter. 'Goodness gracious me, Melvyn, what a ruthless man you are.'

Lord Dartleigh's laugh was a little too jarring and Melvyn was shocked into wondering whether or not he may have over-stepped the mark. He back-pedalled immediately.

'Just a little joke, Harold,' he said, 'a little joke, believe me, nothing more. Our officers would naturally be in protective clothing and under cover. We would, furthermore, ensure that they were positioned upwind of the fallout, so that when they emerged to examine the results, they would be exposed to residual ionising radiation only. Harmless, I can assure you, quite harmless.'

'Oh, don't back down now, Melvyn, whatever you do.' Harold clapped his hands encouragingly. 'I'm on your side, remember? But do tell me, come along, old chap, do – how the heck does one convince men to behave in such heroic but downright stupid fashion?'

Melvyn relaxed. Even his sweat glands started to take a rest. 'It's already been done to a great degree,' he said, pausing for effect as he sensed Harold's intrigue. 'You must have noticed the extreme youth of the average soldier here at Maralinga – even the majority of junior officers aren't long out of military school.'

Harold nodded. He was intrigued.

'The deliberate choice of young, naive servicemen, together with the strictly enforced need-to-know rule, serves our scientific purposes to perfection,' Melvyn continued. 'Men are kept in a state of ignorance, and we're able to feed them the amount and the form of data we feel necessary at any given time. It is my belief that after the first firing, during which all safety precautions will have been firmly observed, a general sense of security will prevail. It is then I intend to suggest more extreme forms of experimentation, along the lines I've mentioned. I have many such plans.' Melvyn's smile was bolder now. No longer sly, he was starting to gloat. 'Those wishing to be involved would participate on a strictly volunteer basis,' he said, 'after which it's simply a case of letting human nature take its course.'

'And which particular course would that be?'

Gideon had not been exaggerating after all, Harold thought, the man was a megalomaniac of the first order.

'There are always those who want to be heroes and push themselves that one step further, and there are always those who are content to follow. We would have no shortage of volunteers begging to lead or be led on the latest enterprise, so long as we minimise the actual threat of danger.'

'And, in the meantime,' Harold said jovially, 'should a catastrophe occur, you'd have a wealth of human material for examination purposes.'

Melvyn presumed Lord Dartleigh was joking, but he wasn't prepared to take the risk. 'We're scientists, Harold,' he said. 'We do not make catastrophic mistakes.'

Balls, Harold thought. Melvyn Crowley was just panting for a mistake, and the more catastrophic its proportion the better. All of which quite suited Harold's purpose.

'Well, keep up the good work, Melvyn.' He stood and offered his hand. 'You're doing your country a great service, and you have the full support of MI6, I can assure you.'

'Thank you, Harold.' Melvyn also stood and the two shook hands.

'I shall look forward to receiving your personal reports,' Harold said, 'on a confidential basis, naturally. I'll be of greater assistance to you that way – we'll be able to cut a few corners in the general bureaucratic process.'

'Of course.' Melvyn once again mopped the beads of perspiration from his brow. This had been one of the most exciting days of his life. 'Thank you, Harold. I'm only too delighted to be of service to MI6.'

'Of course you are, old chap.'

As Harold left, he thought what an excellent SS officer Melvyn would have made during the days of the Nazi regime. Come to think of it, he looked rather like Heinrich Himmler. Harold wondered if Himmler had been bullied at school.

On 27 September 1956, after a fortnight of postponements and eleven aborted countdowns, it appeared the One Tree test was finally about to happen.

At dawn, weather conditions were perfect and meteorological reports predicted minimal change. The detonation was planned for late afternoon and, yet again, the countdown began.

Throughout the day, preparations were made. Animals were strategically placed for experimental purposes. Goats were tethered inside the air-raid shelters, which had been constructed not far from ground zero, while sheep, rabbits and mice were tethered and caged in the open air several miles from the blast. Human dummies in military uniform were placed in several of the vehicles that were strewn haphazardly about in the forward zone, the vast collection of warfare paraphernalia having been standing there for weeks – tanks, vehicles, planes, guns, radar sets and more – all awaiting the effects of a nuclear explosion.

Men, too, were prepared for their specialised tasks. Scientists and the officers of the 'indoctrination force' responsible for examining the equipment shortly after the blast were supplied with respirators and the all-white protective clothing fondly referred to as 'goon suits'.

Engineers and technicians spent hours rigging the scientific recording apparatus in the blast area, and the cameras in the twin observation towers that had been erected at the firing zone, officially known as Roadside, ten miles from ground zero.

At the airfield, ground crew ran final checks on the two

Canberra bombers that were to fly into the cloud shortly after detonation, special canisters fitted beneath their wings to collect air samples. The pilots were standing by their respective air-crafts, waiting to conduct their own checks, and both two-man teams were excited at the prospect of what lay ahead. Like many at Maralinga, they were young and eager for adventure.

'Looks like today's going to be the day,' Maurie said as he and his co-pilot, Len, stood shoulder to shoulder watching the ground crew at work. 'Something to tell your kids about, eh?'

'Yep,' Len agreed. 'First into the cloud at Maralinga – it's the chance of a lifetime all right.'

'I've been thinking, you know – we could end up rich if we sold our story to the papers. *We Flew Through the Mushroom Cloud*.' Maurie painted the headlines with a flamboyant gesture. 'We'd make a bloody fortune.'

'Oh, yeah?' Len laughed. 'What about the Official Secrets Act? What about the oath of silence? They'd have our guts for garters.'

'I don't mean *now*,' Maurie scoffed. 'I mean way down the track when we retire from the air force. We could sell our story to newspapers and magazines all over the world. They'd pay us hundreds! Just think of it, Len, we'd become veritable heroes. We'd be living on easy street for the rest of our lives.'

Len was never sure when Maurie was joking, but the thought was attractive so he decided to humour him. Maurie, after all, was not stupid. 'Who knows?' he said. 'You might just have something there.'

Maurie and Len were not alone in their excitement. At Maralinga, men were queuing up to volunteer for duties at Roadside, where the electronic firing would take place, all eager to witness the event from the closest possible vantage point. No-one was permitted into the forward zone beyond Roadside, with the exception of the specially equipped scientists and members of the indoctrination team who would observe the detonation from trenches just five miles from the blast. All other spectators – and there would be hundreds – were to witness the spectacle from Roadside.

The hourly countdown continued, and the weather conditions remained within the limits of safety – at least that was the way William Penney chose to interpret the meteorologists' reports, which were, in fact, borderline. There would be no further delays, he had firmly decided. The waiting game had gone on for far too long – all was set in place and all would go ahead.

'A groundbreaking occasion, eh, Dan?'

'It is, sir.'

'Groundbreaking in quite the literal sense I should imagine.' Harold gave a satisfied chuckle before continuing in a serious vein more appropriate to the occasion. 'This is a proud moment for Britain, lad, and today's only the first step. By the time we finish at Maralinga, we'll be a major authority on atomic power, no longer reliant upon American know-how. And you and I will have been amongst those privileged to witness this glorious page in our country's history. I'd call that damned exciting, wouldn't you?'

'Yes, sir.' Despite Lord Dartleigh's rhetoric, Daniel agreed with fervour. He was as exhilarated at the prospect of what lay ahead as every man at Maralinga. Today was finally the day! Excitement had spread like a contagion. 'Yes, I certainly would.'

'Good lad.' Harold nodded approvingly, satisfied that his brief but inspirational words had hit home. He gazed happily out the window, enjoying the light breeze, his steel-grey hair glinting in the late afternoon sun. Life really was excellent.

Daniel had been assigned to drive Lord Dartleigh the fifteen miles from Maralinga village to Roadside, where, along with hundreds of others, the deputy director of MI6 would observe the explosion. Sir William Penney had extended an offer for Harold to join him in his chauffeur-driven Humber Super Snipe, in order that the two of them might be seen to arrive together with the official party, as propriety demanded, but Harold had refused.

'No thank you, William,' he'd said in his most aloof manner, designed to infuriate. 'I've been assigned my own chauffeur of late, a young first lieutenant with the transport corps. Wouldn't want to disappoint the poor lad now, would I? He's no doubt eager to be at the prime observation point. Wouldn't be fair to let him down, what?'

Harold's reasoning had been insultingly transparent. Officers of the transport corps were heavily in demand, and First Lieutenant Daniel Gardiner could have availed himself of any number of opportunities that would have seen him at Roadside. William Penney, although irritated by the blatancy of Harold Dartleigh's insult, had accepted the flimsy excuse with apparent grace, and had indeed been grateful to escape the man's company, just as he had no doubt Harold was grateful to escape his.

The feeling would have been mutual if Harold had given it any thought, but he hadn't. He was aware that both his refusal and his excuse could have been seen as insulting, a fact which rather pleased him, but he hadn't been consciously escaping William's company. He'd had Daniel assigned as his driver because he liked the lad, and he wasn't about to change his plans to suit William Penney's sense of propriety. Besides, he would make more of an impact arriving on his own rather than en masse with the official party.

'Do you have a girlfriend, Dan?' On such a momentous day, Harold was full of bonhomie.

'Yes, sir, I do.' At the very thought of Elizabeth, Daniel's face glowed. 'We're engaged to be married.'

'How delightful.' Harold found Dan a most beguiling young man. 'My heartiest congratulations.'

'Thank you, sir.'

'And have you set the date?'

'As soon as I get back from Maralinga, sir.' Daniel grinned, he couldn't help himself. 'In fact, if I have my way, the moment I walk off the plane.'

'Ah, my boy,' Harold's smile was all-knowing and avuncular, 'I think your fiancée may have something to say about that.'

'Oh no, sir, Elizabeth's not one for tradition at all. She doesn't want a white wedding with all the trimmings.'

'Well, good for Elizabeth, I say.'

Lucky girl, Harold thought – young Dan really was an engaging lad. Not conventionally handsome, but attractive in an earnest, boyish way – so much more pleasing to the eye than poor, plodding Ned. By rights, Harold's cipher clerk, Ned Hanson, should have been accompanying him out to Roadside, but Harold had given him orders to remain on duty at the office in Maralinga. Much as he knew Ned longed to be part of the action, Harold found him a boring fellow. He preferred to bask in the refreshingly youthful company of the Daniel Gardiners of this world.

The hour of detonation was now ticking over and the countdown had become minutes. The hundreds of spectators were in position, all facing the direction of the site and waiting for the final moment when they must obey their explicit instructions.

The countdown became seconds. In this hour before dusk, when the land reflected a beautiful light, the voice ringing out from the loudspeakers was jarringly at odds with the desert's serenity.

'*Ten, nine . . .*'

At the start of the final ten-second countdown, the crowd, to a man, turned its back on the site.

'*Eight, seven . . .*'

As instructed, every spectator covered his face with his hands.

'*Six, five . . .*'

Eyes tightly shut, they waited.

'*Four, three, two . . .*'

Then the moment of detonation.

There was a blinding light. Even through closed eyelids, the world flashed suddenly white and was drained of all colour. The backs of necks and the bare legs of men in shorts felt the intense heat of the explosion's gamma rays, and, seconds later, a vivid, orange-red fireball rose in the sky. But the spectators remained with their faces covered and their backs to the blast, waiting for the effects that would follow and about which they had been warned.

The shock waves hit in spectacular fashion, like a physical blow to the body. Men were taken by surprise, some even staggering slightly, caught off balance, and hands left faces to cover ears as the intensity of the reverberations jarred eardrums. In a series of successive explosions, the soundwaves proceeded to take on a life of their own. They resonated about the landscape, racing through the mallee scrub and dodging amongst the mulgas, chasing each other like demented banshees. The desert was alive with sound.

Then, finally, silence.

After minutes that dragged like hours, it was deemed safe to look and, in unison, the spectators turned to face the site.

There, towering in the sky, its stem growing taller, its head billowing larger with every passing second, was the magnificent and perfectly formed mushroom cloud of an atomic explosion.

Harold Dartleigh initiated a round of applause, not forgetting to cast a glance in William Penney's direction.

Others amongst the official party of senior scientists and top-ranking officers joined in, and Sir William accepted the acknowledgement with a curt nod before removing his spectacles and lifting his field glasses to his eyes. But he cursed Harold Dartleigh. In initiating the applause, Harold had successfully drawn attention to himself, as if it were he who was running the show. It was too infuriating for words.

Harold exchanged a quick smile with Gideon Melbray, who was standing barely fifty yards away and who hadn't missed a trick. Then he raised his own set of field glasses to his eyes.

During the half-hour that followed, amazing sights continued to unfold. Within only minutes, two Canberra bombers appeared in the sky. They swung in an arc, as if saluting all who might be watching, then dived into the mushroom cloud and disappeared from sight, eaten up by the dense morass of grey-black.

In the forward area, five miles away and clearly visible across the vast, flat plains, over seventy white-clad scientists appeared from nowhere. They gave the 'safe' signal to the officers of the indoctrination force, and more men materialised to join them, hundreds it seemed. An army in white was marching across the desert. They looked like aliens from outer space.

Binoculars and field glasses kept tilting from land to sky as aliens and aerobatics became of equal fascination to the spellbound spectators.

Maurie had had qualms before they'd dived into the cloud, just as he was sure Len must have had, and the pilots in the other Canberra. It was one thing to be boastful down on the ground and another altogether up here in the sky, he'd thought as

194

they'd faced the great, angry cloud. This was pretty daunting stuff. But orders were orders, and they'd dived.

The moment they'd entered the blackness, radioactivity levels had sent the instruments wild, which had been a bit scary, but the cloud was dispersing as the breeze picked up and most instruments were now becoming operational.

Then they were out the other side and banking, preparing to turn and dive back into the cloud, the other Canberra repeating the manoeuvre below them. Their orders were to continue taking air samples for at least forty minutes.

Once again inside the eerie, all-enveloping gloom, unlike any normal storm cloud he'd encountered, Maurie started to feel elated by the experience. He wondered if Len was too, and he yelled the opening lines of 'High Flight' through his radio mike.

> *'Oh! I have slipped the surly bonds of Earth*
> *And danced the skies on laughter-silvered wings . . .'*

Young John Gillespie Magee's poem, written during the Battle of Britain, had become an anthem to air force pilots, and Maurie and Len knew every word.

Len got the joke, and yelled back.

> *'Sunward I've climbed, and joined the tumbling mirth*
> *Of sun-split clouds . . .'*

Looking through the windscreen at the inky blackness surrounding them, they laughed, before yelling in one accord:

> *'and done a hundred things*
> *You have not dreamed of.'*

We're one up on you, John, Maurie thought. John Gillespie Magee sure as hell hadn't flown through the mushroom cloud of a nuclear explosion.

Test results revealed that the radioactive cloud from One Tree reached a height of 37,500 feet, exceeding the predicted 27,900 feet, and radioactivity was detected as far afield as the Northern Territory, New South Wales and Queensland. The bomb's energy yield of fifteen kilotons was the equivalent of exploding 15,000 tons of TNT, and the same yield as Little Boy, the bomb that had obliterated Hiroshima ten years earlier, claiming in excess of 100,000 human lives.

*They have been walking for days now, Yunamingu, his two wives, his three children and two dogs. Their progress has been slow for the older of the wives is heavy with child. Djunga has presented her husband with all three of his children. A healthy, fertile woman, she could have produced many more over the years, but Yunamingu is careful to observe the tribal law of desert men. He avoids siring more offspring than he can support, particularly during the lean drought years when hunting is poor and food supplies scant.*

*At thirty, Djunga is no longer young, which is why Yunamingu has recently acquired his second wife. But Djunga remains his favourite. Djunga is a quiet woman who talks only when there is a need to talk. Mundapa annoys Yunamingu. Mundapa is little more than a girl, and she talks far too much.*

*The family is heading south to the soak at Ooldea, where, in the coming weeks, they will await the birth of Djunga's baby. As they walk, Mundapa chatters incessantly, but no-one is listening. Yunamingu has dropped back into the scrub behind them in search of goanna, and even the children pay Mundapa no heed. Djunga feels sorry for her husband's new wife, knowing that Mundapa is lonely. The girl is missing the boisterousness of her clan – she is not accustomed to travelling in a small family group. But Djunga, too, has become tired of the sound of Mundapa's voice and she no longer pretends to pay attention. Instead, she watches the dogs sniffing amongst the grasses and allows herself to daydream. Djunga has always been a great daydreamer. In her mind, she is once more a child. The dogs are her father's dogs, and she and her extended family are visiting Ooldea during the days of the white grandmother.*

*Kabbarli was the first white person Djunga had ever seen, but she had not been frightened. Djunga had found Kabbarli a source of great interest – all the children had. Kabbarli had allowed them to lift her strange garments to see what lay beneath, and they had discovered to their amazement that under yet more layers of cloth, Kabbarli's legs were as white as her face. How they had giggled. Kabbarli had also allowed them to peer – very, very carefully – through the metal circles she called 'spectacles'. The smaller of the children had been frightened at the way the world had become hazy through the spectacles, but Kabbarli had comforted them in their own tongue. Kabbarli spoke in the tongues of many people, even those who had travelled great distances to gather at Ooldea.*

*The children had all come to love Kabbarli. So had the mothers and the aunties of the families who had regularly flocked to her camp. Even the men had held Kabbarli in high regard.*

*These days when Djunga travels to Ooldea with her husband and family, her thoughts are always of Kabbarli. She wishes her own children could meet the white grandmother, for her children have had little contact with the white men and she does not wish them to grow up in fear. But Kabbarli has long since departed, and Djunga wonders whether perhaps the white grandmother has gone to meet her ancestors. Her own ancestors would surely welcome Kabbarli, who has been a true friend to so many, and Djunga likes to think that one day they may meet again in the spirit world.*

*Djunga's thoughts are shattered by Mundapa's piercing scream, which is quickly joined by the screams of the children, and then Yunamingu is by her side, his spear at the ready. He barks at them to be quiet, and stands motionless, the whites of his eyes revealing his terror. He whirls on the spot and stands motionless again. They are all motionless now, all deathly silent, frozen in horror as yet more demons appear from out of the scrub.*

*Yunamingu and his family are surrounded by devil spirits – strange, formless mamu with ugly long noses. Even the dogs cower at the sight, without so much as a whimper between them.*

*Then one of the mamu speaks and, although Yunamingu does not understand the words, he realises that these are not spirit beings. These are white men disguised as mamu. But there are too many for him to fight, even if he could summon the courage.*

*Yunamingu is forced to submit to the will of the white men for fear they may harm his family, and, as a truck is driven up, he obeys the instruction to climb into the back. His wives and children obediently follow his example, although the younger children are crying now. Djunga, with her swollen belly, requires help, and she offers no resistance as two of the white men hoist her aboard the truck. Like Yunamingu, Djunga is fearful for the safety of her children.*

*Never before have they travelled in a vehicle of any kind and the experience is frightening. Mundapa wails as she clings to the side of the truck's open tray, and her wails merge with the children's screams to form a chorus of terror.*

*Yunamingu and Djunga make no sound at all, but they too are consumed by fear, and, as two shots ring out behind them like the brittle cracks of thunder, they do not think of the dogs.*

*The ordeal of the truck is nothing compared to that which follows.*

*They are in a white prison, and here even Djunga cannot maintain her silence. She whimpers as the mamu run their sticks over her belly. For she is now convinced that these are mamu in the guise of white men, not the other way round as her husband believes. She hears the click-click-click of the mamu sticks. They are casting a spell on her and her unborn child.*

*Then her naked body is hit with fierce jets of water. The naked bodies of her children suffer the same torment, even the youngest of them, and they begin screaming and writhing, and now Djunga lends her voice to theirs. Water blasts its way into ears and up nostrils, they cannot escape it. Then fresh torture as hands and feet are scrubbed red raw with brushes that feel like spinifex thorns.*

*Again, the evil sticks are run over their bodies, and again, to Djunga's horror, she hears the click-click-click of the mamu's spell.*

*Once more the relentless water and the scrubbing, and once more the click-click of the sticks. Then again and again, a third and a fourth time, until finally it is over and they are being dressed in harsh, cloth garments.*

*When eventually they are bundled back into the truck, Djunga has lost all sense of time. Is it the next day? It seems to be morning. Has she slept? She cannot remember. Have the children eaten? She cannot recall feeding them. The youngest one is vomiting, and she herself does not feel well.*

*Without their disguises, the mamu now appear as white men. One of them pretends to be kind. He speaks their language and tells them not to fear. Yunamingu responds to the kindness and answers the man's questions, but Djunga recognises this as a trick and further evidence of the mamu's cunning. The white man who pretends to be kind is just like the others. He is mamu. They are all mamu. Djunga knows this. Just as she knows a spell has been cast upon her and her unborn child.*

# Chapter Ten

The One Tree test had been an unmitigated success. Operation Buffalo was off to an excellent start.

In the beer garden and canteen at Maralinga, those fortunate enough to have witnessed the event were the envy of others.

'You could actually *feel* it! The *heat*! Incredible!'

'And the shock waves! Like a bloody great punch in the back!'

'Yeah, you wouldn't believe it, would you? Nearly knocked me off my feet.'

Men could talk of nothing else, and the luckless ones who'd been far from the action were already volunteering for duties that would get them as near as was humanly possible to the front-line of the next firing.

There were to be three more detonations over the ensuing month, and, weather conditions permitting, the next test, code-named Marcoo, was barely one week away. Life had taken on a new meaning for the men of Maralinga. Boredom had become a thing of the past.

In the main conference room of the Australian Government

Information Office (AGIO), situated on the second floor of an attractive Georgian building in Rundle Street, Adelaide, Nick Stratton was happy with the way things were going. It was two days after the firing, and this was the first of the open press conferences that would follow the four tests that constituted the Buffalo series. AGIO would play host to the conferences and Nick would be the principal spokesperson at each, with perhaps an occasional representation from AWTSC, or even an appearance from Sir William Penney himself, should it be deemed necessary. At the moment, however, all was going smoothly.

Nick was acquainted with most of the Australian press in attendance, and he'd met the five British journalists who were covering the series two days previously, at the One Tree firing. It had been instantly evident to him that all five were the variety of press he referred to as 'tame' – clearly the British had vetted their own with great care. He had expected as much, but was thankful nonetheless. Nick himself had selected the Australian journalists who'd been invited to observe the detonation, and he'd been most stringent in his choice. The rules had been made abundantly clear to all. Ego-driven, investigative reporters who liked to cause trouble and those with a tendency towards sensationalism would not be tolerated. Any newspaper journalist privileged to witness a test firing did so with the joint permission of the British and Australian governments and, as a specially invited guest, was expected to toe the line.

He was relieved now to discover that at this first major conference, the press at large appeared willing to behave responsibly and observe the rules. He'd anticipated some possibly tricky questions, but his answers to even those queries that could have become issues had been met with a ready acceptance. He presumed, and correctly so, that this was because each of the journalists was hoping to be on his next invitation list.

'Has there been any radioactivity detected outside the restricted area of Maralinga, Colonel?'

Nick recognised the journalist – Bob Swindon of *The Sydney Morning Herald* – not one of those invited to observe the test firing, and not one of those likely to be. Bob was a good journo whose work Nick respected under normal circumstances – but these were not normal circumstances.

He responded in the respectful fashion he'd always found to be effective. 'As you know, Mr Swindon, I'm not at liberty to release the specifics of any scientific data, but I can most definitely assure you that there has been no threat whatsoever to surrounding areas.'

The answer came smoothly – he was, after all, speaking the truth. The reports he'd received had stated categorically that the levels of radioactivity, which had been detected over vast distances, were minimal and presented no particular threat. Nick firmly agreed that any overreaction would be pointless scaremongering.

'Stringent safety measures were maintained at all times, and we can rest assured that these safety measures will continue to be maintained throughout the series,' he said.

He wasn't one hundred per cent sure on that particular score, but that's what he'd been told, and he could only hope like hell it was true.

Maurie and Len weren't at all sure about the safety measures. In fact, Maurie, for all of his former braggadocio, had been severely shaken by the events that had ensued upon their return to base.

As ordered, they'd landed the Canberra at the south end of the runway, where the air-sample canisters attached to its wings were to be released for examination. Guided by ground crew,

Maurie had taxied the aircraft into position, but several minutes later, when he and Len had opened the hatch, they'd found themselves confronted by men in goon suits and gas masks.

'Jesus Christ,' Maurie had muttered.

'Remain in the aircraft,' one of the goon suits had ordered, and the two of them had closed the hatch and stayed rigid in their seats, not daring to move a muscle.

The following sequence of events had taken on a surreal quality, like watching a B-grade science fiction film, Maurie had thought. Or, worse still, like observing something you suspect is about to become your own personal nightmare. Tractor-like machines with electronic arms had approached the aircraft from either side, men in goon suits operating the machines with deft precision. The electronic arms had carefully detached the air-sample canisters from the Canberra's wings and deposited them in open lead-lined boxes. The boxes had then been closed and locked by further men in goon suits, and loaded aboard a truck to be taken away for radiochemical analysis, after which the washing-down process of the aircraft had begun.

It had been around this time that the science fiction film had taken its nightmarish turn, raising a series of questions in Maurie's mind.

Why aren't *we* in goon suits, he'd wondered, looking at his and Len's khaki combination overalls – we're the ones who were up there. The plane's not airtight – hell, it's not even pressurised. And then he'd noticed that the regular servicemen hosing down the aircraft were in shorts and shirts, and that jets of water were bouncing right back at them. Why aren't *they* in goon suits? There's something they're not telling us, he'd thought with a quick glance at Len, who, wide-eyed beside him, was plainly thinking the same thing.

'Step down from the aircraft,' the chief goon suit had ordered, and Maurie and Len had climbed out of the cockpit.

As they'd jumped to the ground, Maurie had noticed the channel of black sludge making its way to the nearby soak-away ditch, but he'd become quickly distracted by the Geiger counter that had been held up to him and the fact that the needle was going off the dial. The Geiger counter being run over Len was doing the same thing. And then the nightmare had become a reality for them both as they'd been put through the showers. Again and again they'd been ordered to scrub themselves, harder and more vigorously each time. Over and over, their skin turning a raw pink, until finally their body readings had been reduced to a level of 'reasonable acceptance'.

To the scientists conducting the examination, the level of 'reasonable acceptance' plainly meant that the safety measures had been observed. But Maurie and Len had been left with the distinct impression that there was a discrepancy between the safety measures in place for the scientists and those in place for the average serviceman at Maralinga.

Following the discovery of an Aboriginal family who'd wandered through the blast area two days after the firing, a spotter with field glasses was placed a mile or so from ground zero to keep watch. His job was to radio a warning to the patrol team should anyone, white or black, unwittingly approach the contaminated site.

Holy Mother of God, young Paddy thought as he gazed through his field glasses. He couldn't believe what he was seeing.

Eighteen-year-old Private Paddy O'Hare of the Royal Engineers had laboured on the construction of the tower. He hadn't been fortunate enough to score a front seat at Roadside and therefore witness the firing, but he'd seen the site in all its glory prior to the test. The ninety-foot aluminium tower had been a splendid sight in Paddy's eyes. There it had stood, a giant modern marvel in primitive scrubland, a testament to man's invention. Paddy had been proud that he'd played a part in it, minor though that part may have been.

But where was the tower now? Indeed, where was the scrubland? Every scrap of vegetation had been annihilated and in its place was a shiny, black-green surface, like glass. Paddy recalled the talk in the beer garden. One of the Australians who'd been at Emu Field had told them about 'bomb glaze'. So this was it, he thought. But surely there'd be a *bit* of the tower left, wouldn't there? Just a *bit*. He scanned the area with his field glasses. Perhaps he was looking in slightly the wrong direction, or perhaps he wasn't looking closely enough. But try as he might, Paddy could find no shred of evidence that the tower had ever existed. The ninety-foot aluminium edifice from which the bomb had been suspended had been fused into nothing.

Holy Mother, he thought, so this was what the black family with their little kiddies had walked through, barefoot and barely clad. No wonder the boffins had decided to set up a watch.

'Do you have any idea what that would have done to them psychologically? A primitive people like that? They'd never even been in a truck before, let alone been showered and scrubbed! The woman was *pregnant*, for Christ's sake!'

Daniel and Pete were sitting outside the barracks in their canvas chairs with the mugs of tea Daniel had brought back from the mess. It was lunchtime, and Pete, who had just returned from the DC/RB area, clearly needed to get things off his chest. Daniel said nothing, just let him rave on.

'The woman was terrified out of her wits. By the time they

called me in there, she was virtually catatonic – I couldn't get through to her at all. They've piled the whole family into a truck now, and they're driving them to the mission at Yalata. They're Yankuntjatjara people who were heading for the soak at Ooldea – Yalata's hundreds of miles from their own lands. They shouldn't have been put through this ordeal. It's wrong! It's so bloody wrong!'

Daniel was wondering what possible alternatives the military or the scientists could have come up with. The family would have had to go through the decontamination process, no matter how terrifying – they'd been exposed to radiation. To return them to their own lands would have been physically impossible, and Ooldea, commandeered by the army as a water source, was closed off to all. Yalata, a hundred miles to the south, was the nearest mission, and surely the only option, particularly for the pregnant woman. Pete was being unrealistic, Daniel thought, and the reason was patently obvious.

'It may be wrong, but it's not your fault.'

Pete's angry tirade came to a halt. He hadn't yet allowed himself time to feel guilty, but the kid, of course, was spot on. The military patrol officers under his guidance should have discovered the family well before there'd been any risk of exposure.

Daniel continued in earnest. 'You do everything that's humanly possible, Pete. Your men can't cover every inch of this terrain.'

'They'd hardly have needed to cover every inch in this case.' There was an unpleasantly sarcastic edge to Pete's reply. 'The family was travelling slowly, with children and a pregnant woman – they must have been in the vicinity for days.'

'You said yourself they have a talent for making themselves invisible.'

'Yeah, yeah. I did. And it's true. Which makes it their own

bloody fault really, doesn't it.' He shrugged. 'Ah well, there's bugger all I can do about it now.' He stood and tipped his tea out onto the ground. 'I need a drink,' he said, and he went into the donga to fill his mug from one of the many bottles of whisky he kept stashed away.

Once again, Daniel was left bewildered. Pete, with his mood swings from passion to indifference in a matter of seconds, remained a puzzling man. Much as Daniel had grown to admire him, he found Petraeus Mitchell possibly the most complicated person he'd ever met.

In truth, Petraeus Mitchell was not complicated. He was angry. He'd been angry throughout his entire life. He'd been angry that his father, after fighting in the Boer War, had re-enlisted fifteen years later and died at the Somme. Hadn't one war been enough for the man? He'd been angry that the mother he'd adored, having been transplanted from her homeland and left with five children, had been literally worked to death by the age of forty-three.

But it was the army that had put the final seal on Pete's anger, turning it from the frustration and regret of his youth to a true bitterness. Many of those who had served as coast watchers during the war and had lived to tell the tale had been left similarly disenchanted. For the job of a coast watcher was a dangerous and lonely one, with little or no backup. It was a job where a man, if discovered, found himself at the sole mercy of an enemy known to be merciless. The coast watcher was not looked after by his own. The fact that Pete had survived such a job for three long years had been nothing short of miraculous, but his time in the army had left him with a cynical view of the world. *Look after number one* had become his creed. *If you don't, no-one else will, because no-one else cares. And why the bloody hell should they?*

It wasn't a view he had held in the past. Despite the anger of his youth, he had never felt a disregard for others. To the contrary, the very anger of his youth had produced a passion to learn, to become the person his mother would have wished him to be.

Johanna Mitchell had been an inspiration to her youngest child. A highly intelligent woman and a skilled teacher, she'd encouraged him to mingle with the children of the black families who'd regularly visited their remote property. She'd instilled in him the lessons she'd learnt from her own parents, who had fought against the injustices wrought upon the South African native. There was much to be learnt from those who were different, she'd told her son, and the Aboriginal culture was the oldest in existence.

Pete had formed friendships with many of the young Unmatjera, a sub-group of the central desert people who'd inhabited the country near his home, and by the time he was twelve he'd spoken fluent Arrernte. When he was fifteen, his mother had encouraged him to sit for the GAE – the South Australian Government's Ability Exams – an educational scheme that was shortly to be discontinued due to the Depression. The boy had been granted a scholarship and fresh doors had opened for him. From that moment on, Pete had known the path he wished to follow.

Johanna Mitchell, sadly, had not lived to see her youngest son further his studies of the Aboriginal culture they had both come to hold in such high regard. She had died shortly before his sixteenth birthday. She never saw him gain his degree in anthropology. She wasn't there to share in his achievements as he worked alongside the young T.G.H. Strehlow, already recognised as one of the foremost authorities on the desert people of Australia. She was never to witness the similar form

210

of recognition afforded her son in the ensuing years. But Johanna Mitchell had, nonetheless, been with him on every single step of his journey. That is, until the army had claimed him.

Following his experiences in New Guinea, even the influence that had governed his life from beyond the grave had become a source of annoyance to Pete. What was the point in trying to fulfil his mother's dreams? The woman was dead, for God's sake! And what purpose did her dreams serve anyway? He was of no value to the Aboriginal people; he was just a puppet in a chain of bureaucracy. So why bother caring? No-one else did. Anger continued to devour Petraeus Mitchell.

Pete reappeared with his mug of whisky and no further mention was made of the Aboriginal family, Daniel wisely avoiding the topic. If Pete wished to talk, then he would, although he may have dismissed the subject from his mind altogether – it was difficult to tell. He was surly, but then that didn't really mean much. Pete was often surly.

Early the following morning, when Daniel awoke, Pete was nowhere to be seen. Then, fifteen minutes later, he came back from the ablutions block clean-shaven.

'Very smart,' Daniel said amiably, although he always found Pete a little odd without his stubble. Receiving only a grunt by way of reply, he slung his towel around his neck, grabbed his toiletry kit and set off for the ablutions block himself.

When he returned to the donga, Pete was nowhere to be seen and, as he wasn't around at breakfast, Daniel presumed he'd left early in his patrol truck. It came as a surprise, therefore, to find the FJ Holden parked near the fettlers' cottages.

'That's Pete's utility,' Daniel said to Gideon as he pulled the Land Rover up beside the corrugated-iron shed and stock-water tank that constituted Watson railway station. Behind them, in a swirl of dust, the two Bedford trucks came to a halt, and Gideon's team started lifting out tarpaulins and ropes in readiness for loading and securing the crates of fresh supplies that would shortly arrive by rail from Adelaide.

Barely 200 yards from the siding stood the row of six asbestos-built houses with corrugated-iron roofs, supplied by the railroad as married men's quarters for the fettlers employed to service the Trans-Australian Railway line. Forlorn, shabby and dilapidated, the houses were nonetheless the height of sophistication compared to the many rough-and-tumble fettlers' camps dotted along the track at other remote sidings.

'What's he doing here?' Daniel was puzzled. Pete's utility was parked directly outside the second of the fettlers' houses. But what business could he possibly have with the fettlers?

The question was rhetorical and Daniel expected no answer, but beside him Gideon smirked knowingly.

'Well, good old Pete knows how to while away the time, doesn't he? Half his luck, I say.'

Again, Daniel was puzzled. Why would Pete be whiling away the time? The Marcoo test was only a few days away. Surely he should be out in his patrol truck.

'Wouldn't mind being in his shoes,' Gideon said with a touch of genuine envy. 'She's quite a looker. Trouble though – he's asking for it in my opinion.'

'What are you talking about?'

But Gideon appeared not to have heard. 'He's being rather blatant, I must say. Usually he parks closer to the siding so it looks as if he's waiting for the train, but this time he's right outside her house. Bold.' Gideon obviously had his reservations about the wisdom of such a move.

'Are you telling me Pete's having an affair?'

They looked at each other, both equally surprised.

'I assumed you knew. He's been having a fling with the wife of one of the fettlers for months.'

Gideon wondered now why he *had* assumed Daniel knew. It was true the two men shared a donga and were friends of sorts, but Daniel was naive and Pete was secretive. There was no reason to believe that Daniel would guess or that Pete would tell. Oh well, too bad, he thought, the cat was well and truly out of the bag now so he might as well fill Dan in on the details. It may even prove to Pete's advantage. Young Dan may be the one person capable of talking sense into the man. Pete Mitchell was playing a dangerous game.

'The wife has an arrangement with the ganger,' he explained. 'She gives the chap a bottle of whisky – provided by Pete, of course – and Tommo, the ganger, sends her husband on one of the long trips down the track, which means he has to camp out. Sometimes he doesn't get home for days – it's an excellent set-up.'

Daniel regarded Gideon with suspicion. How could he possibly know this? Pete wouldn't have told him.

Pete was one of the few who didn't particularly like Gideon Melbray – he found him a little too flashy.

But Gideon wasn't giving away any personal secrets. 'It's true, whether you believe it or not.' He shrugged carelessly. 'Haven't you ever wondered about the once-a-week shave? Why doesn't the man grow a beard?'

Daniel's expression was one of utter bemusement.

'Ada's the reason for the shave,' Gideon said. 'Ada Lampton.'

He remembered his own encounter with the woman. '*You wouldn't even need to bring a bottle of whisky, Gideon,*' she'd said. '*There are other ways I can get around Tommo.*' He could well imagine there would be. '*Come on, lover boy,*' she'd said, snaking her hips

*at him brazenly right out there in the open as the men unloaded the sup-*
*plies from the train. 'I've never had anyone as beautiful as you.'* But
Gideon had resisted the advances of Ada Lampton with ease.
Enticing though she was, she was far too dangerous. Ada was
the sort who liked to cause trouble. Normally, her very danger
would have added to her appeal in Gideon's eyes, but given the
current circumstances she was off limits. He was on a job and
under strict orders. Gideon had no intention of disobeying
Harold Dartleigh.

Across the long, flat desert plain, where the railway track disappeared and the land met the sky, a tiny puff of steam
appeared.

'Good grief, it appears the train's going to be vaguely on time
for once.' Gideon opened the passenger door of the Land Rover.
'Better rally the men, I suppose.' But he made no move to get
out. It was close to midday. Why stand in the sun any longer
than necessary? And the men were squatting in the shade of the
trucks having a smoke anyway – no point in disturbing them.

'You'd be doing Pete Mitchell a favour if you warned him to
be careful,' he said with a nod in the direction of the Holden.
'From what I've heard, Harry Lampton's the worst of a bad
bunch. It wouldn't be a good idea to cross him.'

There was silence for a moment as they both looked at the
shabby row of houses, where the only signs of life were several
rangy yellow mongrels prowling amongst the shadows. The fettlers kept the 'pig dogs' for hunting kangaroo.

Gideon said no more on the subject, and Daniel made no
comment, but he knew he wouldn't act on Gideon's advice, sensible though it might be. He couldn't possibly intrude in such
a way. He felt uncomfortable enough already, as though he'd
been caught peeping through the keyhole of Pete's personal
life. Who was he to issue a warning in any event? Pete Mitchell,

214

of all people, would be fully aware of the danger he was courting. The fettlers' camps were known to attract tough, ruthless
men of whom no questions were asked, for many were on the
run from the law.

'I need to stretch my legs,' he said, and he got out of the
Land Rover. He felt like a spy sitting there looking at Pete's FJ
Holden. Turning his back on the fettlers' cottages, he walked
over to chat to the men as they waited for the train. Daniel
wished that he hadn't been made privy to Pete's secret.

Behind the tattered drawn blinds of the second cottage, Ada was
performing her magic. Lean and taut-bodied, her olive skin
shining with a hard-earned sweat, she rode him in steady
rhythm, her muscles clenching and unclenching with systematic
purpose, working him into her like a piston rod, not too fast, not
too slow, they had a way to travel yet.

This was their second bout in less than an hour, and it would
end ferociously as she rekindled in him a lust he would not have
thought possible. He was no stud, he was a forty-year-old man,
and a jaded one at that. But with Ada he was twenty and a stallion.

Their first bout of sex was always a form of torment. She'd
rub her naked body against his, offering him every part of her,
wantonly opening herself to him, her mouth, her thighs, her
buttocks, but she wouldn't allow him to stay in any one place
too long. When she sensed him losing control, she'd deny all
access, and then she'd eke out the delicious agony with her
lips and her tongue, teasing him to a point almost beyond
endurance, always knowing when to stop, and how to halt the
final moment before continuing. Only when he could take no
more would she give herself to him, and the final shuddering of
his climax would come as an exquisite relief.

She would allow just enough recovery time for a whisky and

a cigarette. She'd fetch a fresh bottle from the secret stock – the stock with which he kept her regularly supplied and of which her husband knew nothing. Then, when they'd finished their whisky and smoke, she'd initiate the second bout. He never quite knew how he came to manage the second time, but he always did. Ada was an expert.

Today, her teasing had taken on the broader dimension of a demand for entertainment, as happened on the occasions when she was particularly bored.

'I want to go for a drive,' she'd said when he'd first arrived.

Pete had heaved a sigh of reluctance. 'Sure,' he'd replied, although all he wanted was the sex. God, just the sight of her was enough to make him hard. It wasn't her beauty, although in her late thirties she was still good-looking, with a touch of the exotic inherited from her Indonesian father. It was the aura of the woman, and the thought of the sexual heights her mouth and her body could drive him to. Pete couldn't get enough of Ada Lampton.

'A drive it is then.' He'd ignored the twinge of guilt he felt at wasting more of the day when he should have been out on patrol.

He'd driven along the rough fifteen mile service track that ran beside the railway line from Watson to Ooldea, Ada urging him to go faster, dust swirling in their wake. She'd laughed whenever they'd hit a soft pocket of sand, the Holden slewing to one side, Pete wrestling the wheel.

'Faster,' she'd urged. 'Go faster.'

'We're not likely to bump into your husband, I take it?' It'd be just his luck to find Harry Lampton working the track between Watson and Ooldea, Pete had thought.

'Nah.' Ada obviously had no such qualms. 'Tommo's sent him way down the line – he won't be back for days.' She'd put her hand on his crotch. 'Come on, lover boy,' she'd said, the touch of her fingers producing an immediate erection, 'go faster . . .'

He'd driven like a maniac to Ooldea, not only to please her but in order to get her back to the cottage and into bed.

During the return trip to Watson she'd continued to play with him, bringing him close to the point of ejaculation, then stopping and playing with herself instead, pulling her skirt up around her waist, exposing herself to him – she never wore panties – and he'd nearly driven off the track.

He'd pulled up beside the cottage and waited for her to get out so that he could park the vehicle over near the siding as usual.

'Leave the ute here,' she'd said.

He'd hesitated. Then her hand was on him yet again, and yet again he'd felt himself instantly harden.

'The men are all at work, there's no train due, and I need to fuck,' she'd said.

Stuff the ute, Pete had thought. He hadn't been able get out of the car quickly enough.

The second bout now nearing its conclusion, he rolled her onto her back and was pounding himself into her when he heard the train. He dimly recalled that she'd said there was no train due, but the responsive thrust of her hips signalled she was on the verge of orgasm, which drove him to fresh heights and his mind became blanketed to all but the frenzy of their coupling. Then her fingernails were raking his back and the crescendo of her moans was mingling with his own animal grunts, and suddenly it was over.

She recovered herself in a matter of seconds, and stood to peer through the slit of the torn canvas blinds at the train that had just pulled into the siding.

He sat up, still fighting for breath. 'You told me there was no train due,' he said.

'I forgot.' The lie was blatant, but she shrugged with unashamed indifference.

Ada's gaze was focused on the man in charge of the team about to unload the crates. God, Gideon was beautiful. She willed him to look in her direction. And he did. She could have sworn he looked right into her eyes. She was aware that he wouldn't actually be able to see her, but she'd put money on the fact that he was fantasising about her. He would know exactly what was going on inside the cottage – he would have seen Pete's ute, as had been her intention. At this very moment he would be wishing like hell he'd accepted her offer, she thought with smug satisfaction. Then she noticed that quite a number of the other men were glancing in the direction of the house. They would all have seen the ute, and no doubt they were all fantasising about having her. The thought excited Ada immeasurably.

Pete stood and joined her. 'Shit,' he muttered as he peered through the blind and saw Daniel. Twice in the past when he'd failed to avoid the train's arrival, he'd seen Gideon and his men, but on both occasions another officer of the transport corps had been with the team. Why did the kid have to turn up on the very day he'd parked directly outside Ada's cottage, damn it! The fact annoyed Pete intensely, although he wasn't sure why. Did it really matter if the kid knew of his tawdry arrangement with the fettler's wife? Or was he angered at being caught out neglecting his duty? Whatever the reason, Pete felt strangely guilty, as if he'd let young Daniel down in some way.

'Why the hell did you lie, Ada?' He took his anger out on the woman. 'You bloody well knew about the train. Why did you lie?'

'Don't you like your mates knowing what you're up to, Pete?' She didn't even bother answering the question, preferring to tease him instead. 'You should be proud – they'll be green with envy. They've all seen me around, they all want to fuck me.'

'Oh, for Christ's sake!' The bitch had set him up deliberately, he thought. This was a sexual game to her.

Unconcerned, Ada continued gazing out at the siding. 'They'll be a while unloading, so you might as well stay.' She turned to him with a predatory smile. 'Why don't we have another whisky, lover boy? Maybe I can get you up and going for a third round, what do you say?'

Aware of his anger, she was goading him. If she couldn't arouse him sexually a third time, which was doubtful, then she'd work him up for a fight, the way she did Harry. The ability to anger men to the point where they lost control was another power that excited Ada. She considered the odd black eye and bloodied lip she suffered as a result a small price to pay for the alleviation of her boredom. Besides, it was something to boast of to the other wives. All five of them knew Harry belted her on occasions, just as they knew about her affair with the patrol officer, but they would never betray her. There was a code of honour amongst the fettlers' wives. They admired Ada's guts.

'Come on, lover boy, let's see what you're made of.'

Her fingers reached down to take hold of him, but Pete wasn't in the mood for her games. He belted her across the face with the back of his hand, taking her by surprise – he'd not hit her before. She staggered sideways, crashing heavily into the pine dresser.

'Bugger you, Ada,' he said, pulling on his clothes and reaching for his boots. 'You're more trouble than you're worth. You can go to hell!'

Seconds later, he stormed out of the cottage, tripping over one of the kangaroo dogs, which bared its yellow fangs at him. He kicked the dog and climbed into his utility without a glance at the train or the men. Bugger Daniel too, he thought. He wasn't the kid's father, for Christ's sake.

Behind him he heard Ada's laughter. 'You'll be back,' she called mockingly. And Pete knew she was right. He was obsessed, not only with Ada but with the escape she offered.

Back at the barracks that night, it was clear that the relationship between Pete Mitchell and Daniel Gardiner had undergone a change. Neither mentioned the subject of the fettler's wife, but somehow she formed a barrier between them. Daniel was uncomfortable about having inadvertently discovered Pete's secret, which he considered none of his business, and Pete wrongly interpreted the younger man's discomfort as disappointment in a father figure he'd come to respect. Both men felt guilty – and both for the wrong reasons.

The fourth of October dawned with favourable weather conditions, and the meteorologists predicted little change. The test was scheduled for late afternoon. The hourly countdown to Marcoo was now under way.

'Jeez, we'll be in with a bird's eye view, eh, Col?'

'Bloody oath we will, mate.'

'It'll be something to write home about, I reckon.'

'Too right it will – if you want to end up court-martialled.' Col Rogerson laughed and his mate, Bud Barton, joined in.

Privates Michael 'Bud' Barton and Colin Rogerson were only two in the group of Australian, British and Canadian servicemen excited by the prospect of getting closer to the blast. A number of their regiments' middle-ranking officers had signed up to be part of the newly formed Commonwealth Indoctrination Force, which, under cover and protectively clad, would stand only a mile or so from ground zero. The group of general servicemen, around forty in all, was to be positioned a further one mile back from the front-line force, and they were to be dressed in varying styles of uniform. The intention was to test whether conventional battledress was adequate for nuclear war. All those taking part in the operation had been assured of its safety; there would be no risk of over-exposure, they had been told, as they would be placed upwind of the fallout. The prospect of being in on the action had been eagerly embraced by those fortunate enough to have been assigned the task.

Preparations similar to those for the One Tree test had been made. The site had been pegged out so that, following the blast, radioactivity in the soil could be tested at varying distances, and animals and equipment had been strategically positioned, also at varying distances from ground zero. The differing factors in the Marcoo test were the absence of a tower – the bomb was to be exploded at ground level – and the direct involvement of sol-diers for experimental purposes. As the nuclear device was far smaller than the One Tree bomb, with a predicted yield of only one and a half kilotons, this practice was deemed quite within the safety measures.

As before, hundreds assembled in order to witness the deton-ation, but the excitement engendered amongst those at Roadside could not match that of the servicemen gathered just two miles from the blast.

'Fingers crossed, eh,' Bud muttered jokingly to Col, although, if the truth be known, he was just the tiniest bit apprehensive.

'Bloody oath, mate – who wants to get fried,' Col replied, which didn't help Bud's nerves.

Col himself wasn't nervous at all – he was excited. Why shouldn't he be? They weren't at war. The army wouldn't put them in this position if there was any risk, and it was sure as hell something to tell his girlfriend about when he got back to Perth. Bugger the Official Secrets Act – he'd swear her to his own oath of silence the way only he could. Marge'd do anything for him. But then he'd do anything for Marge.

They were standing at ease, as commanded, and Col glanced around at his fellow servicemen, who were divided into three groups according to the uniforms they were wearing. He and Bud and their mob were in cotton khaki drill, another bunch was in battledress serge, and the third lot was in gabardine combat suits. It seemed to Col that his mob, in their lightweight uniforms, had copped the raw end of the deal, but he wasn't particularly bothered. They had all been issued with the Atomic Weapons Research Establishment combination underwear, guaranteed to provide protection.

One minute to go.

At Roadside, the crowd stood motionless as the voice counting down the seconds reverberated through the loudspeakers.

Two miles from ground zero, the soldiers also stood motionless as the sergeant barked out each passing second. Until . . .

'*Ten* . . .'

Simultaneously, all turned their backs to the site and, as the countdown continued, all firmly placed the palms of their hands over their eyes, as instructed.

'*Two, one, zero* . . .'

Then the blinding flash of the gamma rays. Even through closed and covered eyes, the spectators at Roadside were startled to see a sudden blaze of white. The men two miles from the blast, however, could see something far more sinister.

Bloody hell, Col thought. He heard himself gasp with shock, a quick intake of breath. They all heard themselves gasp as they saw the bones of their hands. Through their skin and their flesh, they could see their own skeletons, each bone clearly highlighted as if by X-ray. The sight was so distracting they barely noticed the wave of intense heat that followed.

Seconds later, they were ordered to brace for the shock wave, which, when it came, knocked several men over. Then they were ordered to face the bomb site.

In the distance, all vegetation had disappeared, and in its place was a yawning great crater, above which a burgeoning mushroom cloud billowed. Halfway between them and the crater, the men could see the indoctrination force emerge from cover in their protective suits. Officers from their own regiments, they thought, right there in the thick of it. But they were given no time to admire the sight. Their own job had just begun.

For the next forty minutes, the soldiers were given a variety of orders. Those in battledress serge and the gabardine combat suits were sent off in different directions with instructions to march through bushy areas ensuring their uniforms gathered as much contamination as possible. Those in cotton khaki drills were split into two groups, and both were ordered to crawl in the accepted military manner over a distance of thirty yards. The first group was to crawl over a barren, sandy area, and the second through spinifex grasses – it was later discovered that the grasses retained radioactive particles to a far greater degree than the soil.

Col Rogerson couldn't help thinking that, once again, his mob had copped the raw end of the deal. But the next day, who cared? Over breakfast in the canteen, Col and Bud and the rest of them had the best of stories.

'You could see the bones in your hands, honest. Like a bloody X-ray it was.'

'Yeah. And just look at that.'

Those who'd been there compared the burns on the backs of their necks; blisters had already started to appear.

'The scars of battle, mate,' Col boasted, and they all laughed. Something to tell Marge about, he thought.

*Ngangala and his family are Pitjantjatjara – 'Spinifex'*
*people of the Western Desert – and they have been trav-*
*elling south for some time.*

In the good seasons, those when drought does not
threaten, it is a spring pilgrimage of theirs to gather with
others at Ooldea. Ngangala's wife, Pantjiti, likes to
socialise and she believes it is good for the children.
Nantji is ten now, a raucous boy who enjoys the company
of other raucous boys; and six-year-old Minna, who has
a tendency to shyness, can only benefit from contact with
those her own age.

Several times over the past two days they have seen
white men in trucks, but they have not felt threatened.
They have seen white men before as they have skirted missions and towns, and the children are, by now, as adept
as their parents at merging with the landscape. But
Ngangala and Pantjiti have wondered what the white
men are doing out here, so far away from the comfort of
their towns. The white men are strangers to the desert.

It is late in the afternoon on this seventh day of their
travels that they see the smoke signal. It is preceded by a
white flash that lights up the sky. At first, Ngangala and
Pantjiti take this to be lightning. The lightning is then followed by cracks of thunder, and they wait for the storm
to sweep up from the south. But the storm does not
appear. In its place, smoke billows upwards.

At first Ngangala thinks the smoke comes from a

*hunting fire and that it signifies a fine kill. Men have food to share, more than enough to meet their needs, and they are welcoming others to join them in a feast. But he quickly decides this is not so. The smoke is a mighty cloud, unlike that of a hunting fire. Indeed, it is unlike the smoke from any fire he has seen. Strangely shaped, it would be visible from a great distance. Surely it must be signalling a ceremonial event of some significance.*

*Pantjiti agrees with her husband. The smoke is calling people to a great gathering with much festivity. The prospect excites her.*

*They will sleep, Ngangala decides, and they will set off early in the morning. There is a good day's walk ahead, and he hopes to arrive at the gathering before nightfall.*

*In travelling towards the signal, Ngangala and his family must leave behind their familiar tracks and water-holes, but there is no danger for they can survive on mallee root water. Like all desert people, Ngangala and Pantjiti know the particular type of desert mallee tree whose long, lateral roots yield water. They will dig up these roots and crush them to extract the meagre supply they need.*

*They have walked all day. Darkness has fallen, and the desert night has become chill. Ngangala is uneasy now. There is no sign of the fire, nor of the gathering. But there is endless evidence of the white man. They have passed many strange vehicles sitting derelict in the wilderness, and the ground is crisscrossed with the tracks of the white men's trucks.*

*The children are tired and thirsty, and they complain that their eyes hurt. Ngangala and Pantjiti also have itchy eyes, and a thirst that cannot be slaked by mallee root water. They are all tired. They need to sleep. Ngangala looks about for a suitable camp site amongst the scrub. He will make a fire for warmth, but they will not bother cooking the wallaby slung over his shoulder.*

*He speared it at dusk, intending to offer it as his contribution to the gathering upon their arrival. But no-one is hungry now.*

*In the darkness up ahead, he sees a strange light. They all see it. The land appears to be shimmering. Ngangala approaches warily, moving through the mallee scrub with stealth, Pantjiti and the children following well behind, prepared to flee should he signal danger.*

*But Ngangala makes no such signal and, as they join him, they stare in silent, equal wonderment at what lies before them.*

*The scrubland has gone and in its stead is a giant, gaping hole, where the earth glows with a magic, luminescent green light. They are mesmerised by its strangeness and its beauty.*

*Ngangala investigates the phenomenon. He slithers down the slope and into the giant hole, discovering, to his surprise, that the earth there is warm – far warmer than the ground above. The hole is cosy and welcoming – a perfect camp site. There will be no need for a fire tonight. They will set out for Ooldea at dawn, he decides. Water has become their main priority. But for now, they must rest.*

*'We will camp here,' he calls to his wife. 'This is a good place. We will sleep well here.'*

*His family joins him in the crater.*

# Chapter Eleven

Two days after the Marcoo test, patrol officers made a grisly discovery.

'Stop the truck, Charlie. I just saw something.'

Private Charlie Waite did as he was told, although he was surprised Sam had been keeping a lookout at all. They were only five miles south-east of the bomb site, halfway between ground zero and Roadside. There'd be no Aborigines in this area.

He brought the truck to a halt and took the field glasses Sam handed him.

'Over there, in the shade.' Corporal Sam Farrington pointed to a grove of mulga trees. 'Tell me I'm wrong. Tell me I'm seeing things.'

Charlie peered through the field glasses. 'Oh, no,' he said in his thick Yorkshire brogue, and from the way he said it, Sam knew that he hadn't been seeing things.

They drove over to where the woman sat holding her two dead children to her chest. Propped up against a tree trunk as she was, she could have appeared alive, if it weren't for the flies and the ants that had gathered. The man was curled up on the ground beside them, and all four were covered in red blotches where they'd scratched away their own skin.

'They've been contaminated,' Sam said. 'Better not touch them.'

Charlie was thankful for the suggestion. He hadn't relished the prospect of loading the bodies into the truck.

'Poor bastards,' he said.

'Yeah.' Sam contemplated the bodies thoughtfully. 'They don't look as if they've been dead for very long, do they?'

'No, they don't. Poor bastards.'

They gazed for a moment or so longer, and then Sam contacted headquarters on the truck radio.

'A special team's being sent,' he told Charlie. 'We're to stay here and accompany them back to the DC/RB area.'

'Right.'

Charlie averted his eyes from the bodies, he found them disturbing. The little girl was only around five or six, not much younger than his own baby sister. Charlie loved kids – he was eighteen years old and the eldest of five siblings.

Sam radioed through to Pete Mitchell's patrol truck. The news was greeted with a deathly silence at first. Then Pete's voice returned, briskly demanding their location. He arrived on the scene a half an hour later, only minutes before the decontamination team, although he'd travelled a far greater distance.

Sergeant Benjamin Roscoe, the young patrol officer with him, climbed out of the truck's cabin thankful they'd arrived in one piece. Pete had driven like a man possessed. He seemed calm enough though, Benjamin thought. In fact, given the circumstances, Pete Mitchell's calmness was just a little alarming.

'Well, this hardly comes as a surprise, does it?'

Pete acknowledged Charlie and Sam with a brief nod, and the three young soldiers stood respectfully to one side as he knelt before the bodies. He found the sight sickening, but he didn't allow it to show.

'Poor bastards,' Charlie muttered. He seemed incapable of saying anything else.

Poor bastards indeed, Pete thought.

'They must have walked right through the contaminated area,' Sam said. 'Why would they do that? Where were they heading?'

'They were heading for Ooldea and water,' Pete replied brusquely.

The signs of dehydration were obvious as he studied the caked mouths and cracked lips, but he was mystified nonetheless. Desert people rarely died of thirst. Desert people knew the secret water sources and could survive where all others would perish. Was thirst another symptom of irradiation, or had they simply lost the ability to think rationally, he wondered. Whichever was the case, judging by the self-inflicted wounds, there had been torment before death.

To Pete, the position of the bodies told a poignant story. Regardless of their torment, the man and the woman had clearly accepted the inevitability of death. It was obvious the children had died first, as would be expected. The woman had then cradled them in her arms. The man had curled up on the ground beside her. And together they had waited.

He stood as, behind them, a Bedford truck from the DC/RB area pulled up and four officers of the indoctrination force alighted. They were dressed in protective clothing.

'Keep clear, please, sir,' one of them said. His tone was not overly officious – he knew who Pete was – but it was, nevertheless, an order. Pete backed away – a couple of paces only, but it seemed to suffice.

Two of the officers started lifting lead-lined boxes from the back of the truck, while the other two took Geiger counter readings of the bodies. The radiation levels, as expected, were extraordinarily high.

'Looks to me as if they've been in the crater,' one of the officers said to Pete. 'There's bomb glaze residue on their skin.'

Of course, Pete thought. The Marcoo device had been detonated at ground-level and had produced a large crater, which must have attracted the family. Why shouldn't it? A big, warm hole in the ground was a perfect camp site on a chilly desert night.

He watched as the bodies of the man and the woman were loaded into two separate lead-lined boxes. The boxes were suspiciously coffin-like in appearance, he thought, as though they had been designed for this very purpose. The children shared a box between them.

The orders were for all to report to the DC/RB area, where there would be a briefing, and the three trucks set off in a convoy, the Bedford in the lead.

Like a funeral procession, Pete thought, his eyes on the coffins in the back of the Bedford. He felt hollow, devoid of emotion. He had known this would happen, it had been just a matter of time. His mixture of helplessness and guilt was overridden by a sense of utter defeat.

Nick Stratton left headquarters not at all relishing the prospect of carrying out his British commanding officer's orders. But orders were orders, and, distasteful though the task might be, the decision was the right one. There really was no alternative course of action to be taken, he thought as he climbed into the Land Rover and started up the engine. He just wished he wasn't the one who had to spell it out to the men.

The lead-lined boxes were taken directly to one of the principal laboratories in the DC/RB area, where the chief liaison officer, Colonel Nick Stratton, was already waiting. Upon their arrival, the four officers of the indoctrination force were ordered to report to the nearby decontamination unit where they would be divested of their protective clothing, Colonel Stratton instructing them to say nothing of the incident during the procedure. Pete Mitchell and the three general servicemen were to remain in the laboratory until the officers' return, after which the briefing would commence.

Charlie, Sam and Benjamin looked about the laboratory with great interest. They'd never even been through the gates of the DC/RB area, let alone inside a laboratory. So this was where it all happened, each was thinking. This was what Maralinga was all about. Was this where they made the bombs?

Pete wasn't interested in the laboratory. He was too busy staring at the lead-lined coffins. What are they going to do with you, he wondered. Shove you into a pit along with the other radioactive materials? Probably. Sorry, but there's not much I can do about that. Christ, he was fed up with the whole thing – he wanted to just turn his back and walk away. But somehow he couldn't. He remained staring mindlessly at the coffins. Charlie's right, he thought. *You poor bastards*. There was nothing more one could say, really, was there? You poor bastards – you didn't ask for any of this.

He snapped out of his reverie as the officers returned and Nick Stratton took the floor.

The seven soldiers were instructed to stand at ease, and did so in military fashion, legs astride, hands clasped behind backs, which made Pete all the more conspicuous as he perched a buttock on the granite-topped bench in the corner. He intended no personal disrespect to Nick Stratton, who was only doing his job and carrying out orders, but Pete had a distinct feeling he knew which way the briefing would go. The army's bound to want to cover this up, he thought. There'll be a whole heap of bullshit, and then we'll be reminded about the oath of bloody silence, I'll bet.

'This tragic incident is deeply regretted by both the British and Australian armies and all those involved with the Maralinga project,' Nick said.

Yeah, yeah, get on with it, Pete thought.

Nick did. 'However,' he continued, 'I must remind you of the oath of silence you have all sworn.'

Well, he hadn't beaten about the bush. Pithy and to the point, you had to give the bloke that much. It was typical of Nick Stratton, Pete thought with begrudging respect.

'You are bound, every one of you,' Nick's eyes swept the room, making contact with each man in turn, 'to abide by the Official Secrets Act at all times.' His eyes met Pete's, retaining contact for a second or so longer, as if saying, *That means you too, Pete*. Then he continued. 'You men are, therefore, ordered to maintain silence on all you have witnessed with regard to the Aboriginal deaths, regrettable though they are.'

There was a slight snort of derision from the granite-topped bench in the corner, which Nick ignored.

'And it is my duty to warn you,' he said sternly, 'that any man who disobeys this order will be instantly court-martialled.'

The announcement surprised even Pete. Pretty radical, he thought.

'The violation of the Official Secrets Act is a treasonable offence, as I'm sure you're all aware,' Nick continued. 'Just as I am sure you are also aware that those found guilty of treason can face thirty years' imprisonment or the firing squad.'

Pete glanced at the soldiers for their reaction. They were stunned, all seven of them. The four officers remained eyes front, but he could see they were shocked. Young Charlie, Sam and Benjamin were openly exchanging gawks of amazement.

Nick had expected such a reaction. 'Put the fear of God in them,' the brigadier had instructed. 'If the press gets wind of this, we're in serious trouble.' Irksome though Nick found the task, he couldn't argue with the reasoning. They could not afford a public outcry, and fear was certainly a way to keep men in line. He'd wondered whether he should sweeten the pill and give reasons for so dire a threat, but he had decided against it. An order was an order, after all.

'Under no circumstances must the Maralinga project be threatened,' he concluded. That would have to do, he thought. 'Thank you for your attention, gentlemen.'

The briefing at an end, he opened the door. 'You can have your laboratory back now, Dr Crowley,' he said to the white-coated scientist who stepped inside. 'Thank you for your patience.'

'My pleasure, Colonel.'

Nick stood beside the door as the men filed out.

Pete remained where he was. Crowley, he thought. He remembered the man. He'd met him a week or so ago, when he'd been called into the DC/RB area to communicate with the Aboriginal family who'd undergone decontamination treatment. Dr Melvyn Crowley – that was his name. He was the chief pathologist.

'You too, Pete,' Nick said. The last of the men was leaving the room, but Pete Mitchell hadn't moved a muscle.

Melvyn Crowley would be responsible for dissecting the animals exposed to radiation, Pete thought, and he looked around the laboratory, taking in the scene for the first time. This was a pathology unit. The very granite-topped bench he was perched on was designed for the specific purpose of dissecting corpses.

He stood, but made no move for the door. There were only three of them left in the room now. He looked at Melvyn

Crowley, but Crowley didn't look back. Crowley had eyes for nothing but the coffins. And he was positively drooling.

'After you, Pete,' Nick said firmly.

'Shit!'

The expletive was enough to distract Melvyn Crowley's attention from the coffins, and, as he looked at Pete, the excitement in his eyes was readable.

You perverted little creep, Pete thought, you just can't wait to get started, can you.

'I said time to go.' Nick's patience was running out. This was an order now.

Pete looked from one to the other. Melvyn Crowley, his glasses steaming up in ghoulish anticipation, and Nick Stratton, so steeped in military protocol his vision was blinkered.

'You can get fucked, the lot of you,' he snarled, and he stormed from the laboratory.

That night in the officers' mess, Pete Mitchell was noticeably drunk. It was quite early in the evening, but he'd downed several hefty whiskies back at the donga and was now pouring beer on top. Daniel, sensing something was wrong, tried to join him, but Pete waved his cigarette in a gesture of dismissal – he wasn't interested in the company of others. Others weren't interested in the company of Pete either – he could be a morose bastard when he was on the drink, it was agreed, so they left him alone at his table in the corner.

Nick Stratton felt sorry for the man as he watched from across the other side of the mess. Pete Mitchell was taking the deaths of the Aboriginal family very much to heart. It was understandable – he no doubt held himself responsible in some way, but he shouldn't. There was nothing he could have done. In any event, drinking himself into oblivion wasn't going to solve the problem. Nick downed his beer and crossed to the table. Pete glared as he sat, but he didn't wave Nick away as he had Daniel.

'Why don't you take yourself off to bed, Pete,' Nick said quietly. 'There's no point in agonising over something beyond your control.' Pete dragged heavily on his cigarette and continued his baleful glare. 'It was an accident that shouldn't have happened, but you couldn't have prevented it. It's not your fault.'

'You're just like all the rest, aren't you, Nick? You think because they're black, they're expendable.'

Damn, Nick thought, he shouldn't have come over to the table. He should have stayed where he was and kept his mouth shut.

'Who the hell do you think you are?' Pete hissed. 'Who the hell do you think *they* are? Casualties of war? You think you can justify their deaths for some noble cause? I've got news for you, mate. We're not at war.'

But we are, Nick thought. We're at war with communism. We're at war with mother Russia. The race for nuclear power is a whole new war, Pete, unlike anything you and I have known. This is the very purpose of Maralinga. It's why we're here.

He rose from the table. 'Go to bed, Pete,' he said.

'Sure.' Pete rammed his cigarette butt into the overflowing ashtray, stood and skolled the rest of his beer. He needed something stronger anyway. 'What a pity you can't threaten *me* with a cosy little private court martial, Colonel. You'd have to take me to the Supreme Court, and that'd make it a matter of public record. I must be a real cause for worry.'

Nick made no reply, and Pete didn't push the confrontation any further. Hell, why bother? They both knew he was no cause for worry. Pete Mitchell never made waves. Pete Mitchell looked after number one.

Nick watched him go. What a pity, he thought. Pete had lost

his objectivity; he was verging on unstable. It appeared the army had made the wrong choice in Pete Mitchell. But he felt sorry for the man nonetheless.

An hour and a half later, when Daniel arrived back at the donga, Pete had drunk himself into a near stupor. He was sitting on his bunk, barefoot and dishevelled, necking the whisky straight from the bottle.

'Come and join me, mate,' he said. 'Come and have a drink.' He held out the bottle, then realised it was all but empty. 'Hang on a minute, hang on.' He leaned over and started ferreting between his legs for the cardboard box he kept under his bunk.

'I don't want a drink, thanks, Pete.'

'Course you do, course you do.' The cardboard box appeared and, taking out a fresh bottle, Pete handed it unopened to Daniel. 'There you go, be my guest.' Then he pushed the box back under the bunk with his foot.

Daniel could see he didn't really have much option. Pete had now decided he was in the mood for company and wasn't prepared to take no for an answer.

'Thanks,' he said, opening the bottle and fetching a tin mug from the dresser. He poured himself a modest whisky, left the bottle on the dresser, and pulled up one of the donga's two chairs. 'Cheers.' He raised the tin mug in a salute and hoped that Pete would pass out soon.

'It's a bugger of a thing to happen, isn't it?' Pete said blearily. 'A real bugger of a thing.'

'Yes, I suppose it is.' Daniel didn't bother asking what the bugger of a thing was.

'You know what Crowley and his mob'll do to those poor bastards?'

'Nope. No idea.'

'They'll dissect 'em – just like they do the *sheep* and the *goats* and the *rabbits* and the *mice*,' Pete gave added emphasis to each word with a wave of the bottle, 'and any *other* living creature they can irradiate. They'll cut up their bodies and grind up their bones in the name of science, and they'll love every bloody minute of it.' He drained the dregs of the whisky. 'Jesus, they must be over the moon now they've scored a few humans. Crowley sure as hell is – you should have seen the look on his face. Grab us that bottle, will you.'

Daniel fetched the bottle from the dresser and handed it over. He wasn't sure if he understood what he was hearing, but Pete had certainly gained his attention.

'You know what the really bad part is though?' Pete fumbled with the cork of the bottle. 'At least *I* reckon it's the really bad part, and they would too if they had a say in it, which of course they don't because they're dead.' The cork finally came free. He tossed it on the floor and took a swig of whisky. 'The really bad part is the cutting-up part.'

Pete leaned forward, elbows on knees, fingers firmly clenched into a fist around the neck of the bottle. He had an intense desire to communicate with Daniel. Young Dan, unlike the average soldier at Maralinga, had actually shown some concern for the Aborigines. Although, Pete had to admit, even in his addled state, that such a judgement wasn't quite fair on his part. The average soldier at Maralinga had been fed a load of bullshit when all was said and done. They'd been told the local population had been removed from the area – that is, if there'd ever been any local population in the first place. The average soldier could hardly be expected to show concern for those who didn't exist.

'The worst thing you can do to these people, Dan,' he said ponderously, trying to choose his words with care although he was having some trouble, 'the worst thing you can possibly do to them is to cut them up. That's the really, *really* bad part. You understand me?'

'Not exactly.'

The kid wasn't getting his drift, Pete thought. He took another swig of whisky and then spelled it out. 'You don't mutilate them, that's what I'm saying. You don't chop these people up when they're dead! Dismemberment is worse than death. These people have to go to their ancestors intact. Am I getting through?'

'Who exactly are we talking about?'

'The dead family.' Pete was exasperated – who the hell did Dan *think* he was talking about? 'Mum and dad and the two little kids, that's who.'

Dead family? What dead family, Daniel wondered. Pete was rambling in his drunkenness. He must mean the family who'd been put through the decontamination unit. Good God, if there'd been deaths reported, it would have been the talk of the mess.

'I haven't actually heard of any dead family, Pete,' he said carefully.

'Well, of course you haven't, and you won't tomorrow either, or the day after that, or next week or even next year. They've threatened to court-martial anyone who talks – violation of the Official Secrets Act – a treasonable offence, mate. Jesus Christ, I could cop a bullet through the brain for telling you this.' Well, that had certainly hit home, Pete thought with satisfaction. He laughed, enjoying the shock on the kid's face. 'Ah, they're a ruthless bunch your employers, Dan.' He raised the bottle in a toast. 'Here's to the army, mate, yours and mine. A pack of bastards every one of them.' Then, head back, he guzzled long and hard, whisky spilling in rivulets down his chin.

Daniel was indeed shocked, but more by the very suggestion that such a thing could happen than by his actual belief that it had. This was surely no more than the lunatic ravings of a drunk.

'So there you are, that's the way it goes.' Pete was close to passing out now. 'A nice young family finds a cosy hole and curls up for the night and, before you know it, they're being cut into bits. Doesn't seem fair to me . . . Doesn't seem bloody fair at all . . .'

The bottle slid from his grasp and hit the floor. Daniel rescued it.

'Oh, thanks, mate, thanks a lot.' Pete put his hand out for the bottle, but Daniel placed it on the dresser.

There was a moment's pause while the hand hung uncertainly in the air, then Pete seemed to forget all about the whisky. He flopped back on his bunk. 'Bugger of a thing to happen,' he said. 'Bugger of a thing . . .' He kept muttering for a while, and gradually his mutters became snores.

Daniel hefted Pete's feet up onto the bunk and then sat on his own bunk, deep in thought.

It couldn't have happened, he told himself. None of it could have happened. He couldn't afford to believe that it had. Pete was a disturbed man. If Aborigines had been discovered dead, word would have got around, surely. But then, Daniel thought, what word ever *did* get around about Aborigines? He'd only heard about the family who'd been contaminated through Pete. Everything he knew about the Aboriginal predicament at Maralinga he'd learnt through Pete.

He remembered the day he'd gone out in the patrol truck, the day he'd seen the woman and child, and he remembered how the two had seemed to disappear before his very eyes. There *are* local people in the area, he thought, and they *are* difficult to locate, and they *are* in danger. All this he knew to be a fact. So if the dreadful but plausible scenario of the family's death was true, could it be possible that the authorities were so bent on keeping the fact a secret that men were being threatened with court martial? Violation of the Official Secrets Act, no less – a treasonable offence? Daniel found it impossible to believe.

He looked at Pete, whose snores were by now stentorian. He'd confront him in the morning, he decided. One way or another, he must find out the truth.

But in the morning Pete was gone. Daniel waited for him to return from the ablutions block, but he didn't.

He didn't report for breakfast either. The confrontation, Daniel realised, would have to be postponed until the evening.

Pete had left Maralinga before daylight. He'd driven out of the township in his FJ Holden wondering if he'd ever go back, but knowing deep down that he would. If he were really on the run he'd have packed his belongings, wouldn't he? But then he hadn't wanted to wake Daniel. No, that wasn't the truth either. He hadn't *dared* wake Daniel. He had some vague idea that he'd spewed out the whole story last night. Or had he just dreamt that he had? He hoped it had been a dream. If it hadn't, then he'd opened a whole can of worms, and he really didn't want to face that right now.

Dawn was breaking. He pulled up the car and got out to watch the beauty of the sunrise. The land was waking afresh, as if newborn in the first clear light of day, and as he squatted in the dust looking out over the rolling, red Nullarbor sandhills, he thought that this could be the beginning of time. Then he recalled the Aboriginal family. He saw their bodies lying there, so accepting of a death they should never have suffered. What had he done to prevent it? What was he going to do to avenge it? What meaning could he offer for the sacrifice of their lives? One word answered every single query that came into his mind. *Nothing.* The same word summed up his entire existence. What purpose did his life serve? What had he achieved? What did he believe in? *Nothing.*

Pete no longer saw the beauty of the dawn. The miracle of a desert sunrise had never been lost on him before, but it was this morning. His head was throbbing, he had to stop thinking.

He climbed back into the Holden and started the engine. He needed oblivion, and, apart from whisky, oblivion came in just one form. Ada.

He took his time driving to Watson – no point in arriving before the fettlers had set off for work – and as he drove he thought of Ada. Even thinking about her was enough, the anticipation of her body and her mouth successfully clouding his mind.

Two hours later, he pulled up at the siding. Watson appeared as deserted as always. The fettlers' truck used for track maintenance in nearby areas accessible by road was gone, but that didn't mean all the fettlers were. Men were transported by rail for work well down the line and would camp out, often for days. Pete was not so distracted that he couldn't think clearly. Harry Lampton might be down the line, or he might be waiting for the next train. There was no way of knowing which.

He got out of the car, leaned against the tray, and took a packet of Craven A from his top pocket. All he could do was follow the normal procedure and hope that she may be watching. This was the first time he'd arrived unexpectedly. As a rule he and Ada made their assignations well in advance, but their last meeting had ended acrimoniously and no plan had been set in place. The plan was always very simple. He would arrive on a given day at a given time and, if the coast was clear, she would step out onto the cottage's small front verandah. If things had gone awry and she'd been unable to get rid of Harry, she would not appear. He would wait long enough to smoke one cigarette and then he would leave. He had never, as yet, smoked the cigarette. She had always appeared before he'd even lit up.

He took out a Craven A and returned the packet to his shirt pocket. Then he ferreted about for his matches, buying time, each step in the ritual slow, methodical.

Inside the cottage, Harry was having his breakfast – damper topped with thick slices of tinned camp pie and lots of pepper. It was the same breakfast he had when he was out bush, always accompanied by a mug of strong tea, black, scalding hot and with plenty of sugar.

'Hurry it up, Ada, for Chrissake.'

'Keep your shirt on. I can't make tea draw any quicker than it wants to, can I?'

It was a no-win situation either way – she'd cop it if his tea wasn't strong enough. Oh well, too bloody bad, she thought, picking up the cheap tin teapot with a dishrag, but still managing to burn her hand in the process. She poured his mug of tea and dumped it on the table in front of him.

'There,' she said.

'Did you sugar it?'

She dumped the sugar bowl on the table and slammed the spoon down beside it.

'Watch it, Ada,' he said as he piled in four spoonfuls. 'Watch it.' The bitch was still sulking, he thought. As if she had a right to. Christ, she was lucky she'd only copped a black eye. He'd had every right to throttle the life out of her.

Harry had returned home three days previously and, in bedding his wife, had discovered a large bruise on her left breast.

'Where'd you get that?' he'd asked, instantly suspicious.

'I fell against the dresser,' Ada had replied, which had been the absolute truth, but there'd been something smug in the way she'd said it.

He'd messed her about a bit to teach her a lesson, and she'd goaded him as she always did, hinting that he wasn't the only bloke she could have if she wanted to. But this time, with the bruise on her breast as proof, Harry's suspicions had been raised beyond the normal jealous rage she managed to provoke. He'd started ransacking the house for proof of his wife's infidelity and he'd very soon found the case of whisky. He'd belted her to within an inch of her life. A blackened left eye was only the outer manifestation of the beating; she'd also suffered two fractured ribs from where he'd got the boot in.

For three days now, Harry had remained holed up in his cottage, waiting for his wife's lover to return. He'd offered no reason for his refusal to work, but Ada's condition had given Tommo, the ganger, grounds to guess why, and he'd marked Harry 'off sick' on the work roster. Tommo had been only too thankful Ada had not told her husband of his own involvement. Like everyone else, Tommo was scared of Harry Lampton.

Harry sipped his tea. 'It's not strong enough,' he said.

'Well, I told you, didn't I? I can't make the bloody stuff draw any quicker than it wants to.'

He stood and she backed away a little. The left side of her face was swollen, she couldn't see out of her eye and her whole body was aching. She couldn't take another round.

'Chuck it out and get me a stronger one,' he said, handing her the mug.

Harry turned back to the table and, as he did, glanced through the open window. Parked by the siding was an FJ Holden. He crossed the room quickly, positioning himself against the wall, careful to keep out of sight – for a big man, Harry Lampton was light on his feet. He peered out at the railway station. A man was leaning against the Holden smoking a cigarette.

'That's him, isn't it?'

Ada, too, had glanced out the window. She'd seen Pete. She'd been expecting him to turn up any day now, although she was surprised he'd arrived so early in the morning.

'I said that's *him*, isn't it?' Harry hissed.

She nodded.

'Get out on the verandah. Give him the all clear.'

She looked back at the siding. Bugger it, she thought. Pete was taking another drag on his smoke, but she couldn't tell from this distance whether he'd just lit up or whether he was about to finish the damn thing. Perhaps if she could buy some time . . .

She tipped Harry's tea into the basin on the bench and was about to pour him a fresh mug . . .

'Stop mucking around, Ada, you heard what I said.' If she'd been within striking distance Harry would have belted her. 'Get yourself out there.' He picked up the .22 rifle that was leaning against the wall, loaded and at the ready as it had been for days. 'Get yourself out there and call him in.'

Ada shrugged and walked to the door. What was the point anyway? She was only delaying the inevitable. Pete would come back another day, and Harry would still be waiting. She opened the door.

'Stand up straight, you stupid cow, and don't let him see your fucking eye.'

She stepped outside, feeling a stab of pain in her ribs as she straightened her back. Behind her, she heard the rifle being cocked. Then she heard Harry's hissed warning.

'Don't forget, Ada, if he takes off, you're the one in my sights.'

She stood with the window behind her and the knowledge that resting on its sill was the barrel of the rifle. She looked towards the siding and angled her head so the left side of her face was in shadow.

Having milked the cigarette to its bitter end, Pete dropped the butt to the ground. He was on the verge of leaving. And then he saw her step out onto the verandah. Salvation, he thought, grinding the butt into the dust with the heel of his boot. Here was his panacea, his oblivion, and he started to walk the 200 yards from the siding to Ada's cottage.

Ada watched him approaching. She made no move, gave no warning signal. It was him or her. She had no choice.

Harry lined up his target in the rifle's sights. Come on, you bastard, he thought, come on.

Pete was barely fifty yards from the cottage when he noticed something different about Ada. The left side of her face looked strange. His step slowed just a little.

That's it, Harry thought. Perfect range . . . You've had it, you prick.

Ada saw Pete hesitate. If he ran, Harry would think she'd signalled a warning. She smiled invitingly. But the smile was lopsided.

She's been beaten, Pete thought, and the realisation flashed through his mind that it could mean only one thing . . .

In that very instant, a shot rang out.

Pete Mitchell achieved the oblivion he sought. He was dead the moment he hit the ground, a .22-calibre bullet through the brain. Harry Lampton was an excellent marksman. But then the target had been an easy one.

Behind the tattered screens and curtains of the fettlers' cottages, there was movement, but not a sound was heard. No alarm was raised.

Eyes watched as Harry dragged the body into the scrub, a shovel over his shoulder. Eyes watched as, forty minutes later, he loaded his meagre belongings into the FJ Holden. And eyes watched as Harry Lampton, his wife beside him, his roo dog in the back, drove away from Watson.

Through their windows, the fettlers' wives saw it all. So did Tommo, the ganger, and his wife. They saw everything and yet they saw nothing. The eyes of the fettlers were blind to anything that might invite enquiry.

# Chapter Twelve

Daniel was puzzled and a little concerned when Pete didn't return to the barracks that night. The following morning, he checked on the FJ Holden and, discovering it gone, made discreet enquiries amongst the patrol officers. He didn't wish to be over-alarmist in reporting Pete missing. As it turned out, Sergeant Benjamin Roscoe, who normally accompanied Pete on patrol, was as puzzled as Daniel was.

'He didn't front up yesterday,' Benjamin said. 'I didn't see him at all.'

Benjamin had actually wondered whether Pete Mitchell's failure to report for duty might have had something to do with the Aboriginal deaths, but he hadn't said a word. He hadn't dared. He hadn't even brought up the subject with Charlie and Sam, who wouldn't have welcomed discussion if he had. They were all terrified of the repercussions should they be overheard. Each of the men had put the episode behind him. It was as if the Aboriginal deaths simply hadn't happened.

'I wouldn't worry too much though, Lieutenant,' Benjamin added comfortingly. 'Pete tends to flout the rules. He's a bit unpredictable, if you know what I mean.'

Daniel nodded; he knew only too well what Benjamin meant. 'His utility's gone,' he said, 'but he hasn't taken any of his gear with him. I'm just hoping there hasn't been an accident.'

Unspoken thoughts were rife in Daniel's mind too. In the remote possibility that Pete's wild accusations were true, then Benjamin would be one of those servicemen threatened with court martial should he break silence. But Daniel didn't dare ask. If Pete's story *was* true, then he would be placing the man in danger, although he had to admit that the down-to-earth Benjamin Roscoe didn't appear like a soldier under threat of treasonable charges and a firing squad. In the cold light of day, the whole business was starting to seem rather ludicrous.

Benjamin and Daniel both agreed that, in the event Pete's car might have broken down or there'd been an accident, the military police should be informed – the desert was no place to be stranded.

'But let's leave it until tomorrow, Lieutenant,' Benjamin suggested. 'Pete's a pretty smart bushman, he can survive a day or two out there, and we wouldn't want to get him into trouble.'

'What sort of trouble?'

'Well, not so much *trouble*,' Benjamin said, 'more embarrassment really.'

Daniel was mystified by the remark.

'It's possible he might have stayed overnight at Watson,' Benjamin added.

'Oh. Yes, of course. You're probably right.' Daniel felt a little foolish. He'd forgotten all about the fettler's wife. Was he the only person who hadn't known of Pete's affair, he wondered. 'We'll leave it until tomorrow, and if he hasn't turned up by then, we'll alert the MPs.'

When Pete didn't turn up the next day, they reported him missing to the military police, whose first port of call, at

Benjamin's suggestion, was Watson. But there was no sign of Pete at Watson. Nor was there any sign of his FJ Holden.

'Nah,' Tommo, the ganger, said when shown a photograph, 'haven't seen the bloke. What about you, Mave?' He handed the photo to his wife.

'Nup,' Mavis said with a shake of her head, 'never clapped eyes on him.'

The response from the fettlers' wives was the same. No-one had seen either the man or the vehicle, which to the MPs seemed strange as they'd been informed Pete regularly visited Watson. But then fettlers were notoriously unhelpful.

The military police scoured the surrounding area for the utility, and reports were sent to Ceduna and Adelaide seeking Pete's whereabouts, but no news was forthcoming. It seemed Pete Mitchell had simply decided to take off.

Daniel was worried. Pete was indeed unpredictable, as Benjamin had said, but he wouldn't take off without a word, and he certainly wouldn't leave his gear behind. Something had happened. There'd been an accident, Daniel was sure of it.

Nick Stratton was also concerned for Pete's safety, but his reasoning differed from Daniel's. He didn't believe there'd been any accident. He believed Pete Mitchell, in his unstable state, may have cracked completely. Had his guilt over the Aboriginal deaths driven him to such distraction that he'd disappeared into the desert and taken his own life? Tragic as the possibility was, Nick found it eminently plausible.

For most, the mysterious disappearance of Pete Mitchell was overshadowed by a far more exciting event. Just four days after he'd gone missing, the countdown began on the third test in the Buffalo series. As before, a heightened sense of anticipation pervaded Maralinga.

Codenamed Kite, the test was once again to differ in its form of detonation. This time, the device – a Blue Danube bomb – was to be dropped from an RAF Vickers Valiant at a height of 35,000 feet, and exploded in an airburst approximately 400 feet above the ground.

The bomb had originally been scheduled to use a service-issue forty-kiloton core, but plans had been changed.

'What if the airburst fuse fails?' one of the physicists had suggested. 'A surface explosion with a bomb of that yield could result in huge contamination problems.'

Sir William Penney had admitted there was possible cause for concern, and a low-yield bomb core of 3 kilotons had been substituted.

'Just in case,' they'd all agreed.

The Kite test presented particular grounds for excitement. This was to be the first time a British atomic weapon had been launched from an aircraft. The eleventh of October 1956 would mark a historic occasion for armed forces and scientists alike.

Weather conditions were favourable that morning, but, as the day progressed, the upper winds began to veer and it was decided to bring the schedule forward by one hour. The drop would now take place close to two thirty in the afternoon.

At Roadside, the crowd was gathered in its hundreds, field glasses and binoculars trained on the Valiant bomber overhead. But at the start of the ten second countdown the focus shifted and all observers turned their backs to the site.

In the Valiant's cockpit, a tense silence prevailed as the final seconds of the countdown sounded through the headsets of each crew member.

'*Two, one, zero . . .*'

Then the bombardier's voice, calm, unruffled. 'Bombs away.'

A slight bump was felt as the weapon left the aircraft, after which the pilot and crew sprang into action. Upon immediate release of the bomb, the pre-planned manoeuvre was to take the aircraft clear of the weapon's detonation while simultaneously counting down the seconds for the time of the fall. The final second of the predetermined countdown would be the moment of detonation, or so they all hoped.

As the aircraft sped away from the site and the countdown began, every crew member waited breathlessly for the blinding flash, praying that it would occur at the precise moment it should. If the airburst fuse malfunctioned and the detonation took place prematurely, they were in trouble.

Then, on the final second of countdown, the sky turned white. The device had detonated safely as planned, 400 feet above the ground.

Cheers screamed through headsets; men grinned and gave each other the thumbs up. The Kite test had been a resounding success on every level of operation.

The following day, however, there was reason to question the overall success of the Kite test, although only a select few were aware of the fact.

The weather had not behaved favourably as predicted. Winds had veered in an alarming fashion and fallout from the bomb had drifted much farther south than had been expected. Furthermore, rain had been forecast to the south-east of the state. This wet weather had been presumed well beyond the reach of any fallout and therefore harmless, but the presumption had now proved wrong.

On 12 October, the day after the third test in the Buffalo series, the city of Adelaide, approximately 600 miles south-east of Maralinga, was blanketed by radioactive rain. No reports of the danger appeared in the press. Nor was the public alerted to the fact that readings of radiation levels 900 times higher than normal were secretly recorded in the Adelaide area. No-one but a handful of scientists knew. And only one was prepared to go public.

'I've had a disturbing call from Hedley Marston of the CSIRO in Adelaide,' Nick announced at a meeting with Titterton, Butement and Martin of the safety committee. It was two days after the firing and he was there to receive his brief for the press conference to be held in Adelaide the following day. 'Mr Marston enquired whether we intend to make any announcement about the Adelaide readings.' Nick looked from one man to another, his eyes clearly asking, *What readings? What aren't you telling me?*

'Marston's an alarmist,' Titterton, the AWTSC chairman, snapped. 'Low amounts of radioactive particles were detected in the air above Adelaide, presenting no danger whatsoever. The man's a positive menace.'

Titterton was very quick to dismiss the celebrated biochemist. In his view, it had been a wrong move to bring in the Commonwealth Scientific and Industrial Research Organisation to assist with biological experiments. And it had been a particularly wrong move to allow Marston free rein with his tests on the radiation effects upon animals well outside the test zone. The original assumption that his findings would be a helpful measure of fallout over vast areas had proved correct, but the man himself was getting out of hand. Sir William Penney and Professor Ernest Titterton were in firm agreement that Hedley Marston was rapidly becoming a political disaster. Through his experiments, Marston was obtaining potentially scandalous data on radioactive fallout. Even more worrying, he was not bound by the secrecy provisions in place at Maralinga.

'He doesn't understand the political situation,' Penney had

complained time and again. 'If a man of his scientific reputation says the tests are damaging there'll be an almighty row. The communists and other political troublemakers will have a field day. He must be silenced at all costs.'

'I warn you, Colonel Stratton,' Titterton now continued, 'Marston could jeopardise the entire test program.' The *tut-tut* of disapproval that followed seemed directed at Nick as much as at Marston. 'I must say, I'm not surprised he got in touch with *you* when all contact should have been made via the committee – the man appears determined to undermine our credibility. It's irresponsible, to say the least.'

'I agree. He's a security risk we can ill afford.' Alan Butement instantly backed Titterton, as he always did.

Nick glanced at Leslie Martin, the Australian. He usually tried to gauge the truth of the situation via Martin, who didn't have the same vested interests as the British scientists, although Nick sometimes wondered how often Martin was conveniently left out of the loop. In this instance, however, the Australian appeared to genuinely concur with his colleagues.

'He's a bit of a renegade,' Martin agreed, 'with a tendency to exaggerate.'

'Is this what I tell the press conference if his name comes up?' Nick's question was deliberately confrontational.

'His name won't come up,' Titterton said dismissively. 'The general press doesn't even know who he is. You won't hear a peep about Marston.'

Ernest Titterton had every right to be confident. Hedley Marston knew that if he attempted to expose his personal findings, he would be contradicted by his peers and exposed to ridicule. Sir William Penney had, furthermore, demanded that all reference to Adelaide be deleted from the article Marston was writing for publication in a scientific journal, and a further warning had been issued, in the interests of national security. Should any defamatory material appear, it would be instantly quashed, along with Marston's reputation.

'*I* will address the conference, Colonel,' Titterton said in conclusion. 'You will make your statement to the press and, before you call for questions, you will introduce me. In the meantime, you can put Marston right out of your mind.'

Nick was grateful to be relieved of the burden. But he really did not like Ernest Titterton.

On the second floor of the Government Information Office in Rundle Street, Adelaide, all was going as planned.

'And now I'd like to call upon Professor Ernest Titterton, chairman of the Atomic Weapons Tests Safety Committee,' Nick announced. 'I'm sure he'll be happy to answer any questions you may have.'

'Thank you, Colonel.'

Nick stood to one side as Ernest Titterton addressed the press gathering.

'Firstly, may I offer the committee's firm assurance that all safety procedures were observed and all communications strictly in place during the Kite test. Weather conditions were satisfactory for firing, and complete agreement was reached between the Australian committee and the trials director that there was no danger of significant fallout outside the immediate target area.'

Titterton went on in a similar vein for a further minute or so before concluding with his personal guarantee that the committee would continue to monitor all experimentation assiduously. Then he called for questions. There were very few. And not one involved radiation readings recorded in Adelaide.

'Thank you, Colonel Stratton.' In returning the floor to Nick to conclude the conference, Ernest Titterton managed to make it sound like an order.

Arrogant bastard, Nick thought – he wanted to deck the man.

Nick stayed overnight in Adelaide. He had another press conference in Canberra the following day and was booked on a commercial flight early in the morning. He could have flown out that afternoon, but he preferred to spend as little time in Canberra as possible – he found it a sterile place.

After changing into civilian clothes, he dined at the hotel and then took himself off to the seedy bars and clubs of Hindley Street with the express intention of getting drunk. He rarely got drunk, but he was so fed up with the game-playing his job required that he felt an insatiable urge for some form of distraction. Christ, he had every right to get bloody well plastered, he told himself. Safeguarding military secrets and protecting the all-important Maralinga project was one thing, but taking orders from two-faced little Pommie-prick boffins was another thing altogether.

He did the rounds of a few bars, drinking a beer or two in each, before moving on to a downstairs club featuring a piano player, where he switched to Scotch.

'Thank you,' he said to the waitress as she placed his drink on the table.

The club was small and half-empty and he knew the type well. The clientele was male and the staff female, with the exception of two bouncers lounging in the shadows. Even the bartenders and the piano player were female, and the several women seated at the bar or drinking with the customers would be hostesses. This was a club for lonely men.

The good-looking brunette playing the piano segued from 'La Vie En Rose' to 'Tennessee Waltz', and a couple rose from a table to shuffle around the pocket-sized dance floor. A customer leaned against the piano pouring the brunette a glass of champagne, and Nick wondered whether the pianist, too, was on the game. Most of the women would be, he was sure.

'Hello there. Would you like some company?'

He peered up through the atmospheric gloom of the club's lighting into a pretty face surrounded by platinum blonde hair. The lips were full and red, the figure voluptuous, and she appeared vaguely familiar. He hadn't planned on sex, but it suddenly seemed like an excellent idea.

'Please. Join me. Champagne?' Nick knew the rules. Hostesses at such clubs were paid commission on the cheap sparkling wine that was sold at exorbitant prices under the guise of champagne.

'Lovely,' she said breathily, and she sat.

'What's your name?'

She gave him a dazzling smile. 'Marilyn.'

Of course, he thought.

Marilyn turned out to be fun. 'You're a military man, aren't you?'

'How can you tell?'

'Easy. I always know. It's the body language. I'm a singer myself.'

'Really? Where do you sing?'

'Here.'

Five minutes later, the pianist beckoned her over.

'Do you mind if I take Bella some champagne?' she asked, picking up the bottle and her own full glass.

'Of course not.' He smiled. 'I'll get us another one, shall I?'

'Lovely.'

As she crossed to the piano, he signalled the waitress. The previous bottle would go missing, and Marilyn would probably empty her glass into the lavatory or whatever else the girls did to get rid of the stuff – it was all part of the game. This was how the club made its money.

The rendition of 'Baby It's Cold Outside', which Marilyn sang as a duet with the pianist, was pure Monroe in every sense. From the breathy tone to the heavy-lidded eyes, the pout and the wiggle of the hips, Marilyn had her namesake to a tee.

'Sentimental Journey' followed in exactly the same vein, and then she returned to the table.

He applauded her as she sat. 'Excellent,' he said, and she beamed.

He poured her a wine from the fresh bottle the waitress had delivered.

'I'm sorry, I seem to have lost my glass,' she said.

'No matter, the girl brought you another one.' He toasted her with his Scotch. 'You're a very good singer,' he said. Presuming she wished to be perceived as original, he carefully avoided any reference to Marilyn Monroe.

'You'll like the next songs even more,' she promised. 'They're my specialty.'

The next songs turned out to be 'Diamonds are a Girl's Best Friend' and 'The River of No Return'. There was obviously no need to avoid the subject of Marilyn.

'She's my idol. I based myself on her.'

'Yes, I had noticed the similarity.'

A breathy laugh of delight.

They talked and drank, and then they danced, and he bought her supper, and then they talked some more, or rather Marilyn did. She was an excellent conversationalist. It was her job, she said. First and foremost she was a singer, but she was also expected to entertain the customers. It would hardly be fair, would it, to scoff the food and champagne and not offer some form of conversation? She believed in giving good value for money. Marilyn's honesty was disarming. She was really Edie Smith from Mount Barker, she told him, but for show business purposes she'd decided to become Marilyn. 'I'm so good at it now that Marilyn's taken over and I've forgotten who Edie Smith is,' she said with another breathy laugh.

She was intriguing and amusing and Nick was enjoying her company. He looked forward to the sex, but for the moment her presence was enough. He'd missed being with a woman.

Nick Stratton had made it a rule to avoid the complications of relationships. He'd come close only once to marriage. He'd been stationed in Seoul, and she'd been a cipher clerk in the intelligence unit of the US army, a captain by rank. Theirs had been a passionate affair. He'd wanted very much to marry Jennifer, or so he'd thought at the time. But, as it had turned out, they'd proved too alike. 'Face it, Nick,' Jenny had said, 'we're both married to the army.' She'd refused to give up her career and, when the war was over, she'd returned to America. Nick was rather grateful for the fact now. He'd had the odd casual affair since then, but for the most part he was happy to keep his sexual liaisons on a cash basis. He found it simplified things.

'Do you want to come back to my hotel, Marilyn?' he asked as she finished the last of her crème caramel. The supper had run to three courses.

'My place would be better,' she said, 'it's not very far.'

'Fine.' He pulled out his wallet, about to settle the bill.

'I can't leave yet though. I have another bracket.' She smiled apologetically. 'Is midnight all right?'

He looked at his watch – an hour to go. Of course, he thought, it would be a house rule that the girls stayed until midnight, ensuring the management sold its quota of suppers and champagne. It also explained why the place had suddenly become busy. Men purely after sex had only one hour of club prices before leaving with the girl of their choice.

'Sure,' he said. 'Shall I get another bottle?'

'Lovely.'

In the taxi on the way to her nearby flat, she kissed him, sensually, provocatively, a promise of what was to come, and Nick was instantly aroused. It had been a long time.

As they undressed each other, he saw in the light of the bedside lamp that she was a good deal older than she'd appeared in the club – late thirties, certainly. Not that it turned out to matter at all. The sex was excellent. Just as Marilyn gave good value at supper, so she also gave good value in bed.

But when it was over, Nick realised they hadn't discussed what that value was. She hadn't quoted him a price, and he'd stupidly not asked. He lay looking up at the ceiling for a moment or so, recovering his breath, while she lay panting beside him. She had probably faked her orgasm, he thought, but if so she was a very good actress. He could have sworn her passion was real, which had made the experience so much more enjoyable.

'Oh, that was *so good*,' she said, stretching luxuriantly and sounding for all the world as though she meant it.

'It certainly was,' he agreed.

He climbed from the bed and started to dress. Discussing business was always more comfortable with one's clothes on.

She sat up, the sheet demurely clutched about her breasts, and watched him.

'Thank you for the supper and champagne,' she said. 'I enjoyed your company very much. I really did.'

'The feeling's mutual.'

It was as if they'd been out on a date, he thought. She was making it very difficult for him to ask *how much*. Easier to leave a present, he decided – he'd met women before who preferred to ignore any form of transaction had taken place. He took a ten-pound note from his wallet and slid it tastefully under the statuette of the ballerina that sat on the mantelpiece. He expected her to pretend not to notice, but she didn't pretend at all.

'How generous,' she said, as if it was the most unexpected gift in the world. 'Thank you,' and she blew him a kiss.

'My pleasure. Bye, Marilyn.'

As Nick left, he was vaguely aware that the evening had cost him close to a week's wages, but for some strange reason he didn't feel as if he'd been taken advantage of.

Edie Smith from Mount Barker played the game her own way. She vetted her clients with great care. Sometimes she told them an element of truth, as she had tonight, and some-times she invented a whole new tale to keep a customer entertained throughout supper. But she only ever went home with those she considered gentlemen, and preferably gentle-men she fancied – she enjoyed sex. Edie was content with her singer's wage and club commission, she wasn't interested in chasing a trick a night. And she never quoted a price because there was no need. The standard 'short time' rate most of the girls at the club charged was five pounds, and her gentlemen invariably came up with twice that amount. She considered it extremely generous on top of the outlay they'd made on champagne and supper. But Edie knew she was worth it. She'd given excellent value for money. They'd scored Marilyn Monroe, no less.

Back at the hotel, Nick managed four hours' sleep before showering and catching a taxi to the airport. He felt a little seedy after too many Scotches, it was true, but he also felt a whole lot better.

Around the same time Nick's taxi arrived at the airport, Gideon Melbray and his team pulled up at Watson railway station. They'd left Maralinga before dawn to meet the train delivery that was due early that morning.

Gideon climbed out from the passenger side, ostensibly to stretch his legs, but really to escape the young private who'd been driving the Land Rover. He wished the transport corps had supplied him with Daniel. For God's sake, he thought, it's too early in the morning – doesn't this boy ever shut up?

Nineteen-year-old Toby also climbed out – still chatting away in his thick Manchester accent, but Gideon ignored him. Behind them, the two Bedford trucks pulled up and Gideon gave them a wave. He couldn't wait to be relieved of Toby's relentless company.

'Do you have any toilet paper?' As it turned out, Toby was seeking relief of his own – although even a lavatory break seemed to warrant a chat. 'I should have gone at the barracks before we left,' he said, 'but I didn't feel the urge.' He caught the roll of toilet paper Gideon tossed to him. 'And I didn't want to cause any delay, what with the convoy and all –'

'Shovel's in the back,' Gideon said.

Toby hefted out the shovel and slung it over his shoulder. 'I shan't be long,' he said and he headed off towards the clump of trees 100 yards or so away.

'Take your time,' Gideon called after him.

Barely twenty yards from the trees, Toby faltered. He was sure he could hear growling up ahead – low, threatening growls coming from the mallee grove. Then he saw the animal emerge, a big, rangy, mangy, yellow roo dog – one of the fettlers' beasts.

It trotted clear of the trees with what appeared to be a hambone in its mouth and, just ten yards from him, settled down to gnaw at it. But as Toby watched the animal warily, he noticed that it wasn't a hambone at all. It was a human forearm, complete with wristwatch.

He dropped the shovel. The bile rose in his throat, his whole stomach heaved, and seconds later his breakfast lay spewed on the ground. Then he was running back towards the convoy, yelling and gesticulating wildly. 'Oy! Oy!'

The men turned to see the gawky lad from Manchester bearing down on them, arms flailing ridiculously like a demented bird, the forgotten roll of toilet paper still in his hand. What the hell had happened?

Gideon beckoned to one of the soldiers and together they raced to meet him. If it was a case of snakebite then the boy was mad to run like that – it would only pump the venom more quickly through his system. But they quickly realised it wasn't a case of snakebite. Toby was babbling something about a human arm and a dog, and he was pointing back where he'd come from.

They could see the dog. Gideon told Toby to return to the convoy, and he and the soldier went forward to investigate. Sure enough, it was true. The dog was chewing on a human arm. The limb was white and in the early stages of decomposition, but Gideon was pretty sure he knew whose arm it was.

Beside him, the soldier gestured towards the trees up ahead, and Gideon nodded. He, too, could hear the sound of growling. He picked up the shovel and held it at the ready as they walked towards the grove of mallee trees.

The sight that greeted them was a gruesome one. Three roo dogs were feeding on the remains of a human corpse. Dingoes had exposed a shallow grave during the night, and in the early hours of the morning the dogs had picked up the scent and come in for their share. The animals were displaying little aggression towards one another – the growls were more a warning to outsiders. A clearly established pecking order existed amongst the fettlers' dogs, and each knew its place. The pack leader was feeding on the carcass at the graveside, and the two subordinates were well clear, with a limb apiece.

The dogs didn't appear to find the humans a threat, or perhaps they were too distracted. The leader of the pack growled as Gideon walked forward to look at the grave, but it was merely a warning not to touch the carcass. Gideon had no intention of doing so. Between the dingoes and the dogs, what was left of the body was barely recognisable as human, but the animals had shown little interest in the head. And the head remained distinctly that of Pete Mitchell.

So Harry Lampton did murder him, Gideon thought. In the eight days since Pete's disappearance, Gideon had pondered the matter and only two scenarios had sprung to mind. Either Pete had run off with Ada, who'd been conspicuously absent of late, or Harry had found out about the affair and killed them. It seemed the latter was the case, although there was no sign of Ada's body – perhaps she'd been spared.

Gideon hadn't bothered to share his suspicions with the military police – he hadn't even mentioned Ada's name. He had no desire to become embroiled in a police enquiry. Now, however, with Pete Mitchell being rapidly devoured by roo dogs, it appeared unavoidable.

'I'll radio the MPs while you and the men clear the dogs away,' he said to the soldier.

*The sky is clear and the moon is bright. It is the hour before dawn, and Djunga is giving birth. She has left the mission at Yalata and has crept out into the desert with two women in attendance. Her husband's younger wife, Mundapa, is not present, for Mundapa is too inexperienced – she has yet to give birth to a child of her own. The women tending Djunga are not of her clan, but this does not matter – at such times all women are sisters.*

*The two stand either side of Djunga, their hands clasping each of hers tightly, supporting her as she squats and pushes with all her might. She has been pushing for a long time now and, although the night is chill, she is sweating from her efforts. Never in her three previous births has she had to push so hard or so long. In the past, birthing has been an easy process so easy that within hours Djunga has been going about her everyday duties. But in the past, her babies have helped her. They have been eager to come into the world, and she has barely needed to push. This baby does not wish to come out. This baby is not helping at all.*

*Djunga remembers when she last felt her child kick hard in her belly. It had been several days ago, and the baby had kicked so forcefully she thought her time had come. She had been prepared to go with the women out into the desert that very afternoon, but the moment had passed. Since then, the movement in her belly has become weaker, and now, as she pushes, she tells herself that this baby is lazy. She is cross with this baby for not wanting to come into the world. But even as she tells herself this, she is fearful, for she knows that something is not right, and she dares not think of that which she most dreads.*

*She pushes harder and harder. Her teeth are clenched, her head is thrown back, and the tendons of her neck are taut ridges under the skin. She is close to exhaustion and, although she has not once screamed with the pain, rasping sounds now come from the back of her throat.*

*Then the baby's head appears, and the knowledge that the final moment is upon her lends Djunga renewed strength. Minutes later, with her last vestige of energy, she pushes the child from her body.*

*The baby slithers into the waiting hands of one of the attending women, and Djunga slumps to the ground. She rests on her buttocks and watches as the second attendant kneels between her splayed legs and sets about cutting the cord. But there is no sound from the baby. The woman smacks its tiny body. But the baby does not cry out. The baby is dead.*

*Many women in Djunga's clan have lost children, particularly during the lean drought seasons. Malnourished themselves, they cannot feed the babies in their bellies and the children die prematurely or are stillborn. But this is not Djunga's way. Djunga has always given birth to healthy babies.*

*Now, in the first light of dawn, as she looks at the tiny body, Djunga hears the click-click-click of the mamu sticks. It has been nearly three weeks since her terrifying ordeal and, although she has been unable to erase the memory from her mind, she has been reassured by the healthy life she has felt in her body. But during these past several days, as the baby's kicks became weaker, she has lived in dread. Now all her fears have proved true. The mamu did indeed cast a spell upon her. This child was destined to die from the moment they ran their evil sticks over her belly.*

*The women help Djunga dig a hole and she buries her baby. Then the three of them return to the mission.*

# Chapter Thirteen

The discovery of Pete Mitchell's body became the talk of Maralinga. Word spread about town that he'd been shot through the head, and further word quickly spread of his affair with the fettler's wife. The men found it a novel experience having something to gossip about. Infidelity, jealousy and murder were permissible topics of conversation, eminently more open for discussion than the arcane affairs of Maralinga.

The topic was under even greater discussion at Watson.

'Yeah, it'd be Harry Lampton all right. He's got a record you know – been inside. He's a bad bastard, isn't he, Mave?'

With the police enquiry now firmly focused on the small railway settlement, Tommo's attitude had changed. He was going out of his way to be helpful, and so was his wife.

'Rotten to the core,' Mavis agreed. 'And Ada's no better. She's a right little slut that one. She was the one caused the trouble, I'll bet.'

'Not that we seen anything, mind.' Tommo flashed a look at his wife. 'Just a feeling you get, you know?'

Interviews with the fettlers' wives proved much the same. They all agreed that it had to have been Harry, and that Ada slept around. But there wasn't a witness to be found amongst them.

The military police now had their prime suspect, however, and a description of Harry Lampton, together with the details of his criminal record, was widely broadcast. The hunt was on.

Once again, the news spread like wildfire, and two days after the discovery of the body Gideon Melbray was running a book on where and when Harry Lampton would be apprehended. The bets rolled in. It seemed that in death, Pete Mitchell was proving the perfect all-round distraction for a township of bored and restless men. Neither gossip nor gambling was conducted in the presence of Daniel Gardiner, however, for the men could see that he was taking Pete's death very much to heart. Dan's grief was understandable, they agreed – the two had shared a donga, after all; they'd been friends. Well, as much as anyone could be friends with a loner like Pete Mitchell.

It was true Daniel was tormented by Pete's murder. But his torment did not lie so much in the death of a friend – the news of which had not surprised him – as in the cause of death and the perpetrator. For the past week, he had steadily convinced himself that everything Pete had told him the night before his disappearance had been the ramblings of a drunken man. Now, he was plagued with doubt. According to the reports, Pete had been shot through the head. To Daniel, the coincidence was chilling.

*Jesus Christ, I could cop a bullet through the brain for telling you this . . .* He could hear Pete's voice. *They're a ruthless bunch your employers, Dan.* He could see Pete's face as he raised the whisky bottle in a toast. *Here's to the army, mate, yours and mine. A pack of bastards every one of them.*

Over and over the words echoed in his mind, arousing in him a terrible suspicion. *I could cop a bullet through the brain . . .* Was Harry Lampton a scapegoat? There were those who knew Pete had been having an affair. Murder by a jealous husband would be the perfect set-up if his death had been planned. But precisely *who* would have planned it? *They're a ruthless bunch your employers* . . . No, Daniel told himself, such a conspiracy was not possible. *Here's to the army, mate . . . A pack of bastards . . .*

For two long, sleepless nights Daniel agonised over his suspicions and all they implied. If Pete had been deemed a threat to military security and disposed of, then everything he had said that drunken night must have been true. An Aboriginal family had been irradiated, their deaths had been labelled top secret, men had been threatened with charges of treason if they talked . The whole story, every facet of it, seemed to Daniel implausible. Pete Mitchell had been a disturbed man, he'd been heavily drunk that night – his death was surely coincidental. But coincidence or not, Daniel knew he wouldn't rest until he'd discovered the truth. There was just one problem though. Where was he to turn? Who was he to ask? If there *was* a conspiracy, then he was in the thick of it, and he dared not risk the same fate as Pete.

He would make no enquiries amongst the military, he decided. Not yet. Not until he felt it was safe to do so. He would start with the fettlers. They might well know something they weren't telling the police. Fettlers were renowned for avoiding any involvement with the authorities.

Early the following morning, before breakfast, Daniel popped into the transport office. He went directly to the front desk where he greeted the day duty sergeant, a beefy Cockney in his mid-thirties.

'Good morning, Norman.'

'Morning, Mr Gardiner, sir.'

'Put me on detail for the lunchtime run to Watson, will you.'

'No can do, I'm afraid, sir, you've already been assigned.'

269

'Really? Well, un-assign me, there's a good chap.'

'Would if I could, sir, but it's beyond my control.' Norman gave a regretful shrug as though he cared, although he didn't really. 'Lord Dartleigh has requested you drive him to Ceduna.'

'Ceduna?' The assignment was something of a surprise. It was half a day's drive – six hours at least – and much of it over rough roads that were little more than dirt tracks.

'That's right, sir.' Norman consulted his roster chart. 'The request came in yesterday evening. You're to collect him from his quarters at 0800 hours, you're to be in mufti, and the trip will require an overnight stay. You've been booked into the Ceduna Community Hotel.'

'Oh, I see.'

Norman could tell that the young lieutenant wasn't at all happy with his assignment, and he felt a genuine twinge of sympathy. He wouldn't fancy being stuck in the middle of nowhere with a toff like Dartleigh either – he had no time for the gentry himself, stuck-up bastards the whole blooming lot of them. 'It seems his lordship is bored, sir – too long between bombs – needs a bit of R and R.' Norman gave a derisive snort. 'Well, don't we all. Half his luck, I say.'

'Thank you, Sergeant.' There were times when Norman stepped right out of line.

'Sorry I can't be of more help, Lieutenant.' Although he sensed a slight reprimand, Norman didn't care in the least. He didn't care about anything except serving the remaining three months of his posting, collecting his substantial pay and getting away from this Godforsaken place. 'I just sign out the vehicles, sir, you know how it is.'

Norman was right about Harold Dartleigh: he was bored; it was too long between bombs and he needed some R and R. He too

270

couldn't wait to get away from Maralinga, but, unlike Norman, he wouldn't have to wait three months.

Just one more test to go, Harold thought as he stared out of the Land Rover's passenger seat window at the endless desert rolling by. Just four more days until the final firing in the Buffalo series and then he'd be on a plane home. He'd been counting the days for some time now. He would need to return to Maralinga every several months or so – one must maintain a presence – but Gideon would keep him regularly posted, and his trips would be brief, no more than a week or so. Of course, there would be Operation Antler, the second of the major test series next year, but that was thankfully a whole ten months away.

The plains of spinifex were giving way to salt pan territory now, none of which in the least impressed Harold. God, it was a hellhole, he thought. He'd been stuck in this primitive wasteland for over four wretched weeks and it had been altogether too long. He frankly didn't know how the men bore it.

'How much longer do you have to go, Dan?' he asked.

'Quite a distance, sir.' The question took Daniel by surprise, he'd been deep in thought. 'We're only halfway to Yalata – at least another three hours. We'll pick up speed when we get to the Eyre Highway.'

'No, no, lad,' Harold said with a touch of impatience, 'I mean how much longer do you have to serve at Maralinga?' The boy seemed rather distracted, he thought.

'Oh, I see. Sorry, sir, I misunderstood. Another six months – my posting's up the end of April.'

'Six months!' Harold gazed out the window. The stark, parched red earth with its salt-encrusted surface looked to him like some hideous lunar landscape. 'Goodness gracious,' he murmured, more to himself than to Daniel, 'how on earth will you bear it?'

271

'I rather like the geography of the desert, sir.'

'You do?' Harold turned to stare at his driver. The boy was insane. 'Why?'

'It's so extraordinarily primitive.'

'Yes, it's certainly that.'

'And it's so varied.'

'Really?' Harold once again looked out the window. He couldn't quite see the variation himself. But then Dan was a sensitive lad. Such an attractive quality in a young man, he thought. 'Perhaps I suffer a touch of agoraphobia,' he said, 'but there's just a little too much *space* for my liking.'

He settled happily back in his seat, prepared for a chat. The boy's company would alleviate the boredom of the scenery – it was why he'd chosen Dan, after all. Imagine being locked in a car for six hours with Ned Hanson! And then another six hours all the way back!

'A whole six months, eh? You'll be chafing at the bit by the time you get off the plane, I warrant.'

'I daresay you're right, sir,' Daniel replied. 'It'll be good to be home.'

'No, no, no, my boy, I mean you'll be chafing at the bit to get married, what? Elizabeth, that's her name, am I not correct? She doesn't care at all for tradition, she doesn't want a white wedding with all the trimmings, and you're going to marry her the moment you step off the plane.' Harold beamed triumphantly.

'That's right, sir. Fancy you remembering that.' Daniel flashed a smile at Harold Dartleigh; he couldn't help but feel flattered.

'I always remember things about people who interest me, Dan.' It was true, Harold did. Just as he remembered absolutely nothing about those he found dull. He had no idea whether or not Ned Hanson was married, and Ned had been working with the department for years. 'So tell me about Elizabeth. She sounds absolutely enchanting.'

'She's a journalist, sir.'

'Ah. A liberated woman.'

'Indeed, sir, a most liberated woman. In fact, Elizabeth's the most liberated woman I've ever met.'

'How admirable. And for whom does she write?' The subject of Elizabeth was of no interest at all to Harold, but he was seeking entertainment and young Dan, in speaking of his fiancée, was bound to delight.

Daniel could see that Lord Dartleigh was in the mood for a chat. He had preferred the silence of the drive when they'd both been lost in their own thoughts, but it was flattering that the man should show such an interest, and with great pride he told Harold of Elizabeth's job at *The Guardian*.

'*The Guardian*? Really?' Harold was somewhat surprised, but the announcement did not elevate Elizabeth to any particular level of fascination. He was, however, pleased to observe that he'd been correct about Daniel. The boy was positively glowing. 'And a feature writer no less,' he continued, 'most impressive. Your Elizabeth is obviously a very clever girl.'

Daniel could well imagine Elizabeth's response to being referred to as 'a very clever girl'. *How extraordinarily patronising*, he could hear her say.

'She is, sir, she's very clever indeed.'

The conversation had aroused a longing in Daniel. Elizabeth was always in his thoughts, but it had been some time since he'd spoken her name out loud, or heard it spoken by another. Now, talking of her brought her painfully close and he yearned for her company. Their correspondence had become unsatisfying in its enforced superficiality. He had communicated to her in full the powerful effect the desert had had upon him, and these days he wrote of only trivial matters. There was no point in composing poetic love letters, even if he'd had the talent – Elizabeth was not one for sentiment. And apart from his love, what else of any importance could he communicate? Certainly nothing about Maralinga. Daniel had never felt so isolated. There was no-one in whom he could confide, and now, more than ever, he needed a confidant.

'So where did you two meet, Dan?' The boy had gone quiet, which rather irritated Harold. 'Do tell me, I'm absolutely fascinated.'

But Daniel didn't hear the question. A sudden thought had occurred to him. He *could* confide in Elizabeth. Of course he could. This trip was a God-given opportunity. He could post a letter from Ceduna. With the realisation came a great sense of relief, as if a weight had been lifted from his shoulders.

'Come along now, Dan, don't be coy.' The smile had frozen on Harold Dartleigh's lips. The boy should be flattered by his attention, but he seemed to have drifted off. How dare he. 'Where did you meet your Elizabeth?'

'Aldershot, sir.' Daniel, upon registering the steely edge to the voice, was quick to make up for his inattentiveness. 'It was the spring of 1954, the day of the centennial celebrations. Elizabeth was working for *The Aldershot Courier-Mail* and I was marching in the grand parade.'

'Ah, how romantic.' Harold calmed down. He'd been about to get quite tetchy. 'Do go on.'

Daniel painted a picture of Aldershot as it had been that day, seeing it all so vividly himself: the hundreds of soldiers marching down High Street; the thousands of spectators cheering them on; and the one lone woman amongst the gathering of press at the entrance to the park.

'I'm sure every single soldier in that parade was looking at her,' he said, and laughed. 'I certainly know I was.'

'Charming,' Harold said as he settled back in the passenger seat. 'Utterly charming,' and he closed his eyes. 'Wake me when we get to the highway.' The boy was an absolute delight, but it was going to be a very long drive. He'd doze for an hour or so, he decided.

Ceduna was an attractive town. Overlooking Murat Bay on the Great Australian Bight, it was set amidst grain farms, natural bush and a coastline of rugged rocky bays and white sandy beaches. It was also the last major settlement to the eastern side of the Nullarbor Plain and, as such, a hub for travellers, offering an essential point of embarkation for those about to undertake the desert crossing, and providing a welcome haven for those weary voyagers arriving from the west.

Harold found the town enchanting. In fact, the moment he'd been granted his first sight of the sea he'd been filled with an indescribable happiness. How truly oppressive the desert was, he thought, and yet all the time this pretty coastal area had been here offering the perfect escape. He really should have made the trip earlier.

Daniel drove into the township and down to the beachfront, where stately Norfolk Island pines lined a broad promenade, and an impressively long loading jetty forked its way across a white stony beach and out into the broad sweep of the bay. Overlooking the foreshore was the Ceduna Community Hotel, an elegant single-storey stone structure, which had undergone many renovations since its original construction in 1902. Architecturally, the hotel was the town's most distinguished building, and the pride and joy of its citizens.

'Goodness gracious, how very attractive,' Harold said as they climbed out of the Land Rover and stretched their cramped limbs. Things were getting better by the minute, he thought. 'Come along, Dan, I'll buy you a beer.'

'If you wouldn't mind, sir, I'd like to freshen up a bit first.' Daniel was exhausted.

'Ah, yes, yes, of course, you're bound to be a bit tired.' Harold looked at his watch. It was nearly three o'clock in the afternoon – a bloody long drive, he thought, the lad had done well. 'You'll probably want a bit of a kip, what?'

'I would rather, yes, sir.'

'Goodo. We'll meet for dinner then.'

They checked in at reception.

'Dartleigh and Gardiner,' Harold said to the woman at the front desk, 'two rooms have been reserved for us, I believe.'

Daniel was surprised to hear Harold Dartleigh introduce himself so humbly, but he quickly recognised the reason for the omission of title. A peer of the realm would create quite a stir in Ceduna, and Harold Dartleigh would have no desire to call attention to his presence. Nor would he wish to invite any discussion about Maralinga. As deputy director of MI6, Dartleigh had clearly decided the two of them were to travel incognito with neither title nor military rank attached to their names. It also explained, Daniel realised, why he himself had been instructed to wear mufti.

They were given the keys to their respective rooms – Harold had been booked into the one and only double, and Daniel was told he'd been allocated 'second single from the end'. This turned out to be one of the many single and twin rooms that led off from the hotel's long central passage. Despite the building's architectural elegance, its accommodation was basic – not unlike the dongas at the barracks, Daniel thought.

'See you in the dining room at seven,' Harold said before he disappeared into his room. 'Sleep well.' He intended to take a walk along the beach himself. He'd slept for a full three hours during the trip and felt absolutely marvellous.

Daniel freshened up in the bathroom down the hall and, after collecting some stationery from the receptionist, returned to his room with the intention of writing to Elizabeth. But he couldn't keep his eyes open. He'd write his letter after dinner, he decided, when his mind was clearer. He lay down and was asleep within seconds.

Harold was buoyant over dinner. The trip to Ceduna had rejuvenated him already. 'The sea air works wonders,' he said effusively as they sat in the dining room having a pre-dinner beer. 'You really must make sure you take a good walk along the front, either after dinner or before we leave tomorrow,' he instructed. 'It'll do you the world of good.'

'I certainly will, sir, I shall look forward to it.'

'My God, but I'm starving. Shall we have some wine with dinner?'

'If you wish, sir.'

'I wish.'

Harold clicked his fingers, but the waitress was busy and didn't notice. The dining room, as usual, was crowded – the Ceduna Community Hotel did good business. 'Excuse me, my dear,' he said loudly, tapping the salt cellar on the table to attract her attention. 'We'd like to order.'

As it turned out, the hotel served a three-course set meal. 'Vegetable soup for starters, local snapper for mains, and there's rice pudding for sweets.' The waitress reeled off the menu.

The wine, when it finally did arrive, was not up to scratch, but Harold did not complain, he'd expected as much. The food, to his surprise, was most palatable. The soup was perhaps a little thin in texture, more like a broth really, but tasty enough, and the fish was fresh and quite delicious. Not being a fan of rice pudding, he skipped the dessert and was a little piqued that there wasn't the option of a cheese board, but again he did not complain. He was in far too good a mood.

'A triumph, Dan. A positive triumph, I'd say, wouldn't you?'

'Yes, sir, it was an excellent meal.' Daniel had enjoyed every single mouthful, although he could have done without the wine. He'd have preferred another beer himself.

'The trip I mean, lad, the whole trip. A marvellous idea. Why didn't I think of it sooner? We could have popped down here between each of the tests. The perfect getaway, wouldn't you agree?'

*Popped down here?* Daniel wondered at the phrase and, more particularly, at the ease with which it sprang from Harold Dartleigh's lips. Had the arduous drive escaped the man's attention?

'Yes, sir, this is certainly a very pretty spot.'

Daniel was rapidly coming to the not unsurprising conclusion that Lord Dartleigh lived in a world alien to most; a world where the privileged were granted their every wish and where servants sprang unquestioningly to a master's bidding. Daniel, although accustomed to the British class system in general, and most particularly to the well-established pecking order of the military, had had no personal contact with the aristocracy and he found the phenomenon fascinating.

Following dinner, Harold insisted upon another constitutional, and he further insisted Daniel join him. Together, they strode vigorously down the promenade of O'Loughlin Terrace and back; then they strode just as vigorously out to the end of the interminable jetty and back, by which time Daniel felt it was within his rights to retire. Harold, however, was keen to socialise a little longer.

'Just one quick port in the lounge, what do you say?'

Harold had made his enquiries. The hotel's bars observed the six o'clock closing regulations, but the lounges remained legally open to house guests and to those bona fide travellers willing to sign a permit to the effect they had travelled at least sixty miles. Needless to say, there were many 'travellers', bona fide and otherwise. The Ceduna Community Hotel did a roaring lounge trade.

'Come along, lad, don't dawdle.'

Harold was already heading through the door to the general lounge, and it seemed Daniel had little option but to follow.

There were no vacant tables, and they were forced to join two other hotel guests, a very respectable-looking couple in their forties who'd been in the dining room earlier. Harold ordered drinks from the waitress – a port for him and a beer for Daniel – and then he initiated introductions.

'Harold Dartleigh, how do you do,' he said with aplomb as he offered his hand. 'And this is young Daniel Gardiner. We're both English, as I'm sure you can tell. And you're from . . .?'

In one swift move he'd switched the focus to the couple, putting the onus upon them to explain themselves, which they did. Vic and Gloria Davison had arrived in Ceduna just that afternoon. They'd come from Perth and were on their way to Adelaide to visit their daughter who'd recently married. It had been an exhaustingly long five-day journey so far.

'And the *dust*,' Gloria said. 'The *dust* is so *appalling*! It gets into *everything*, don't you find?'

'Oh, yes,' Harold agreed, 'yes, I do indeed.'

The drinks arrived and, sensing his escape, Daniel started downing his beer as quickly as he could. He was grateful to the couple – Harold Dartleigh appeared to find them interesting.

'We thought it'd be such an adventure doing the trip by car,'

Gloria said, 'but I've learnt my lesson. It'll be the train next time, won't it, Vic?'

Vic nodded.

'And besides, I don't drive, so it's really not fair. It puts a lot of pressure on Vic. He's completely worn out, poor darling.'

Having sipped his port, Harold pushed the glass aside with a grimace. 'I'd fire the cook that put that in a jelly *trifle*,' he muttered darkly.

Gloria laughed.

'You're making short work of that beer, Dan,' he said as he signalled the waitress. 'Can I get you another?'

'No, thank you, sir, this'll do me fine. I might turn in shortly, if that's all right?' The query inferred that he'd like to get a good night's sleep in preparation for another six-to-seven-hour drive the following day, but Daniel didn't want to say anything that might invite comment from their companions. Judging by the couple's reaction, he'd already created an interest in referring to Harold Dartleigh as 'sir', but how else was he to refer to him? He'd been given no instruction.

The slip of the tongue, if indeed it had been one, did not appear to have worried Harold in the least. 'Of course, my boy, you take yourself off and have a good long sleep, you've earned it.' The waitress arrived at the table, and he turned to the couple. 'Vic, Gloria, may I buy you a drink?'

'Not for me, thanks,' Vic said. 'I'll be off to bed soon too – I'm tuckered out.'

'Just a beer then, thank you.' Before the waitress could leave, Harold made a point of handing her the glass of port. His lack of comment was a comment in itself, although the waitress appeared unfazed as she plonked the glass on her tray and disappeared.

Weary though he was, Vic's eyes had lit up with curiosity. 'What exactly is it that you *do*, Harold?'

Gloria nodded eagerly. She found Harold Dartleigh without doubt the most intriguing and charismatic man she'd ever met.

'Aah,' Harold's smile was enigmatic, 'that's classified information, I'm afraid.' He tapped the side of his nose with his forefinger in the classic gesture. 'Can't breathe a word,' he said, and cast a meaningful glance at Daniel. 'Top secret, isn't it, Dan?'

'Yes, it is, sir.' He's playing with them, Daniel thought.

Vic and Gloria laughed uncertainly. They weren't sure if this was a game or not, but by laughing they felt they could save face.

'Oh, I'm quite serious,' Harold assured them. 'I'm quite, *quite* serious, believe me.' They stopped laughing abruptly and there was a moment of awkward silence. Then, having successfully halted the line of questioning, Harold beamed jovially. 'Now tell me about Perth,' he said. 'I've never been there. Such a pretty city, I believe.'

Daniel sensed for the first time the dichotomy that was Harold Dartleigh. On the one hand, the effete aristocrat, and on the other, the ruthlessly smooth operator who could put the fear of God into people without them even knowing why or how.

He downed the last of his beer and waited to take his leave, but it was difficult choosing the moment. Gloria, thankful that all had reverted to normal and anxious to make amends for having appeared over-inquisitive, was waxing lyrical about her home town of Perth.

'Excuse me, Gloria, Dan wants to go to bed.' Harold had no compunction at all about interrupting the flow. 'Off you go, Dan, there's a good lad.'

Daniel stood.

'We'll make it ten o'clock in the morning, shall we,' Harold said. 'No, no,' he corrected himself. 'Let's make it half past – I want to explore the town before we leave. No need to set off too early, what?'

'Very well, sir.' Excellent, Daniel thought – he'd be able to send his letter directly from the post office. He'd been a little dubious about the prospect of leaving it with the receptionist. 'Goodnight, sir.' He bade the couple farewell and went to his room.

*Dearest Elizabeth.* As he started to write, Daniel did not ponder his words. They poured out of him.

*Please forgive me for any worry I might cause you in writing as I do, but I have some grave concerns and no-one with whom to share them. The fact that I'm able to share them with you now means that I am not sending this letter from Maralinga, as you will have gathered. I have for some time been Lord Dartleigh's assigned driver, and, most fortuitously as it has turned out, Dartleigh decided upon a trip to Ceduna, a small coastal town several hundred miles from Maralinga. In doing so, he has inadvertently granted me the chance to write to you free of censorship, and I cannot resist the opportunity. You are the only person in whom I can confide, my darling, and, although you are powerless to provide any answers, I know that simply speaking to you on paper will ease the burden.*

*This is what has happened – I will be as succinct as I can.*

*The man with whom I have been sharing barracks accommodation was an ex-Australian army lieutenant by the name of Petraeus Mitchell. He was serving in a government capacity as Aboriginal liaison officer, responsible for relocating any local population discovered in the area.*

*Pete was a tormented man in many ways, a heavy drinker, prone to black moods, but I liked and respected him a great*

282

*deal. We had become friends. Anyway, a week or so ago, in a*
*drunken state, he told me of unimaginable happenings at*
*Maralinga, events that were quite shocking. He said that men*
*had been threatened with court martial if they spoke of what*
*they'd seen.*

Daniel paused. He could not risk telling Elizabeth about the
Aboriginal deaths. If by chance Pete's story was true, then in
repeating it he would be violating the Official Secrets Act and
risking his own court martial.

*I cannot tell you the specifics of Pete's allegations – for obvious*
*reasons, which you will understand – but shocking though they*
*were, I couldn't bring myself to believe there was any truth in*
*what he said. He was rambling at the time, practically*
*incoherent, behaving like a madman. He actually laughed and*
*boasted that he could 'cop a bullet through the brain' for what*
*he was telling me. Those were his exact words.*

*Well, the awful part is, Elizabeth, this is exactly what has*
*happened. Pete has been murdered, shot through the head,*
*supposedly by the jealous husband of a woman with whom he*
*was having an affair. I know that the affair with the woman is*
*true, not something concocted, and, under normal*
*circumstances, the event, ghastly though it is, would be*
*understandable. Itinerant workers here in the outback – like*
*Harry Lampton, the fettler currently being sought for Pete's*
*murder – are tough, ruthless men. But the coincidence haunts*
*me.*

*I have decided to make my own enquiries, if only to achieve*
*some peace of mind. I truly do not believe there is a conspiracy,*
*Elizabeth, and, even as I write this, I am starting to feel self-*
*consciously melodramatic. You see what a help you are to me,*

*my darling? In the meantime, however, I cannot help agonising over the awful coincidence of Pete's death. If I can only discover some irrefutable evidence that establishes Harry Lampton as the killer – perhaps a witness amongst the fettlers – then I will rest assured that my fears are as foolish and as groundless as I'm sure they are.*

*Forgive me, my darling, for pouring all this out to you, but, as I have said, there is no-one in whom I can confide, and it is such a relief for me to be able to write openly of it. I shall sleep more soundly tonight having unburdened myself, I can assure you, although I realise it is probably the ultimate act of selfishness on my part. It is not my intention to worry you, I promise. I will not place myself in any danger and I will not behave rashly. My enquiries will be made with the utmost discretion.*

*Oh, my dearest Elizabeth, how very much I do miss you, and how very much I do love you.*

*I remain yours forever and forever and forever, Danny.*

The following morning, Daniel was at the post office the moment it opened its doors for business. He bought an overseas stamp, popped the letter in the bright red mailbox, and felt happier than he had in days.

Harold Dartleigh's mood remained ebullient as they set off on the long drive back to Maralinga.

'I feel positively reborn,' he said. 'I shall return to Ceduna next year when I'm back for the Antler series. The sea air has done me the world of good.'

Last night had also done him good, he thought. There was nothing more satisfying than knowing one could have a woman right under her husband's nose.

'Oh, what a pity to be left all on one's own,' he'd said, when

Vic had insisted upon winding his weary way off to bed. 'Are you sure I can't tempt you to a final nightcap?'

Vic had read his wife's hesitation. 'You stay for a drink if you like, love,' he'd said. 'I'm off to bed, I've had it.'

A complacent man, assured of his wife's fidelity, Harold had thought – always a fatal mistake.

Gloria had stayed.

'Alone at last,' he'd said jokingly. Or was it a joke? Gloria had laughed, a girlish, breathless laugh, the sort he recognised – middle-aged women always found him irresistible.

Gloria had been his for the taking. He'd known she would be from the moment he'd joined the couple at the table. Except, of course, he hadn't taken her. He never did. He was always faithful to Lavinia. But he did so enjoy the game. Harold was a terrible tease.

'Goodnight, Gloria,' he'd said forty minutes later. 'I've enjoyed your company immeasurably.'

Her disappointment had been palpable, and Harold had delighted in the thought that she'd been prepared to cuckold her husband, no doubt for the first time in a twenty-five-year marriage. Such moments were a wonderful boost to one's ego.

'So you had a decent night's sleep then, Dan?'

'Yes, sir, I did.'

'I must say, you look well-rested. The sea air's obviously worked wonders for you too. I thought you seemed a little peaky on the trip down.' Harold's bonhomie knew no bounds.

'I was rather out of sorts, but I feel very much better, sir, thank you.'

'Excellent. A bit of a change now and then would do all you lads good, I should think.'

Daniel wondered how twelve hours or more of heavy-duty driving over rough terrain could be termed 'a bit of a change', but he wasn't about to argue. Harold Dartleigh was, after all, quite right. The trip to Ceduna had done him the world of good.

Harold peered regretfully back at the last glimpse of coastline. 'It must be hard for you boys sometimes,' he said. The sea disappeared from sight and he turned to stare down the endless dusty highway. 'Very hard, being stranded out here in the middle of nowhere without family and without women. Lonely, I should think.'

Daniel couldn't really dispute the fact. It *was* lonely. Particularly now that Pete had gone – he hadn't realised how much he'd come to rely on Pete's company. But he felt somehow bound to give a positive reply.

'Oh, I don't know, sir, we have a lot of laughs. There's plenty of camaraderie amongst the men –'

'Bollocks! Camaraderie, my arse!'

Harold Dartleigh's reaction was so completely unexpected Daniel wasn't sure how to respond.

'There should be a great deal *more* camaraderie, boy.' As Harold warmed to his theme, it was plain he expected no response. 'The army is successfully demoralising the men, in my opinion. The need-to-know policy's been taken to such extremes it's denying the freedom of friendship.'

Harold was actually referring to William Penney's policy rather than the army's. Penney's insistence that the men be kept in ignorance irritated Harold intensely. There were times when even *he* was denied information, and all because of Penney's ridiculous obsession with his own power. Thank God he'd placed Gideon undercover, Harold thought, and thank God he'd cultivated the odious Melvyn Crowley. William Penney, in his megalomania, would close the doors even on MI6 if he could. Damn the man's hide.

'Men need to let off steam, Dan.' Harold looked out at the

desolation surrounding them – in only minutes, it seemed the desert had swallowed them up. 'Particularly in a depressing hell-hole like Maralinga.'

Harold Dartleigh's views surprised Daniel. He'd have thought the need-to-know regulations would be right on target for MI6.

'Well, don't you agree, lad?' Harold was inviting comment now – he was in the mood for conversation. 'The camaraderie of men is of the utmost importance in a place like Maralinga, wouldn't you say?'

'Yes, indeed I would, sir.'

'So why the reticence? Come along, Dan, let's have your say. I feel like a chat.'

'I suppose I'm just a little surprised, sir. Given your position, I'd have thought you'd consider security in every form to be of the utmost importance.'

'Oh, I do, my boy, I do, believe me. But Maralinga's security lies in its isolation. The remoteness of its location makes it a veritable fortress. And do you know the next most important security factor to be taken into consideration after the choice of location?' Harold paused, and Daniel wondered whether it was a trick question. But it wasn't. 'The loyalty of one's team, Dan.' Harold triumphantly answered himself. 'And do you know what breeds loyalty?'

This time Daniel took a punt. 'The camaraderie of men, sir?'

'Exactly!' Harold clapped his hands and Daniel felt as if he'd just gone to the top of the class. 'Loyalty and comradeship should be encouraged at all times, particularly under conditions such as those at Maralinga.'

Harold was very much enjoying his own argument. He really should be running Maralinga himself, he thought – Sir William Penney and the military were both employing the wrong tactics.

'To nurture ignorance is to invite inefficiency,' he proclaimed. 'And to breed fear, as the army has done, is counterproductive on every level.'

*To breed fear, as the army has done.* The words struck an immediate chord with Daniel. Could Harold Dartleigh be indirectly referring to the army's threat of court martial? The man seemed very passionate in his views, and if soldiers *had* been threatened with court martial then the deputy director of MI6 would be bound to know of it.

'What's the matter, Dan?' The boy had been paying rapt attention, but he'd suddenly drifted off as he had during the drive south. Harold was in such a good mood that, rather than finding the fact irritating, he felt a touch of concern. 'You've gone very quiet, lad. What's up?'

'I'm so sorry, sir, I do beg your pardon. I didn't mean –'

'You've been preoccupied lately. Come on, boy, spill the beans. What's weighing on your mind?' Harold was imbued with a rush of avuncular affection. If young Dan had a problem, he'd like to help. Perhaps the lad was being bullied, or perhaps some senior officer was making his life hell.

Daniel wondered whether he dared test for a reaction, and, as he carefully broached his subject, he studied Harold Dartleigh from the corner of his eye, searching for a giveaway sign.

'A close friend of mine died recently, sir. I'm afraid I've found it rather upsetting.'

'Yes, well, death tends to upset us all, doesn't it.' Harold's interest waned dramatically and he looked out the window. How disappointing, he thought.

Undeterred, Daniel continued. 'His name was Pete Mitchell. He was my roommate at the barracks.'

'Ah, Pete Mitchell . . .' Harold's interest was immediately

rekindled and his eyes lit up. 'The liaison chappie responsible for the Aboriginal business. Yes, yes.'

Daniel's breath caught in his throat. He felt himself physically gasp. Surely Harold Dartleigh couldn't mean the Aboriginal deaths. He'd hoped to garner some hint about the veracity of Pete's story, but he was shocked to hear the subject referred to so openly.

'What Aboriginal business would that be, sir?' he asked, keeping his voice as steady as possible and his eyes focused on the road.

'You know . . . locating them . . . seeing them off the land . . .' Harold gave an airy wave of his hand; he really had no idea what an Aboriginal liaison officer did. 'All that sort of thing.'

Realising that Dartleigh had been speaking in generalities, Daniel nodded a little too readily and a little too eagerly. 'Yes, sir, that's right,' he said, 'that was Pete's job.' He was praying fervently that his reaction had gone unnoticed.

It hadn't. Very little escaped Harold Dartleigh. So the boy knew about the native deaths, he thought. How very interesting. He hadn't known himself until Melvyn Crowley had told him. Of course, Melvyn considered the natives' deaths a major breakthrough, but then Melvyn was a ghoul. A very handy man to have on side though, Harold told himself. If it weren't for Melvyn, he would be unaware of the army's threat of court martial. Gideon, for all his contacts, had heard nothing – the men were plainly too frightened to talk. Just as well Melvyn, with his ear firmly pasted to the laboratory door, had overheard every word. He'd come up with a full report too, including an account of all those present. Good old Melvyn, Harold thought – he was indeed indebted to the man. Personally, he couldn't give a tinker's toss about the natives, nor about the army's threat of court martial, which he supposed was necessary under the circumstances, but he did so detest being left in the dark.

'A terrible business,' he said, 'quite, quite terrible.'

'What's that, sir?' Daniel was nervous. Harold Dartleigh's mood had become contemplative and it worried him. He wasn't at all sure what to expect.

'Your friend's murder, of course.'

Harold had no intention of putting young Dan on the spot. Pete Mitchell had obviously told the boy about the dead natives – rather inconsiderate, he thought, feeding the lad information that could lead to his court martial.

'I didn't know you and Pete Mitchell had been roommates, Dan. No wonder you're upset,' he said sympathetically. 'A gruesome affair, most unpleasant all round.'

'You know about Pete's death then, sir?'

'Of course I do. I know everything about it – the whole of Maralinga does.'

Surely the boy must be aware of the book Gideon Melbray was running, Harold thought. The capture of Pete Mitchell's killer was the hottest bet in town. But possibly, in the interests of good taste, the men had kept Gideon's book a secret from young Dan.

'I believe the killer's a chap from Watson,' he said. 'A fettler by the name of Harry Lampton.' He'd put ten pounds on Harry Lampton turning up in Kalgoorlie – a gold-mining town had seemed a good choice to Harold.

'Well, yes, sir, Harry Lampton's the chief suspect.'

Harold's senses were instantly on the alert. There was something in the way young Dan had said that, he thought. But he kept his response casual.

'You have your doubts, eh, Dan?'

'About what, sir?'

'You think it might not be the fettler?'

'Oh, no, sir, I didn't say that.' Daniel was flustered in his reply. 'I mean, everything points to Harry Lampton of course . . .'

'Yes, but naturally you'd want to be *sure*, wouldn't you?'

Harold's finely tuned antennae had come into play. He was sifting through every single nuance of every single word they'd spoken, and things were adding up. He didn't need to confront the boy. *Who do you think it was, Dan?* There was no necessity for such interrogation. He knew exactly who Dan thought it was.

'You'd want to be sure because Pete Mitchell was your friend. And when a friend meets a terrible end like that, you'd want to know that the true culprit had been apprehended. Isn't that right, Dan?'

'Yes, sir, that's right.' It was the simple truth, and Harold Dartleigh seemed so understanding that Daniel had no trouble admitting it. 'The sooner Harry Lampton's found, and the sooner he's proved guilty, the happier I'll be.'

'Well, we'll have to get cracking then, won't we?'

'I beg your pardon, sir?'

'The only problem is, from what I've heard, the military police haven't been able to come up with any witnesses. The fettlers have closed ranks, I believe. Of course, a motley bunch like that always does when the police snoop around, what?'

'Yes, sir, that's right.' The conversation had taken a most unexpected turn, but it seemed Daniel had found an ally in Harold Dartleigh. 'I'd thought of making some enquiries at Watson myself.'

'Ah, no, Dan, no, no, wrong move. The fettlers wouldn't open up to you any more than they would to the police. But a civilian with hefty bribe money – now that would be a different matter altogether. I'll put a man on to it, you just leave it to me.'

Daniel felt a rush of relief. The mental agony of the past few days suddenly lifted. If there had been any conspiracy to silence Pete Mitchell, he thought, then Harold Dartleigh would undoubtedly have known of it. But clearly he didn't. Everything pointed to Pete's death being the coincidence it had appeared to be.

'I don't know what to say, sir. I'm very grateful, very grateful indeed.'

'No need to be, Dan. I can't have my driver distracted from his duties, what? Don't you worry, we'll get to the bottom of this. Nothing goes on around Maralinga that I don't know about or can't find out. You pop into my office in a few days and I'll let you know what I've come up with.'

'Yes, I will, sir. Thank you.'

'Now, if you don't mind, I might try and have a bit of a nap before we get to the really bumpy parts of the drive. All right with you?'

'Yes, yes, of course, sir.'

Harold leaned back and pretended to doze. He wasn't at all tired, but he couldn't be bothered talking any more. What a very interesting turn of events, he thought. He could certainly see why young Dan had been so preoccupied.

He ran through the sequence in his mind. Natives killed, soldiers threatened with court martial, Pete Mitchell blabbed it all out to the boy and ended up with a bullet through his skull. Well, no wonder the lad thought the army had murdered his friend. And who knew? Perhaps he was right. Pete Mitchell wasn't a soldier, after all – he couldn't be tidily dealt with in a court martial that no-one would hear about. The quickest and most efficient way to silence him would be to kill him. Harold would certainly have done so himself in similar circumstances.

Harold was grateful to young Dan, and had every intention of honouring his promise. He'd put Gideon on the job, he decided. If anyone could get information from the fettlers, Gideon certainly could. Personally, he didn't care one iota whether Pete Mitchell's death had been a matter of military expediency or the result of a jealous husband's rage, but he would *not* be left out of the picture. First Penney, and now the army – it simply wouldn't do.

Three days later, a familiar excitement pervaded Maralinga. Once again the routine of military life was about to be shattered by the thrill of a nuclear explosion.

The final test of the Buffalo series was codenamed Breakaway. The bomb, with a core of 10 kilotons, was to be suspended from a tower, as had been the case in the One Tree test, but the difference on this occasion was the time of detonation. Breakaway was to take place in the dead of night.

'Well, we're beggars for punishment, aren't we?' Bud muttered.

Privates Bud Barton and Col Rogerson, rather than waiting to be assigned special duty, had this time volunteered.

'You've got to be in it, mate,' Col had said. He was always the ringleader. 'They say the explosion's spectacular at night.'

'Oh, yeah? Who's they?'

'Well, you know, that's what they reckon.'

It was shortly after one o'clock in the morning and a dozen or so men were assembled in the outer perimeters of the forward area. They were wearing uniforms made of a new style of fibre the army was keen to test. A crescent moon was etched in the cloudless desert sky and stars glittered like gemstones, but the night's serenity was broken by the officer's voice barking out each second of the final minute's countdown.

'Bloody stupid, that's what we are,' Bud continued to grumble when Col made no reply. He didn't know how he let himself get talked into these things.

Col grinned, undaunted. 'Don't be such a whinger. Imagine the stories you'll have down the track.' Col was excited. This was something else to tell Marge about when he got back to Perth.

The countdown reached ten and the men turned their backs. '*Three, two, one, zero . . .*'

This time, Bud's and Col's hands were not splayed over their faces. This time their fists were firmly ground into the sockets of their eyes. But, strangely enough, as the world turned white, they still saw the bones of their fingers.

For those watching several miles away at Roadside, the sight was truly spectacular. When the shock waves had passed, they unveiled their eyes and turned to look at an unbelievable sky. The night was lit up as bright as day, and a giant red and gold fireball hung in the air.

Those in the forward area were greeted by an altogether different sight. They uncovered their eyes but did not turn around. They stood frozen in horror at the chaos before them.

'Shit,' Col muttered. 'Holy shit.'

They were surrounded by dozens of blinded rabbits.

The officer in charge made an instant decision. He did not order the men to crawl on the ground as had been his instructions. A quick ten-minute march sufficed, and then they were in the trucks heading back to Maralinga.

At dawn, clad in protective clothing and wearing gas masks, a team of scientists and several squads from the indoctrination force and the radiation detection unit arrived at the forward area several miles from ground zero. The scientists set about collecting their recording apparatus, and the officers commenced their laborious examination of the now burnt-out vehicles and equipment that had been strategically placed.

They could see, in the shallow far-distant valley, where the tower had been, the earth's bald surface now reflecting an ominous glassy-green. The teams would not venture that far. Readings would not be taken at ground zero for several days yet.

It was Captain Brian Fadden, a Canadian engineer from the radiation detection unit who first noticed the blackened Land Rover. He was puzzled. Who had put a Land Rover in the line of fire? The equipment normally used for experimentation purposes was worthless. Why destroy a valuable vehicle? What sort of idiot had made such a stupid decision, he wondered.

The same sort of idiot who'd put a dummy in the thing, he realised as he walked over to have a look. Now, how smart was that? The uniform and equipment placed on a dummy set at this range would be incinerated. And, of course, it was. The whole dummy was incinerated, charred beyond all recognition. It was just a blackened effigy of a human being.

Except that it wasn't an effigy. Oh my God, Brian thought, and he raised the alarm.

# Chapter Fourteen

Kenneth and Prudence Gardiner were delivered the news in person on 23 October by a Major Neville Chadwick, who introduced himself as aide-de-camp to Lieutenant General Barraclough, British army.

'You are the father of Lieutenant Daniel Gardiner, sir?' the major asked when Prudence, upon request, summoned her husband to the front door. Kenneth nodded, and the major, grateful that he didn't have to confront the mother alone, continued. 'I'm afraid I have bad news for you both.' His pause was infinitesimal – one could not break such news any way but brutally, and the sooner it was over the better for all concerned. 'It is my duty to inform you that Daniel was killed on 21 of October at approximately 2.30 pm Greenwich Mean Time in Maralinga, South Australia.'

There were no histrionics from either parent. The numbness of their disbelief robbed them of emotion. As the major continued, they even found themselves making intelligent queries, although they barely heard their own questions, let alone the responses. During later discussions, however, they would find that every word that had been uttered was clearly etched in their minds.

Ten minutes later, the major departed, leaving his details. The army would be in touch shortly regarding the memorial service, he said, and they were to telephone him any time of the night or day should they have any further queries.

Over the next twenty-four hours, as the afternoon stretched into a sleepless night, Kenneth and Prudence discussed everything the major had told them. They sifted through the information, trying to make sense of what had happened in a logical fashion, anything that would aid them in avoiding the awful reality. It would be some time before they would be capable of accepting the inevitable truth that their son was dead.

As a result, Elizabeth did not learn of Daniel's death until two days later. Fiancées did not rank as next of kin, so she was not informed by the army. The odious task fell upon Prudence.

'I apologise for ringing so early, Elizabeth.' Prudence, guilty at the thought of letting it go one day longer, had telephoned the flat at eight in the morning. 'But I wasn't sure what time you left for work. I'm afraid we have received some dreadful news.' Like the major, Prudence got straight to the point. 'Dan has been killed.' When there was no response from the other end of the line, she continued briskly, 'I'm sorry to be the bearer of such terrible tidings. I'm aware it must come as a shock. It did to us too, of course.'

Prudence Gardiner was not unsympathetic in her feelings for Elizabeth, but she could not allow any show of sentiment for fear she herself might start to crumble. She and Kenneth were keeping their grief private – even from each other, it seemed, which Prudence found a little hard. She would like to have shared the burden of her anguish, at least with her husband.

'We were informed two days ago,' she continued. 'I must

apologise for not calling you sooner, but we're only just now coming to terms with the news ourselves.'

'When . . .? How . . .?' Elizabeth's voice was barely audible as her shock manifested itself in utter confusion. She could not comprehend what she was hearing. England was not at war. How could Danny be dead? There had been no battle.

'Four days ago. It was an accident, so Major Chadwick told us . . .' Prudence took a deep breath and repeated the major's words verbatim. 'An accident that occurred as a result of the detonation of a nuclear device. The army has offered to arrange a memorial service with full military honours. I'll let you know the details as soon as we've decided on the day.' Prudence's tone was brusque now, she needed to get off the phone. 'It will probably be the Saturday after next, here in Crewe, of course. Naturally, you're quite welcome to stay with us.'

'A memorial service?' Elizabeth was more confused than ever.

'Yes, that's right. Major Chadwick says the circumstances of Dan's death make it impossible for the army to ship his body home to England. He'll be buried at Maralinga. It's another terrible blow to us, of course.'

'But –'

'And now I really must go, Elizabeth.'

Prudence could talk no longer. She and her husband had discussed the subject, and there were no words left to say. Ken seemed to understand the necessity of their son being buried in a foreign land. Personally, she didn't, and she was sick to death of hearing *the army knows best*.

'I'll be in touch in the next day or so when the arrangements are made,' she said, and she softened a little. 'I'm sorry, my dear. I'm so very, very sorry for us all. Goodbye.'

Elizabeth's reaction as she hung up the receiver was much

the same as Kenneth's and Prudence's had been. She was numb with disbelief. One quick phone call and she was expected to accept the irrefutable fact that Danny was dead? She couldn't. She couldn't possibly.

For some time she sat quite still, staring at the phone, unable to cry or to feel anything, unable to move or even to think. Then, as her mind started to clear, she told herself that she must take action. She must find out what had happened, the cold, hard facts. She would not believe Daniel was dead until she knew the truth.

*It was an accident, so Major Chadwick told us.* Major Chadwick, she thought. She needed to talk to a Major Chadwick. She was on the verge of ringing Prudence back to get the man's details, but had a better idea and telephoned *The Guardian* instead – the direct line of Reginald Dempster, foreign correspondence editor.

'Reg, it's Elizabeth. I'd like you to do me a favour.'

'Of course. Are you all right? You sound a bit odd.'

'I need to get in touch with a British army officer, a Major Chadwick . . .'

'Ah, yes, I know the chap.' The fact was not remarkable – there were very few in the upper echelons of power that Reginald Dempster did *not* know. 'He's aide-de-camp to Lieutenant General Barraclough –'

'Can you ring me back with his phone number? I'm at the flat.'

'Yes, of course. Are you sure you're all –'

'Thank you. And would you mind telling Lionel that I won't be in today.'

'Right you are. Don't move. I'll get back to you in a minute.' Reginald didn't bother asking again if she was all right. She clearly wasn't.

Reginald Dempster was as good as his word, and within sixty seconds Elizabeth had Chadwick's number. She rang the offices of Lieutenant General Barraclough and was informed by the female receptionist that the major was not available.

'Do you wish to leave a message?'

'Yes, please. I'd like him to ring me as soon as possible. My name is Elizabeth Hoffmann and I'm Lieutenant Daniel Gardiner's fiancée.' She gave the receptionist her phone number, then added, 'Tell him I've just received a call from Lieutenant Gardiner's mother.'

Major Chadwick proved as prompt as Reginald Dempster. Within sixty seconds, the phone rang. It was exactly 9.30 am.

By now, Elizabeth's numb state of shock had worn off and her nerves were threatening to get the better of her as the truth slowly seeped home. A mother did not announce her son's death without certain knowledge. Why, she wondered, was she putting herself through this fresh agony? But she had to hear it for herself, even though she knew what the major would say.

'Lieutenant General Barraclough extends his deepest sympathy, Miss Hoffmann, as indeed do I. Had we known of your official capacity as Lieutenant Gardiner's fiancée, we would have personally informed –'

'Just tell me what happened, please, Major.'

'Yes, of course.' A tough young woman, Neville Chadwick thought, judging by the tone anyway. 'Daniel was killed on 21 October at approximately 2.30 pm Greenwich Mean Time.' He listed the official facts, as she obviously wished him to. 'He was stationed at Maralinga, South Australia at the time, and his death was an unfortunate accident that occurred as a result of the detonation of a nuclear device.'

The major waited for some reaction, but there was none, so he continued. 'Regrettably, the circumstances of Daniel's death make it impossible for his body to be shipped home to England. He will be buried at Maralinga. But, as I'm sure Mrs Gardiner informed you, the army is arranging a memorial service with full military honours.'

Again, the major waited for a response. Again, there was none.

'Your fiancé died in the service of his country, Miss Hoffmann.' Neville Chadwick's voice took on a gentler tone. Perhaps the young woman wasn't as tough as she'd sounded – he wished she'd say something. 'The army deeply respects his supreme sacrifice, and in recognition –'

But Elizabeth had stopped listening. 'Thank you, Major,' she said, and she hung up.

From the moment she'd heard the major's voice on the phone, she had known the very words he would say – she'd heard them quoted verbatim by Prudence. *Daniel was killed on 21 October . . . His death was an unfortunate accident . . . He will be buried at Maralinga . . .* But this time the awful finality of the words had hit with a brutal force, tearing into her like bullets, driving home the inescapable truth.

She sank into a chair, clutching the armrests as if she were drowning, her chest heaving. She seemed unable to breathe properly. Danny's dead, her mind was saying over and over, Danny's dead, Danny's dead. And then it was no longer her mind that was saying it. She could hear herself keening the words as she rocked back and forth, tears flowing freely down her cheeks. 'Danny's dead, Danny's dead, Danny's dead.'

Had Prudence Gardiner been witness to Elizabeth's robust display of grief, she might have felt envious. There were times when she longed to give voice to her pain, but pride and stoicism prevailed in the Gardiner household. Prudence was even careful to disguise the evidence of those privately shed tears she gave way to during the night. She did so for Kenneth's sake, convinced that beneath her husband's show of strength lay a fragile man.

This morning was no exception.

'It's from the prime minister,' Kenneth said as she joined him at the table. Having collected the mail, he'd called out to her as soon as he'd seen the envelope. 'Listen to this.'

She sat.

'*Dear Sir,*' Kenneth read, '*Please allow me to extend my personal condolences. Your son, Captain Daniel Gardiner . . .*'

He looked up from the letter. '*Captain* Daniel Gardiner,' he said. They had been informed that in recognition of his ultimate sacrifice, Daniel was to be posthumously promoted. 'Did you get that, Prudence? *Captain* Daniel Gardiner.'

She nodded; yes, she'd got that. He continued.

'*Your son, Captain Daniel Gardiner, an officer and a gentleman who has made the ultimate sacrifice for his Queen and country, is owed the respect and gratitude of the nation. My thoughts are with you and your family in your hour of loss. Sir Anthony Eden. Prime Minister.*'

'And look at that, just look at that.' Kenneth pointed to the bottom of the page. 'Signed by the man himself. That's not a stamp, that's a personal signature that is.'

'Very impressive,' Prudence agreed.

'It certainly is, very impressive indeed.'

She left him sitting at the table with the prime minister's letter, knowing that he'd study it until he could quote every word.

At the door to the kitchen, she paused to look back. He hadn't noticed she'd gone. She'd wondered whether she should tell him she'd rung Elizabeth that morning, but she hadn't bothered. It would mean nothing to him. Ken lived in a world of his own. A world where his son's death had a meaning, she thought with a touch of bitterness. His son was a hero who had died for his country, and now Ken had a letter from the prime minister to prove it.

Prudence disappeared into the kitchen to brew a pot of tea. She vehemently disagreed with both Ken and the prime minister. She considered her son's death a meaningless waste of a fine young life, but she kept such thoughts to herself. She dared not shatter her husband's illusions.

The following morning, Elizabeth, too, received a letter, but it was not from the prime minister. Exhausted after a sleepless night of weeping, she'd thought she was drained of tears, but as she sat at the kitchen table staring down at the envelope with its all too familiar handwriting, she felt the threat of a fresh onslaught. Fingers trembling, she opened the letter.

> *Dearest Elizabeth,*
> *Please forgive me for any worry I might cause you in writing as I do, but I have some grave concerns and no-one with whom to share them . . .*

The postal services had proved most efficient. Daniel's letter had arrived exactly eight days after he'd popped it in the bright red mailbox at the Ceduna post office.

Reginald Dempster was just settling down to tackle the salad lunch his secretary had delivered to his office. A rather stout man in his early forties, with a genial face and reading glasses perched in perpetual readiness on the top of his head, Reginald very much enjoyed fine food and wine. As a rule, he lunched at his club in Fleet Street, several blocks from *The Guardian*, but for the past month, having decided to lose weight, he'd instructed his secretary to bring him a salad two days a week. He gazed down at the plate with distaste, thinking of the roast pork and crackling the club served from its carvery. He detested salad, and the diet wasn't working anyway, he hadn't lost a pound.

There was a tap on the glass door of his office and he looked up, astounded to see Elizabeth Hoffmann. He jumped to his feet.

'Good God, girl, what are you doing in here?' he said as he opened the door and ushered her to one of the two guest chairs opposite his desk.

She'd rung him earlier that morning with the news. 'Danny's been killed,' she'd said bluntly. 'Will you tell Lionel I won't be in today? In fact, you'd better tell them all. I won't be in for some time.'

Reginald was most concerned to see her now. 'Go home, Elizabeth, you need to rest.' She looked terrible, he thought, she obviously hadn't slept. 'You shouldn't have come into work.'

'I haven't,' she said. 'I'm not here to work. I want you to do me a favour.'

'Of course.' Behind the fatigue in her eyes, Reginald recognised the light of battle. The look was familiar to him – they'd worked together a great deal – but this time there was something manic in her intensity. 'Anything you say. What are you after?' He circled his desk and sat, swooping his reading glasses onto his nose and grabbing a pencil.

'A man called Harry Lampton, a fettler by trade, is the chief suspect in a murder case in South Australia. He shot his wife's lover.'

Reginald started scribbling the details in his notebook.

'The victim was a man by the name of Petraeus Mitchell,

known as Pete, and he was serving in a government-appointed position as Aboriginal liaison officer at Maralinga.'

Reginald's eyes darted up from his notepad. Elizabeth's fiancé, Daniel, had been stationed at Maralinga. He peered at her over the rims of his reading glasses.

'Yes,' she said, recognising the query, and Reg did indeed have a right to make one, she thought. 'Danny and Pete Mitchell shared barracks accommodation. They were friends. I want to find out what happened.'

'To Danny or to Pete Mitchell?' Reginald was just a little confused.

'Both. But let's start with Harry Lampton. Can you make enquiries?'

'Of course I can, and of course I shall. But you're being very enigmatic, Elizabeth. Do you want to tell me what this is about?'

'I'm not altogether sure myself,' she said, which was the truth, but Reg was owed an explanation and she was quite prepared to give one. 'I received a letter from Danny this morning . . .'

'Oh, dear.' Reginald pushed the reading glasses back to their customary position, his face a picture of concern. 'Oh, dear,' he said, 'how very upsetting for you.'

'Danny wasn't convinced that Harry Lampton was the guilty party,' Elizabeth continued briskly; sympathy was the last thing she needed. 'He thought there might have been some form of conspiracy. Pete Mitchell had told him of highly confidential happenings at Maralinga, and Danny was suspicious when Pete was killed shortly afterwards. He wrote in his letter to me that he was going to make enquiries. Then, three days after he posted that letter, Danny himself was killed. Accidentally, and in a nuclear detonation I might add, which means his body can't be returned to England.'

A lengthy pause followed, during which Reginald looked at her as if she were mad. Finally, he found his voice.

'Do you know what you're *saying*, Elizabeth?' Perhaps she was demented in her grief, he was thinking. 'Do you know the *magnitude* of your implications? Do you have any *idea*?'

'Yes, of course I do, Reg, don't treat me like an idiot. I'm saying the army may have murdered Danny.'

'Oh my God, girl.' He glanced about his office, startled, as if the very walls themselves might betray what they'd heard. 'That's sheer madness.'

'Yes, it may well be,' she agreed, 'but I won't give up until I find out.' She stood. 'Of course, if you don't wish to help me I'll quite understand.'

'Of course I want to help you.' Reginald rose to his feet. 'But what do you expect of me?' He lowered his voice and once again glanced guiltily at the walls. 'I can hardly ring my military contacts at Maralinga and ask them if they're killing off their own chaps, can I?' Then, realising what he'd said and to whom, he hastily apologised. 'I'm so sorry,' he stammered, 'I didn't mean to offend . . .'

Elizabeth actually managed the faintest of smiles. Reg told the worst jokes in the world, but he was unwittingly funny at times, and always when he least intended to be. 'Let's just start with Harry Lampton,' she said.

'Harry Lampton it is.' He walked her to the door. 'Now go home, Elizabeth. I'll ring you, I promise. Given the time difference, I probably won't have anything for you until tomorrow, so go home and get some sleep.'

'Thanks, Reg. I appreciate your help.'

He opened the door for her, but she hesitated in leaving. 'I didn't mean to put you on the spot just now. I shouldn't have said what I did; I should have kept my thoughts to myself.'

Elizabeth realised she'd been most unfair. Indeed, what did she expect of him? His career could well be ruined if he alienated his valuable contacts. 'I'm sorry,' she said, 'it was really thoughtless of me. I don't expect you to become embroiled in this business. I won't compromise you in any way, I promise.'

She kissed him on the cheek, and Reginald melted, as he always did. His had been a hopeless case of unrequited love from the outset, a situation which he totally accepted, knowing that Elizabeth saw him as a father figure.

'But just between you and me,' she added, 'I meant what I said. I don't intend to give up until I find out the truth.'

'Yes, I know.' That was the worry, Reginald thought. 'Now go home, you need sleep. Go home and go to bed, there's a good girl.'

Elizabeth went home, but she didn't go to bed. She read the letter again. She read it over and over, despite the fact that she already knew it by heart.

Reginald, as always, was true to his word. He rang her exactly twenty-four hours later. Once again, the innocuous salad lunch sat on his desk, but this time he was not distracted by the thought of roast pork and crackling. Far more disturbing matters were on his mind.

'I have some news for you.'

'Yes?' Elizabeth felt herself tense.

'Harry Lampton was apprehended in Kalgoorlie four days ago. He's been flown to Adelaide where he'll stand trial for the murder of Pete Mitchell, and, according to my source, it's a cut-and-dried case. Lampton's wife has turned evidence against him – she witnessed the shooting – and I believe other witnesses amongst the fettlers have also come forward.'

So Pete Mitchell's death had been the coincidence Danny had hoped for, Elizabeth thought. She was relieved to hear it.

307

'Thank you, Reg,' she said. 'Danny would have liked to have known that. I'm very grateful to you.'

'Yes, well, there you are then.' Reginald's voice was just a little over-hearty. 'Nothing suspicious at all, the fettler did it, a crime of passion. Explains everything I'd say, wouldn't you?'

'It explains Pete Mitchell's death, yes,' Elizabeth agreed. 'It doesn't explain Danny's.'

'Yes, it does, Elizabeth.' Reginald dropped the heartiness. Her reaction was just as he'd feared it might be. 'It explains the fact that there was no conspiracy afoot at Maralinga. Pete Mitchell was killed by a jealous husband, and Danny's death was an accident – a terrible, shocking accident certainly, but an accident nonetheless.'

'I don't believe that, Reg.'

'You must, my dear, it's the truth.'

'But you haven't read the letter –'

'I don't need to.' Reginald's voice was firm and authoritative. 'I have had direct confirmation from an impeccable source high in the military chain of command at Maralinga. Daniel's death was accidental, I can promise you.'

'No, it wasn't. No, I don't believe that at all. And you won't either when you read the letter. I'll bring it in and show you. Honestly, Reg –'

'Don't pursue this.'

'What?' Elizabeth was taken aback.

'Don't follow this path. Leave the matter alone.'

'You know something,' she said. 'What is it? What have you found out?'

'I have found out no more than the truth, Elizabeth. And the truth is, Daniel's death was an accident! You must stop torturing yourself and accept that! I insist that you do so!'

There was silence on the end of the line. Reginald regretted having had to speak with such force, particularly under the circumstances, but he was thankful that he appeared to have finally convinced her. 'This is a very difficult time for you, my dear,' he said gently. 'You have my deepest sympathy, you know that.'

'Yes, I do. Thank you.'

'Now you will try and rest, won't you?'

'Yes. I'll try.'

'Good. That's good. Ring me if you need anything, and I'll see you when you're ready to return to work.'

He hung up, took one look at his plate of salad and headed off to his club for lunch, deeply relieved that the episode was over. When he returned an hour and a half later, however, he found her waiting in his office.

'I hope you don't mind,' she said, 'but I couldn't wait outside in the newsroom. Too many people wanting to offer their condolences and I'm not up to that yet.' She took the letter from the top pocket of her blazer.

'Elizabeth –'

'Read that.' She unfolded it and placed it on his desk. 'Read that and then tell me you still believe Danny's death was an accident.'

Reginald heaved a sigh and sat, taking his reading glasses from his top pocket where they'd lived throughout lunch. He hated this. He dreaded the prospect of having to tell her the truth.

After reading the letter with great care, he positioned his glasses on his head and leaned back, surveying her thoughtfully.

'You see?' Elizabeth's challenge was triumphant. 'It changes everything, doesn't it?'

He was silent. To his mind the letter changed nothing at all. If anything, it confirmed the truth. But how was he to tell her?

Sensing he was troubled, Elizabeth was quick to reassure him. 'Oh, don't worry, Reg, I don't expect you to do anything with the letter. That part's up to me. I just wanted you to read it so that –'

'What do you intend to do?'

'I don't know really.' She hadn't thought that far ahead. 'Take it to some top military authority here in London, I suppose. I was hoping you might tell me who I should –'

'It wouldn't accomplish anything, Elizabeth.' There was no alternative, he realised. She had to be told.

'You *did* find out something, didn't you?' She searched his face for a clue; there was something he wasn't telling her. 'Come on, Reg. What is it the army's keeping a secret?'

'You won't give up until you find out, will you?'

'Nope. You know I won't.'

'Indeed I do. In which case, you'd best hear it from me.' Reginald wished with all his heart that he didn't have to say the words. 'Daniel took his own life, Elizabeth.'

She stared at him, dumbfounded.

'I'm sorry, I'm so sorry, I didn't want to have to tell you. The army is keeping the truth quiet, for the family's sake, and naturally that means for your sake too.' The army was probably keeping the truth quiet in order to avoid any focus upon Maralinga, Reginald thought with a touch of cynicism, and also because such incidents were not good publicity for the armed forces in general. This would certainly not be the first suicide the military had covered up 'for the sake of the family', but Elizabeth did not need to know that.

'It's most regrettable you had to find out, my dear.'

'Why on earth should the army think he'd killed himself?' Elizabeth was more amazed than upset.

'Apparently he was very much affected by the death of his

310

friend.' Reginald tentatively offered the answer to a question he wished he hadn't been asked. He'd heard from his military contact at Maralinga that Daniel Gardiner had been so distressed by Pete Mitchell's gruesome murder he'd become quite unbalanced. 'According to the report, Gardiner was a deeply disturbed young man,' his contact had said. 'Went to pieces after his best friend was murdered and half-eaten by dogs, very grisly affair. Anyway, he was determined to do a good job on himself. Poor chap drove out to the forward area in the dead of night and parked right where he knew both he and the vehicle would be incinerated. Shocking business all round. We're keeping mum about it. Reg – for the sake of the family, you understand – so not a word, there's a good chap.'

'I was told that, following Pete Mitchell's murder, he became deeply disturbed,' Reginald said, praying that Elizabeth would not ask for more detail.

Far from seeking more detail, however, Elizabeth was outraged. She picked up the letter and waved it in his face. 'But you've read this, for God's sake,' she said. 'This isn't the letter of a man on the verge of suicide.'

Reginald begged to differ. 'It is the letter of a troubled man, Elizabeth,' he said with care.

'Troubled, yes, but hardly about to kill himself.'

Elizabeth riffled through the letter and, pointing out a line, she thrust the pages at him. 'Look at that, just look at that: . . . *even as I write this, I am starting to feel self-consciously melodramatic. . .* That's what he says.' She was becoming agitated. 'How sane is that, I ask you? It's certainly not the comment of a man bordering on suicide.'

'No. It's more the comment of a man covering his turmoil in order not to worry his fiancée.'

Reginald found the fact that Daniel had written such a letter at all highly suspect. To him, it displayed the classic signs of a troubled young soldier, lonely, far from home and with no-one to turn to. Having served as a foreign war correspondent in many regions of conflict, Reginald Dempster had often seen such young soldiers fall into a state of despair. The only difference on this occasion was the fact that there had been no actual battle.

Elizabeth came to a sudden halt. She'd been about to rant and rage. How could Reg possibly give credence to such a ridiculous notion, she'd thought. Now she realised that Reg gave far more than credence to the notion; he implicitly believed it to be the truth.

'You really do think Danny killed himself, don't you?'

'I'm afraid I do, Elizabeth, yes. I'm sorry.'

'I see.' She stood. 'I won't accept it, you know.'

Reginald also stood. 'That is your prerogative, of course.'

'I'll fight it. I'll demand the army conducts an investigation.'

'You won't get anywhere, my dear. The report is confirmed. The army will take no action. They won't even listen to you.'

'Then I'll elicit the help of Daniel's parents. The army will have to listen to them.'

'They will probably pretend to, yes, but it still won't lead anywhere. Even if the parents support your enquiries, the report will remain the same, and you'll cause the family untold grief. You must say nothing.'

'So what do you suggest I do?'

'I suggest you acknowledge the truth. Daniel took his own life.'

'No. No, he didn't.' She carefully folded the letter and replaced it in her blazer pocket. 'But I can promise you, I'll find out who did.'

Elizabeth sailed from his office, and Reginald watched

through the glass doors as, head held high, she weaved her way amongst the desks of the crowded newsroom, ignoring the sympathetic looks coming from every direction. A woman with a mission, he thought; a mission that might well undermine his career. She would not divulge his name as her informant, he knew, but word would undoubtedly get back that it was him. He'd never be trusted again.

He watched as, with a nod to the reporter who had opened the door for her, she disappeared from the newsroom. Despite the personal threat she posed, Reginald had to admire her. Elizabeth Hoffmann was on a crusade, and that too was her prerogative.

As it eventuated, Elizabeth did not undermine Reginald Dempster's career, but not through any conscious decision on her part to avoid doing so. Grateful though she was for his help and his friendship, Reginald's career did not once enter her mind as she sat through the interminable memorial service pondering her course of action. Reginald's words of advice, however, did. And it was his advice that ultimately swung the balance.

'My son served his country honourably.' Kenneth Gardiner was addressing the congregation from the pulpit. 'And he died in that service. Be it in peacetime or be it in war, no man can do more than lay down his life for his fellow countrymen . . .'

Elizabeth found the man offensive. His pomposity angered her. How could he honestly believe that the waste of his son's life was heroic? She wondered how he'd react if he knew the army had written Daniel's death off as a suicide. She wanted to stand up and scream it out at him. *The army doesn't think your son's a hero, you stupid man! The army thinks your son killed himself!* She resisted the urge.

Beside her in the pew sat young Billy. He was in uniform, twenty years old and fresh out of Sandhurst, a lieutenant just as his brother had been. He was looking up at the pulpit and trying to stem his tears, but Elizabeth knew that, although he lacked his father's pomposity, he was no less deluded. In Billy's eyes, his brother had died a noble death.

And seated beside Billy, there was Prudence. Straight-backed, dry-eyed Prudence, who didn't believe her son's death was heroic at all and who bitterly resented his meaningless loss. Elizabeth had seen it in her eyes just the previous night when, over the family dinner table, Prudence had allowed the veil to lift – only slightly, and only for one brief moment, but it had been enough.

Elizabeth had arrived in Crewe the day before the service, bent on eliciting the family's support in approaching the army with a request that Daniel's death be investigated. She had no intention of bringing up the matter until after the memorial service, and had thought long and hard about how she might make her approach. She would show them the letter first, she'd decided. Hopefully the letter would convince them, as it had her, that Daniel's death had not been accidental and that he'd met with foul play. There was only one problem, however. She could no longer be sure of the letter's impact.

In the week since her meeting with Reg, Elizabeth had tried to be objective about Daniel's letter. She had originally con-sidered it hard evidence – indeed, the principal weapon in her fight to be heard – but Reg Dempster had interpreted its meaning quite differently, and she was now aware that others would too. Although her personal opinion remained unchanged, in studying the letter with the investigative eye of a journalist, she recognised its ambiguity. Pete Mitchell's murder having proved the simple crime of passion it had been purported to be,

Daniel's obsession with the case could be seen as unbalanced, even paranoid.

Elizabeth could only hope that upon reading their son's letter, the Gardiners' initial reaction would be the same as her own. In any event, she had decided it was the preferable approach, rather than telling them outright the army was covering up their son's death as a suicide, which was her own very firm belief. Imparting that particular piece of information would be the next step, and one she did not at all relish.

They'd been four at the dinner table the night of her arrival, Billy having been granted a week's leave on compassionate grounds. Elizabeth had not met young Billy before, but, like Daniel, he'd been posted to Aldershot fresh out of Sandhurst and that had made for easy conversation. While Prudence served up the steak and kidney pudding and Kenneth fetched a bottle of beer, Elizabeth and Billy talked about the Hippodrome and the military parades in Princes Gardens, and even the teashop near the post office in Victoria Road.

'The best cheesecake in town,' Billy said, his boyishness reminding Elizabeth achingly of Daniel. 'And about ten different sorts,' he added. 'It's impossible to choose.'

'Yes, that's the only trouble,' she agreed. 'Danny and I could never make up our minds.'

There was the slightest pause and Elizabeth wondered if she'd said the wrong thing. Prudence seemed to hesitate over the final serve of pudding, and Kenneth remained poised by his chair with the bottle of beer.

'We used to go there a lot,' Elizabeth said with an apologetic query to Billy. Were they not supposed to mention Daniel?

'Yes, I know you did.' Billy gave her a reassuring smile. 'Dan told me. He said it's where you finally agreed to marry him.'

'That's right,' she said, 'over cheesecake.'

The awkward moment had passed and the two of them embarked upon reminiscences about Daniel. Prudence doled out the plates of pudding and passed around the bowl of Brussels sprouts; she appeared to have relaxed and was enjoying hearing her son spoken of with such love. Kenneth, however, did not seem to share his wife's enjoyment.

'Beer, Billy?' The tone held a slight reprimand.

'Thanks, Dad.'

'Elizabeth?'

'No, thank you, Mr Gardiner, I'm happy with the water.'

'Right.'

Kenneth poured the beers, and Billy, his father's reprimand having fallen on deaf ears, embarked upon another childhood story.

'I remember the time when Dan got caught raiding old Mr McClusky's apple orchard. He was twelve and I was ten, and I was scared to death of the McClusky place because the old boy had three Rottweilers. Anyway, the dogs bailed Dan up in a tree and he had to stay there for over an hour until old Mr McClusky arrived with the local copper.'

'Why did he risk the Rottweilers in the first place?' Elizabeth asked.

'It was a dare.'

'Who dared him?'

'I did. I was always getting Dan into trouble. He'd accept every dare I came up with. I remember one time he rode his bike –'

'There's something I'd like to show you, Elizabeth,' Kenneth interrupted, and this time Billy registered a reprimand, although he couldn't think what it was he'd done wrong.

Kenneth Gardiner left the dining room briefly and silence reigned until he reappeared twenty seconds later with a piece of paper.

'Have a read of that,' he said proudly, and he handed her the letter from the prime minister.

Elizabeth did as she was told, and when she looked up from the letter, she wondered what on earth she was expected to say. There was no need to say anything, she discovered.

'Impressive, isn't it?' Kenneth pointed to the signature. 'Personally signed too.'

'Yes. Yes, I can see that.'

Taking the letter from her, Kenneth carefully placed it on the sideboard, away from the food and out of harm's way. It was his intention to have it framed. Then he returned to the table, but he did not sit.

'I propose a toast,' he said, picking up his glass, 'to Captain Daniel Gardiner, who made the ultimate sacrifice for his Queen and country.'

Billy leapt to his feet. He realised now why he'd incurred his father's displeasure, and he felt guilty. On the eve of Dan's memorial service he should have shown more respect.

Prudence and Elizabeth stood also, and all four raised their glasses.

'To Dan,' Kenneth said.

'To Dan,' they repeated.

The bittersweet pleasure Prudence had been enjoying had suddenly been snatched from her, and there was resentment in her eyes as she looked at her husband over the rim of her water tumbler. The young ones had been celebrating her son's life with their reminiscences, and now Ken had ushered the empty nothingness of sacrificial death back into the room. She understood his reasons, but she nonetheless cursed him.

That was when Elizabeth had seen the veil lifted.

Kenneth took over the conversation. 'It's a tremendous blow to us all that Dan's body can't be brought home to England,' he said to Elizabeth. 'Prudence finds it most upsetting, as I'm sure you must too.'

'Yes, I do.' Elizabeth glanced at Prudence, but the veil was once more in place, she was giving away nothing. 'In fact,' Elizabeth added, emboldened by her feeling for the woman, 'I wondered whether there might be some grounds of action you could take to have that decision rescinded.'

Kenneth felt a flicker of annoyance, but it quickly disappeared – women, after all, did not understand such things. 'I don't think so, my dear.' His answer was patronising. 'Dan died as a result of a nuclear detonation, after all.'

He and Billy exchanged a knowing look. If there *had* been any remains they would have been highly irradiated, but one didn't say such things in the presence of women.

'I'm aware of the effects of a nuclear detonation, Mr Gardiner, but I still think an appeal to the authorities –'

Kenneth stopped it right there. 'The army knows best, Elizabeth.' He didn't even need to look at his son to know that Billy was nodding agreement. 'The army knows best.'

Again Elizabeth glanced at Prudence, but Prudence's eyes did not meet hers. 'The apple crumble needs to come out of the oven so that it can cool,' she said to no-one in particular, and she left for the kitchen.

Now, Elizabeth sat in the church, fighting back the urge to scream at Kenneth Gardiner as he concluded a eulogy that must surely, she thought, be as sickening to his wife as it was to her.

'My son knew the ultimate price he risked in the choice of his career,' Kenneth said, 'and he was prepared to pay that price. Dan loved the army with a passion, and he loved serving his country.' Kenneth Gardiner fought manfully to control the sudden tremor in his voice. 'I'm proud, very proud, to have had such a son.'

He returned to sit beside his wife, his eyes staring fixedly ahead, and Elizabeth was surprised to see Prudence quietly take her husband's hand in both of hers. The simple gesture said everything. Without his belief in the purpose of his son's death, Kenneth Gardiner would be a broken man. And, furthermore, his wife knew it.

The service continued. There were other eulogies, and, although none matched Kenneth's in pomposity, they were delivered by military men for the most part and therefore along similar lines. Elizabeth no longer heard the words. Her mind was elsewhere. Only minutes earlier she'd wanted to burst Kenneth's bubble of complacency. She wasn't so sure now. She wasn't sure she could do it to any of them – Prudence or Kenneth or Billy. All was neatly in place. Daniel had died accidentally in the service of his country. The family needed no further complications. In showing them the letter and trying to elicit their help, she would be exposing them to the Maralinga military's suicide report, and to what purpose? Reg had told her categorically that the army would take no investigative action, and there was not a man in the country who knew the workings of the British army better than Reg Dempster. What was it he'd said? *Even if the parents support your enquiries, the report will remain the same, and you'll cause the family untold grief. You must say nothing.*

Then and there, with Reg's words echoing in her mind, Elizabeth made her decision. She would follow his advice and say nothing to the family. She would not, however, heed his further advice and acknowledge Daniel's death as a suicide. She remained totally committed. She would find out the truth, but she would do so alone. And she would need to be alone, she realised. If the army would not listen to the family, then they were hardly likely to listen to her. She would need to infiltrate the system.

Her thoughts were interrupted by the glorious tenor voice of Mario Lanza. It flooded the church with its richness, reverberating amongst the old stone walls and arches.

One of Danny's favourites: 'You'll Never Walk Alone'. How very appropriate, she thought as the tears sprang involuntarily to her eyes. For the first time throughout the service, Elizabeth felt herself moved, and, beside her, moist-eyed himself, Billy smiled, pleased that his personal selection had hit the mark.

'I picked that one,' he whispered. 'Dan loved Mario Lanza.'

'I know.' She fumbled for her handkerchief.

'So does Mum,' he said with a meaningful nod.

Elizabeth looked at Prudence standing beside him. She had finally allowed herself to let go and the tears cascaded unchecked down her face.

'A good choice, Billy,' Elizabeth said.

A good decision too, she thought. She would leave the family to grieve in their own way, but she would discover the truth, if only for herself. And discover it she would, no matter how long it took.

# BOOK III

# Chapter Fifteen

Following the completion of the Buffalo series of tests, the township of Maralinga underwent a radical change. Virtually overnight, a residency of several thousand was reduced to just several hundred, and life took on a more relaxed style. Army disciplines, although still observed, became less rigorous, and duties, which now revolved principally around maintenance, less arduous. Leave was granted more readily, and those lucky enough to score a week of freedom headed straight to Adelaide and the pubs, clubs and bars of Hindley Street, leaving their mates to loll enviously in the pool. As November crept into December, the heat continued to spiral.

The 'accident' was no longer discussed and hadn't been for some time – more out of respect for Daniel Gardiner and his family than in observance of any official oath of silence, although the army had indeed sworn the men to secrecy. At the start, despite orders, there'd been a great deal of talk amongst the men; in fact, they'd talked of little else, the news of Daniel's suicide had so shocked them. Those who knew him were aware he'd been severely affected by Pete Mitchell's death – it had been common knowledge, they told the military police – but they'd not realised the degree of his devastation. Gideon Melbray, however, the last person to see Daniel alive, and on the very night of his death, had found him in a terrible state. 'I've never seen him so drunk,' Gideon told the MPs.

When Daniel hadn't turned up in the officers' mess that evening, Gideon had called around to his barracks to confirm the train delivery arrangements for the following morning. 'Dan wasn't a big drinker as a rule,' he said, 'but he was crying drunk that night. He went on and on about Pete's death – seemed obsessed that there'd been some sort of plot to kill the fellow. He wasn't making any sense at all, so I told him to go to bed and sleep it off. Never thought it'd come to this.'

Harold Dartleigh, although extremely surprised that young Dan should take such desperate action, was in agreement that the lad had appeared somewhat obsessed with the murder of Pete Mitchell.

'Don't know why he had suspicions,' Harold said. 'I'd have thought it was a pretty simple case myself. Chappie has an affair and ends up getting shot by the woman's husband – classic crime of passion, what? But young Gardiner was desperate for positive proof that the fettler had actually done it. I even agreed to have enquiries made for him – just to help put his mind at rest, poor boy.'

Harold hadn't felt it necessary to tell the MPs that not only had he had enquiries made, thereby encroaching upon their territory, but that he had achieved a breakthrough just the previous day, the very afternoon of Daniel's death. In response to a healthy bribe, Tommo the ganger had admitted to seeing everything from start to finish, and with the promise of further money had agreed to come forward as a witness – but only when Harry Lampton was safely in custody. 'You won't get a word out of me while Harry's on the loose,' Tommo had said, 'and you won't get a peep out of the others neither.'

Harold Dartleigh, having honoured his promise, was disappointed that young Dan would never know the trouble he'd gone to on his behalf. But then, he had to admit, his motives hadn't been altogether altruistic. There'd been a degree of personal satisfaction in discovering that the army hadn't killed off Pete Mitchell as Dan had clearly suspected. That was one bonus to come out of this whole sad business, Harold supposed. It was a relief to know that the army hadn't been keeping him in the dark.

These days, Daniel's death was rarely mentioned, and on the odd occasion when it was, it was always referred to as 'the accident'. The men used the term not only because they'd been ordered to do so for the sake of the family – a kindness with which they entirely concurred – but because they wished to believe it *had* been an accident. They needed absolution. Even those who'd barely known Daniel felt guilty to have been so unaware of a fellow soldier's distress.

Although life on the range was more relaxed and the troops less hard-worked, the scientists of Maralinga were as busy as ever. Nuclear experimentation did not cease at the end of a major test series and, following the general exodus, the hardcore team of boffins remaining in residence devoted themselves wholeheartedly to the minor test trials.

The minor trials had been allocated the colourfully eccentric codenames of Kittens and Rats and Tims, with further tests planned for introduction that were to be known as Vixens. Their purposes were quite specific. Kittens examined various forms of triggers or initiators required to start the nuclear chain reaction in an atomic weapon; Rats and Tims measured the compressibility of materials used in the make-up of a nuclear device; and the planned Vixens were intended to investigate the effects of accidents that might befall a nuclear weapon, such as a fire in a weapons store or the crash of a plane carrying a nuclear device.

While less spectacular than the major detonations, the minor tests offered limitless opportunities, for they could be conducted in far greater secrecy with less accountability and therefore more freedom.

'It seems you blokes are out of a job these days,' Nick said at his meeting in Adelaide with the principal directors of AWTSC. 'I hope we're not being kept in the dark.'

The remark was made in a jocular fashion so as not to offend, and Leslie Martin, the Australian, smiled obligingly, but Ernest Titterton and Alan Butement were not amused. In their opinion the colonel was out of line. It was his job to liaise not comment.

'I hardly think so, Colonel Stratton,' Titterton replied dryly. 'Approval from members of the safety committee is not necessary for these individual firings. The British are simply required to issue a safety statement to the Australian authorities in advance of the test. This is the agreement that has been reached between the two governments.'

'Yes, I'm aware of that, Professor Titterton –'

'I have here a report from the British trials superintendent, which covers the recent firings.' Titterton placed a manila folder on the table in front of him. 'You may wish to take it to Canberra for your meeting with the minister next week, although I'm sure it won't be necessary. And should a press conference be called, you'll find any general statement you want in there. Everything is very straightforward.'

'Thank you.' Shoving the folder under his arm, Nick stood abruptly. 'Good afternoon, gentlemen,' he said, and left the meeting.

Ernest Titterton was plainly telling him that his job was that of a public relations officer only, and that he should stick to it. Nick could find no grounds for disagreement – in principle the man was right – but it was not pleasant to be reminded of the fact and with such deliberation. Yet again, Titterton had managed to annoy him intensely.

Dr Melvyn Crowley and his team of pathologists and bio-chemists had never been busier. Dead animals were being discovered on a daily basis – rabbits, kangaroos, emus and even wild camels – all forming an excellent source of random survey. Then there was the additional workload the team had inherited due to Dr Hedley Marston's 'present state of health'.

Melvyn Crowley was aware that Hedley Marston's 'present state of health' was a euphemism and that Sir William Penney wanted the independently contracted CSIRO scientist out of the picture.

Marston was deemed a security risk, and his work was to be reallocated to those in-house scientists who could be trusted. The decision meant that a number of biochemists upon whom Melvyn had relied for assistance were now required to travel far afield collecting and analysing data that had previously been Dr Marston's realm. In the true spirit of scientific research, how-ever, Melvyn had raised no objections. He preferred to work on his own as much as possible anyway, with assistants who would unquestioningly accept his leadership, rather than colleagues who might challenge it. A man as dedicated as he was needed full autonomy.

Melvyn considered himself a pioneer and Maralinga his per-sonal gateway to untold discoveries in the effects of nuclear warfare. Here, away from the limited perspective of society, actual experimentation on humans could bypass in one fell swoop years of tedious laboratory work. A number of tests involving troops' exposure to minor levels of radiation had already been carried out, but Melvyn longed to take bolder strides. He'd secretly hoped for a mishap during one of the detonations – nothing shockingly catastrophic, but something that might have resulted in a death or two. To Melvyn Crowley, the most valuable research commodity possible was a human cadaver that had been exposed to the full effects of radiation. The loss, just six weeks previously, of such material had been his greatest disappointment.

'It's such a terrible waste, Harold,' he'd said at the time. 'There must be something you can do, surely?'

He had contacted Harold Dartleigh urgently the moment the body had been delivered to the DC/RB area. Dog-tag identification had proved it to be that of a young lieutenant by the name of Daniel Gardiner.

'I'm told they're not going to release the corpse to me,' Melvyn had complained to Harold as they sat in the offices adjoining his laboratory. Young Trafford, his laboratory assistant, was filing documents in the corner cabinet. 'Apparently I'm not going to be allowed to examine it –'

'By *examine*, I presume you mean *dissect*,' Harold had interrupted, and Melvyn had seen his lip curl in distaste.

'Well, I am a pathologist, after all,' Melvyn replied, his voice displaying as much disdain as he dared allow show to a peer of the realm.

'For God's sake, man, Lieutenant Gardiner was your fellow countryman.'

'The corpse can provide us with invaluable information,' Melvyn had continued, ignoring the interruption. 'The army should recognise the need for –'

'The army recognises the need for its officers to be buried with full military honours and, whenever possible, *intact*!'

'We are men of science, Lord Dartleigh.' Melvyn had made the bold leap from mild disdain to blatant superiority. 'We do not over-sentimentalise. Our purpose is the advancement of knowledge that will serve mankind.'

He realised too late that his tone had been a mistake – the sort of mistake that under normal circumstances might have left him with cause for regret. But Harold Dartleigh was off to England the following day and, luckily for Melvyn, couldn't be bothered pursuing the issue. Instead, he'd simply refused to help.

'I'm afraid I can't intervene for you on this score,' he'd said. 'The army will not release the body to you and, in the interests of self-preservation, I strongly suggest you do not attempt to pursue the matter. Men do not take kindly to those who wish to dissect their friends, whether for the advancement of science or not.'

Harold had stood and turned to young Trafford, giving him a jovial beam. 'You, young man, had best take great care. God forbid where you might end up should you meet with an accident.'

Melvyn had walked Harold to the door, fuming inside but unable to risk offending the man further.

'Keep up the good work, Melvyn,' Harold had said. 'I shall expect to receive ongoing reports from you in London. In the meantime, you have my full support in all areas, as you well know. Bar the dismemberment of our fellow countrymen,' he'd added with a laugh.

'Yes, of course, Harold, of course,' Melvyn had responded deferentially, but once Harold had left he had reverted to his usual autocratic manner.

'So that's it,' he'd said to Trafford in annoyance. 'If Dartleigh can't get the body released to us, then no-one can. The army's certainly not going to sign it over. Just as well they turn a blind eye to the blacks is all I can say.'

Now, six weeks later, Melvyn remained determined in his quest to acquire a human cadaver. His latest target was the child of the woman who had suffered irradiation after the One Tree test. He had expected her to give birth prematurely to a still-born and had been most eager to gain possession of the corpse. Surprisingly, the woman had carried her child full-term, but had given birth in secret, after which there had been no evidence of the baby. The search for where she might have buried it had so far proved fruitless. But Melvyn had not given up hope.

'Did you make further enquiries at Yalata?'

He asked the same question every few days upon arrival at his office and the answer was inevitably the same. 'Yes,' Trevor would say, 'still no sign of the body.'

Today, however, the answer was different.

'Yes, I called them again,' Trevor said without looking up from the reports he was working on. 'They've made a thorough search of the entire area surrounding the mission and there's nothing to be found.'

'Tell them to keep looking,' Melvyn barked.

'They say there's no point. She could have buried the baby anywhere.'

'You mean they're giving up?'

'Yes.'

'Damn. Another wasted opportunity.' Melvyn stormed off to the laboratory, frustrated and ill-tempered.

Trafford Whitely continued working on his reports, display-ing no remorse at all about lying to Dr Crowley. He'd made no further enquiries at Yalata; even if he had, he knew they would have led nowhere. The woman's stillborn child would never be found.

Trafford was thankful for the fact. He'd found the notion of stealing the corpse repellent. The autopsies conducted on the Aboriginal family who'd died after camping in the Marcoo crater had been a different matter altogether. Indeed, the dismemberment and thorough examination of the corpses had, to his mind, been essential. But to secretly dig up a baby's body, and without the family's permission, seemed both a macabre act and a terrible invasion.

Melvyn Crowley's further orders to those of his team working out in the field had appeared equally ruthless to Trafford.

'It's quite possible there are other dead blacks out there,' Melvyn had said. 'Keep your eyes open, and if you find a corpse, report directly to me so we can bring it in secretly. No-one else needs to know, and we'll be doing the army a favour anyway.'

Trafford Whitely was a young man of ambition. He had applied for a position on the medical research team strictly in order to advance his career, in the full knowledge that the desert living conditions would be uncomfortable and the work demanding. Both factors he had happily taken in his stride, but there were times when he had difficulty coming to terms with his superior's code of ethics.

Christmas at Maralinga was a bizarre affair for the British troops, who yearned for snow and the crisp, cold bite of their customary Yuletide. But it was rendered even more bizarre by the attitude of the Australians.

'There you go. Just look at that,' said Col Rogerson.

It was Col and his mate, Bud Barton, who started it. They chopped down a mallee tree, planted it in a halved 44-gallon drum and decked it with tinsel and baubles they'd bought in Adelaide during their recent leave. They carted the tree into the centre of the dry, dusty beer garden a week before Christmas, just to get everyone in the mood – a gnarled, stunted thing, ridiculous in its finery. And, strangest of all, they'd draped cottonwool over its branches.

A group of twenty or so men gathered around to admire the tree – or, rather, the Australians admired it, giving Col and Bud a healthy round of applause. The others seemed more bemused than anything.

'What's the cottonwool for?' Paddy O'Hare asked the question on everyone's lips.

'It's snow, you stupid Irish git.'

'Oh, it's snow, yes, I see.' Paddy's good-natured face lit up in a grin. 'Well, that's grand, that is.' He was touched that Col and Bud should go to such trouble to give them all a taste of home. 'That's very thoughtful of you, Col, and very inventive what's more.'

'No, it's not. We do it every year.' Col looked about at the other Australians present, most of whom were nodding. 'Just about everyone I know does it.'

'Just about everyone you know does what?' young Toby asked in his thick Manchester accent.

'Puts cottonwool on their Christmas tree,' Col said with a touch of impatience. Was Toby an idiot?

Bud intervened. 'They're usually fir trees though. You got to admit, Col, it looks more like the real thing with a conifer.' He studied the Christmas tree critically. 'I reckon maybe we should get rid of the cottonwool. It does look a bit funny.'

Bud's response didn't clarify things at all for the British, nor for the several Canadians present. Be it a conifer or a eucalypt, why the Australians would wish to put pretend snow on their Christmas trees was an unfathomable mystery.

Further mysteries along similar lines were revealed over the next several days. A mail delivery arrived and with it hundreds of Christmas cards. The men made decorations of them, stringing them all together and hanging them around the canteen and the beer garden, and the British were amazed to discover that the cards the Australians had received were the same as their own. Snowmen, mistletoe and red-breasted robins abounded.

Then, to top it all off, there was the announcement of Christmas lunch, which was broadcast several days in advance so that the men had something to look forward to. The army chefs were going to bake whole turkeys and legs of ham, the men were told, and there would be plum pudding with brandy sauce to follow.

The Australians were excited.

'It'll be just like home,' Bud said.

'Do you reckon they'll put threepences in the pudding?' Col asked, and the others laughed.

The British couldn't work up the same enthusiasm. They were amazed that anyone could relish the prospect of a baked dinner served at midday in temperatures well exceeding 100 degrees Fahrenheit. But the truth had finally registered with them: despite all impracticality, and even in the hottest regions of the continent, Australians embraced a northern hemisphere Christmas. Presumably this was because their country had been colonised by the British, it was decided, but the custom seemed nonetheless bizarre. There were whole generations of born-and-bred Australians celebrating traditional white Christmases without ever having seen snow. The British troops found the practice quite astounding.

Any misgivings they had, however, proved happily unwarranted. Christmas Day was a resounding success. Regardless of the heat, the men managed in true festive spirit to stuff themselves with turkey and ham and plum pudding, after which they took their bloated bellies to the pool where they spent the afternoon lolling in and out of the water.

The real partying took place in the evening when the grand piano was wheeled out of the VIP mess and into the beer garden. The piano had been the preserve of the top-ranking officers and visiting dignitaries during the major tests, and on many a hot, balmy night it had been wheeled outside to provide entertainment under the stars as the VIPs lounged about with their ports and cigars. Tonight, however, it sat incongruously in the other ranks' beer garden, beside the mallee Christmas tree, which now sported fairy lights.

A number of the men could play the piano, some better than others, although no-one really cared so long as the tune was something they could sing along to. Then they discovered a favourite: Benjamin Roscoe was not only a talented pianist, he knew every number that had been in the top ten hit parade over the past five years.

'Shake, Rattle and Roll' . . .

'Rock Around the Clock' . . .

'Sixteen Tons' . . .

The orders came in fast and furious, and Benjamin segued with ease from one song to the next. As an added bonus, he also knew every lyric of every number and was happy to give voice, which was of great assistance in the singalong.

'The Yellow Rose of Texas' . . .

'Mambo Italiano' . . .

'Heartbreak Hotel' . . .

By now, no-one but Benjamin was allowed near the keyboard. The piano was his domain as he belted out every hit number the men could come up with.

'That's Amore' . . .

'Mockin' Bird Hill' . . .

'Hound Dog' . . .

The beer flowed, the night grew raucous and men grew

hoarse as the songs of the fifties reverberated across the desert plains.

The new year of 1957 was ushered in with little change at Maralinga. The scientists' work remained stimulating as the minor tests continued, but the troops became bored and restless. For many, football and cricket were no longer the pleasurable distraction they had been, losing their appeal in the relentless heat of midsummer, and the principal escape became the pool. Everyone craved the excitement that had attended the major test trials, but the Antler series was not planned until September, and there would be many long months before preparations commenced.

February rolled by, and some of those whose posting had come to an end were happy to escape the tedium. Fresh young replacement troops arrived, eager and as full of excitement as they themselves had been just twelve months previously. Col Rogerson and Bud Barton were two of those leaving. They'd signed on together, their year was up, and they were heading back to Perth.

The night before they left, their mates toasted them in the beer garden.

'Wish it was me,' Big John said, 'you lucky, lucky bastards.' Big John was a renowned whinger, but in this instance Col and Bud tended to agree with him. Even Col, who'd found Maralinga so thrilling, had had enough by now. He'd been a bit off-colour for the past six weeks – chronic diarrhoea was wearing him down.

'It's this place that makes you crook,' he'd said to Bud, when Bud too had copped a case of the runs. 'Just as well we're getting out, mate. Jeez, I can't wait to throw myself into the surf at North Cott.'

Col was actually looking forward to far more than the beaches of Cottesloe. As soon as he got back to Perth, he was going to propose to Marge. He announced the fact to his mates in the beer garden.

'Next time you blokes see me, I'll be a married man,' he said, which called for more rounds of drinks and more toasts.

Col got very drunk that night, but he made no complaints on the flight back to Perth the following day. His hangover was proof of an evening well spent.

It was early March, and Nick Stratton was surprised by his commanding officer's orders.

'Why would they want a press conference?' he queried. 'There's nothing to report.'

'Apparently *The Advertiser* has requested an update,' the very British brigadier said with the air of one who considered such a suggestion presumptuous. 'Being the state newspaper they no doubt want to be seen as responsible, but we can't grant them exclusivity. I want you to inform the interstate press and arrange a general conference for next week.'

'Will we need a safety committee member present?'

'No, they're not interested, and they say it's not necessary – you can just issue a general statement. But in case someone's got wind of the minor test trials, they think you should bring up the subject and offer some minimal information – to be on the safe side.'

'Right you are.'

The following week, armed with the latest report from the British trials superintendent, which had been supplied by AWTSC, Nick headed for Adelaide.

There was quite a gathering in the AGIO conference room. He hadn't expected so many. Perhaps there's a shortage of murders and scandal, he thought with a touch of cynicism. But then he reminded himself that this was the first general press conference since the last of the major test trials and so a healthy turnout was hardly surprising.

He walked to the podium at the far end of the room, greeted the assembled press members, then got straight down to business.

'There's not a great deal to report, so I'll cover the basics, and then if there are any questions you wish to raise feel free to fire away.'

He placed the folder on the podium. Having familiarised himself fully with its contents, he had no need to refer to it for information, but he found it a handy prop.

'I have here the latest report from the British trials superintendent that was forwarded to the Atomic Weapons Tests Safety Committee,' he said. 'As I'm sure most of you are aware, the next major test trials are not due to take place for another six months – the Antler series, planned for September. In the meantime, however, many of you may *not* be aware that experimentation does continue at Maralinga. Minor tests are currently being conducted on various components, and these tests are being carried out with the full approval of both the British and Australian governments. All safety precautions are observed, and there is close liaison at all times between the British trials superintendent and the Australian range commander. Comprehensive reports such as these,' he tapped the folder in reference, 'are regularly received by the safety committee whose members are quite satisfied with all aspects of management in regard to the tests.

'And that's about it, gentlemen.' Nick smiled and gave a mock shrug of apology. 'I'm afraid things are rather dull at Maralinga.' There was a smatter of appreciative laughter. 'Does anyone have any questions?'

'Yes. I have a question. I have several, in fact.'

It was a woman's voice, loud and clear, and it came from the rear of the conference room. Heads swivelled to look in her direction.

'Can you tell us more about these tests, Colonel?'

The woman was sitting in the very back row, virtually invisible to all but those beside her. Nick peered for a clearer view. He was nonplussed. Like most of the men present, he'd been unaware there was a female in the room.

The woman stood and identified herself. 'Elizabeth Hoffmann from *The Advertiser*,' she announced. 'You say "minor tests" are being conducted on '"various components". Can you be a little more specific, Colonel Stratton? Exactly what are the tests and what are the components?'

Elizabeth's invisibility had been carefully orchestrated. As the only woman present she had not wished to call attention to herself and thereby lose the element of surprise, so she'd slipped into the conference room shortly before the arrival of the colonel when most of the reporters had already gathered. She was wearing a navy skirt and matching lightweight cotton jacket, the jacket masculine in cut and not unlike those worn by some of the men present. Flanking her in the back row were Jonathon 'Macca' Mackay, her colleague from *The Advertiser*, and her newfound friend, Bob Swindon of *The Sydney Morning Herald*. They'd been only too eager to liven up the normally staid proceedings. Indeed, they couldn't wait to see what effect might be wrought by the feisty Elizabeth Hoffmann.

They weren't disappointed. Jaws gaped at the sight of the handsome young woman in the masculine jacket, her dark hair cropped short. She was tall, statuesque even, and she stood boldly challenging the colonel in a way most men wouldn't dare.

Having asked her question, Elizabeth did not sit. She'd

gained the element of surprise she was after – Stratton had been caught out, she could see it in his face. She remained standing as she awaited his answer. Confrontation was now of far greater value than surprise.

'I am not at liberty to disclose military secrets . . . *Miss* Hoffmann, is it?'

'Yes, that's right.'

'Well I'm sure you'll appreciate, Miss Hoffmann, as your colleagues have done,' Nick glanced around the room in friendly recognition of the many familiar faces, 'that for security purposes, both the British and Australian governments, along with all branches of the military, will not, and indeed cannot, divulge the specifics of any test trials conducted at Maralinga.'

Although his tone was not insulting, it was the standard reply Nick reserved for those upstart journalists who were ignorant of the rules. Elizabeth Hoffmann was obviously new to the game and needed to be made aware of the parameters that had been set. He wondered why *The Advertiser* had assigned a woman to report on the Maralinga project in the first place.

'I appreciate the security factor, Colonel,' Elizabeth replied, her voice projecting clearly from the back of the room. She was aware she was being patronised. 'These are perilous times and we need to tread warily. But I believe the public has a right to be informed about the basic purpose of these trials. They do, after all, involve the use of nuclear materials, isn't this so?'

'Naturally they do, Miss Hoffmann, which is hardly surprising, as I'm sure all those present will appreciate.' This time his tone was distinctly condescending. 'The Maralinga range was established for the sole purpose of nuclear experimentation.'

Nick was not in the least unnerved by the woman's questions, which were plainly based upon ignorance rather than fact, but he was very much distracted by her looks and her manner.

She was incredibly striking and, even from a distance, her eyes met his with a challenge that was fearless. He couldn't help but find the mixture of womanliness and strength extraordinarily attractive, and the fact irritated him intensely. Elizabeth Hoffmann was clearly aware of the effect she had on men and was using it to gain an advantage. He was annoyed with her for doing so, and annoyed with himself for responding.

'As I've said on many an occasion,' once again he included the general assembly, 'I am not at liberty to discuss the specifics of the trials, but the safety aspect is most certainly within my domain. In fact, as liaison officer, it is my principal duty to report on the precautionary measures set in place. So, Miss Hoffmann, in answer to your question . . .' There was no patronising edge to his voice now as he addressed her personally. He spoke patiently and evenly, aware that he must not allow his irritation to show. He would not permit her that advantage. 'Although certain nuclear materials are used under strictly controlled conditions, I can assure you that the minor trials do not involve nuclear explosions.'

Having answered her question, to his mind quite satisfactorily, Nick expected her to sit down, but she didn't, so he turned his attention to the rest of the gathering. 'Responsibility for safety on the range during these tests lies with the British trials superintendent . . .'

As he embarked upon a general description of the trials' safety protocol, he was disconcerted by the fact that Elizabeth Hoffmann remained standing. She was being deliberately provocative, he decided, and he determined to ignore her. But he found that he couldn't. Her attention was focused upon him with such intensity that his eyes were continuously drawn to her. It was as if she were demanding he address her, and her alone.

'Following each test,' he continued, 'in accordance with the

340

agreement between the British and Australian governments, the superintendent gives a detailed report to the Australian range commander who is responsible for range security between each of the trials . . .'

Elizabeth was most certainly studying Nick Stratton with the deepest intensity. She was deciding what sort of man he was and which tack she should take. His earlier condescension had aroused in her a desire to retaliate; she'd wanted to shock him out of his complacency by informing him that she actually knew quite a bit about the tests. 'I believe the concentration is on trigger mechanisms and the compressibility of materials in a nuclear device, Colonel,' she'd been tempted to say. She was glad now that she hadn't taken such an openly hostile stance as it wouldn't have served her purpose. Nick Stratton was a military man who did things by the book, and if he saw her as a troublemaker he would simply have her barred from any involvement with the project. Bob Swindon had told her as much.

'He's a tough cookie, Elizabeth,' Bob had said. 'Not a bad bloke, but you wouldn't want to cross him. And be warned, he doesn't like smart-arses. Believe me, I should know,' he'd added with a grin. 'I've been a bit over-smart myself from time to time, which is why I'm not invited to the firings.'

Bob Swindon was right, Elizabeth decided: she would need to tread with care.

As she studied Nick Stratton, she found him an impressive man – a man of integrity by all appearances. She wondered whether he was fully informed of all aspects of the tests, or whether, like most according to her source, he was being kept in the dark. Either way, she must get to know the colonel. He was, without doubt, her most valuable link to Maralinga.

'So, as you can see, and as I mentioned earlier,' Nick said in conclusion, 'there is full cooperation and liaison between all parties, both British and Australian, which is in accordance with the requirements laid out by the safety committee.'

He decided to wrap up the conference on a humorous note, particularly as Elizabeth Hoffman remained so conspicuously on her feet.

'I think that's just about it,' he said with a smile. 'Unless, of course, you have any further questions, Miss Hoffmann?'

Everyone laughed and Elizabeth, recognising that the comment had been made in good humour and happy to be the butt of the joke, returned the smile. Then she boldly pushed the joke one step further.

'I do have a final question, Colonel, yes.'

There was more laughter, particularly from those seated alongside her. Bob Swindon and Macca Mackay were taking great delight in the proceedings.

'I believe these minor trials are known as Rats and Kittens and Tims,' Elizabeth said in all apparent innocence. 'Is there any particular purpose in the choice of such quaint terms?'

She asked the question as if she'd heard the code-names openly bandied about, but in playing such a game she prayed she wasn't going too far. Was she intriguing the colonel as she hoped? Or was she being, as Bob Swindon had put it, a smart-arse?

How could she know that, Nick thought. How could she possibly know that? No general announcement had been made; these were still early days.

As their eyes met across the room, he tried to suss her out. This was no innocent query. What game was she playing?

'There's no particular purpose whatsoever in the choice, Miss Hoffmann.' His reply was casual and amiable. There was nothing to be gained by either denial or cross-examination, both of which would overdramatise the situation; and there was no harm in the codenames being known anyway. Besides, he thought wryly, what alternative did he have now that she'd put the word out.

'The army is famous for its colourful use of code language and we wouldn't want to disappoint, would we? After all, we've had One Tree, Marcoo, Kite and Breakaway in the Buffalo series. A few Kittens and Tims and Rats seem rather tame in comparison, wouldn't you say?'

'I would, Colonel.' Elizabeth smiled broadly, pleased that she'd intrigued rather than offended. What a clever answer, she thought. 'I most certainly would. Thank you very much,' she said. And she sat.

There was something congratulatory in her smile, Nick thought. She'd been one up on him and now she was congratulating him on his rejoinder, as if she'd found him a worthy competitor. He didn't know whether to be flattered or angered.

'Thank *you*, Miss Hoffmann,' he said as he picked up his folder. 'And thank you, gentlemen. That concludes our meeting.'

As he walked back to his hotel in North Terrace, Nick's mind was on Elizabeth Hoffmann. He would have liked to ask her how she'd learnt of the code-names, but he hadn't wished to do so in the company of her colleagues. He wondered whether he should ring her at *The Advertiser* and ask if she'd like to meet for a chat. He was still wondering an hour later as he packed his few overnight belongings and prepared to leave for the airport. He was returning to Maralinga that afternoon.

He glanced at the phone. There was still an hour or so to go, he thought, still time for a coffee or a drink. But he knew he wouldn't ring her. Who was he kidding? He wasn't really interested in the source of her information; he was interested in the woman herself. Best to practise common sense and steer clear, he told himself, as he latched his Gladstone bag. Elizabeth Hoffmann was not the sort with whom one had a casual fling, and a casual fling was all he wanted from any woman.

He'd have a drink in the lounge before he left, he decided. The hotel room was a little claustrophobic.

The phone rang. He answered it.

'There's a lady here to see you, Colonel,' the receptionist said. 'A Miss Elizabeth Hoffmann.'

'I'll be right down.'

He picked up his bag and headed straight for the foyer.

'Hello, Colonel.' Elizabeth offered her hand and, as they shook, he noted that her grip was as firm and confident as a man's, which didn't altogether surprise him. 'I hope you'll forgive the intrusion,' she said.

'It's not an intrusion at all, Miss Hoffmann. I have an hour to fill in before I leave for the airport. Will you join me for a drink?'

'Thank you. I'd love to.'

When they'd settled themselves in the lounge, he ordered a Scotch for himself and she opted for a pot of tea. It was a bit early in the day for her, she said, she still had an afternoon's work to get through.

'This is something of a surprise, I must say.' Nick leaned back in his armchair with a querying look.

'Yes, I suppose it is,' she agreed, then went on to explain. 'My colleagues told me you always stay at the Grosvenor, so I thought I'd pop around on the chance that you might have a spare moment.'

'And I do. But for what purpose, Miss Hoffmann?'

'Perhaps to accept an apology?' Elizabeth didn't feel remotely apologetic, but she'd been unable to come up with a better pretext for a visit. 'I sensed your annoyance at the conference and I'm sorry. I didn't intend to be quite so confrontational.'

Nick laughed at her blatant transparency. 'Of course you did, that's an out-and-out lie. You were as provocative as you could be right from the start.'

Oh no, I wasn't, Elizabeth thought, I could have been a lot more provocative, believe me. But she smiled, grateful for his good-natured response. 'Surely that's a journalist's job, Colonel,' she said.

'Then why the apology? Aren't you being a little contradictory, Miss Hoffmann?'

'Yes, I suppose I am,' she admitted, 'but I wanted to make sure that I hadn't offended you. You see, I've only been at *The Advertiser* six weeks. I'm still new to the job and I wouldn't want to –'

'You wouldn't want to cruel your pitch, is that it?'

'Yes, that's precisely it.'

'I admire your honesty.'

Nick did. In fact, he found her honesty remarkable. She appeared to have not a shred of the artifice he'd encountered in most women. Particularly in most good-looking women. Perhaps he'd misjudged her.

The tea and Scotch arrived, and when the waitress had gone, he offered his own admission, which seemed only fair.

'I have to admit I *was* a bit annoyed,' he said. 'I took offence at the way you used your femininity to gain an advantage.'

'In what way?' Elizabeth wasn't sure what he was getting at.

'Well, the way you remained standing for a start. You were the centre of attention, all eyes were upon you. It was extremely provocative.'

'I thought we agreed that's a journalist's job.'

'Not when a journalist looks like you, Miss Hoffmann. In remaining the central focus you provoked nothing but distraction. A rather cheap trick to gain the upper hand, I thought.'

Elizabeth tried to keep a rein on her anger, although the colonel's attitude, so typical of that which she had encountered from men on a regular basis, infuriated her.

'I can't help my appearance, Colonel,' she said stiffly. 'I do my best to counter it, I can assure you.' She gestured at her blazer. 'I do not dress seductively, I wear virtually no make-up and if I cut my hair any shorter I'd be bald. Quite frankly, if men can't handle my appearance then that is their problem, not mine.'

'Oh dear.' Nick realised that perhaps he could have expressed himself a little more delicately. 'My turn to apologise. I'm sorry, I didn't mean to sound so blunt.'

Elizabeth gave in with relatively good grace, although she recognised the man was making no apology for *what* he'd said, only the way he'd said it. But then, of course, he knew no better.

'That's perfectly all right, Colonel,' she said. 'I did my training in Aldershot – I'm quite accustomed to the attitude of military men towards women in the workforce.' Even as she made the dig, she smiled to let him know that he was off the hook. 'I can assure you though, I am an excellent journalist.'

'I don't doubt that for one moment, Miss Hoffmann. So tell me, how did you know about the code-names?'

'Ah, that would be giving away far too much,' she said. 'A good journalist never reveals her source of information.'

She sipped her tea thoughtfully, wondering how much she should tell him in order to keep him intrigued without annoying him. The balance was delicate. Which way should she play things?

Nick didn't push the matter any further, construing her

silence to mean that the subject was closed. He didn't care about her source of information anyway; he was far more interested in the woman than the journalist. No doubt some soldier on leave had been showing off while he tried to get her into bed, he thought. And who could blame any man for trying to bed Elizabeth Hoffmann?

'Aldershot, eh,' he said with interest, keen to make up for his previous blunder, 'the home of the British army. Well, you'd certainly earn your stripes as a cadet reporter there, I would think. So how and when did you become a feature journalist?'

As she regaled him with the story of her interview for *The Guardian*, Nick found himself riveted. The thought of her storming an editor's office dressed as a man and smoking a cigar was not only amusing, it was somehow erotic. And yet she seemed unaware of the fact. There was an extraordinary sexuality about Elizabeth Hoffmann, but she didn't appear to know it.

They chatted for a further half-hour, or rather Elizabeth did. Nick mainly asked the questions. Then he looked regretfully at his watch.

'Time I was heading off, I'm afraid.'

As they stood, he added casually, 'I'm back next week, Wednesday, just overnight. I don't suppose you'd be interested in dinner?'

He wasn't scheduled to be in Adelaide the following week at all, but he could make an overnight stopover on his way to Canberra, he decided. By now, all good intentions to practise common sense and steer clear of the woman had deserted him. Elizabeth Hoffmann was a positive magnet. What red-blooded male could resist such a challenge?

'Thank you, yes. I'd enjoy that.'

'Excellent. How about I ring you at *The Advertiser* when I get in, probably mid-afternoon, and we'll make our plans then?'

'That suits me perfectly, Colonel.' Elizabeth offered her hand.

'Do you mind if I call you Elizabeth?' he asked as they shook. 'Outside the office, of course,' he added.

'I don't mind at all, Nick.' She smiled. 'Thanks for the tea. Have a safe trip. I'll see you on Wednesday.' And with a quick wave, she was gone.

Elizabeth knew Nick Stratton found her attractive. She hadn't at first. At first she'd thought that he found her a genuine cause for irritation. But when he'd displayed no interest in discovering her source of information, she'd suddenly realised why. She'd stopped wondering how to keep him intrigued, recognising that there was no need. He was already intrigued, but not by her mind. She had to admit that she was just a little disappointed in the colonel. He was an impressive man, and she would have preferred his interest to have been of a more cerebral kind. Under normal circumstances she would have offered him no encouragement, but these were not normal circumstances. If she was to discover what was going on at Maralinga, she would need Nick Stratton's assistance, and if devious means were called for, then so be it.

For the first time in her life, Elizabeth found herself practising feminine wiles she hadn't even known she possessed.

# Chapter Sixteen

In the four months since Daniel's death, Elizabeth's resolve had not faltered nor her conviction diminished. She remained steadfast in her determination to discover the truth, and more than ever she refused to believe Daniel had died either by his own hand or accidentally.

As the rawness of her grief had settled, she'd studied his letter for further clues. She did not view it as the product of a disturbed mind as others might; others, after all, did not know Danny. Certainly, he'd been in a degree of turmoil at the time of his writing, she could see that, but the cause of his turmoil was abundantly clear to her. Danny was an idealist with a love of the army and a strong sense of justice. When he'd suspected his friend's death might have been a possible military assassination, his faith in the army had been severely shaken, but a man like Danny did not suicide for such a reason. Nor did he suicide through grief suffered over the loss of a comrade. A man like Danny would be driven to discover the truth. Was this why he had met his death?

She went over and over the contents of the letter, no longer needing to refer to it directly, every word now etched in her mind. *Had* the army threatened men with court martial if they spoke of what they'd seen? Pete Mitchell had evidently said so, but Danny himself hadn't appeared too sure. And if men *had* been threatened with court martial, then what was it they had seen?

There were many questions to be asked, but of one thing Elizabeth was certain. To find out what had happened to Daniel, she would need to find out what was going on at Maralinga. And she couldn't do that from the other side of the world.

After handing in her notice at *The Guardian*, she'd applied for a position with *The Advertiser* in Adelaide and had been instantly accepted, the editor only too keen to gain the services of E. J. Hoffmann, whose feature articles in the London *Guardian* were so impressive.

Elizabeth's adventure had begun the moment she'd set foot on board the SS *Strathaird* at Tilbury Docks one icy-cold morning in early December. As the ship had pulled out into the harbour, she'd leant over the railing waving to her parents who'd come to farewell her, and she'd kept on waving even when they'd been swallowed up by the crowd, just in case they could still see her. Alfred and Marjorie Hoffmann, too, had continued to wave from the dockside, even though they'd no longer been able to distinguish their daughter amongst the hundreds jostling for position on the *Strathaird*'s decks.

Unlike the majority of her fellow passengers who were migrating under the post-war assisted-passage scheme offered by the Australian government, Elizabeth was paying her own way. She was therefore free to return to her homeland at will, without serving out the scheme's obligatory two years, but this did not make her chosen course of action any the less momentous. The instant she had decided to leave England, Elizabeth had known that her life was about to undergo a radical change.

She'd enjoyed the sea voyage. Even the Bay of Biscay's rough crossing and the overwhelming heat of Port Said had not deterred her, and the Suez Canal she'd found quite remarkable. Unfortunately, disembarkation had been forbidden due to the Suez Crisis, but boat traders had provided an exciting distraction, swarming the ship and selling every conceivable trinket to its captive passengers.

Most of all though, Elizabeth had loved the vast expanse of ocean and the sense of wonder she'd felt as she'd stood on the deserted deck watching the sunrise over the endless blue water, or when, late at night, she'd looked up at the stars in a sky she'd never seen, a sky clearer and more vivid than the one she'd known in the northern hemisphere with different constellations. At such times, she'd thought of her life and of Daniel's and of the plans that they'd made, and her thoughts had not saddened her but rather strengthened her purpose. She'd felt he was with her in her search for the truth.

The first Australian port of call had been Fremantle, and then it had been on to Adelaide, where the *Strathaird* had arrived just six weeks after departing Tilbury Docks. The next leg of Elizabeth's adventure had begun.

She'd bought a map of the city and booked into the Ambassadors Hotel in King William Street. It had proved comfortable enough, but of far greater importance was the fact it was just around the corner from the offices of *The Advertiser* in Pirie Street.

As on previous occasions, while not actually lying, Elizabeth had failed to stipulate her gender in her application, and when she'd fronted up to *The Advertiser* to make herself known, she'd anticipated some hostility, if not from the editor then certainly from her fellow journalists.

'Good God, you're a woman.' The editor, a jovial man called

351

Peter Johnston, known to all as P. J., had been astounded. 'Why didn't you tell me?'

'You didn't ask, and I didn't think it necessary given the fact that you'd accepted my credentials,' she'd replied pleasantly. Then she'd waited for the outburst. To her amazement, there'd been none.

'Fair enough,' P. J. had said. 'Welcome to *The Advertiser*, Miss Hoffmann. Good to have you aboard.'

Elizabeth had been surprised. Not only had the editor welcomed her, but her male colleagues, apparently respecting her work and her track record, had displayed none of the professional antipathy towards a woman in the ranks that she'd experienced during her early days at *The Guardian*. There'd been the customary problem of unwanted attentions from some, but she'd managed to discourage without offending, and the men had quickly come to regard her as one of their own.

She had sensed immediate animosity, however, from the one female amongst the senior hierarchy. Edna Sparks, a New Zealander in her forties, was the leisure and entertainments editor and held sway over a broad spectrum of the paper that dealt with the more lightweight matters, particularly those appealing to the female readership. Edna had regarded Elizabeth with baleful suspicion from the outset, and Elizabeth had had no idea why.

'Jealousy, that's all it is,' Laurie Knight, sports columnist, had said dismissively. 'Edna's got it in for all the young things, particularly the lookers. You want to watch her though, Liz, she's tough. You get on the wrong side of Edna and Sparks'll fly.' He'd given her a nudge and a wink, as if the remark was his own, but the pun had been bandied about as long as Edna had been in power, which was well over a decade.

Elizabeth had smiled dutifully. Laurie was well-intentioned

enough, but he was one of those who had to be kept at arm's length. Why were the sports columnists always the most insistent, she'd wondered; and she really wasn't too sure about being known as 'Liz'. She had yet to realise that Laurie Knight was not the only Australian with a penchant for diminutives and that it was more than likely she'd be stuck with 'Liz'. She had taken his advice with regard to Edna though, and had steered clear of the woman whenever possible.

Laurie's glib assumption, which was not uncommon amongst his fellow journalists, was actually incorrect. Edna Sparks, having fought for her position in a man's world, was certainly tough, but she felt no particular animosity towards young women, good-looking or otherwise, unless they were after her job. As a company woman, married to her work and to the newspaper, Edna had no time for petty jealousy; it was not productive. Her initial antipathy towards Elizabeth had sprung from neither the threat of competition nor the envy of youth. She had been concerned that Elizabeth Hoffmann might prove a disruptive element. The other young female employees performed secretarial and typing pool duties and knew their position in the hierarchy. They would not dare encourage the men's attentions during working hours – any flirtatious behaviour was conducted outside the office. Elizabeth, however, had been brought into the workplace as an equal, and Edna could see that the men found her a distraction. It would be only a matter of time, she'd thought, before Elizabeth Hoffmann would cause trouble.

But as Edna had watched and waited for the warning signs, she'd quickly recognised that Elizabeth Hoffmann had no intention of causing trouble. Indeed, she'd found herself admiring the skilful manner in which the young woman fielded the men's attentions, neither offending nor encouraging, but relating to her colleagues in a friendly fashion and on a strictly professional basis at all times. Within barely a fortnight, Edna Sparks had reversed her opinion completely. Elizabeth Hoffmann was a credit to women in the workforce, she'd decided. There should be far more like her.

'Would you care to join me for lunch? I know an excellent little cafe that serves the very best sandwiches.'

The invitation was offered in the quaint New Zealand accent that no-one dared ridicule because it belonged to Edna, and Elizabeth looked up from her work flabbergasted. Only days previously the woman had been scowling at her across the news-room floor, hatchet-faced and eagle-eyed, as if waiting for a moment to swoop in for the kill.

'Love to,' she said.

They sat opposite each other in one of the booths of the little corner milk bar where the chicken and salad sandwiches were indeed delicious, and while Edna made no apologies, she admitted to her original suspicions.

'I was so sure you'd cause trouble,' she said, 'but I must say I admire the way you handle the men.'

'In what way?'

'No nonsense. You keep them in line. I like that.'

Elizabeth laughed. 'You make me sound like a sergeant major,' she said, but she knew exactly what Edna meant. 'Actually the men make it easy for me, Edna. Even those on the make seem to respect my work. It wasn't at all the case when I started out at *The Guardian* I can tell you. I've no idea why,' she said thoughtfully as she stirred her tea, 'but for some strange reason, Australia seems more tolerant towards female journalists than Britain is.'

'Oh, we Antipodeans aren't quite as backward as you British tend to think.'

The tone of voice wasn't as harsh as the comment itself, but in glancing up from her cup Elizabeth nonetheless expected to encounter criticism. She encountered nothing of the kind. As Edna smiled, her hawk-like face softened and her eyes gleamed with an intelligence that was suddenly attractive.

'From a historical viewpoint, it's not really unexpected, you know. New Zealand led the suffrage movement, granting women the vote in 1893, and Australia followed in 1902. Britain didn't come to the party for another whole sixteen years.'

'Yes, you're right, of course. I'd forgotten that.'

'And did you know that both countries also boasted pioneer women journalists prior to the turn of the century?'

'No, I certainly didn't. How very interesting.'

'Oh yes, it is indeed.' Edna launched into a passionate account of her fellow countrywoman Stella Allan, who'd become the first female parliamentary reporter in New Zealand and Australia. 'That was in 1898,' she said. 'She was Stella Henderson then, it was before she married. She was only in her mid-twenties.'

After recounting Stella Allan's story, she moved on. 'And of course there was Louisa Lawson who pioneered *The Dawn: A Journal for Australian Women* in 1888. She employed female typesetters too, which was a further cause for controversy . . .'

It was a full twenty minutes before Edna came to a halt. 'I've carried on a bit, haven't I,' she said with no attempt at apology. 'It's a subject very close to my heart.' She looked at her watch. 'We'd better be getting back to work.'

'What a pity,' Elizabeth said, 'I could listen to you for hours.' She meant it wholeheartedly. 'And I must say I'm very thankful that the Antipodeans appear to continue one step ahead with regard to women's rights – in the world of journalism anyway. It's quite a relief.'

They split the bill between them and left.

'How are you settling into Adelaide, Elizabeth?' Edna asked as they walked back to Pirie Street. She had decided she would not adopt the diminutive as her male counterparts had done – 'Liz' did not suit the young Englishwoman at all. 'Have you found somewhere to live yet?'

'No, I'm still at the Ambassadors. I've decided to stay in a hotel until I find the right place.'

'And what do you see as the right place?'

'I'm not sure, I haven't really had time to start looking in earnest, but I'd thought of somewhere by the sea.' Elizabeth smiled self-effacingly. 'It's probably frightfully British and frightfully unrealistic, but in coming all the way to Australia one fantasises about living by the beach.'

'It's not unrealistic at all. I have a contact who handles several rental properties in Glenelg and Brighton.' Edna had contacts all over Adelaide, advertisers mostly who were keen to keep on side with her. 'I'm sure he'll have something that will suit you. Leave it to me.'

Elizabeth did, and a week later she'd moved into a large, airy flat on the first floor of a once-imposing terrace house in St Johns Row, Glenelg. The house, which had seen better days, had been converted into two holiday apartments and the balcony of Elizabeth's upstairs flat commanded splendid views of the beach.

*The building is faintly reminiscent of those seedy, once grand seaside hotels that abound in English coastal towns,* she'd written to her parents. *The beach itself bears no resemblance at all to our beaches, however – in fact, it quite puts them to shame. There are no pebbles here, just miles and miles of glorious white sand, like one sees in the postcards, and the promenade is lined with magnificent Norfolk Island pines. Every morning I walk barefoot along the beach, after which I*

356

*shower and then catch a tram into work – Glenelg is less than half an*
*hour's ride from the city. I must say, it is a wonderful way to start the*
*day . . .'*

Elizabeth had been deeply indebted to Edna Sparks.

'I can't thank you enough, Edna. Really, I –'

'Rubbish. A phone call, that's all it was.'

Edna's response may have been abrupt and dismissive, but a friendship had been forged and both the women knew it. Despite the discrepancy in their ages and their vastly different backgrounds, Elizabeth Hoffmann and Edna Sparks had a great deal in common, not least being their lack of female friends. As career women working in a male-dominated world, friendships with those of their own sex had been rare and they quickly grew to value each other a great deal.

The heat she'd encountered during her sea voyage had not altogether prepared Elizabeth for the relentlessness of a South Australian midsummer, particularly when, in mid-February, a four-day heatwave hit Adelaide. She'd found the 100-degree temperatures extremely trying.

*Thank goodness I have the flat,* she'd written to her parents. *The days in town are simply stifling, but to come home to the breeze off the water makes everything bearable. I even conquered my fear of the ocean on Saturday and, instead of paddling ankle-deep in the shallows as I normally do, I threw my whole body into the sea, along with the hundreds who swarm to Glenelg every weekend. All Australians can swim wonderfully and are fearless of the water. I felt so incredibly clumsy spluttering and floundering about that I have now determined I shall learn how to swim. It cannot be that difficult, surely . . .*

Elizabeth had embraced the dramatic change in her life with a practicality that was typical, developing a genuine enthusiasm for her new job and her new country, but she had not for one minute lost sight of her purpose. After allowing herself six weeks to settle in at *The Advertiser*, she'd decided the time was right to request she be assigned to the Maralinga project.

Peter Johnston, the editor, was a pragmatic man and had instantly recognised that reportage by an English journalist, particularly one fresh from the prestigious London *Guardian*, would not only be apt under the circumstances but bound to impress.

'You'll need to liaise closely with Macca, of course,' P. J. had said. 'He's been principally responsible for our Maralinga coverage. But I'm sure he'll be delighted to have you on his team.'

Jonathon 'Macca' Mackay, senior feature writer and regular political columnist, had been more than delighted. He'd basked in the knowledge that he'd be the envy of his colleagues.

'Working hands-on with her, eh? You lucky bastard.' Laurie Knight had been the only one to make a suggestive comment, which he'd emphasised with his customary nudge and wink.

In deference to Elizabeth, Macca had not responded in kind, but neither had he taken offence. Laurie was only voicing what a lot of the others were thinking. The men respected Elizabeth but it didn't stop them lusting after her.

Macca's own feelings towards Elizabeth were not in the least lascivious. A devoted family man in his late thirties with two young children, he had a very pretty wife whom he absolutely adored. But he admired a handsome woman as much as the next man, and the prospect of being the envy of his mates greatly amused him.

Elizabeth warmed to Jonathon Mackay from the start. A ginger-haired Australian of Scottish descent, Macca was good-natured, easy to work with and a great deal of fun. He was also extremely helpful, supplying her not only with every single report the newspaper had run on Maralinga but also a wealth of material on the earlier British nuclear testings at Monte Bello and Emu Field.

'A bit of homework for you, Liz,' he'd said as he'd piled her desk high with files from the archives department. 'Best to be historically up to date, don't you reckon?'

Elizabeth certainly did, and she'd studied every report and every article with the utmost care. Several days later she'd reported to his office, which looked out over the newsroom and her own desk, eager to move on to the next step. But things had taken a surprisingly frustrating turn.

'So where to from here, Macca?'

'How do you mean?'

'I've finished my homework. Historically I'm a full book. So who do I talk to about the current state of play?'

'You don't. You wait until *they* talk to *you*.'

Macca's response to her bewilderment was sympathetic.

'I hate to disappoint you, Liz, I know you're raring to go, but I'm afraid you'll have to wait until they call a press conference.'

'But surely there's someone who fields questions? Nothing confronting that would breach security regulations, just a general interview.'

'Nope. They don't allow individual interviews with the press. They call conferences and they issue statements and they tell us just as much as they feel we should know. They're very self-protective.'

'By *they* I presume you mean the military?'

'The military and everyone else.' Macca reeled off the list: 'The British government, the Australian government, every branch of the armed forces from both countries, and let's not forget the scientists. Maralinga's a closed shop, Liz. And it's not really surprising when you think about it. Reds under the bed . . .' He shrugged philosophically. 'The whole bloody country's terrified.'

Reds under the bed, Elizabeth thought. The fear of communism was obviously as rampant throughout Australia as it was throughout Britain – she wondered why she found the fact vaguely surprising. Probably because Australia seemed such a world away, she told herself. But it wasn't any more, was it? The fears of the Australians were more than justified with Britain's nuclear testing ground flourishing in their midst.

'Then I suppose my best bet would be to come from the unofficial direction,' she said. 'Try for an interview with a soldier on leave. Aim for a human interest story – "Life on the Range", that sort of thing.'

Macca gave a loud hoot of laughter. 'You have to be joking!'

His response was disbelieving rather than derisive. Elizabeth's suggestion seemed unrealistically feminine and very much out of character for the hard-nosed journalist he knew her to be. He didn't wish to appear mocking though, so he curbed his mirth as best he could.

'Don't you reckon "Life on the Range" might be just a little fanciful, Liz?' Then he registered the glint of something that could have been mischief in her eyes. 'Oh,' he said, 'you *were* joking.'

'Was I?' Her response was enigmatic. 'The human interest angle would at least give me somewhere to start, and a soldier on leave would expect that sort of approach from a female reporter, wouldn't you say?'

Macca's grin quickly faded. 'Right, I get it. You're not joking at all. You're sounding me out.'

Elizabeth nodded. 'So what do you think my chances are?'

'Bugger all, I'm afraid.' Macca briskly spelled out the facts. 'Soldiers on leave are not permitted to give interviews to any members of the press. Even those who appear harmlessly female,' he added with meaning. 'Soldiers are also banned from talking about Maralinga to any member of the public anywhere at any time. I've actually heard there are military spies posted around the most popular gathering places in the city to ensure men don't speak out of turn.'

'In other words,' Elizabeth said wryly, 'you're suggesting the unofficial approach is not the way to go.'

'It most definitely is not.'

'Then perhaps I'll ruffle a few official feathers instead, try a more confrontational tack.'

'Don't give it a thought. The moment they smell you mean trouble, you'll be straight out the door.'

'If that is the case, Macca, I consider it absolutely appalling, and you should too.' Elizabeth didn't care in the least if she sounded stuffy; she was becoming annoyed. 'Whatever happened to the freedom of the press?'

'There's no such thing in the middle of a Cold War.'

Macca's glib reply annoyed her further and she was about to interject, but he didn't give her a chance.

'Government security, Liz – we have to play it safe or we won't get a look-in. You'll just have to wait for the next press conference – there's nothing else you can do.' Aware of her frustration, he made an effort to mollify her. 'Why don't you write a general piece in the meantime – something with political comment that won't offend?' He thought for a second or so. 'How about "Australia's inestimable value to Britain in the face of America's nuclear non-proliferation policy"? That could be interesting, don't you think?'

Much as Elizabeth liked Macca, she found his complacency infuriating, and his attempt at mollification only succeeded in increasing her overwhelming sense of frustration. Why should she write a safe, cosy piece just to please the government? But of far greater importance, how was she to make any possible inroads into Maralinga? It was maddening to have come so far only to be told by the likes of Macca Mackay that her hands were tied and she could go no further.

Only days later, however, Elizabeth had had every reason to thank Macca Mackay. On the Friday following their frustrating exchange, Macca had unwittingly opened up the avenue of opportunity that was to prove invaluable. It started with a seemingly innocent introduction in the lounge of the Criterion Hotel in King William Street not far from *The Advertiser* office. 'The Cri', as the pub was fondly known, was a favoured watering hole for journalists, both local and those visiting from interstate.

'Liz, this is Bob Swindon of *The Sydney Morning Herald*,' Macca said. 'We don't hold that too much against him though, he's originally an Adelaide boy. Bob, this is Liz Hoffmann, ex London *Guardian*. Liz has been with *The Advertiser* six weeks.'

'Seven actually. Hello, Bob.' Elizabeth offered her hand. 'Elizabeth Hoffmann,' she said in the vague hope that for once the hint might be picked up.

It wasn't. 'G'day, Liz.' The handshake was big and hearty like the man himself. 'I've heard about you.' News having travelled far and fast as it did in the world of journalism, Bob Swindon had most certainly heard about the good-looking young journalist from *The Guardian*. 'Nice to meet you love,' he said. Christ, she must get sick of being chatted up, he thought as they shook hands.

Bob Swindon made a habit of playing an avuncular role with young women these days. He'd decided, with some regret but a great deal of common sense, that his womanising days were over. Fat and fifty was no longer a dignified image for the Lothario he'd once been; at least, that was his humorously self-deprecating way of putting it. A decade of high-blood-pressure medication having seriously affected his ability to perform in the sexual arena, the decision had, to a certain degree, been made for him.

'You and Liz have a lot in common, Bob,' Macca said.

'Is that so?' If he were twenty years younger, Bob thought, they sure as hell would have. 'In what way?'

'Liz is a renegade like you. She's the sort who likes to make waves.' Macca flashed a disarming grin at Elizabeth. 'And she's highly critical of the fact that I'm the sort who doesn't, isn't that right, Liz?'

'Well, um . . .' Elizabeth felt caught out. She'd not said so to his face, but Macca couldn't have voiced her feelings better.

Macca laughed good-naturedly. Elizabeth Hoffmann was the most readable woman he'd ever met, and he liked her for it.

'So what are you two rebels drinking? My shout. A shandy for you, I take it, Liz?'

'Thanks, Macca.'

A shandy was the closest Elizabeth had been able to come to the national penchant for beer, but the situation had been exactly the same with her colleagues in London so there'd been no need for adjustment. Personally she would have preferred a glass of claret, but no-one seemed to drink claret in pubs.

Bob opted for a beer and Macca disappeared to the bar.

The pub was always busy on a late Friday afternoon and he was gone for quite a while, during which time Elizabeth and Bob found that they did indeed have a lot in common.

'So if you're a renegade, Bob, tell me how I crack a decent story about Maralinga.' Having been offered the perfect opening, Elizabeth dived right in. 'Macca tells me I have to play it safe. What would you do?'

'I'd play it safe. Macca's right.'

'Really?' Elizabeth studied the man with suspicion. Was Bob Swindon fobbing her off because she was a woman?

'Oh, I grant you Macca's a conservative journo, you're on the money there.' In the face of her scepticism Bob felt the need to explain. 'He's a beaut bloke and a bloody good writer, but his wife and kids are his whole world. Danger doesn't attract Macca like it does you and me.' He didn't question the fact that danger attracted her – it quite plainly did. 'Macca'll take the safe path every time, he's famous for it. In this instance though, you'd be wise to follow his example.'

'And if I don't?'

'You'll find yourself on the outer. Government security demands we "renegades" are barred from the project.'

'Yes, that's what Macca told me. So are *you* barred?'

'Well, I'm not one of those journalists invited to observe the firings, which I suppose says something. But I go along to the press conferences and I toe the line like the rest; there doesn't seem much option really. Or perhaps my renegade days are over,' he added with a slightly theatrical sigh of resignation.

Elizabeth rather doubted that to be the case. 'It's blackmail then. I have to play the game if I want to observe the firings.'

'Oh, you won't get a look-in at the firings. They won't invite you to Maralinga under any circumstances.'

'But I'm a journalist who's been assigned to report on the project – why wouldn't they invite me?'

'You're a journalist who's a woman, that's why.'

As he said it, Bob Swindon realised that in the brief time they'd been conversing he'd actually lost sight of the fact that Elizabeth Hoffmann was a woman. Good God, he'd been talking to her as he would a man, he thought, how bloody depressing. Had his fading fat-and-fifty libido deserted him to such a degree he was blind?

'I see,' Elizabeth said tightly. 'So no women are permitted to enter Maralinga.' She felt a flash of annoyance at the thought that yet another avenue was closed, and an avenue that she'd considered of the utmost importance. She should have known better than to expect anything different, she supposed. The Australian press might show leniency towards women, but the army was the army the world over. 'Even a member of the press from a leading newspaper would be denied entry if she happened to be female, is this correct?'

'Absolutely.'

'Well, well, well, they do make things difficult, don't they?'

She stared across the lounge. The burgeoning crowd was jostling for seats as more people poured in from the bar and the street, but she didn't see them. She didn't see anything as her mind ticked over. There must be another way, she thought. If she couldn't get inside Maralinga itself, then she needed to get inside the mind of someone who could. Returning her attention to Bob Swindon, she abandoned all caution. Caution would not gain her an ally.

'I want to know what's going on at Maralinga, Bob,' she said. 'One renegade to another – can you help me? Do you have a contact that might be able to offer some information?'

Hit once again by the full force of her energy, Bob realised that his blindness to her gender had not been a result of his fading libido at all. Elizabeth Hoffmann possessed a power that transcended gender. Furthermore, her passion was contagious. He felt a sudden irresistible compulsion to help her.

'There is perhaps someone,' he said.

'Yes?'

Their eyes locked and Elizabeth knew she'd found her ally.

'A bloke I went to uni with, strangely enough. I haven't seen him for years but we go back a long way. We're both from

Bordertown, grew up together, families knew each other, all that. I heard he'd been doing independent field work on the tests and I phoned him from Sydney about six months ago. He agreed to an interview, possibly for old times' sake, but more probably because he knew he could trust me – I have a track record for getting myself into trouble but not those who grant me information. Anyway, he seemed more than keen on the idea. Then out of the blue the interview was cancelled and I never heard back. I believe they've been keeping him quiet.'

'Who is he?'

'His name's Marston. Hedley Marston. He's a biochemist with the CSIRO here in Adelaide. The general public doesn't know of him, but in scientific circles I believe he's quite famous. Funny really, because when we were at uni he failed mathematics and didn't score a degree.'

'Do you think he'd see me?'

'You might be the only journalist he *would* see.'

'Why do you think that?'

'You're not known to the authorities like me, and you're not the image they expect of a journalist – word wouldn't get back that he'd spoken to the press. Marston wants to go on record, I'm pretty sure of it. I'm also pretty sure he's been threatened in some way. You'd have to gain his confidence, of course, make him feel secure, but who knows, maybe he'll feel safer talking to a woman. A few feminine wiles certainly wouldn't go astray.'

'I'm not sure I have any.'

'Oh, you have.' Bob stifled a smile – she was actually serious. 'Trust me, you have.'

'If so, I don't use them,' she said a little primly.

'Yes, I've gathered that. Perhaps now's the time to start.' He looked across the lounge to where Macca was wending his way through the crowd, beer glasses held high. 'I'll give Marston a call to pave the way,' he said. 'That'll probably get you through the door, after which it'll be up to you.'

'Thank you.' Elizabeth offered her hand and once again they shook. 'I can't tell you how grateful I am.'

'Don't leave yourself too open to disappointment, love.' Bob reverted to the avuncular as he added a word of warning. 'There's no room for hot-shot reporting here. If Marston does offer up any controversial data, you won't be able to go public. There are national security regulations in place and the paper won't publish inflammatory material. No-one will.'

'I know that.'

'Good. Marston will know it too, but it's my guess, rightly or wrongly, that he wants to go on record for the future. Probably his way of saying "I told you so" when his findings are eventually allowed to be published. You'll be an ally to him then, but right now you won't get any form of exposé out of this.'

Macca arrived beside them.

'But hell, who needs an exposé,' Bob said encouragingly. 'I'm sure you'll find some way to use whatever information you discover.'

'Oh, yes.' Elizabeth agreed wholeheartedly. 'I'm quite sure I will.'

'What exposé? Is there a plot afoot here?' Macca plonked the drinks on the table.

'There most definitely is,' Bob said as he grabbed his beer. 'Renegade stuff, Macca – doesn't involve you.'

Macca sat, saluting the others with his glass.

'So what are you doing in town, Bob?' he asked when he'd taken a swig. 'There's nothing going down at Maralinga. What's the big story?'

'No big story, I'm not here on business. Or rather I am, but it's personal business.' He paused a second or so for dramatic effect. 'My three-year-old mare's racing in the Autumn Stakes at Cheltenham this weekend.'

'Really?' Macca was most surprised. Bob Swindon was well-known as a track aficionado and punter, but not as a racehorse owner. 'I'm impressed,' he said.

Bob's smile was one of pure pleasure. It had been his intention to impress. He was thrilled with his new acquisition, which was indeed his life's dream.

'She's only half my mare actually,' he admitted, 'the other half's my brother's. We bought her last year and raced her as a two year old. She's trained and stabled here, costs a mint, and she'll be my retirement plan or my ruination, I'm not sure which.'

'What's she called?' Elizabeth asked.

'Speed of Light.'

'Ambitious,' Macca said with the wry lift of an eyebrow.

Bob took the comment as a compliment. 'Yeah, good name, isn't it? The punters'll like it. She did very well as a filly, so we're hoping. This is her first adult meet and she's up against a strong field. I doubt she'll place. She may even come in last, but that doesn't bother me, it's bloody good training.' He downed a healthy swig of his beer. 'Horses are like people in my opinion. Mix a horse with the wrong company and it'll pick up bad habits. Pit it against the best and it might well come out a winner.

'Which reminds me, Liz,' he said, taking a business card from his pocket and jotting a phone number on the back, 'give me a ring – I'm here for a week. I'll be most interested to hear how you go.' He handed her the card. 'Hope you score a win.'

Elizabeth smiled. 'I'll score a win, Bob. And I bet I'll score it without the use of feminine wiles.'

He took her literally – Bob could never resist a bet. 'Want to make it five quid?'

'If you like.'

'You're on,' he said.

They raised their glasses and clinked while Macca looked from one to the other in complete mystification.

What an exciting woman she was, Bob thought. God, how he wished he was twenty years younger. But then if he was twenty years younger, he'd be so busy trying to get her into bed he probably wouldn't appreciate what she had to offer beyond the obvious. Jesus, life was an irony.

Elizabeth did score a win. And she did so without resorting to the use of feminine wiles. Not as a matter of principle – she'd heeded Bob's advice and had been quite prepared to do so – but there'd been no need. Honesty and intelligence had quickly registered with Hedley Marston.

Bob Swindon's reasoning had been closer to the truth than he'd realised. Hedley Marston had recently completed a detailed manuscript of his findings for publication in a scientific journal, but he had been continuously thwarted by the cabal of scientists, bureaucrats and politicians bent on keeping the details of the nuclear tests and their aftermath a well-hidden secret. With little or no idea of when his manuscript would finally see the light of day, or indeed how much of the truth would appear in its ultimate publication, Marston was keen to go on record with someone he could trust. And for some strange reason he chose to trust Elizabeth Hoffmann.

'I have received a telephone call as you're no doubt aware, Miss Hoffmann. You come highly recommended by Bob Swindon. I take it you know him well?'

Marston was studying her astutely through horn-rimmed spectacles, a pleasant-faced man in his fifties with a bald domed head and rather large ears. Elizabeth realised she was being tested.

'I don't know Bob at all well,' she said. 'We met only several days ago, last Friday to be precise.'

'Then why would he sing your praises?'

'I believe he senses that I can be trusted. I work the same way Bob does, Mr Marston. My word is my bond and I never betray a confidence.'

His lips curved into a smile. It was a delicate mouth, she noticed, well-shaped, almost feminine amongst features that were otherwise ordinary.

'Bob always was a good judge of character,' he said. 'Sit down, Miss Hoffmann.'

'Thank you, sir.' She'd obviously passed the test.

Hedley Marston talked for an hour, not only about his findings but about the way in which he'd been silenced, and Elizabeth found much of what he had to say shocking.

In his monitoring of the background radiation over Adelaide, the twenty-four-hour sample he'd taken the day after the airdrop test had shown levels hundreds of times above normal, he told her, but the safety committee had maintained his readings were exaggerated and had accused him of being an alarmist.

His examination of the iodine content in the thyroids of dead animals following each of the tests had proved that vast tracts of Australia had been subjected to radioactive fallout. Members of the safety committee had contradicted his results and threatened to discredit him amongst the scientific community.

Elizabeth scribbled down his revelations in shorthand, offering no comment and making no interjection.

The controlled experimentation he'd conducted in farming areas had shown that most of the exposure to livestock came from contaminated food, which posed a far longer-term risk than contaminated air. Not long after he'd presented these particular reports, it had been decided he was overworked and he'd been taken off the program. 'Health problems' had been cited.

He told her how his reports had been altered or discredited, and how his attempts to publish his findings had been thwarted at every turn. The power of the nuclear cabal was limitless.

Finally, he brought up the subject of the minor nuclear tests. These were still in their relatively early stages, he said, the Kittens, the Tims, the Rats, and the soon to be included Vixens, but the experiments were numerous and were run virtually unchecked. Furthermore, they were planned to continue for years.

'I'm no nuclear physicist,' he said, 'but the irresponsible use of uranium and beryllium and, above all, plutonium is courting disaster on all levels. The scientists at Maralinga are having a field day. They have a desert to play in and limitless materials to play with. It's like giving children boxes of matches.'

Marston paused before making his final announcement. 'The minor tests are bound to result in huge amounts of radioactive contamination. In my opinion, they'll pose an even greater ongoing risk than the atomic bomb detonations.'

He'd come to an abrupt halt, and Elizabeth, who'd remained silent throughout, looked up from her notepad at a loss for words.

'How can they get away with it?' she said finally.

'The world's a frightened place. The threat of communism and the race for nuclear power gives them the perfect excuse, or so they believe.'

'But to deny the public access to such information, to discredit your findings, to alter your reports, to prohibit you from publishing . . .'

'You don't understand, Miss Hoffmann.' The eyes behind the horn-rimmed glasses had hardened, signalling a dire warning. 'We are dealing with ruthless liars in high places.'

She was silent for a moment, wondering if she should leave. The interview seemed over.

'What will you do?' she asked.

'I will continue to monitor the situation and take readings, despite no longer being an official part of the program, and one day, when it's safe to publish my findings, I shall do so. For the moment I must remain silent. If I don't, they will ruin me.'

*Ruthless liars in high places*, Elizabeth thought. How ruthless? If they would destroy the career of a prominent scientist in order to silence him, would they murder a soldier who threatened to expose the truth?

'But surely the collusion between politicians and scientists can't guarantee total security, Mr Marston,' she said, trying to keep her voice steady – she felt on the brink of discovery. 'What of the soldiers on the range? They're working in the thick of things. They must have some idea of what's going on.'

'They have no idea at all.' He dismissed the notion without giving it a thought. 'The troops are kept in complete ignorance; they don't know a thing.'

She persevered. 'But if by any chance a soldier *did* know something, and if he threatened to speak out, what would happen to him?'

'The question's superfluous. He wouldn't be told anything to start with, and if he somehow found out, he wouldn't talk anyway. There is such a thing as the Official Secrets Act, you know.'

Elizabeth's flutter of excitement faded. She was surely following the wrong path. Danny would never have broken his oath of silence. She was aware too that she might be pushing the boundaries with Marston. His response had been peremptory and she sensed a certain arrogance in him now. He was not interested in discussion. He'd wanted his story recorded, their time together was up, and any further interrogation was unwelcome. She doggedly pursued the subject nonetheless. Whether the path she was following was right or wrong, her question demanded resolution.

'Yes, sir, I'm aware of the Official Secrets Act. But you refer to ruthless men in high places, Mr Marston – men who would destroy your career rather than allow you to speak out. So, as a matter of interest – hypothetically speaking – if a soldier *did* discover data such as yours, and if he threatened to talk, would his life be in danger?'

Marston seemed to find her question amusing. 'What are you asking? Do you mean, would they *kill* him?'

'Yes, sir, that's exactly what I'm asking.'

'My dear Miss Hoffmann,' he smiled whimsically and his reply was good-natured, albeit just a little condescending, 'A soldier on the range would hardly be considered a threat. If they were going to kill anyone, they would start with me.'

'Of course, sir.' Well, that answers that, she thought. She returned his smile as she stood. 'I'm rather barking up the wrong tree, aren't I?'

'Yes, you are rather.'

As soon as she was back at *The Advertiser*, Elizabeth rang Bob Swindon and they arranged to meet in the lounge of the Criterion at the end of the work day.

When she arrived, he was already seated with a half-finished beer.

'That'll probably be a bit flat,' he said, gesturing to the shandy that sat on the table waiting for her. 'I got here five minutes early and wanted to beat the queue. How'd you go?'

'You owe me five pounds,' she said as she sat.

'Good girl.' He fished his wallet from his pocket. 'Any feminine wiles called for?'

'Not a one.'

'Probably not surprising,' he said, slapping a five-pound note on the table. 'They're a dry old lot, those boffins.'

'What a ridiculously sweeping generalisation, and how on earth would you know anyway?' Elizabeth countered.

'Quite correct, I wouldn't,' he replied unperturbed. 'But I take it I was right about Marston? He wanted to go on record?'

'Oh, yes, you were right there. He definitely wanted to go on record. Breakthrough material, I have to say . . .'

'Really?' There was a feeling of expectancy as he waited for her to go on.

'None of which I can tell you, Bob, as you would well know. I gave my word.'

'Yes,' he said hastily, 'yes, of course you did.'

'I promise you'll have the whole story as soon as I get the go-ahead from Marston,' she said. 'Although God only knows when that will be. In the meantime –'

'I know, Liz, I know,' he interrupted. 'I wouldn't expect anything more of you and I respect your silence.'

'Rubbish. You were dying for me to spill the beans just then.'

He shrugged. 'A bit of wishful thinking – you can't blame a bloke for that. So where do you go to from here? You can't publish any of his information, I presume.'

'No, but it gives me some ammunition, and possibly a bit of room to manoeuvre. As a new reporter fresh on the scene, I might be able to ask a couple of seemingly innocent questions. You know, rattle them enough that they have to come up with an answer.' She took a sip of her shandy and frowned as she put down the glass. 'But then how do I go about it? I have to wait until the powers that be graciously deign to grant us a press conference.'

'Why don't you twist their arm?' She looked at him blankly.

'Have a word with your chief. There hasn't been a general press conference for months. I'm sure if *The Advertiser* requested an update, Maralinga's PR department wouldn't be able to refuse. The state's daily newspaper has a responsibility to its readership, after all.'

'What an excellent idea.' She scooped up the five-pound note. 'I'll buy you a beer on the strength of it.'

'But you haven't drunk your shandy.'

'You were right, it's flat. Don't go away,' she said, 'we need to talk,' and she headed off to the lounge's service bar in the corner.

Elizabeth realised that, in some ways, she was back to square one. Despite her brief flurry of excitement, her meeting with Marston had not offered a solution to the mystery of Daniel's death. The mystery of Maralinga, however, was becoming more tantalising by the minute, and she was convinced that the two were linked. Hedley Marston had been an independently contracted biochemist, principally responsible for the collection of data on radioactive fallout. If he had proved through his animal thyroid examinations that such widespread and long-term danger existed, then what other shocking facts were being covered up at Maralinga?

The words of Daniel's letter were ever-present in her mind. Pete Mitchell had said men had been threatened with court martial if they spoke of what they'd seen. But what had they seen? Marston himself had dismissed the troops as any threat to security on the grounds of the Official Secrets Act. What could those soldiers have witnessed that was so shocking they would need to be reminded of their oath of silence?

She returned to the table with the drinks. 'Tell me what to expect at this press conference, Bob,' she said, leaning forward on her elbows, eager for information. 'Who'll be chairing, who'll be speaking and how many?'

'My guess is there'll be only one speaker, and it won't really be a conference as such, more of a press statement with questions to follow. They won't consider the request for an update warrants anything more.'

'Pity. Good about the questions though. Who'll be delivering the statement?'

'Their liaison officer, an Australian army colonel by the name of Nick Stratton. He's the link between the Aussies and the Poms and the scientists and the bureaucrats, and as such he's virtually the voice of Maralinga.'

'Really? What a handy man to know,' she said thoughtfully.

'Yes, but not an altogether easy one.' Bob thought it necessary to offer a word of advice. 'He's a tough cookie, Liz. Not a bad bloke, but you wouldn't want to cross him. And be warned, he doesn't like smartarses.'

'Then I'd better behave myself, hadn't I?'

Elizabeth very much looked forward to meeting Colonel Nick Stratton.

# Chapter Seventeen

During the days that followed the press conference, Nick Stratton thought about Elizabeth Hoffmann a great deal. He couldn't remember when he'd last been so strongly attracted to a woman. Possibly never, he thought, and then warned himself not to be foolish. Such a woman would hardly be an easy conquest and as he had no wish to become involved, he should really keep well away. But what the hell, he decided, why not test the water? If he sensed he stood a chance with her sexually then he'd pursue her further. If not, a simple dinner out was harmless.

He rang her as soon as he arrived. 'I'm in town,' he said, which wasn't exactly true; he was telephoning from the airport. 'Is dinner still on for tonight?'

'Of course, I look forward to it.'

'Do you have a favourite restaurant?'

'Not a one. I don't dine out much.'

'Nor do I,' he admitted. 'I eat at the Grosvenor when I'm in Adelaide. How would that suit you? The dining room's pleasant and the food's always good.'

'The Grosvenor it is then.'

'Excellent. We'll make it about seven thirty. Where do I pick you up?'

'You don't. I'll meet you in the foyer.'

Nick realised about halfway through the main course that his reasoning had been based upon self-delusion. A simple dinner out was not harmless at all. In fact, a simple dinner out had proved his fatal mistake.

Throughout the soup of the day – a pleasant prawn bisque – they'd stuck to small talk. He'd asked her how long she'd been in Australia, and she'd told him only two months. She'd arrived in the height of midsummer, she said.

'I found it unbearable at first, particularly the heat-wave that hit us last month, but I have a flat in Glenelg so I get the breeze off the water.'

'Glenelg.' He stored it away as his first piece of information. 'Good beach, Glenelg – do you swim a lot?'

'I'm learning,' she said proudly. 'I give myself a lesson every Saturday morning.'

'Well, if you need a teacher, let me know. I'm an excellent swimmer.' The remark was not boastful, just a simple statement of fact.

'Of course you are,' she said. 'All Australians are. It makes me frightfully self-conscious. There I am drowning and a five year old swims past me like a fish – it's most demeaning.'

He laughed, enjoying her company. He found her delightful even in small talk, although he was waiting for her to broach the subject of Maralinga. He was quite sure she wouldn't be able to resist.

They briefly discussed wines. He'd ordered a shiraz to go with the main course, and she admitted to a fondness for a good red wine.

'It's actually the only alcoholic drink I *do* enjoy,' she said. 'I get by on shandies when I'm with the gang, but to me the beer spoils the lemonade.'

'You do realise that in this country that remark is close to sacrilegious.'

'Yes, it is in England too.'

'You should pay a visit to the vineyards just outside Adelaide,' he suggested. 'The Barossa Valley produces some of the best wines in Australia.'

'So I'm told.'

The main courses arrived – duck for her, steak for him – and that was when the small talk came to a halt.

'Tell me, Nick,' she said after the waiter had poured the shiraz and departed, 'am I permitted to ask a few questions off the record?'

He pretended surprise. 'A few questions about what? You surely can't mean Maralinga.'

'Yes, I do,' she replied in all earnestness. 'I wasn't here for the previous series like the other journalists – I have a lot of catching up to do.'

'You can ask as many questions as you like,' he said pleasantly. 'Just don't expect answers.'

'Oh, I wouldn't presume to overstep the mark.'

'Like hell you wouldn't.' He smiled as he picked up his glass. 'Have a sip of your wine first. Tell me what you think of it.'

They sipped simultaneously, his eyes querying hers over the rims of their wine glasses.

'Delicious,' she said, 'I like it very much.' She did, although it differed greatly from the French wines favoured by her father.

'Penfolds. Right here in the Barossa Valley.' He put the glass down and started on his steak. 'So ask away, I'm all ears.'

'The Atomic Weapons Tests Safety Committee . . .'

She started out harmlessly enough, enquiring about the safety committee's purpose, its founding members and the way it worked. The information was openly available to the press, she was already cognisant with the basic facts, and Nick answered her questions freely. Then she changed tack.

'What do you think of the committee's overall effectiveness?'

'In what way?' His response was guarded.

'Well, it seems a little biased, wouldn't you say? Two of the three founding members are British, and both have worked on previous British defence projects – would they really have Australia's best interests at heart?'

'It's not my job to offer personal opinion,' he replied. She'd just voiced his personal opinion to perfection.

'Yes, of course. I'm sorry, I shouldn't have asked. The question slipped out. I'm really very sorry.' She returned her attention to the duck, which she'd barely touched.

'The question didn't slip out at all, and you very well know it.' Things had just jumped to a different level, Nick thought. She was testing how far she could push him. He rather enjoyed her audacity. 'You had every intention of asking me that, didn't you?'

Elizabeth was aware she was walking a fine line. She could maintain his interest through mindless chatter – he clearly found her attractive – but mindless chatter would not gain her information about Maralinga. She needed to charm and intrigue equally.

'Yes, I suppose I did,' she admitted. Honesty had always served before, she thought, a dose now surely wouldn't go astray. 'I shouldn't have expected an answer though. That was hardly fair.' She put down her cutlery, the duck once again forgotten. 'You see, Nick, I'm interested in the power of the committee.'

He continued to devour his steak without comment, but she knew she'd garnered his attention.

'At the conference, you talked of the full cooperation and liaison between all parties, both British and Australian, and you said that this was "in accordance with the requirements laid out by the safety committee". But I can't help wondering what sort of power the committee has to lay out requirements, and just what those requirements might be.'

He stopped eating and took a sip of his wine, waiting for her to go on.

'Oh, please don't misunderstand,' she added hastily, 'I'm not asking for your opinion. I'm just offering my own.'

'And what is your opinion?'

'I think the Atomic Weapons Tests Safety Committee is a sham,' she said boldly, defying him to differ.

Elizabeth was voicing Hedley Marston's views. According to Marston, AWTSC was an out and out sham. The committee had been set up by those in high places, he'd said, and its members continued to obey orders from above. Not only did the safety committee fail to protect Australia, it lied about its own findings and obfuscated the findings of others. At first, she'd wondered whether in his bitterness Marston might not be distorting the facts, but she'd found his arguments too persuasive, too intelligent. If he was right, and she believed he was, did Nick Stratton know the level of deception being practised? Marston had said all soldiers were ignorant of the true facts, even high-ranking officers. Was Nick covering the truth, or was he being kept in ignorance?

As their eyes locked across the table, Elizabeth tried hard to read his reaction.

'I see,' he said slowly, as if he were giving the matter a great deal of thought. 'The safety committee's a sham – that's your confirmed opinion, is it?'

They were sizing each other up. She nodded. His normally stern face was sterner than ever, and she had a feeling she may have gone too far.

Nick was wondering how she came to hold such views. Who had she been talking to? He'd presumed she'd learnt of the test codenames from a soldier on leave – a man out to impress in order to get her into bed. But a soldier would have little knowledge of the safety committee and probably even less interest in it. She must have been talking to a scientist, he thought, and a jaded one at that. He was surprised that a scientist should so openly express an opinion, but then the scenario would probably have been the same, wouldn't it? The man would no doubt have been on the make, and men bent on conquest were known to behave foolishly.

'Let me get this right, Elizabeth,' he said. 'You're offering your opinion, and you don't expect any form of comment from me. Is that correct?'

'Yes, absolutely,' she assured him. 'I mean, absolutely no. I don't expect any comment from you at all.'

'What utter rubbish.'

Oh dear, Elizabeth thought, I *have* gone too far.

'You're grilling me for information, aren't you?'

It was only then she realised that he was enjoying the game. Until that moment she hadn't even realised it was a game, but she could see quite clearly now he was right. Furthermore, it was a game she knew she could play.

'Of course I'm grilling you.' Her smile was both challenging and seductive. 'Do you think I'm likely to get anywhere?'

'Well, you'll never know if you don't try, will you?'

He raised his glass and she returned the salute with her own. They were openly teasing each other. The ground rules had been set in place. The game had commenced in earnest.

As they toasted each other, Elizabeth was surprised by the relative ease with which she'd embraced the art of flirtation. Bob Swindon would be proud of her, she thought.

For Nick, the toast was the moment when he realised there was no turning back and that he would continue to pursue Elizabeth Hoffmann for as long as there was the remotest chance of her capitulation.

He looked critically at her plate as he put down his glass. 'Are you going to eat that duck or not?' he asked.

'Of course I am. I'm ravenous.' She attacked the duck lustily. 'Delicious,' she said through a mouthful of thigh meat. 'Absolutely delicious.'

It was like watching a healthy racehorse enjoying its oats, he thought.

The evening continued pleasantly. They relaxed in each other's company. She didn't push for further information and he didn't overstep the mark when they said goodnight. He shook the hand she proffered, wondering how long it would take before he could kiss her.

'Thanks for a lovely evening, Nick,' she said as the taxi pulled up. She'd refused his offer to escort her home. 'Don't be ridiculous,' she'd scoffed, 'you'd only have to get another taxi back from Glenelg. What a terrible waste of money.'

'I'll give you a ring next week, Elizabeth. We must repeat the experience.'

'Yes, I'd like that.'

He stood on the kerb and waved as the taxi took off.

Further evenings out followed, and the odd lunch too – over the next several weeks, Nick found any number of excuses for regular trips to Adelaide.

The game between them became progressively more daring.

She would bring up the topic of Maralinga and he would tantalise her with bits and pieces of information he considered harmless. Then she would push him just that little bit further, offering opinions, trying to draw him into conversation, sometimes even succeeding, and when he started to become testy she would back off and apologise for having gone too far. Nick knew he should ban such discussions, but he wasn't sure if he could maintain her interest without teasing her along, and so the game continued.

Nick Stratton found Elizabeth Hoffmann mercurial, maddening and very, very clever, all of which only added to her attraction. But he was making no inroads in the sexual stakes. By mid-April he'd progressed no further than a kiss on the cheek. On the several occasions when he'd started to home in, she'd artfully avoided mouth-to-mouth contact, and the kiss on the cheek had now become standard practice, replacing the handshake upon greeting and departing. It was infuriating. He was being treated like a workmate. Furthermore, she always insisted on catching her own taxi home, thereby excluding him from any contact with her personal life. He dared not risk scaring her off by attempting to ravish her the way he wished – she was far too intriguing – but he'd reached a definite stalemate. It was time to take action, and the first step was to meet her on her home ground.

He arranged a weekend's leave and booked a hire car in advance. Then he telephoned her mid-week.

'Do you want to visit the wineries on Saturday?' he asked. 'I'll be in town and I'll have a car.'

'Love to,' she said.

'Right. I'll pick you up around ten. What's your address?'

Elizabeth hesitated. She liked Nick Stratton: she found him stimulating company, and he was certainly useful. She was aware that the material he shared with her was heavily censored, but it was nonetheless insightful and she was slowly but surely learning much about the basic structure of Maralinga. She'd avoided inviting him into her personal life, however, knowing full well he was bent on seduction.

Oh, well, she thought, too late now – she could hardly insist upon meeting him in town. She gave him her address, hoping that she wouldn't have to fight him off when he dropped her home.

He arrived on the dot of ten to discover her waiting outside the house in St Johns Row.

'Good day for it,' he said as he jumped out and opened the passenger door for her. The day was indeed glorious: crisp, cloudless and sunny. 'The Barossa's spectacular in autumn.'

The Barossa Valley, roughly an hour's drive north-east of Adelaide, was prime wine-producing country and exceptionally beautiful. They spent two hours driving through the lush, rolling foothills, visiting the wineries and walking beside the river. Then Nick called a halt for lunch.

The restaurant looked out over endless vineyards stretching down the slopes to the shallow valley below, and the leaves of the vines were a riot of colour, from rusty reds to yellows and even the deepest of purples.

'You're right,' Elizabeth said, 'it is spectacular.'

They were loath to leave when they'd finished their meal and they lingered over their wine, savouring the beauty of the place.

'How incredible,' Nick said, leaning back, arms folded, observing her with an air of amusement.

'What's incredible?'

'It's been a whole five hours and you haven't once mentioned Maralinga.'

'Good heavens above, I haven't, have I?' She was surprised as she realised that he was right. 'Would you like me to?' The challenge was there once more, in her voice and in her eyes.

'Suit yourself.'

The game was on again, he thought, but he was tiring of it now. The bar would have to be raised if she wanted more information.

'The minor tests,' she said, 'the Tims and Rats and Kittens . . .' She paused, considering how to word a statement that was really a question.

'The tests with the colourful codenames supplied by your mysterious source,' he prompted archly.

'That's right.' She smiled at the reference to their first meeting, then continued in all seriousness. 'Surely these experiments could create an ongoing risk.'

'In what way?'

What was she up to, he wondered. In which particular direction was she heading this time?

'They employ the use of materials that are highly radioactive,' she said, 'uranium, beryllium, plutonium . . .' Elizabeth was once again looking for a giveaway sign. She was more convinced than ever that Nick Stratton was ignorant of the true cover-up at Maralinga, and the true cover-up had become a source of great interest to her. 'I can't help wondering,' she said, 'whether these tests might pose a contamination problem in the future.'

'You're certainly a full book on the subject. I take it this is further information gained from the mysterious source who cannot be named?'

She registered the superciliousness in his tone, but not the degree to which she'd angered him.

'I've been to the library,' she said. 'I've been reading up on the subject.' It was true, she had.

386

'How very clever of you.'

Nick deeply resented her line of questioning. He'd realised that she was testing the extent of his knowledge and he was insulted. This was the first stupid move she'd made, he thought. Did she honestly believe he was so naive he didn't know he was being fed half-truths and possibly even lies from above? As liaison officer, he was the spokesperson for the British and Australian governments and was given material approved by both for public consumption – virtual propaganda, little more. This was the frustration of his job admittedly, and it irked him, but security demanded such safeguards be set in place. Armies and governments throughout the civilised world conducted top-secret projects in exactly this manner, he thought, and if the notion was beyond Elizabeth's comprehension then it was she who was naive.

He drained the last of his red wine. 'Let's go,' he said abruptly, rising and picking up his jacket from the back of his chair.

'I'm sorry,' she said as she stood. 'I didn't mean to offend –'

'You're free to think whatever you wish, Elizabeth, but I'd advise you to keep your thoughts to yourself.'

'Please don't be angry, Nick.' She was bewildered by the force of his reaction, but contrite nonetheless. It had been unfair of her to push him so hard when he was not at liberty to respond. 'I'm really, really sorry. It's been a lovely day. I didn't mean to spoil things.'

'You haven't.' Her apology was genuine and he was forced to accept it, but God she was a maddening woman. 'We'll make a detour and visit Hahndorf on the way back,' he said.

They spent well over an hour exploring the German-settled village of Hahndorf. Elizabeth was enchanted by the picturesque pocket of Europe nestled so incongruously amongst the Australian eucalypts, but Nick's mind was elsewhere.

During the drive, he'd analysed his knee-jerk response, wondering why he'd so overreacted. Was he really insulted because she may have discovered he was little more than a mouthpiece? He hadn't enjoyed being reminded of the fact it was true, but in hindsight why should he care? He did his job and he did it well. Was he perhaps worried about her source of information? He didn't for one minute believe she'd gained her facts from the library – but was her informant a threat to security? No, he didn't believe that either. Her informant was a Maralinga scientist who'd been big-noting himself during his trips to Adelaide in an attempt to win sexual favour. And that was where the true problem lay, he realised. He couldn't help wondering whether the man had met with success. Elizabeth appeared to know a lot about the Maralinga tests – at times he suspected more than he did himself – and she could not have gained her knowledge during a brief conversation over a beer at the Criterion. Had she teased this man for information the way she was teasing him? Had she and the scientist had an affair?

He pictured the two in bed making love, Elizabeth and some faceless man, and realised with a sense of shock that his over-reaction at the restaurant had been one of pure jealousy. Good God, he thought, he was envying a mythical lover of his own invention. Now, as they wandered the quaint streets of Hahndorf, Nick couldn't get the image of Elizabeth and her lover out of his mind, and yet the man quite probably did not exist. Elizabeth was a very proper middle-class Englishwoman; she would hardly offer her body as payment for information. His frustration was making him thoroughly irrational.

It was dusk when they pulled up outside the house in St Johns Row. He walked her to the front door.

'Would you like to come in for a cup of tea?'

Common courtesy demanded she make the offer, although in doing so Elizabeth hoped she wasn't asking for trouble.

'No,' he said, aware of her trepidation. 'I'll get back to the hotel, it's been a long day.'

'I've had a wonderful time, Nick. Thank you so much.'

'I enjoyed myself too. Thank you for your company.'

She averted her head for the kiss on the cheek, but he took her face in his hands and turned her to him. The rules were about to change.

She did not pull away. She'd known she couldn't keep him at arm's length forever, and she'd been waiting for him to force the next step. She'd been unsure of what her reaction might be when he did, but now, as their lips met, she decided to acquiesce. A goodnight kiss could do no harm.

Sensing her wariness, he was careful to keep his passion in check and he kissed her with the utmost tenderness. Then, as her resistance wavered, he gathered her to him, feeling her surrender, her mouth opening slightly to the gentle insistence of his. He became lost in the feel of her. For this moment she belonged to him, he thought. For this one moment Elizabeth was actually his.

The longing of the past six weeks poured itself into Nick's one moment of possession and, when the kiss was over, Elizabeth was bewildered. She didn't know how to react. He'd done nothing improper. He'd made no attempt to caress her intimately. It had been a simple kiss. Why did she feel as though they'd just made love? Why did she feel so terribly guilty?

'Goodnight, Nick.' Unsure of what to say, she left it at that.

'Goodnight, Elizabeth.'

As he drove back to town, Nick couldn't have felt happier. The bar had been well and truly raised; he could now move on.

\*

'Good morning.' He was back the next day at ten o'clock, standing on her front doorstep in shorts and T-shirt, a towel draped around his neck.

'Nick, what on earth are you doing here?'

'I had the car for another day,' he said, 'there was no point in wasting it. How about a swimming lesson?'

'What?'

'You told me you were teaching yourself to swim – you said you give yourself a lesson every Saturday.'

She stared at him blankly.

'Don't you remember?'

She nodded. Yes, she remembered mentioning the fact briefly, but that had been over six weeks ago.

'Well, you missed out yesterday, so I thought we'd make up for it with a Sunday session. What do you say?'

'Oh, no, I don't –'

'It'll be winter before you know it,' he said. 'You should seize the opportunity while the weather's still good.' She remained hesitant. 'Particularly with an expert teacher to hand.'

'Isn't it a bit cold?' She was wavering.

'Don't be such a sissy.'

No one called Elizabeth a sissy. 'All right, you win.'

'Excellent. I'll wait in the car while you get ready.'

As she donned her swimming costume, Elizabeth supposed she should be annoyed by this intrusion upon her personal life, but she couldn't really blame him. He'd obviously presumed yesterday's kiss gave him licence to call on her. Elizabeth herself had decided to ignore the kiss. She had dwelt upon neither the kiss itself nor her reaction to it, which she'd dismissed as a romantic flutter of girlishness on her part. It had been foolish of her to feel guilty; she'd done nothing wrong. But she must be careful not to encourage him any further, she told herself as she pulled on her tracksuit. Things must not be allowed to get out of hand.

She grabbed a towel and headed downstairs.

He left the car parked where it was and they walked down Jetty Road to the beach. It was not particularly hot and the beach was no longer crowded with summer hordes, but the day was bright and sunny and the crispness of autumn did not deter the true devotees. A number of fitness fanatics ploughed backwards and forwards through the water, and scattered about on the sand were those hardened sun bakers determined to prolong their tans for as long as humanly possible.

Nick and Elizabeth stripped down to their bathing costumes and waded into the ocean. Nick tried hard not to ogle her body, but with some difficulty. She was a tall girl who carried herself well, but she never dressed provocatively. Who could possibly have guessed, he thought, that beneath the sensible blazers and skirts lay such magnificently moulded breasts and buttocks and thighs? He could barely take his eyes off her as she strode into the sea. More than ever she reminded him of a thoroughbred racehorse in peak condition.

They waded out waist-deep.

'Right, now show me what you can do,' he said. Seconds later, he couldn't contain his laughter as she floundered about, arms thrashing wildly, head tossing up and down, gasping for air. So much for the thoroughbred racehorse, he thought.

'What's wrong?' she spluttered as her feet found the sandy bottom and she stood. 'Why are you laughing? I was swimming all right.'

'No you weren't. You were drowning.'

'I most certainly was not,' she protested. 'I've watched other people and that's the way they do it.'

'Other people breathe.'

'I was breathing.'

'No, you weren't.'

'Yes, I was. I've studied them swimming overarm and that's exactly what they do. They lift their head to the side and breathe in as their arm goes back . . .' She waved an arm in the air and turned her head to one side by way of demonstration. 'Just the way I did,' she added defiantly.

'And what do they do when their arm goes forward?'

'They put their head back in the water.'

'And they breathe out.'

'Do they?'

'Yep, every time.'

'Oh.' A brief pause. 'I didn't know that.'

He demonstrated the breathing technique and made her practise leaning forward in the water with her feet still on the ocean floor. 'Deep, even breaths,' he said, and he patted his midriff. 'Use your diaphragm, push the air out from here.'

Then he incorporated the arm action. 'Lead back with your elbow,' he showed her how, 'and stretch well forward with your hand, really grab the water.'

He taught her the correct head movement: 'No need to heave your whole head up – just turn your face to the side enough to get air.' And, holding her hands while she floated, he taught her how to kick properly. 'Your feet are your outboard engine,' he told her, 'don't let them sink.'

'Right,' he finally said, 'now let's put it all together. Float on your stomach again, arms out front, I'll support you.'

She did, and he cradled one arm under her waist, holding her steady in the water. 'Off you go,' he said, 'nice and easy, and don't forget to kick.'

He walked beside her, supporting her with one hand and correcting her style with the other. 'Stretch right out,' he said, running his hand along the length of her arm to her wrist, extending her reach. 'Don't cut your stroke short.'

She did as she was told.

'Good, that's good. Watch your head – you're lifting too far out of the water, it's a waste of energy.' He placed the palm of his hand between her shoulder blades. 'No lifting from here, just a turn to the side,' he said, sliding his hand to the back of her neck. 'From here,' he said, 'turn from here.'

Again, she did as she was told.

'Good, very good, but don't forget to really push out that air.' He nudged her with his supporting arm. 'I can't feel your diaphragm working.'

Nick was an experienced instructor. He'd taught many to swim over the years, and he was now so focused upon tuition that he wasn't really aware of their bodily contact. Elizabeth was. Much as she was concentrating on her performance and on obeying his commands, she was aware of his every touch. She could feel the muscles of his forearm as he supported her. She could feel the brush of his fingers along the length of her arm. She could feel his hand on the bare flesh of her back and her neck. She wasn't accustomed to such intimacy – it made her self-conscious and ill at ease. At the same time, she was annoyed with herself. How stupid she was being, how stupid and prudish – the man was only giving her a swimming lesson. She tried with all her might to focus solely upon his instructions, but she could not ignore the distraction of his touch on her naked skin.

The water was chilly and finally he called a halt. 'We'd better leave it at that,' he said, 'you're getting goose bumps.'

He was cold himself, he needed some action. 'I'll see you on the beach – I'm just going to warm up a bit.'

She waded ashore and, as she towelled herself dry and donned her track suit, she watched him cutting his way through the water. It was an impressive sight. He was a powerful swimmer with an elegant style.

'You make it look so easy,' she said ten minutes later when he'd jogged up the beach to her.

'It *is* easy. You'll be swimming like that yourself in no time.'

'I hardly think so,' she scoffed.

'Of course you will. You've conquered the breathing and that's the main part. Swimming's all about breathing.' He grabbed his towel and started drying himself off. 'You did very well, Elizabeth, very well indeed.' He meant it. 'You should feel proud of yourself.'

'Thanks, Nick.' For some strange reason she found herself basking in his praise.

They jogged back up Jetty Road in order to keep warm, and when they arrived at the house she made the offer of a hot shower. It was only fair, she thought, the poor man was shivering as much as she was.

He followed her upstairs to her apartment, where she showed him the bathroom and gave him a fresh towel.

'No, no, you go first,' he said, 'you're freezing.'

He was insistent, so she led him through the lounge room's French windows to the balcony where he could wait in the sun. Then she disappeared briefly to the bedroom and returned with a large woollen cardigan, which she tossed to him.

'I'm sorry I don't have anything more appropriate,' she said, 'I don't stock men's clothes, but that should keep you warm. I won't be too long, I promise.'

'Take your time,' he called after her.

He struggled into the cardigan, which, although not small, was a very tight fit on a six-foot man of his build, and sat looking out at the ocean. Things were moving along very nicely, he thought.

She reappeared barely five minutes later. 'Your turn,' she announced, popping her head through the French windows.

He stood. 'You shouldn't have rushed,' he said as he stepped inside. 'I was quite happy just –'

She burst out laughing. The cardigan, loose-fitting on her, looked quite silly on him. Furthermore, it was mauve.

'You look absolutely ridiculous,' she said.

'You don't.'

Her wet hair was scraped back from her face, she wore a simple red sweater and black trousers, and he didn't think he'd seen a woman more glorious. She was barefooted too, which seemed to have a special significance, as if she were somehow undressed. The next step was only natural.

As before, the kiss started out slowly and tenderly. Elizabeth had not anticipated it, but she didn't resist. She was aware that she should, having vowed not to encourage him any further, but she found herself once again surrendering. Then, before she knew it, surrender had become desire. Suddenly the kiss was no longer a simple kiss and she was no longer a passive participant. She was aroused. She wanted him to make love to her. She wanted the touch of his naked skin against hers, the feel of him inside her . . .

She broke away, flustered and breathless. Her moment of sexual abandonment had lasted only seconds, but she was shocked.

'I'm sorry, Nick,' she said. 'I'm sorry, but I think you should go. I'm sorry. I'm really, really sorry if I've led you on in any way, but –'

'Don't apologise, Elizabeth, please,' he said. She looked so very frightened. 'I'm the one who should be apologising. I didn't mean to take advantage . . .' He stopped; he had meant to. Of course he'd meant to. And he would again, but only when he felt she was ready. 'I'm sorry. I didn't intend to frighten you.'

He kissed her on the cheek and quietly left. He hadn't frightened her at all, he thought. She'd frightened herself. It was only a matter of time now, and he was happy to wait. He was happy to wait for as long as it took – now that he knew she wanted him.

He climbed into the car and drove off, unaware he was still wearing the mauve cardigan.

It was over two months before they finally made love.

She avoided seeing him altogether for the first month, offering flimsy excuses when he rang and asked her out. Then, in the first week of June, he turned up again on her front doorstep.

'I thought it was high time I returned this,' he said, holding up the mauve cardigan. 'The boys at the base say it doesn't suit me.'

Elizabeth laughed. She hadn't realised how much she'd missed his company. She'd been too riddled with guilt to think of anything but her moment of weakness. How could she have lusted after another man, and so shamelessly, when Danny had been dead little more than six months? She was appalled by her behaviour.

'It's good to see you, Nick. Would you like a cup of tea?'

After that, things moved slowly but nonetheless surely. During the next month or so he made regular stopovers in Adelaide en route to his Canberra meetings, and they went to the cinema or dined out. At first they reverted to the kiss on the cheek, Elizabeth trying to maintain the barriers and Nick careful to observe the parameters she set. But he made sure he had a hire car to hand these days and insisted upon driving her home. As a result, the nightly farewells at her front door followed a natural progression. The kiss on the cheek once again graduated to the mouth, just a gentle brush of the lips to start with, but it escalated rapidly and they were soon both aware that the inevitable was looming.

Then, one cold winter's night in July, as their lips parted and the steam from their mouths mingled, Elizabeth decided she couldn't take any more. Yet again they'd done nothing except kiss, but yet again she'd been devoured by sheer carnal lust. He'd made no attempt to caress her or to thrust himself upon her in any way. But she desperately wanted him to.

'Don't go back to the hotel,' she said.

They went upstairs.

Nick Stratton was an experienced lover and a highly accomplished one at that. In avoiding serious relationships with women, he had not avoided pleasuring them in bed. In fact, he'd made it quite an art form, for his own sake as much as theirs. A woman's sexual pleasure was to him the most erotic aspect of copulation.

Now, as he made love to Elizabeth, his pent-up longing to possess her, far from impeding his performance, only enhanced it. He'd kept himself in careful check for months and he had no trouble keeping himself in check now as he teased her to the brink of ecstasy and beyond. Then, when she'd slightly recovered herself, he started all over again. He revelled in the control he had over her and the pleasure he could give her.

When she was close to exhaustion, and when he felt his own climax nearing, he worked her once again into a fever pitch for the mutual finale, still maintaining the presence of mind to withdraw at the last minute – just to be on the safe side. He always did. He never took chances. But as he held her quivering body close, his own release meant little anyway. He would have preferred to have gone on forever, driving her into a frenzy of sexual delirium. His greatest personal pleasure lay in the exercise of his power.

He rolled away from her and they both lay on their backs catching their breath.

Elizabeth stared up into the darkness. She could feel, like tiny electric shocks, involuntary muscular spasms in the very core of her being, as if her body, like her mind, was trying to come to terms with what had transpired. When she'd recovered herself sufficiently, she turned to him. She couldn't make out his eyes, but his face was clearly silhouetted in the moonlight spilling through the window that looked out onto the far end of the balcony.

'I didn't know it could be like that,' she said.

He'd guessed as much. He'd sensed tonight had been something of an awakening for her.

'You're a very sexual woman, Elizabeth.'

'Am I really?'

She was pleased he should think so, and felt rather as she had when he'd told her she'd done well in her swimming lesson.

'Oh, yes, indeed,' he said with heartfelt sincerity. How extraordinary that she didn't know it herself, he thought. 'You're not very experienced though, are you?'

She wasn't sure if the remark was an insult or a compliment, but either way it seemed to imply criticism. 'I'm not a virgin, you know.'

He smiled in the darkness. He'd made a simple observation, but she was instantly defensive and on the attack. How typically Elizabeth, he thought.

'I'm aware of that,' he said.

'Oh. So it showed, did it?' Her reply was arch. 'Well, of course it would, wouldn't it? I mean to someone as experienced as you obviously are.'

Elizabeth had no idea why she was being so brittle and girlish. What did she expect of the man? That he take her in his arms and tell her he loved her? How puerile. She'd been like a bitch on heat. She'd wanted raw, animal sex and he'd given it to her beyond her wildest expectations. She should be grateful instead of behaving like a wounded ingenue.

'I'm sorry,' she said, her voice lost and bewildered in the dark, 'I'm being unfair. I don't know why.'

'I do.'

He leaned over and switched on the bedside lamp. She was startled by the light, but said nothing as she sat up drawing the bedclothes around her.

'How old are you, Elizabeth?'

'Twenty-six.'

'I'm forty,' he said. 'I'll be forty-one next month, and I've never married. Of course I've had many women during my life, of course I'm experienced. It's natural.'

'I know that, Nick. I'm sorry, I didn't mean –'

'And do you know what else is natural?'

She sensed the question was rhetorical, but she shook her head anyway, like an obedient student in response to a teacher.

'Your sexuality,' he said. 'Your sexuality is the most natural thing in the world; it's nothing to feel guilty about.' He kissed her lightly. 'You're a healthy, highly sexed woman. Now that you've discovered that, don't be ashamed. Be proud.'

He put his arm about her and they snuggled back into the bed, where they lay quietly, her head on his shoulder. He waited for her to say something, and when she didn't he wondered whether he was invited to stay the night or whether she'd like him to leave. He would prefer to stay. He'd like to make love to her again. In fact, he'd like to make love to her again right now, but he needed a little more recovery time these days. He remembered how in his twenties he'd needed virtually no recovery time at all, not for a second bout anyway.

'Would you like me to go?' he asked after several minutes' silence, but she didn't hear him. She too had been lost in thought.

'I've only slept with one man before,' she said, 'and only several times during one very short weekend. That was over a year ago now. We were engaged to be married, but he was killed last October.'

Nick made no response. This was sounding altogether too serious. It was tragic that her fiancé had been killed, but what was he expected to say?

No response was necessary, however. Elizabeth was not seeking sympathy.

'I loved him very much,' she continued, 'and I always will. But we were both young and both inexperienced. We never had time to get to know each other sexually.' She turned to face him, propping herself on one elbow. 'So you see, you're quite right, Nick. Tonight has been a sexual revelation for me. And I'm grateful for your advice, very grateful indeed.' She paused. She'd given the matter serious consideration and had come to a definite conclusion. 'I did shock myself, and I was feeling guilty, but I heartily agree with you. To suffer guilt or to feel shame would be foolish. In fact, it would not only be foolish, it would be the height of hypocrisy on my part.'

He threw back his head and laughed out loud. 'My God, what a formidable force I've unleashed.'

'Yes, you have rather, haven't you?'

'No, Elizabeth. No, I haven't at all.' He quickly sobered up, although he was still smiling – he found her mixture of worldly intelligence and blind naivety utterly disarming. 'You've always been a highly sexual creature. Everyone else seems to sense it except you. Someone was bound to unleash you at some time.'

'That doesn't sound particularly flattering,' she said, although she was clearly not offended.

'I'm just lucky it happened to be me.' He reached out and traced the tips of his fingers very, very slowly down her neck and across her shoulder and down the length of her arm. 'I'm ready again if you are.'

'Of course I am.' Her skin was tingling.

He drew her to him. His months of patience had not been in vain. The conquest of Elizabeth Hoffmann had proved well worth the wait.

# Chapter Eighteen

Elizabeth had wholeheartedly embraced her sexual liberation. Or so she told herself. And she certainly made the pretence that she had, to herself and to Nick as their relationship blossomed into a fully fledged affair. But deep down she knew it was all bravado. She was in love with Nick Stratton. She tried to persuade herself that love and sex were separate issues and that she was confusing the two, but it didn't work. She loved the man, it was as simple as that. She loved him in every sense of the word.

Her liberation was true in one respect, however. She was surprised to discover that she experienced neither the guilt nor the disloyalty she would have felt only a short time ago for loving a man other than Daniel. She could love two men, couldn't she? She could love two men in two very different ways. There was no shame in that.

Daniel remained very much in Elizabeth's thoughts. She was no less committed to solving the mystery of his death than she had been when she'd first arrived in Australia. Indeed, the controversial facts she'd learnt from Hedley Marston had fuelled her interest in the entire mystery that surrounded Maralinga.

But uncovering the truth about Daniel's death remained her first priority and she wondered briefly, now the situation had changed, whether she should try to enlist Nick's direct help. Surely he would understand her need to determine the truth. Perhaps he even knew the facts himself – what if it were that simple? But by doing that she could be placing him in an invidious position. He might even be offended that she should so presume upon their relationship. She dared not take the risk, she decided. Their affair was hardly based upon solid ground.

Elizabeth had no illusions about their relationship. Nor did she have any illusions about Nick. Perhaps he loved her in his own way – he was certainly obsessed with her, she was aware of that – but she doubted his true capacity to love. She felt a little sorry for him in some regards. He was a man who put up walls, and she wondered why. In any event, she was realistic about their affair. She never told him she loved him, knowing it wasn't something he wanted to hear. He clearly wasn't interested in any form of commitment, and one day, when the novelty had worn off, he would look for a fresh conquest.

Nick was most certainly obsessed with Elizabeth. As their affair continued throughout July and into August, his interest, far from waning as it normally would, only increased. At first he put it down to her sexuality. He found her extraordinarily exciting in bed. So erotic, indeed, that at times he had to fight for control and it became a battle with his own body. A battle he always won, he made sure of that, but she was a test of his power. As the weeks passed though, he had to admit that even when they weren't making love, she continued to fascinate him. She was clever and witty and funny, all of which he'd recognised from the start, but she was also strong and capable, a woman of integrity. He admired her.

Admiration was a dangerous factor, and a warning voice occasionally sounded in Nick's brain, but he felt safe in ignoring it. If he was becoming a little infatuated, did it really matter? The affair would eventually run its course, as all affairs did. They would tire of each other and move on. Elizabeth accepted the relationship on exactly the same grounds and made no demands upon him. Where was the harm in their mutual enjoyment?

'Happy birthday,' she said, saluting him with her wine glass. 'It's a Penfolds shiraz by the way.'

'So I noticed.' He smiled as they clinked glasses.

'Bon appétit. Don't let it get cold.' She set about attacking her own steak by way of example.

She'd insisted he tell her when his birthday was. 'Next month, you said – "I'll be forty-one next month", those were your very words. Well, it's next month now, so when's the actual day? I haven't missed it, have I?'

'The eighteenth.' It had been simpler to give in to her badgering.

'Ten days to go. Excellent. You must wangle a trip into town and I'll cook you a birthday dinner.'

He'd arrived on a relentlessly wet and wintry night to find the table in the lounge room romantically candlelit, with a bowl of crisp bread rolls and a bottle of wine in the centre. He'd been touched by her efforts, but he hadn't seen her for over a week and there were priorities more important than birthdays.

'Don't worry,' she'd said, 'everything's perfectly organised – the dinner can wait,' and they'd made a detour to the bedroom as she'd known they would.

It had been a good forty minutes before they'd emerged.

Now, as she watched him sawing his way through a steak that was like leather – doing his best to make it look easy, which she found rather gallant – Elizabeth wondered where she'd gone wrong. She'd given up on her own steak. It was quite inedible.

'I'm sorry the steaks are so tough. I don't know why they should be. The butcher told me it was an excellent piece of rump, aged and all that, which is supposed to make it tender, or so he said.'

'How did you cook them?' he asked, jaws working furiously.

'Oh, not for too long,' she assured him. 'I know true meat lovers don't like their steaks overcooked. I fried them up just before you got here and then put them in the oven to keep warm.'

'Ah.' He nodded. 'That might be where the trouble lies. The salad's nice,' he said encouragingly. 'I like the dressing.'

'Oil and vinegar. I don't dare make my own. I've tried to several times but it's always abysmal. I'm a terrible cook.' She topped up their glasses. 'If I were you, I'd fill up on the bread rolls and wine and wait for dessert. Peter's ice-cream and tinned fruit salad, with cheese to follow. Even I can't make a mess of that.'

'Ice-cream and fruit salad's a real treat to an army man.'

'I'm sorry.' She gazed regretfully at the dried slabs of meat on their plates. 'I thought if I chose something really simple I might get it right for once.'

He realised that her flippancy was an act and she was genuinely dismayed the steak had proved a disaster. What did it matter if she couldn't cook, he wondered, although the fact did come as something of a surprise. He'd never known a woman who couldn't cook, and Elizabeth was normally so proficient at everything she turned her hand to.

'Well, it's a relief to discover there's something you can't do,' he said jokingly.

'I can't swim.'

'That's true.'

'But at least I can *learn* how to swim. I can't seem to learn how

405

to cook.' She took a healthy swig of her wine. 'I have a theory. True cooks are born. They have a passion. I don't. I've tried, I really have, but it's just not there. Even the basic ability isn't there, which I find rather sad. It makes me less of a woman.'

'What?' He looked at her blankly; she was joking of course.

'I lack the nurturing capabilities of the normal female.'

She wasn't joking. 'If you were any more of a woman, Elizabeth, you'd have to be locked up.'

She smiled, appreciating his effort to jolly her along, but still feeling something of a failure.

'I have an excellent idea,' he said. 'Let's keep the dessert for later and go straight to the cheese. Bread rolls, cheese and a good red wine – you can't get much better than that.' He crossed to the Gladstone bag, which he'd dumped on the coffee table, and opening it up he took out a bottle. 'I naturally arrived with supplies,' he said, 'we won't run out.'

Elizabeth cleared away the steaks and fetched the cheeses: a New Zealand cheddar and a French brie, which she'd gone to a lot of trouble to find. Edna Sparks had directed her to a superb little delicatessen that specialised in a line of imported foods. They settled down at the table once again while outside, through the French windows, the deluge continued.

'Damn,' she said, 'I've even managed to mess this part up.'

The brie was firm; she'd forgotten to take it out of the refrigerator.

'No matter,' he assured her, 'it'll warm up soon. We'll start on the cheddar.'

'Maybe a talent with food is genetic,' she said thoughtfully. 'My mother can't cook. Well, she says that she *doesn't*. She views her choice not to cook as a statement, but it may very well be that she can't. Perhaps I've inherited her disability – what do you think?'

'Perhaps.'

She'd certainly inherited her mother's eccentricity, he thought. Although he knew if he were to suggest such a thing she would vehemently deny it, considering herself the only sane member of her family. Nick enjoyed listening to Elizabeth talk about her parents. They featured quite regularly in her conversation and, from what he could gather, both were bizarre. Little wonder, he thought, that they'd bred such a remarkable daughter.

'What about your mother, Nick?'

'Eh?' What did she mean, what about his mother?

'Is she a good cook?'

'I wouldn't have a clue.'

He'd been so caught out by her change of focus, he'd had no time to formulate any answer but the truth.

'Oh.' The bluntness of his reply brought her to a halt.

'We don't see each other.'

Elizabeth longed to ask 'why not?' but decided it would probably be too intrusive, so she stuck to the original topic. 'Was she a good cook when you were little?'

'I don't know. I really can't remember.'

He didn't appear in the least annoyed, but as he obviously wasn't interested in talking about his mother she switched to the cheese.

'I think the brie's softened up a bit,' she said.

'I'm not trying to avoid the subject, Elizabeth.' Which was strange, he thought. Normally he would. 'I like hearing you talk about your family. I don't mind telling you about mine.'

'Oh, good.'

She settled back happily with her wine. How interesting, she thought. He'd not talked of his family before.

He'd never known his father, he said. He'd been killed in the First World War. 'When he left for the front, my mother was pregnant with me, but neither of them knew it. When my mother found out, she hated him for leaving her. She hated him even more when he died in the trenches and she was stuck with a six-month-old baby to bring up on her own. She remarried when I was about two years old. A man called Des. He was a good enough bloke, but after she'd given him two sons and a daughter of his own, he wasn't all that interested in raising another man's child, so I was a bit on the outer right from the start.'

As Nick told his story with a brevity that was typical, everything fell into place for Elizabeth. So that's why he couldn't wait to join the army, she thought. He'd spoken quite openly about his professional life. She knew every step of his military career. Upon graduation from Duntroon, he'd been posted to New Guinea, where he'd served as a platoon commander, rising to the rank of major by the end of the war. He'd worked in Japan with the Occupation Forces, and in 1951 he'd seen active service in Korea with the 3rd Battalion Royal Australian Regiment. Finally, he'd ended up in a desk job in Canberra promoted to the rank of lieutenant colonel. 'The army's been my life,' he'd told her. 'As a boy I couldn't wait to join up. For as long as I can remember, all I ever wanted to do was join the army.' But he'd never said why. He'd never once mentioned his family.

'I don't see Mum and Des any more,' he said now. 'There doesn't seem much point. They're in their sixties, retired on the Gold Coast; they've got their own life and their grandchildren and they're happy by all accounts. I used to keep in touch with my half-siblings – the four of us were quite close when we were little. I was a big brother to them back then. But we grew apart years ago. They've got kids of their own now; they don't need me coming in and out of their lives.'

'So the army's your family.' It all made sense.

'Yes, I suppose it is,' he admitted. 'I've always loved army life. I still do.' He gave a wry smile. 'Although I sometimes think active service is easier than the diplomatic kind. Particularly the diplomatic kind required at Maralinga.'

'Why did you accept the job then?'

'Promotion, what else? The position of liaison officer came with the rank of colonel. The army's all about promotion, you can't afford to stand still. You have to work your way up rung by rung, even if sometimes you don't like the specific job or the posting on offer.'

He was back on safe ground now; he could talk about the army all night. He was rather surprised that he'd told her about his personal life, even as briefly as he had. And he'd done so of his own volition, he realised; she hadn't pressed him for the information. How strange. He'd certainly changed since he'd met Elizabeth.

They scoffed most of the cheese and half the second bottle of wine, and then retired once again to the bedroom where another sexual battle took place as Nick fought to maintain the control that threatened to elude him.

The dessert served as a midnight feast. They sat in bed with large bowls of ice-cream and tinned fruit salad, and watched through the window as the balcony became awash under the relentless downpour.

'It's been a special night, Elizabeth. Thank you.' He smiled as he turned to her. 'Normally birthdays come and go and I don't notice them – even as a kid they meant little to me.'

'Me too. Birthdays were always ghastly because my parents forgot them.'

'This one's been a beauty.'

He kissed her, and she could taste pineapple.

They'd moved a step closer that night, Elizabeth thought, but she warned herself not to be foolish and raise her expectations. Nick quite possibly did love her, but he was a loner and he always would be. That was his tragedy. She must not allow it to become hers.

Maralinga was once again a hive of excitement as, throughout August, preparations for the second major test series became progressively more intense. The first of the three detonations that constituted the Antler series was codenamed Tadje and was scheduled to take place on 14 September.

By the end of August, the hordes had started pouring in. First came the scientists and specialists who would be directly involved in the tests, then the bureaucrats, military personnel and other VIPs of varying description who would observe the firings. Conspicuously absent amongst these latter arrivals was Harold Dartleigh. Harold was leaving things until the last minute. Once the series started he'd be marooned in that Godforsaken wilderness for the duration, he told himself – a whole month, no less. He would arrive for the briefings several days before the Tadje firing, and not one minute sooner.

'I won't be able to see you for the next fortnight or so,' Nick said, 'not until after the first test of the series. There'll be a press conference following the firing, of course, and I'll be coming to Adelaide for that.'

It was early afternoon. They'd just made love and were lying naked in each other's arms, the bedclothes tossed to one side, their bodies still warm from their exertion.

He'd flown into Adelaide for a late morning conference at the AGIO offices and the plan had been to meet for lunch, but they'd skipped lunch and come straight to the flat. She'd told him when he'd telephoned that she could take the afternoon off. She was working on a feature that she could easily write at home, she'd said, which wasn't true. She'd cancelled an interview to be with him.

'I have to make a couple of trips to Canberra,' he continued, 'but I can't really justify an excuse for a stopover here, things are too busy.'

She'd miss him, she thought, but she didn't say so. She continued to play the game the way he liked it played.

'We'll just have to wait until the press conference then, won't we?' she said cheekily. 'I shall harass you as much as I can and you can take it out on me in bed afterwards.'

He laughed and propped himself on his side with his chin in his hand, looking down at her as she lay there. She was so bloody gorgeous, he thought. He longed to make love to her again, but recovery time was necessary, so he kissed her instead, a slow, languid kiss, sensual rather than erotic, and, without the urgency of copulation, a deeply pleasurable experience.

'I'll miss you, Elizabeth,' he said lightly. Then he lay back, drawing her to him and pulling the bedclothes up around them – winter's final throes lent a chill to the air, and they'd both cooled down now. 'It's only two weeks, I know, but what on earth will I do without you?'

The kiss, the nurturing embrace and, above all, the sentiment, playful though it was, rather took her by surprise and she heard herself ask something she'd never thought she would.

'Have you ever been in love, Nick?'

Far from being daunted by the question or confronted by her asking it, he replied in all honesty.

'Once, yes. I was stationed in Seoul and she was a captain in the US army intelligence unit. I asked her to marry me. She knocked me back, thank goodness.'

'Why do you say thank goodness if you loved her?'

'I don't know.' He shrugged. 'Perhaps I *didn't* love her, although I certainly thought I did at the time. I was heartbroken when she said no. But I'm glad she did now – it wouldn't have worked out. I'm not the marrying kind. Besides,' he added, planting an affectionate kiss on the top of her head, 'if I'd married Jenny I wouldn't be here with you, would I?'

'No, I suppose you wouldn't.'

There was a moment's pause.

'Tell me about your fiancé, Elizabeth.' The conversation had taken such an intimate turn that it seemed a natural enquiry, and he was interested to know. 'How did he die? Or would you rather I didn't ask that? I'll quite understand if you don't want to talk about it.'

'No, no, I'm very glad you asked.' There would never be a more appropriate time, Elizabeth thought; she couldn't have orchestrated a better opening if she'd tried. 'I've been wanting to tell you for some time now, Nick.'

She sat up, leaning her back against the bedstead, the blankets pulled around her, and Nick, recognising her need to talk, did the same.

'My fiancé's name was Daniel,' she said. 'Lieutenant Daniel Gardiner, and he died at Maralinga.' She was aware of his shock, but she didn't wait for a response, continuing in the same matter-of-fact manner. 'Exactly how he died is a mystery. The official report says "accidental death", the unofficial report says "suicide". I don't believe either to be the case.'

He was staring at her dumbfounded, barely able to believe what he'd heard. 'You're young Dan's fiancée?'

'I was. Yes. Did you know him?'

'Of course I did. Everyone knows everyone at Maralinga.'

'Do you know anything about his death?'

'No more than you obviously do.' Was she interrogating him, he wondered. It certainly sounded that way. 'His death was reported accidental for the sake of the family and also for security purposes. How did you know it was suicide? Who told you?'

'It wasn't suicide, Nick.' She ignored the question. 'Danny would never have killed himself. He had too much to live for. We were in love, we were to be married in April. It wasn't suicide, and it wasn't an accident. They're covering something. I don't know what, and I don't know who, but I intend to find out. That's why I came to Australia. Will you help me?'

'Help you? In what way could I possibly help you?'

Elizabeth didn't notice the slightly distant tone. She was too excited by the prospect of acquiring an ally in Nick.

'You could make some enquiries for me.'

'Enquiries into what exactly?'

'The investigation.'

'And what investigation would that be?'

'The investigation into the accident . . .' She'd suddenly registered the scorn in his voice and she became flustered. He was ridiculing her, or so it sounded. 'There must have been an investigation. You could find out who was the last person to see Danny alive, that sort of thing . . .'

'What could have led you to believe, Elizabeth, that I would offer you my assistance? If you have seriously developed the demented notion that the army murdered your fiancé, how on earth could you expect –'

'Not the army, Nick, I didn't say the army. Well, I didn't *mean* the army, I meant some*one*. I don't know who or why, but someone killed Danny.'

He threw back the bedclothes and stood. It was too ludicrous, he thought, sitting here naked discussing military assassination plots.

'Please listen to me, please,' she said desperately.

'I can listen while I dress,' he said, pulling on his trousers. 'I have to be leaving for the airport soon – the plane's scheduled for take-off at four.'

413

'I had a letter from Danny that he posted from Ceduna only several days before he was killed. In it he talked about his friend Pete Mitchell. Pete had been murdered and Danny suspected foul play –'

'Pete Mitchell was killed by a jealous husband.' He didn't look at her as he tucked his shirt into his trousers and sat to put on his boots.

'I know that, but Danny didn't at the time and it worried him. Pete had told him just before he'd been murdered of something terrible that had happened at Maralinga. Danny didn't say what it was, but men had been threatened with court martial if they spoke of what they'd seen.'

Nick looked up sharply.

'And,' she continued, 'he was worried that Pete's murder was in some way connected.' Elizabeth was relieved to have finally gained Nick's full attention. His eyes were now riveted upon her. 'Danny intended to make his own investigations into the murder, but he died only several days after he posted that letter. Pete's death proved unrelated to whatever it was the men saw and to the threat of court martial, Nick, but what about Danny's? Don't you think two coincidental deaths is rather stretching credibility?'

'So you believe some nameless, faceless person murdered Dan to prevent him exposing the reason why men were threatened with court martial, is that it?'

Again the derision, but this time, even though she was unable to give him a direct answer, Elizabeth's response was not in the least flustered.

'I don't know what I believe. But I intend to find out what it was those men saw. It may not be the answer, but at least it's a starting point.'

'I see.' He stood and shrugged on his jacket. 'Well, you're

certainly a woman of surprises, Elizabeth. I must congratulate you. I would never have guessed.'

'Guessed what?' He was offended, she thought. Why?

'That all the time you were posing as an investigative reporter you were using me to gather personal information.'

She supposed he had a right to be annoyed, but she couldn't help feeling he was overreacting a little.

'I admit that I had a hidden agenda, Nick, but I was also doing what I'm employed to do and that is to cover events at Maralinga. I wasn't posing as an investigative reporter. I *am* a reporter, it's my *job* to investigate, and you're the principal source of information regarding Maralinga.'

'Do you make a habit of sleeping with your principal source of information?'

So that's why he's angry, she thought. She didn't deign to answer.

Her silence only aggravated him further. 'I presume that's just another part of the job, is it? You used me, Elizabeth, why don't you admit it? You used me unashamedly.'

'No more than you used me, Nick.' Her eyes met his squarely. 'Be honest.'

They gazed at each other for several long seconds. Then he turned and walked away.

He's leaving, she thought. And he's leaving for good. So where's the harm in telling him the truth?

'I didn't sleep with you to gain information,' she said.

He stopped at the door and looked back.

'I slept with you because I love you.'

Did he believe her? From the look in his eyes it was impossible to tell, and it didn't matter anyway. But she was glad she'd said the words out loud. She didn't like living with a lie.

'I know what it was the men saw, Elizabeth.' His voice was

cold. 'I know what they saw and I know why they were threatened with court martial. I should, after all: I was the officer who issued the threat. Does that make me a suspect, do you think? Could the nameless, faceless person possibly be me?'

He left, closing the door quietly behind him.

All was in readiness and, with only several days until countdown commenced, Maralinga was abuzz with anticipation. The final batches of VIPs had settled in and, with over 3000 residents, the township was now functioning at full capacity. But there was one more late arrival.

Harold Dartleigh stepped out of the de Havilland into a perfect spring morning. The sky was a cloudless blue, and the vibrant colours of the Nullarbor appeared newly washed as fresh green growth sprang from the ochre-red earth. But Harold didn't notice. All he could see was the wretched wasteland of desert stretching for miles and, as he walked towards the airport terminal, those preposterous oleanders lining the pathway in welcome. Monstrous plants, he thought, ugly as sin, even in blossom. Little wonder they thrived in this wilderness. No respectable English plant could survive out here.

Ned Hanson, his cipher clerk, was on hand to greet him.

'There was little for me to do back at the office, sir,' he explained, 'so I thought I'd come out and offer you a personal welcome.'

Oh, Christ, Harold thought. 'How very kind,' he said.

During the drive into Maralinga, Ned chatted away, first about the reports he'd been sending, then, when that didn't produce much reaction, the weather – Ned was not a man comfortable with silence. Beside him, Harold stared listlessly out of the Land Rover's passenger window. He would miss young Daniel during this trip, he thought.

Things picked up several hours later though. When Ned had left the office for the second lunchtime shift as arranged, a familiar face appeared in the doorway.

'Welcome back to Maralinga.' Carefully latching the door behind him, Gideon slid with his customary grace into the wicker chair opposite Harold's desk. 'You've been pining for us all, I can tell.'

Thank God for Gideon Melbray, Harold thought.

They quickly got down to business, the main topic of the day being the minor test series. Gideon brought Harold up to date on the progress of the Kittens, Tims and Rats.

'Your account is certainly far removed from the reports that are forwarded to me from this office,' Harold remarked dryly.

'Ah, yes, poor old Ned's been left very much in the dark, I'm afraid, but then so has everyone else. The boffins are having a field day out there.' Gideon waved a hand about vaguely as if indicating the entire desert area of South Australia. 'With no eyes upon them they can do what they want and they're getting away with bloody murder.'

'Good for them. I have no problem with that, but how dare Penney not keep MI6 informed.' Harold scowled. 'The man's power truly has gone to his head.'

'We knew they'd close ranks on us though, didn't we? That's why I'm here, after all.'

'Yes, indeed.' Yet again, Harold congratulated himself on the foresight he'd shown in placing Gideon undercover. 'I presume you're gaining your information from the phone taps?'

'Oh, yes. The little red phones have proved a positive goldmine. They chat away on their personally interconnected lines like garrulous teenagers. And then they hand their boring, predictable reports in to poor old Ned – it's really quite laughable.'

'Laughable to you perhaps, Gideon,' Harold said stuffily. 'I,

417

frankly, find nothing at all amusing about information being withheld from the deputy director of MI6 and a peer of the realm no less. Who the hell does that upstart Penney think he is?'

Gideon didn't respond to his superior's fit of pique. Harold could become quite pedantic when his blue blood was on the boil. 'And, of course, there's always Melvyn,' he said instead, changing the subject. 'Melvyn's a fund of information.'

'Melvyn Crowley, yes.' Harold was distracted from the diatribe he'd been about to deliver on William Penney rising so disgracefully above his station in life. 'I've had some interesting calls from Melvyn. Indeed, we've become quite pally. I must certainly pay him a visit.'

Crowley was a madman of the first order and an odious sycophant, Harold thought, but his views on human experimentation were intriguing to say the least. He rather looked forward to another chat with the little Nazi. Well, well, this was becoming like old home week, wasn't it? He was settling in, after all.

The fourteenth of September dawned clear with favourable weather conditions, and as the morning progressed meteorological reports remained positive.

The final go-ahead was given. The first of the Antler test series was now underway.

The device this time was of low-energy yield – 1 kiloton – and, as in previous tests, it was to be exploded from a tower, the detonation scheduled to take place at two thirty in the afternoon.

By one o'clock there were hundreds gathered at Roadside. The final countdown to Tadje had commenced.

*Etta walks beside the railway line. She is following the tracks that disappear far away to the west where the desert meets the sky. She has been following the tracks for ten days now, ever since the mail truck from Coober Pedy dropped her off at Tarcoola. Very soon she will reach Ooldea.*

*The railway tracks and the fettlers' camps have been Etta's lifeline, the railway leading her ever closer to her family, and the camps providing her with sustenance. She has travelled at a regular pace, stopping at each siding and each camp along the way – Malbooma, Wynbring, Barton, Immarna – and the fettlers have readily exchanged food and water for sexual favours. Some of the men were content to ignore her pregnant belly, lifting her cotton dress and taking her from behind, while others she served with her mouth. Etta is accustomed to serving white men.*

*Now, as she strides along, her arms swinging freely, her belly no discomfort, Coober Pedy seems a lifetime ago. She has no regrets. The white men with whom she lived there did not harm her, but she wishes she was not with child. She does not know which of the two white men fathered the baby inside her and she does not care, but if she was not with child she could have stayed with them in Coober Pedy. She liked Coober Pedy.*

*Etta is a Kokatha girl. She is seventeen years old and has always been rebellious, even as a child. Her extended* family group of a dozen or so are converts to Christianity and accustomed to mission life. They do not stay long in one place, however, regularly disappearing from the missions to continue a nomadic existence.

Etta met the white men one year ago. Her family group had set up camp near the mission at Yalata. Her mother and aunties liked the services conducted by the Lutheran minister there, and her father and uncles liked the food the mission provided for its flock.

The two white men had driven across the desert from Kalgoorlie and had stopped to fill their water bags at Yalata. Etta had flirted with them. She liked to flirt. The men were on their way to Coober Pedy to mine for opals, they said. A pretty black girl like her could come with them if she wanted to. They would look after her.

Etta had said nothing to her family. She'd just climbed into the cabin of the Holden utility and driven off with the white men.

She had loved Coober Pedy. It was a place of great magic where strange people came from faraway lands and some even lived in houses under the ground. The white men had set up camp on the outskirts of town and she had been happy enough with them. She did their chores and slept with them when they wanted a woman, performing whatever sexual duties were required. She had food enough and they never beat her and she was content.

It was only when her belly started to swell that she realised she was pregnant. But she didn't tell the white men. She kept her secret for as long as possible. It was *not difficult. She was young with a neat, tight body and her belly didn't show beneath the loose cotton dresses she wore. She successfully hid her condition even during copulation, exciting the men with her mouth and then presenting them with her bare backside. They hardly looked at her when they took her anyway.*

*Etta had been well into her time before the men had found out, and when they had, they'd been angry. They'd paid the mail truck driver two pounds to take her on his run as far as Tarcoola, and they'd threatened to bash her if she came back to Coober Pedy. A baby had not been part of the bargain.*

*Now, as Etta approaches Ooldea, she prepares the lie she must tell. Her family must not know that the child she carries is a white man's child. If her family were to know this, they might well disown her. When the baby is born, they will cast her aside she is sure, but she dares not think about that now. She feels that her time is not very far off, certainly less than one full moon. She must find her family before then.*

*The sun is leaning towards the west when she comes upon the fence. It is early afternoon and Ooldea lies just ahead, but she can go no further. Who has built this great fence of wire, she wonders. And where are those of her people who would normally be gathered here? Who is keeping them from Ooldea? Ooldea is a meeting place for many, many people. It is where she had hoped to find her family. And if not her family, then at least others who will take her in and help her when her time comes. What will she do now? Where will she go?*

*As if in answer, a sign appears in the sky to the north. A mighty cloud has formed, growing in magnificence, surely signalling the gathering of many. Perhaps her own family is amongst this gathering.*

*Etta leaves the safety of the railway line, but she feels no fear. She has her own tracks to follow now. This is familiar territory. She has travelled this area often with her family. She knows the waterholes and the signs of her people.*

*She sets off towards the great smoke signal. It is several days' walk away at least, possibly further. But this does not matter. The smoke beckons her. It is a personal sign, and she has time enough.*

# Chapter Nineteen

The Antler test series was off to a flying start. Every facet of the Tadje firing had run with clockwork precision. The lessons learned during the Buffalo series had proved invaluable.

In Adelaide the following day, the AGIO conference room was packed. The interest of the press had been sharply rekindled. Tadje was the first major test to be conducted for nearly a year, and the first of a brand new series. All eyes were once again upon Maralinga.

Given the importance of the occasion and the keen response from the press, several prominent figures were in attendance, including a senior official of the Australian government, the chairman of the safety committee, and Sir William Penney himself. As a result, Nick Stratton's job was to MC proceedings rather than to act as spokesman.

After introducing the officials who were seated behind him up on the dais, Nick called upon Sir William Penney to address the gathering.

Sir William rose and walked forward to the podium, and Nick returned to his seat. As Penney talked through the technical aspects of the Tadje firing, Nick didn't listen to one word the man said. Elizabeth was not visible from where he was sitting and he was marking time until the next introduction. He could see her quite clearly from the podium.

Sir William's speech was concise. He thanked the press for their attention, returned to his seat, and Nick was quickly back at the podium. While introducing the foreign affairs diplomat from Canberra, his glance kept flickering to Elizabeth where she sat in the very last row, and he willed her to look at him. But although she appeared to be giving him her full attention, not once did her eyes meet his.

He returned to his seat while the foreign affairs diplomat droned on about Australia's commitment to Britain and the strength of the bond forged with the mother country. Then it was time for the introduction of Professor Ernest Titterton, chairman of the Atomic Weapons Tests Safety Committee. Again Nick willed Elizabeth to look at him, and again she didn't. During each of the introductions she assiduously avoided eye contact.

When the speeches were over, Nick returned to the podium and opened the floor to questions. Most were directed to specific speakers, but he remained standing by to answer any general queries and to field those that might prove troublesome. He kept glancing towards Elizabeth, waiting for her to make her presence known, as he was sure she would. But, to his surprise, she said nothing, and after half an hour or so the questions petered out.

'Is that it then?' His eyes raked the room before coming to rest upon Elizabeth. 'No more questions?' he asked. 'Last chance.' It was an open invitation. In fact, it appeared rather like a dare.

Finally her eyes met his. She held his gaze for a second or so, gave a barely perceptible shake of the head and looked away.

Nick brought the conference to a conclusion.

*

'You should have come up with a question, Liz. Stratton was obviously after another confrontation.'

Over beers at the Criterion, Bob Swindon had a good-natured go at Elizabeth. He and Macca Mackay had been seated beside her at the conference and both had been surprised by her silence, particularly as Nick Stratton had seemed to be personally seeking her contribution.

'I think he enjoyed the verbal stoush last time,' Bob said, 'and I must say it livened things up.'

'Things didn't need livening up this time, Bob. There was a genuine report to be delivered; no sense in turning it into a farce.'

'Don't tell me,' he said with mock horror, 'that you were inhibited by the presence of the big guns.'

'I most certainly was not,' Elizabeth replied tartly. 'Why on earth should I be?'

'Of course, silly me.' Bob quickly backed off; he couldn't imagine Elizabeth being inhibited by anyone.

'I'm sorry, I didn't mean to snap. It's just that I don't see any point in putting on a show for the sake of it.'

'Fair enough.' He changed the subject. 'Have you had any further contact with our friend Hedley Marston?'

'No, why do you ask?'

'Oh, I just wondered if you'd heard he's been awarded an honorary Doctor of Science degree by the Australian National University.'

'Really?'

'So I suppose that means they haven't been able to blacklist him altogether.'

'I should hope not.'

The two were interrupted by the arrival of Macca, who had Georgie Swann and Ron Woods in tow, and the conversation immediately turned to the Tadje detonation of the previous day.

Macca, Georgie and Ron were *The Advertiser*'s three-man team who attended the firings, and Bob Swindon demanded to hear every single detail of the proceedings, as he always did. Bob swore he got far more information over beers at the pub than he ever did from a press conference.

Elizabeth had heard it all before. She'd asked the very same questions of Macca just that morning, so she made her excuses and left. She wasn't in the mood to socialise anyway. Seeing Nick again had left her unsettled.

During the tram ride home she pondered Bob Swindon's light-hearted accusation. Bob was right, she thought, she *had* been inhibited, but not by the big guns. She'd been inhibited by Nick. She'd toed the line and maintained her silence all because of him. He'd been in charge of the proceedings and she hadn't wished to disrupt the conference for his sake. How spineless, she thought crossly. How girlish and spineless and completely out of character. It wasn't as if Nick had expected her to behave herself. In fact, he'd openly encouraged her to speak up.

Why had he done that, she wondered as she stared out of the tram window into the gathering dusk. Why on earth had he done that? It was as if he'd *wanted* her to disrupt the conference. Why? She was mystified.

She walked the several blocks from the tram stop and by the time she reached the house, dusk was turning to night.

He was waiting for her on the front porch. At first she was startled by the figure looming in the shadows.

'I'm sorry,' he said, 'I didn't mean to frighten you.'

'Nick. What a relief.' She made light of the moment. 'I thought I was about to be attacked.'

'May I come in?'

'Of course.' She led the way upstairs and into the kitchen.

'Would you like a cup of tea? I'm making a pot for myself. I've been at the Criterion and I'm a little shandied out.'

'I'd rather have a Scotch. That is, if you haven't thrown away the bottle.'

'No. I haven't thrown away the bottle.'

She only kept Scotch in the house for him. She never drank spirits herself. She gave him the bottle and he poured himself a drink while she put the kettle on.

'Are you hungry?' she asked. 'Can I get you something to eat?'

'No, no, thank you. I'm fine.'

A slight awkwardness existed between them. The change in circumstances required some adjustment. Food and drink had always been secondary to lovemaking, and by now they would have been in the bedroom.

'The conference went well,' she said.

'Yes. A good turnout.'

Their chat followed general lines as she made the tea, both of them carefully avoiding any personal issues. Then they adjourned to the lounge room, Elizabeth taking the teapot with her. As they sat at the little table by the French windows, she posed the question she'd been longing to ask.

'Why did you urge me to take a stand, Nick?'

His shrug seemed to say *isn't that obvious*, but Elizabeth remained mystified. It wasn't at all obvious to her.

'You seemed to be daring me,' she said, puzzled. 'It was as if you *wanted* me to cause trouble, as if you wanted me to –'

'I just wanted you to be you, Elizabeth.'

He said no more than that, which didn't really seem to answer the question, but she nodded obligingly as if it had. 'Oh, I see,' she replied.

'No, you don't. You don't see at all.' He drained the last of his Scotch. 'You had Penney and Titterton and that bore from

Canberra right there in front of you. You should have been on your feet confronting them, if only to rattle the bastards.'

Elizabeth took instant umbrage. 'That's unfair! I didn't want to disrupt things for your sake.'

'I can look after myself, thank you. I don't need to be molly-coddled.'

'I wasn't *mollycoddling* you, for God's sake!' She was insulted. 'I was only trying to be –'

'Well, don't. Don't try to be anything other than you. Don't change, Elizabeth. Don't ever change. Be true to yourself.' He stood. 'I'm going to get the bottle.'

He left for the kitchen and reappeared seconds later with the Scotch. She looked at him suspiciously as he sat and poured himself another stiff measure.

'Have you been drinking?'

'I had a couple earlier,' he admitted, 'but I'm not drunk.' It was true, he wasn't. 'And I didn't come here to talk about the conference. I came here to offer you my help.'

'Help in what way?'

'In finding out who killed Dan. That is if anyone did – I'm not so sure about that. But at least I'll help you find out the true facts of his death.'

Elizabeth felt an overwhelming surge of relief. At last she had an ally, she thought. At last she wasn't alone.

'You don't believe it was suicide then?'

'Not any more.'

'What changed your mind?'

'You said it yourself. He had too much to live for.'

He looked at her, her eyes shining with excitement and renewed hope. Christ almighty, he thought, the boy was going home to marry a woman like that. Why the hell would he kill himself?

428

He took a swig of his Scotch. 'I have to admit that I found it difficult to believe in the first place. From the little I knew of Dan he didn't seem the suicidal type. Most of the others didn't think so either, which is why the news was so shocking at the time. But the report was conclusive so no-one disputed it. Sometimes the least expected men are the ones who crack under pressure. You see it a lot in conflict zones. Dan's mates would have been sick with guilt that they hadn't realised he was in such a state.'

'So if you don't believe it was suicide, and if you don't believe he was murdered, what *do* you believe, Nick?'

'Oh, I think someone was responsible for his death, certainly, but I doubt it was deliberate. Pure supposition on my part, but they could be covering the fact that he was killed in some terrible botch-up. If his death was the direct result of human error, the army would have to mount a homicide investigation and word could get out. They wouldn't like that.'

'They'd go to such lengths?' Elizabeth was horrified.

'Stranger things have been known to happen, believe me,' Nick said dryly. 'Don't forget, Maralinga's a top-secret project. Security is a major priority. It's understandable.'

'It's not understandable at all,' she said, outraged. 'It's utterly reprehensible that a man's death should be faked to look like a suicide.'

'And then turned back into an accident for the sake of the family,' he added. 'Don't forget that part.' She was about to interject, but he held up his hand. 'Stop it right there, Elizabeth. Calm down. Outrage isn't going to get you anywhere. This is total supposition – I'm just trying to come up with a plausible explanation.'

'Yes, yes, I'm sorry.'

'I'm probably altogether wrong, and you might be too. I'll make some careful enquiries, but what if it turns out Dan really *did* suicide? Are you prepared to accept that?'

'If the evidence is irrefutable, I'll have to, won't I?' She stood. 'But I think you should read his letter.'

She disappeared briefly into the bedroom and, upon returning, handed him the letter without a word. Then she sat and watched as he read it.

Nick tried to sift objectively through the letter's information, looking for clues or some sign that might point him in the right direction, but he found himself personally affected by it. Beneath the expression of turmoil, the young man's love was palpable, as was his belief in the loyalty and support of the woman he loved. It was clear to Nick that Daniel gained his strength from Elizabeth. In fact, the letter said as much about the person to whom it was written as it did about the writer.

When he'd finished reading, Nick carefully put the pages down on the table. He felt a strange affinity with young Daniel.

'What do you think?' she said.

'About what?' he asked, hedging.

'Do you believe that's a man on the verge of suicide?'

'No. I don't.'

'Thank you. A colleague of mine in London said I wouldn't have a leg to stand on if I were to present it as evidence. He said they would interpret it as the writing of an unbalanced, disturbed mind.'

'He's right. They would.'

She was silent for a moment. 'So where do we start, Nick?'

'Where do you want to start?' He knew exactly what was coming next.

'With the threat of court martial,' she said. 'What was it the

430

men saw? Why did Danny think Pete Mitchell had been killed for speaking out?'

Nick had come prepared for this very moment, but strangely enough that didn't seem to make it any easier. He downed the remains of his Scotch and took a deep breath.

'An Aboriginal family was irradiated,' he said briskly. 'The parents and two children had camped in a bomb crater and their bodies were discovered some miles away several days later. The patrol officers who found them, and the members of the decontamination team who transported the bodies back to base for disposal, were threatened with court martial if they talked. I was the officer ordered to issue that threat. The episode was never mentioned again, even within the deepest confines of Maralinga. It was as if it had never happened.'

'How shocking,' Elizabeth said. 'How truly shocking.'

'The deaths were shocking, yes,' he agreed. 'The fact that we kept the matter a secret, however, was essential. For security reasons no other course of action could possibly have been taken.'

Nick felt restless. He contemplated another Scotch, decided against it, and sat drumming his fingers on the table-top. Elizabeth barely noticed his restlessness. She was too distracted.

'But how could such a thing have happened? Reports were issued stating the local Aboriginal people had been removed from the area,' she said.

'That's a load of bullshit. The situation's impossible to police so they ignore it. There might well be other bodies lying out there undiscovered, who knows?'

He wanted to shock her. He felt like being brutal. He was irritated and edgy. Didn't she realise the magnitude of what he'd just done? But his shock tactics didn't work. Elizabeth

431

had moved on from shock as her mind busily added up the facts.

'Pete Mitchell was the government-appointed Aboriginal liaison officer,' she said, 'and Danny wrote that he was a "tormented man". Was this why?'

'It was certainly one of the reasons.'

Nick resigned himself to the fact that she was too busy playing detective to encompass anything else, so he poured himself another Scotch and downed a quick belt before continuing.

'Pete was deeply distressed about the lack of consideration given to the Aboriginal people's predicament. A number of the patrol officers were too. They still are.'

'Understandably so.' She paused before asking the question uppermost in her mind. 'Do you think this terrible incident of the family's irradiation has any direct bearing on Danny's death, Nick?'

'No, I don't. But you said yourself, it's a starting point, remember?' She nodded. 'Well, I agree with you there.' He looked down at the letter still open on the table. 'It all started that drunken night when Pete told Dan about the Aboriginal deaths and the threat of court martial. Pete's subsequent murder led Dan on a trail of investigation, and that's where we have to start ourselves. Who did he speak to? What wheels did he set in motion?'

Elizabeth studied him shrewdly. 'You no longer believe this is a case of human error, do you?'

'I didn't say that.' Nick was wary. The letter had certainly given him a fresh perspective, but he wasn't at all sure what he believed and he wasn't about to encourage any fanciful notions on Elizabeth's part.

'I just said that we should start our investigation where Dan did. And that means the fettlers. I'll pay a visit to Watson tomorrow.'

'Do you think they'll be willing to help? They sound like a pretty tough bunch to me.'

'They'll do anything if the price is right. Do you have any spare cash lying around?'

'About twenty pounds, but I can get more out of the bank tomorrow.'

'No, that'll be fine. We'll pool our resources – fifty quid should do it.'

She jumped to her feet and crossed to the dresser where she took a pile of notes from the top drawer.

'Clever,' he said. 'No burglar would think to look there.'

She ignored the comment, thrusting the notes at him. 'And we need to find out who was the last person to see Danny alive, Nick.' Elizabeth was excited now. With Nick's help she was finally making progress. 'If you could discover who it was, and the circumstances under which they –'

'Oh, I know all that.'

'What?' She came to an immediate halt.

'Everyone at Maralinga knows that.'

Very quietly, she sat. 'Who was it? Tell me. Tell me everything.'

'A bloke by the name of Gideon Melbray was the last person to see Dan alive. Gideon's the senior requisitions officer with the British Department of Supply, and he and Dan worked together quite a lot. They were probably good mates, I really wouldn't know, but on the night of Dan's death Gideon called around to his barracks and discovered him crying drunk. Dan was evidently carrying on about a plot to kill Pete Mitchell and making no sense at all –'

'But Danny didn't drink,' Elizabeth intervened sharply. 'Apart from the occasional beer, that is. I never once saw him drunk.'

She was suspicious already, Nick could tell, but then she was so keen to hold someone responsible he supposed it was only natural.

'Yes, so Gideon said. He was surprised himself. It was out of character, he said, Dan wasn't a big drinker.'

'So what happened? What did Gideon do?'

'He told him to go to bed and sleep it off. What else could he do?'

'What else indeed?' Elizabeth's tone was arch.

'Gideon was apparently horrified the next morning when Dan was discovered dead. He said he'd had no idea that –'

'So this Gideon Melbray was the sole witness to Danny's anguished mental state!' Elizabeth was unable to contain herself any longer. 'Isn't that just a little too pat?'

'Take it easy, Elizabeth, take it easy.' Nick once again held up his hand in a bid to halt her. 'Of course there would have been reports other than Gideon's – the police made a thorough investigation – but Gideon's story was the one that got around the base at the time. He was the last person to see Dan alive, he's the sort of bloke who chats to all and sundry, and naturally his story became the talk of Maralinga –'

'I'll just bet it did!' 'Which, let's face it, is perfectly normal under the circumstances!' In his exasperation, Nick raised his voice, overriding her interruption and finally shutting her up. He gave her a second or so to calm down. 'I'll check out the other reports with the military police, I can promise you. Rest assured, Elizabeth, I won't let you down.'

'I'm sorry,' she said sheepishly. 'I got carried away.'

'Yes, you did. And what's the point? There's no sense in that, no sense at all – it's not productive.' He gave the table a decisive smack with his hand. 'Right, so we now have a plan. I check out the fettlers and call on a couple of MP mates. I'll let you know what I come up with next week.'

He stood, swiftly draining his glass. 'I'll only get one more trip into town between now and the next firing. They've scheduled the second test for the twenty-fifth.'

She also stood. The brusqueness of his manner surprised her. He was in a very strange mood, she thought. In fact, he'd been in a strange mood from the moment he'd arrived but she hadn't really noticed until now. She'd been so excited about gaining his help that she hadn't given a thought to anything else. But now she was puzzled. She was puzzled about a lot of things.

'Why are you doing all this, Nick? Why are you helping me? What made you decide to tell me about . . .' She tailed off. 'Oh my God!' Her eyes widened in amazement and she clapped a disbelieving hand to her mouth. 'Oh my God, the Official Secrets Act. You've broken your oath of silence.'

'Yes.' The penny's finally dropped, he thought. 'Yes, I have.'

'But that's a treasonable offence. You could be court-martialled.'

'If someone betrayed me, I could, yes. I could even face a firing squad if the military decided to exercise the full measure of the law.' His smile was wry. 'I suppose that means I'm in your hands, Elizabeth.'

'Why?' She was dumbfounded. A man like Nick Stratton! The army was his life. It was incomprehensible. 'You of all people – I don't understand. Why would you do such a thing?'

'I believe you have right on your side and I want to help you.'

'No, it's more than that. It's much, much more than that. Why, Nick?'

Then she read the answer in his eyes. His eyes quite clearly said: *can't you guess, Elizabeth?*

'You love me,' she said.

He said nothing, but his silence was answer enough.

'Since when?'

435

'Probably for some time,' he admitted. 'I just didn't know.'

'When did you find out?'

'Not long after I left you that afternoon. When I got over my wounded pride and the notion that you'd used me, and when I realised what you'd said.'

'What? That I love you?'

'Yes. You took me by surprise, I have to admit.'

'And this is your way of reciprocating?'

'I suppose it is.'

'You could have just told me, you know. That's the normal way.'

'I don't put much faith in words myself. Words are too easy, they usually mean little.'

She smiled. 'Actions speak louder, is that what you're saying?'

'Yes, that's exactly what I'm saying.' The answer really was that simple, he thought. 'You need my help, Elizabeth, and I want to offer it to you in any way that I can.' He would offer this woman his life if necessary and, indeed, perhaps he already had.

'I accept,' she said. 'I accept wholeheartedly.'

Later, as they made love, Nick no longer fought a personal battle with his body in order to maintain supremacy. Their union ceased to be a challenge and a test of his power over her, becoming instead a mutual exchange. He gave himself as freely to Elizabeth as she did to him, and when it was over and they lay in each other's arms, he couldn't remember ever in his life having felt such a sense of belonging.

Tommo slipped the fifty pounds into his top pocket. 'You better come in,' he said, and aimed a kick at the mangy yellow dog sniffing around Nick's feet. 'Get out of it, you mongrel bastard.'

The dog slunk away into the shadows of the verandah, and Nick stepped inside the shabby little cottage.

'Stick the kettle on, Mave, we've got a visitor,' Tommo yelled, and Mavis, a thin, sunburnt woman, appeared from the backroom.

'Don't bother with the tea,' Nick said pleasantly. 'I don't want to put you to any trouble.'

'For fifty quid, mate, a cup of tea's no trouble, I can promise you that.' Harry gave an ostentatious wink to his wife. 'Put the kettle on, Mave.'

'No tea.'

Recognising the voice of authority, Mave halted halfway to the wood stove in the corner.

'No tea,' Nick repeated, 'just a few answers to a few questions.'

'Whatever you like.' Tommo slumped into the soggy sofa. 'Only trying to be friendly.'

'Both of you, if you wouldn't mind.'

Mave joined her husband on the sofa, and Nick pulled up a kitchen chair from the nearby table and sat opposite them.

'Do you recognise this man?' He showed them the photograph of Daniel that Elizabeth had given him.

'Nup.' Tommo's reply was instant, but Mave hesitated, glancing at her husband as if seeking permission. She'd copped it for opening her mouth in the past.

'Fifty quid, love.' Tommo nudged her encouragingly. 'Tell the man what he wants to know. Mave never misses a trick,' he said with a gap-toothed grin.

'Yeah, I seen him,' Mave said, 'but not for some time now. Used to turn up for the train deliveries.'

'What did you tell him about the murder of Pete Mitchell?' Nick got straight to the point. He saw no reason not to;

Tommo and Mavis had both given evidence at the trial of Harry Lampton.

'Eh?' Mave looked at him blankly.

'He was around here asking questions about the murder.'

'No, he wasn't,' Mave said, 'not him.' She waved a finger at the photo.

Tommo nodded; for fifty quid he wanted to be helpful. 'No, he wasn't, mate. The only ones asking questions were the coppers and the other bloke.'

'What other bloke?'

'Jesus, I wouldn't know. Would you, Mave? The bloke who paid us the money – I wouldn't know his name. He never told us and I never asked.'

'Oh, I know his name all right,' Mave said. 'The pretty one. Ada always lusted after him, the slut. She never stopped talking about Gideon Melbray.'

'Gideon Melbray?' Nick said. 'You're sure?'

'Course I am.'

'He was making enquiries about Pete Mitchell's death?'

'Yeah, that's right.' Tommo dived in; he was sick of Mave being the centre of attention. 'He paid us to come forward as witnesses. Half upfront if we agreed and half when Harry was caught.'

'And he paid us a *hundred quid* what's more,' Mave said with pursed lips and a meaningful nod.

'Ah, well, I'm afraid I don't have access to that sort of money.'

As Nick stood, Tommo quickly jumped to his feet. Shit, fifty quid was fifty quid. Fucking Mave, he thought, you don't offend a bloke who gives you fifty quid!

'Don't take any notice of the missus, mate. Anything I can do for you, any time, you just let me know. My door's open, mate, my door's open any time.'

When Nick had left, Tommo gave Mave a quick belt around the ears. Dumb cunt, he thought. Did she think fifty quid grew on fucking trees?

'Why would Gideon Melbray be making enquiries about the murder, I wonder?'

It was five days later and Elizabeth and Nick were seated on the balcony overlooking Glenelg beach, a pot of tea on the table before them. Their priorities were back to normal. The tea had been secondary; they'd made love the moment Nick had walked in the door. They were now discussing his findings, and Elizabeth was riveted.

'And how would he get his hands on that amount of ready cash?' she went on. 'You told me he was with the Department of Supply. It seems rather a lot for a government employee, don't you think?'

'The money wasn't his. He wasn't making enquiries on his own behalf, he was in the employ of someone else.'

'Who?'

'Harold Dartleigh.'

'Ah,' she said.

As she didn't appear particularly responsive to the news, Nick felt the need to explain. 'It's Harold *Lord* Dartleigh to be precise, and he's –'

'Oh, I'm quite aware of who Dartleigh *is*,' she said. 'Harold Rodin Dartleigh, 6th Baron Somerston, and deputy director of MI6.'

How dumb, he thought, she was a British journalist, of course she'd know who Harold bloody Dartleigh was. 'Sorry.'

'But how do you know it was Dartleigh who paid Gideon Melbray to make enquiries?' Elizabeth wasn't interested in apologies.

'I don't, although it's a pretty fair assumption. According to the fettlers, Gideon was the only one sniffing around the fettlers' camp apart from the military police, and, according to my MP mates, Dartleigh promised Dan he'd have some enquiries made. It all adds up. Dartleigh wanted to help put Dan's mind at rest, he told the police – he said he was very worried about him.'

'Why would he choose Gideon Melbray to make his enquiries? Where's the connection between them?'

'There isn't one that I'm aware of, apart from the fact that Gideon's a gregarious bloke who knows everyone at Maralinga and regularly does favours.'

'No, I don't go along with that. For a man in Harold Dartleigh's position there'd have to be a stronger link, surely.'

'Yes, I tend to agree with you.'

Nick had his own ideas about the Dartleigh/Melbray connection, but he waited to see what she'd come up with. Elizabeth changed tack though. Her teacup nestled in her hands, she gazed out at the expanse of sun-dappled water.

'It's strange that Danny didn't mention Dartleigh's offer of help in his letter,' she said. 'He drove Harold Dartleigh to Ceduna only several days before he was killed, and it's obvious they spoke intimately during the trip. I wonder why he didn't ;. . . Then the thought occurred to her. 'Of course,' she said, 'the offer of help must have been made on the return journey to Maralinga, *after* Danny had posted the letter.'

'Yes, I'd say so. Dartleigh told the MPs that Dan had talked to him at length. He'd seemed obsessed with the murder of Pete Mitchell, Dartleigh said. Even though all the facts pointed to a simple crime of passion, Dan was desperate for positive proof that the fettler had actually done it.'

'The intimation being that Dan wasn't quite of sound mind perhaps?'

'Yes, perhaps.'

Nick was trying hard not to sway Elizabeth. He considered it important she draw her own conclusions, but their reasoning was certainly following the same path.

'A view not dissimilar to that of Gideon Melbray,' Elizabeth said dryly. 'How coincidental that the mate who was the last to see Danny alive and the superior in whom he confided only days before his death should be in such agreement about his mental state. And furthermore, unbeknownst to anyone else, the two knew each other well.'

'Yes.' She was right on the money, Nick thought. 'According to the MPs, the corroboration of their evidence confirmed the suicide findings,' he said.

'I see.' Elizabeth put down her teacup, discovering as she did so that it was empty anyway. 'There certainly appears to be some collusion.' She picked up the pot. 'Would you like some more tea?'

'No, thanks,' he said, checking his watch, 'I have to leave in five minutes.'

She seemed very calm, he thought, given the circumstances. He'd expected an angrier reaction to this hint of a possible conspiracy.

But Elizabeth had no time to be emotional; her mind was preoccupied with other things.

'What if Gideon Melbray had some connection with MI6, Nick?' she said as she poured herself a cup of tea. 'What if he was some sort of undercover backup for Dartleigh? They do that kind of thing, don't they? Plant a secret agent to keep an eye on everyone for security purposes?'

'Yes, they certainly do.' The very same thought had occurred to Nick.

'So what if Danny's death was covered up by MI6? What if

the army had nothing to do with it?' She dumped the teapot back on the table with an alarming thump. Things were starting to make sense. 'What if something happened – perhaps some terrible botch-up like you said – and in the interests of national security MI6 made it look like a suicide? What if nobody else but Dartleigh and Melbray knew? Or if someone else did, they were being kept quiet by MI6?'

'That's a hell of a lot of "what ifs", Elizabeth.'

'Yes, it is, isn't it?' She flashed him a delighted smile. 'And each one eminently possible. What a pity you can't stay a bit longer,' she said as she added milk to her tea. 'I could get you a Scotch and we could celebrate.'

'I think we may need something a little more concrete to go on,' he said wryly. 'I get the feeling a celebration party might be just a bit further down the track. Of course, I could be wrong . . .'

Elizabeth ignored his sarcasm. She was planning her course of action. Whether or not her surmise was the right one, Gideon Melbray and Harold Dartleigh appeared to be the men who held the answers. Nick had done well with his enquiries, but the next step was up to her.

'Are they likely to be coming into town soon?' she asked.

'Who?'

'Gideon Melbray and Harold Dartleigh, of course. Who else?'

He might have guessed – Elizabeth was making plans.

'I wouldn't have a clue,' he said, 'although I strongly doubt it. Gideon's a permanent fixture throughout Maralinga. He seems to love the place, never goes on leave – Mr Popular, in fact, the life and soul of every party.'

'And Harold Dartleigh?'

'Dartleigh can't stand Maralinga. He fronts up just prior to the major test series and takes off the moment they're over.'

'He doesn't come to Adelaide for the press conferences, does he? His presence isn't recorded in any of the previous reports.'

Dartleigh was the important one, she thought. Dartleigh was the one she needed to confront face to face.

'He hasn't yet, no.'

'Perhaps you could persuade him? In the interest of public relations it might be appropriate. A man in his eminent position, both socially and professionally, couldn't fail to impress.'

'So that's your plan?' How very typical of Elizabeth, he thought. 'You're going to front him at a press conference, are you?'

'Of course. What better arena could I have? He'd have to answer me in some way or another.'

'You'll cause a furore.'

'I certainly hope so.'

'All right.' He stood. 'I can't promise anything, but I'll give it a go.'

As she rose to her feet, he drew her to him and they kissed. 'I'll ring you and let you know whether or not Dartleigh's coming,' he said as they parted. 'See you at the press conference next week.' Then he grabbed his jacket and was gone. She waved to him from the balcony as he drove off.

Elizabeth was left on tenterhooks. The second test of the Antler series, codenamed Biak, was scheduled to take place in just four days. Providing meteorological reports proved favourable and all went according to plan, it had been announced that the press conference would take place the following day. Perhaps, she thought, just perhaps, she was only five days away from discovering the truth.

Upon his return to Maralinga, Nick sought out Harold Dartleigh, but was informed by his cipher clerk, Ned Hanson, that Lord Dartleigh had gone to Ceduna. Ned wasn't sure for how long.

'I wanted to drive him myself,' Ned said, 'but he told me I was far too valuable here, I had to stay and man the office. Bit of a shame really, I'd have liked the trip.'

On checking with the transport office, Nick discovered that Dartleigh had booked a Land Rover and driver for three whole days, which hadn't at all endeared him to the sergeant on desk duty.

'With the bigwigs in town we need every driver and vehicle at our disposal, Colonel,' the sergeant said. He wanted to say 'Bloody lord muck, who the hell does he think he is?' but for all he knew the colonel might be mates with Dartleigh so he kept his trap shut. 'His lordship will be back the day before the scheduled firing, sir.'

'Thank you, Sergeant.'

Nick finally cornered Harold Dartleigh late in the afternoon on the day of his return. He literally bumped into him walking along Ottawa Street. Nick was on his way to the swimming pool and Harold, having just left the hospital, was walking in the opposite direction on his way to his office in the administration block.

'Lord Dartleigh, I've been wanting to have a word with you. Would you have a minute?'

'Ah, Colonel Stratton.' Harold came to a brief halt. 'Yes, yes, of course I have a minute, old chap. What can I do for you?'

Harold Dartleigh's response was most affable, but he once again set off up Ottawa Street, so Nick changed direction and walked alongside him. He was only too happy to do so; he'd much rather conduct their conversation in the privacy of Dartleigh's office. He decided to buy a little time until they got there.

'I believe you've been to Ceduna, sir. Did you have a pleasant trip?'

'Oh, yes, yes, delightful little place, perfect escape from all this.' Harold waved his hands about in a disparaging gesture at the all-pervading desert. The forefinger of his left hand was freshly bandaged. 'Got a nasty little cut though,' he said, wiggling the damaged digit. 'Had a fall wandering about on the rocks of the foreshore, sliced right through my damn finger. The shellfish are quite beastly, I'm told, the possibility of poisoning and all that. Just went and got myself a shot of penicillin. Best to be on the safe side, what?'

'Yes. Yes, indeed.'

'Damned painful though, I must say.'

Having reached the intersection of London Road, they turned left and crossed the street, and it was only when they were standing right outside HQ and the buildings of the administration block that Harold finally called a halt.

'So what is it you wanted to chat about, Colonel?'

Nick realised he hadn't needed to buy time at all. Dartleigh had no intention whatsoever of inviting him into his office.

'I was hoping, Lord Dartleigh, that I might persuade you to attend the press conference following the Biak test.'

'Good heavens above, man, why?'

'I'm sure the members of the press would like to meet you, sir, and it would be an excellent public relations exercise.'

'But I see those chaps at the debriefings after each of the firings.'

'No, sir.' Nick firmly but patiently corrected him. 'At the debriefings, you see only those journalists invited to Maralinga to observe the detonations. I'm referring to the national press conference in Adelaide.'

'Ah, yes, yes . . . *Adelaide* . . .' Harold was already turning up his nose. 'I don't feel there's much purpose in –'

'I strongly believe that your appearance would be more than

a gesture of goodwill, Lord Dartleigh.' Nick interrupted before the answer became an outright no. 'Your presence would be perceived as a mark of great respect. After all, a man of your rank and position symbolises the true link between the mother country and Australia.' What a load of bullshit, he thought, but flattery was the way to a man like Dartleigh. 'Indeed, sir, you symbolise the link between Britain and the entire Commonwealth of Nations.'

'Ah, yes, one does. It's quite true, one does.'

'I take it you'll attend then?'

'We'll see, Colonel. We'll see.'

Harold started to move off, but Nick persisted.

'I'd rather like to announce your appearance to the press, if I may.'

'Oh, I hardly think that necessary, old chap. They'll be there anyway, won't they? I'll let you know on the day.' Harold gave a wave of his non-damaged hand and disappeared into the building that housed his office.

Nick telephoned Elizabeth who'd been impatiently awaiting his call.

'No news about our guest.' Through force of habit, he spoke cryptically. It was probably not necessary, but he always liked to be on the safe side. 'I asked him to the party, but he doesn't want to commit in any way. We won't know if he's coming until the last minute, I'm afraid.'

'Oh dear, how very annoying.'

'Yes, it's a bugger, isn't it? Fingers crossed though. I'll see you at the conference.'

He hung up and Elizabeth was left still on tenterhooks.

Throughout the night, weather conditions remained propitious, and at dawn the meteorological reports proved favourable. The countdown had already started. The Biak test, the second in the Antler series, was to go ahead as planned.

The bomb, with an energy yield of 6 kilotons, was to be exploded from a tower, and the detonation was to take place at ten o'clock on the morning of 25 September 1957.

*Etta is terrified. First the world turned white – the whole of the desert and the scrubland and the sky turned white in one great, blinding flash. Then the evil spirit beings attacked her. She felt their fists as they punched her and she fell to the ground.*

*Now she staggers to her feet and, in sheer terror, runs from the mamu. But they chase her, maddened, screaming their rage. They are too fast for her. They race ahead of her, through the mallee scrub, dodging amongst the trees, hiding in the grasses. They are invisible these mamu, but everywhere she turns she is met by their screeching voices.*

*They have surrounded her, and she sinks to her knees. Their voices are no longer angry. They are playing with her now, taunting her. They surely mean to kill her. She sobs with fear as she awaits her death.*

*Then all is silent. The voices have ceased.*

*Etta looks about, whimpering, expecting any moment the mamu will make themselves visible. Where are they hiding? The morning is clear and the sun bright, but she can see little.*

*Her vision is clouded and there are spots before her eyes. The mamu have blinded her.*

*She feels the child kicking eagerly in her belly. She is only days away from her time and she is frightened. She cannot have her baby here in the presence of the mamu. She must run. She must run far, far away from them.*

*She tries to stand, but she is exhausted, and the last of her reserves seem now to desert her. She slumps onto her back, the desert sand warming her skin through her thin cotton dress. She is defeated.*

*Then she sees the great cloud.*

*The great cloud rises majestically in the sky, just like the cloud she saw from the railway line near Ooldea. But this cloud is far mightier. It is more than a sign; this cloud must surely be a powerful spirit being.*

*As Etta stares up into the sky, her fear slowly subsides. Her vision is clearing and she knows the mamu have gone. The great cloud spirit has broken their spell and frightened them away.*

*Again, the child in her belly kicks, reminding her that she will soon give birth. She hoped to have a woman of experience with her when her time came, but she has not found her family, nor those of her people whose women would have tended to her, and she has resigned herself to the prospect of bearing the burden of childbirth alone.*

*But she is no longer alone, she tells herself. The great cloud spirit is with her, the great cloud spirit who chased away the mamu that would have killed her.*

*She struggles to her feet. She has regained her breath and now has the strength to stand. She must find water and a comfortable shaded place. There she will wait and give birth to her baby.*

# Chapter Twenty

Elizabeth sat in the back row of the conference room, flanked as usual by Bob Swindon and Macca Mackay. Macca had been joined by his fellow journalist Georgie Swann and his photographer Ron Woods, both of whom had accompanied him to Maralinga to observe and record the Biak firing. The men were chatting animatedly to each other as they awaited the arrival of the official party, but Elizabeth wasn't listening. She could think of nothing but her possible confrontation with Harold Dartleigh. She'd spent a sleepless night in anticipation and was now keyed up at the prospect, but Nick hadn't been in touch and she had no idea what to expect. Was Dartleigh coming or wasn't he? It was nerve-racking.

There were fewer journalists in attendance than had been at the conference following the Tadje detonation. It was Macca's view that those travelling from interstate were probably saving themselves for the report on the final test of the series. If rumour proved correct, it promised to be spectacular.

'I've heard they're going to suspend the bomb from a balloon,' Macca told Bob in semi-hushed tones.

'You're joking!' Bob replied.

'No, he's not.' Georgie, seated beside Macca, exchanged a look with Ron who nodded. They'd heard the same thing themselves out at Maralinga. 'Three balloons actually,' he said, peering around Macca to address Bob several chairs away. 'Three balloons linked together, one above the other.'

Macca gestured for Georgie to keep his voice down, although given the general hubbub of the gathering it probably wasn't necessary. 'We're not supposed to know that,' he said to Bob. 'At the debriefings we're always warned about disclosing information. Could get us into trouble,' he said with a warning glance to Georgie.

'I don't see how the balloons can be "disclosing information",' Georgie said nonchalantly. 'The blokes we were talking to at Maralinga didn't give a shit. The gear's all out there ready to go, they told us –'

'And what's the bet there's not one mention of balloons today,' Bob interrupted dryly. Yet again, he'd learnt more from a gossip with the boys than through any official channel. Press conferences were just so much bullshit in his opinion. 'What do you reckon, Liz?' She was very quiet, he thought.

'Yes, I'm sure you're right, Bob,' Elizabeth replied automatically. She hadn't really heard what he'd said – something about the balloons to be used in the final test of the series. She'd had the full rundown on everything from Macca and she'd found it most interesting, but she could think of nothing now except the possibility of seeing Harold Dartleigh face to face. Was she going to have the chance to confront him or not? She felt nervy and on edge.

Several minutes later, the official party made its entrance. Through the open double doors of the conference room strode an AGIO officer, an official representative from Canberra and Colonel Nick Stratton. As they walked to the dais at the far end of the room, an attendant closed the doors behind them. Lord Dartleigh was clearly not expected to make an appearance.

The AGIO officer introduced Nick, who then addressed the gathering.

'Good morning, everyone. Today, as on a number of previous occasions, you'll be receiving your information directly from me.' He placed his manila folder on the podium. 'I have here a full report from the safety committee and will be happy to answer any questions you may have at the end of the proceedings.'

He opened the folder for appearances' sake – he didn't need to refer to it – and as he did, he looked squarely at Elizabeth. *I tried,* his eyes said. *I tried my best, but . . .* He gave the slightest of shrugs.

She disguised her disappointment behind a grateful smile. *I know you tried, Nick, I know. It doesn't matter.*

'The Biak firing took place at ten o'clock yesterday morning. It was a tower detonation, as before . . .'

*I'm sorry. I'm really sorry.*

*Don't be sorry. I love you.*

'. . . and the energy yield of the device was 6 kilotons.'

His eyes had no trouble sending the message that he found such difficulty in voicing. *I love you too,* they said.

'I'm sorry about the way things worked out, Elizabeth,' he said as she lay with her head nestled against his shoulder. 'I know today must have been a terrible disappointment for you.'

'How could a day that ends like this be a disappointment?' She rolled onto her side, perched on an elbow and slung a shameless leg over his thigh, the fullness of her breasts rubbing wantonly against his chest.

He laughed. 'Give a man time, for God's sake,' he said, but it wouldn't take long, he wanted her again already.

Elizabeth disentangled her leg and flopped back on her pillow to look up at the ceiling. She hadn't actually intended to be provocative, just comforting.

'It *was* a bit of a disappointment,' she admitted. 'I'd got myself quite worked up about confronting Dartleigh, but it's hardly your fault – you did what you could.'

'I think he was fobbing me off from the start. He probably never intended to front up. When I approached him early this morning he seemed to have completely forgotten about the conference.'

'It's not your *fault*, Nick, stop agonising.'

'I'm not agonising, I'm bloody annoyed. Christ, he's an arrogant bastard. But don't you worry, I haven't thrown in the towel yet. Although we're running short of time, I must say. The final test's less than two weeks away, and we have to corner him between now and then. He'll head straight back to London when the Antler series is over.'

She propped herself on her side again to look at him. 'What do you intend to do?'

'I intend to have an eminently plausible reason why he has to come to Adelaide.' Her breasts were once more caressing his chest, which was distracting. 'It shouldn't be too difficult. A few of the big guns are flying in from Canberra for a meeting at AGIO next week. I'll suggest to them that, in the interests of national security, they express a desire to meet the deputy director of MI6. Even Dartleigh won't be able to refuse a personal request from representatives of the Australian government.'

'Excellent. I shall storm the meeting.'

'Well, we might have to work out a place and a time when –'

'Later. Let's talk about that part later.'

She leaned her head down to kiss him, and the smell and the

warmth and the womanliness of her was irresistible. Recovery time over, Nick gathered her to him.

Members of the indoctrination force discovered the Aboriginal girl two days after the detonation. They radioed back to the DC/RB area.

'She's irradiated,' they said, 'her readings are going off the dial. She's alive, but only just, and she's heavily pregnant.'

'Bring her in,' was the reply.

By the time the girl arrived she was barely conscious.

Melvyn Crowley was waiting at the decontamination unit to greet the new arrival. He was all suited up in protective clothing, as was his assistant, Trafford Whitely.

Melvyn immediately set about examining the girl, but Trafford, realising that she appeared to be trying to communicate, did not lend assistance. Instead, he bent close to the parched lips in an attempt to discern the barely audible whisper. She was speaking English he was sure. Then he made out the words 'baby' and 'save'.

Intent upon offering some form of comfort, he stroked the girl's bare arm with his gloved fingers, ignoring Melvyn Crowley's irritated glance. 'Yes,' he said, 'we'll save your baby.'

The huge brown eyes seemed to look deeply into him and Trafford wondered if she could tell he was lying. They would be unable to save her baby. But she obviously didn't know that, for all he could see in her gaze was gratitude. He wanted to weep. She was so young, he thought, so very young.

'What is your name?' he asked softly.

Very faintly, he heard her say 'Etta'.

'The child's alive,' Melvyn Crowley said.

He had been about to bark at Trafford to address the job at hand, but his irritation had vanished as he'd heard the heartbeat through the stethoscope. Amazingly enough, the baby's vital signs were healthy. The child was very much alive, even though its mother was near dead. Melvyn couldn't have been more excited.

'We need to get it out as soon as possible,' he said.

Trafford stroked the girl's arm once more before he left. 'We'll save your baby, Etta,' he said.

The huge brown eyes thanked him.

He turned away and followed Melvyn Crowley from the decontamination unit to the outer area where they were divested of their protective clothing.

'Have her put through the decontamination process,' Melvyn ordered. 'Once her body readings are acceptable we'll take the baby out.'

A child irradiated in the womb, he thought. Breakthrough examination material – perfect. He couldn't have asked for better.

'But once her readings are acceptable, shouldn't we get her to the hospital?' Trafford said.

'Why? She'll be dead by then anyway.'

'The child won't be. The child's still alive.'

'But for how long?' Melvyn was becoming impatient; how dare young Trafford question him. 'Good God, boy, the baby's readings will go through the roof. We can't deliver a contamin-ated child in a non-protected area. Besides,' he added, 'this whole business has to be kept as quiet as possible. If word spreads, the army won't like it one bit.' He turned on his heel. 'Now have her decontaminated and get yourself scrubbed up and ready to assist me. I'll be in the laboratory.'

'Yes, Dr Crowley.'

While the girl was being put through the gruelling process of decontamination, Trafford, unbeknownst to his superior, issued his own order.

'Radio the hospital and tell Dr Bradshaw I'd like him to come to the DC/RB area as quickly as possible,' he said to one of the junior assistants. 'Tell him to say nothing to anyone, but warn him he's to deliver a child by caesarean.'

Trafford could just imagine the look on Cliff Bradshaw's face when he received the message. It was hardly the sort of summons one would expect at Maralinga.

He left instructions with the MPs at the main gate and took himself off to the scrubroom adjoining the main pathology laboratory, where he would await Clifton Bradshaw's arrival.

Captain Clifton 'Cliff' Bradshaw of the British medical corps was Trafford's senior by little more than a year. Like Trafford he was an ambitious but highly principled young man, and the two had become friends. It was unusual – scientists and military kept to their own as a rule – but Cliff and Trafford shared the mutual bond of their medical background. Coincidentally, both had graduated from Oxford, although they'd barely known each other at university. Their friendship had been forged at Maralinga. It was a friendship that would prove to last a lifetime, due principally to the events of this day.

When the girl was finally returned to the laboratory she was unconscious and her vital signs minimal. She would not regain consciousness.

Melvyn watched with eager anticipation as the two assistants from the decontamination unit lifted her naked body from the gurney to the examination table. He was so excited by the prospect of what lay ahead that he didn't notice Trafford usher Clifton Bradshaw through the door. Cliff was gowned, scrubbed up and ready to operate.

The men departed with the gurney, and Melvyn dragged his eyes from the body to issue instructions to his assistant. It was then he noticed to his utter astonishment that there was a third person in the laboratory.

Trafford made the introductions. 'Dr Crowley, this is Dr Bradshaw,' he said. 'I'm sure you will have met each other from time to time. Cliff, this is Dr Crowley, our head pathologist.'

'Yes, we've bumped into each other on a number of occasions,' Cliff said congenially. 'Difficult not to in a place like Maralinga.' He saluted the older man with the wave of a sterilised hand. 'Only too happy to be of assistance, sir.'

Assistance? Melvyn looked dumbfounded from Clifton to Trafford and back again. What assistance? He didn't need any fucking *assistance*!

'I thought that as we couldn't take the girl to the hospital, we could bring the hospital to the girl,' Trafford said. 'Cliff's a medical practitioner. He's experienced in child delivery and I was sure you'd want to exercise every caution, Dr Crowley, given the fact that the baby's vital signs are still strong.'

A murderous light shone in Melvyn's eyes. *You little bastard.* 'Of course, Trafford . . . how clever of you to show such foresight.' *You fucking little bastard!* 'I'm indebted to you, Dr Bradshaw.'

He stood to one side, gesturing to the examination table, the girl, the tray of instruments, a gesture that said *she's all yours*, but the murderous light didn't leave his eyes. *You young bastards, the pair of you.* Melvyn wanted to kill them both.

As Clifton stepped forward to the table Trafford joined him to assist with the operation and the two exchanged the quickest of glances. Trafford was right, Cliff thought. There was something of the madman about Crowley.

The moment he looked down at the girl he knew she was gone, but he felt her pulse anyway. 'We've lost her,' he said.

Poor little Etta, Trafford thought. She'd died unnoticed in the minute or so they'd been talking.

'We'll have to move fast.' Clasping the scalpel Trafford placed in his open palm, Cliff made the incision.

With Trafford assisting, Clifton Bradshaw worked speedily and efficiently, the two young men forming a slick, professional team. Melvyn watched from the sidelines, fuming. This is *my* laboratory, he thought. That cadaver and that child belong to *me*. But he was powerless and he knew it. He seethed with impotent rage.

Within only minutes the baby was lifted, squirming, from the dead woman's womb. It was a girl, and she wanted to live. She opened her mouth, her tiny lungs filled with air, her angry little brown face twisted and she cried out her existence to the world.

When they'd cut the cord and cleaned her up, they took a reading of the baby's levels with the radiac survey meter, Trafford running the external probe over the tiny naked body and Clifton listening through the headphones. All eyes, including Melvyn Crowley's, were keenly trained on the Geiger counter's dial and indicator. But to the utter astonishment of all three men, there was no reading.

'There's no evidence of ionising radiation in this baby,' Cliff Bradshaw announced.

'My God,' Trafford said, amazed, 'she's clean.'

'Impossible,' Melvyn Crowley snapped.

'Have a listen yourself.' Clifton handed him the headphones.

Melvyn jammed them on his head and once again Trafford ran the probe over the baby. Once again they all studied the dial, and once again the Geiger counter showed no reading.

'I don't believe it,' Melvyn said, snatching off the headphones. 'It's not possible.'

'How do you know?' Clifton queried. 'The womb's a very protective place. It seems eminently possible to me.' As there was no blanket in sight, he started wrapping the child in a clean towel. 'And you must admit, Dr Crowley, stranger things have happened in medical science.'

'But the thyroid would show radioactive levels, I'm sure . . .' Melvyn was desperate, everything was going wrong. 'And there's bound to be traces of strontium-90 in the bones . . .'

'We'll run a urinalysis at the hospital,' Clifton said, 'but it's my guess we'll find no evidence of strontium-90. As for the rest . . .' He looked at the Geiger counter and shrugged. 'The RSM 2 says she's clean and it's a pretty reliable machine. You can hardly cut her up to prove the thing wrong, can you?'

He smiled as if the comment was an attempt at black humour, but it wasn't. He hadn't altogether believed Trafford when he'd said that Crowley would happily murder the child for experimental purposes. He believed him now. Melvyn Crowley belonged to another world.

'Anyway, enough chat,' he said, picking up the baby. She wriggled in his arms, her perfect little hands escaping the confines of the towel, her tiny fingers clutching the air. 'Time to get this one to the hospital.'

'You do realise that if you take it to the hospital, word will quickly circulate, don't you? I mean about . . . *this*.' Melvyn gestured to the bloodied table and the corpse of the girl.

'I have no idea what you're talking about,' Clifton replied. He was beginning to see no reason why he should even pretend civility to a man like Crowley.

'As Trafford well knows,' Melvyn said with a damning look at his assistant, 'a similar irradiation incident occurred last year and troops were threatened with court martial if the news became public.'

Clifton cast a querying look at his friend.

'It's true,' Trafford said. He'd naturally made no mention to Clifton of the Aboriginal deaths. Cliff was in the army, after all – why place him in such a threatening position?

'We must be discreet then, mustn't we,' Clifton said. 'The fewer of us who know, the fewer of us there will be who will have to live with that threat. And the sooner the child can be placed safely in the care of Aboriginal welfare authorities, the better for all of us, wouldn't you say?'

Melvyn was stumped and Trafford wanted to cheer.

'What a tragedy,' Clifton said as he looked at the body on the table. He'd been so focused upon the child it was the first time he'd addressed the situation of the young mother. 'How sad. She's not much more than a child herself.'

The baby started to cry, as if demanding he redirect his attention to the living, and he gave her the tip of his little finger to suck on.

'Drive me to the hospital, Trafford,' he said. 'The miracle baby of Maralinga wants to be fed.'

They left Melvyn Crowley to fume. And fume he did.

Melvyn cursed Trafford for his betrayal. He'd have the young ingrate transferred immediately, he decided, although the sure knowledge that Trafford would welcome transferral was irksome. If only he could have the little bastard dismissed, he thought, or dishonoured or disbarred or at least in some way discredited. But with Trafford's good chum Cliff on the scene as a witness that would be an impossibility.

Melvyn didn't know which of the two he despised most, Trafford or Clifton Bradshaw. How dare they snatch such an opportunity from him! Indeed, how dare they deprive the scientific world of his findings! There was so much fresh knowledge he might have contributed for the benefit of mankind. He glanced at the corpse. At least he still had her. That was some comfort. But he could have had so very much more.

Two days later, when he heard the baby had been flown to

Adelaide, Melvyn was even more livid. He had presumed she would be taken to the mission at Yalata where he would be able to keep an eye on her condition, which would hopefully decline. But Etta's child, 'the miracle baby of Maralinga' as she was now referred to by the few who knew of her existence, had been swallowed up by the system. She would be given a home with a family keen to adopt, and would be forever beyond the clutches of Melvyn Crowley.

Nick had been angered and frustrated when he'd discovered Harold Dartleigh had disappeared to Sydney.

'What do you mean *no-one knows where he is?*' he'd demanded of Ned Hanson. 'Surely he informed you of where he's staying. You must be able to contact him somehow.'

'I'm afraid not, Colonel. He has no wish to be contacted. He was quite definite about that.' Ned Hanson's weary sigh had been audible. He found the vagaries of his superior frustrating too. 'Lord Dartleigh's gone on holiday and doesn't wish to be disturbed. He'll be back two days before the final test.'

Bloody indulgence, Nick had thought as he'd stormed out of Ned's poky little office, which adjoined Harold's. Why the hell did the British government bother paying Dartleigh? The man was a waste of taxpayers' money!

He'd immediately telephoned Elizabeth with the news.

'Our friend's gone away on holiday for ten days,' he'd said. 'He's in Sydney, but no-one knows where.'

'Oh, dear.'

'Exactly. So he won't be available for next week's meeting. In fact, he won't be available full stop.'

'Right.' He'd sounded so fed up that Elizabeth had decided not to offer any further comment on the subject. 'You're coming into town yourself though, aren't you?' she'd asked hopefully.

'Yes.'

'Oh, I am glad. I'll look forward to seeing you then, shall I?' She always took her cue from Nick and never gave away a thing on the phone.

'The meeting's at three o'clock. I'm not sure how long it'll last,' he'd said meaningfully, 'so I've decided to stay in town for the night. I'll give you a ring when it's over and maybe we could meet for a drink when you've finished work, what do you say?'

'I say that sounds like an excellent idea.'

Now, five days later, they sat on the beach looking out at the ocean. It was late in the afternoon, daylight was fading and the bank of clouds low on the horizon promised a pretty sunset. They'd caught a taxi from the city. These days, during his brief visits, Nick didn't bother with hire cars. Taxis were easier, and he no longer needed the excuse of a car to hand in order to drive her home.

They'd broken their normal pattern of making love as their first priority. Nick, feeling in some way that he'd let her down, had suggested they go for a walk on the beach. 'There's a lot to talk about,' he'd said.

They'd changed into casual clothes and walked barefoot, their shoes in their hands, beside the water's edge. They'd walked, and they'd talked. He'd been keen to make up for the disappointment of Harold Dartleigh's non-appearance.

'Shall I try and entice Gideon Melbray to town?' he asked. 'I'm not quite sure how I'd go about it, I have no official connection with Gideon, but I'm happy to give it a try.'

'No, Nick.' Her reply was adamant. 'You might arouse suspicion, and I don't want you to become directly involved. Your career could be threatened.'

'Oh, don't worry, I'll come up with something plausible. It's just a case of finding the right angle.'

'Anyway, I don't see a great deal of value in Gideon Melbray.'

She'd surprised him. 'Why not? Isn't he your other key person of interest?'

'He wouldn't tell me anything I don't already know. Besides, Gideon's only the messenger. I need to get to the man at the top.'

'But making contact with Dartleigh is –'

'And that man might not even be Harold Dartleigh.'

Their walk came to a halt. He was confused. 'What exactly are you getting at?'

'I'm absolutely convinced that MI6 is behind all this, Nick.'

He wasn't sure how to respond. Since when had it been irrevocably decided that MI6 was 'behind all this', he wondered. Hadn't they agreed that the theory had been based upon supposition? But Elizabeth wasn't seeking a response. She went on without drawing breath.

'Given Harold Dartleigh's involvement, it's pretty obvious to me that MI6 is responsible for faking Danny's death to look like a suicide. Whatever they were covering I've no idea, but it's MI6 who needs to answer for what happened.'

Nick marvelled at the simplicity of her reasoning. For Elizabeth, everything seemed to have fallen neatly into place. She was so supremely sure of herself, he thought. But then she always was. Positivity was perhaps one of her greatest assets.

'Harold Dartleigh might or might not have been acting on orders from above,' she briskly continued, 'but either way he's answerable to the organisation that employs him. And that organisation is in turn answerable for the actions of its employees, wouldn't you agree?'

'Answerable about what and to whom?' Was she really serious? She was talking about MI6.

'In this case, answerable to me. Danny was my fiancé and I demand to know what happened.'

'Oh, right.' She was about to charge off tilting at windmills, he thought, how very typical, and how very futile. 'What course of action do you intend to take?' he asked for want of anything better to say.

'I have a colleague in London with excellent connections. He'll most certainly know who I should contact within MI6. I'll start at the top, and if I can't make any inroads I'll threaten to go public. I'm sure if I rattle the sabre loud enough they'll be forced to take action, or at least to come up with some answers. Harold Dartleigh's head may roll – or the head of the person who gave him his instructions, who can tell? But I intend to get my answers.'

'Ah.' He'd been so distracted by the futility of her plan that the practical aspect hadn't as yet occurred to him. It did now. 'So you'll be heading back to London.'

'Yes.'

'When? How soon?'

'I'm not sure yet. Certainly not for another month – I'd need to hand in my notice at the paper.'

'I see.' There didn't really seem much more to be said. She'd plainly made up her mind. 'Shall we go back to the flat?'

'No. Not just yet.'

That was when they'd decided to sit on the sand and wait for the sunset.

They were silent now as they watched the golden orb of the sun slowly sink into the sea. Then, all of a sudden, the last glimmer disappeared, leaving the clouds aglow with pinks and oranges that fanned out across the sky like a multicoloured roof to the world.

'How beautiful,' Elizabeth said. 'I'd never seen such beautiful sunsets until I came to Australia.'

'Yes, it's certainly lovely.' God, I'll miss her, he thought. 'The days are getting warmer,' he said, still gazing out at the ocean. 'We must get in a few swimming lessons before you go.'

'Yes, we must.'

She didn't want to leave him, but she would if she had to. She'd conduct her fight from London if necessary, although she hoped it wouldn't come to that. She still had one more plan up her sleeve. A plan she could not share with Nick.

That night, after they'd made love, the two of them lay awake for some time, each lost in their own thoughts.

Elizabeth was forming the approach she would take with her editor the following day. She must pitch her idea with care, but she was sure P. J. would agree. He was an adventurous man.

Nick's mind was in a far greater state of turmoil. During their talk on the beach, he'd dismissed Elizabeth's decision to confront MI6 as a waste of time – they would simply close ranks and she'd get nowhere, he'd thought. But now a dreadful possibility struck him. Was there the remotest chance that Daniel Gardiner might have been under investigation by MI6? It seemed most unlikely. But Dan had formed a close friendship with Pete Mitchell, a strangely complex man. Could Pete have converted Dan to whatever cause had obsessed him? Perhaps Pete's death had not been the simple crime of passion it had been reported to be. In which case, perhaps young Dan's hadn't been so simple either. Much as he tried to dismiss such thoughts, Nick couldn't help but worry. His original premise about the possible cover-up of a botched death for security purposes was one thing, but the MI6 investigation of a British soldier working in a top-secret area like Maralinga was quite another. Could Elizabeth be on the verge of disturbing a hornets' nest?

The following morning, after a sleepless night, he wondered whether he should bring up the subject, although he didn't relish the prospect. He could well imagine her reaction. He decided to say nothing. There was no time for discussion anyway. He had to leave for the airport.

'I'll see you at the conference after the firing next week,' he said. 'I'll arrange things so that I can stay overnight.' They'd talk about it then, he thought.

'See you at the conference,' she said, and they kissed. She wished she could tell him of her plan, but she didn't dare.

The final test of the Antler series was codenamed Taranaki and, with an energy yield of 27 kilotons, the bomb was the largest yet to be detonated at Maralinga. The firing was to take place on 9 October, and the device was to be suspended from a system of three balloons held at 1000 feet over the desert. The test organisers were convinced this particular firing technique would considerably reduce both the close-in and long-range fallout.

Weather conditions were carefully monitored throughout the previous night and throughout the morning of 9 October. With a weapon of such size, all precautions must be strictly observed. But the meteorological reports continued to prove favourable and the final go-ahead was given. The hourly countdown to Taranaki had begun.

At Roadside, the spectators were gathered in their hundreds as usual. Scientists, military, bureaucrats and press all had their binoculars and field glasses trained on the three distant spheres in the sky and the barely visible object dangling beneath them. Gigantic though the balloons were, from where the observers stood they were mere dots to the naked eye.

It was four o'clock in the afternoon. Fifteen minutes to go.

Then ten, then five, then one . . . Then the voice through the tannoy started counting down the seconds, until finally . . .

*Ten, nine . . .*

Binoculars were left to dangle around necks as the crowd turned its back to the site.

*Eight, seven . . .*

Everyone stood legs astride, feet planted firmly as instructed. They'd been warned about the shock waves.

*Six, five . . .*

Hands were placed over eyes, palms tightly pressed into sockets.

*Four, three, two . . .*

Finally the moment of detonation and the blinding flash that drained the world of all colour. The backs of necks felt the heat of the gamma rays. But no-one moved. No-one spoke. They all stood waiting.

The atomic shock waves hit with brutal force and a number amongst the crowd lost their footing, staggering, off balance. Hands left eyes and fingers were jammed into ears as a devastating series of explosions ricocheted about the scrub.

Then, as suddenly as it had happened, the madness was over and the desert returned to silence. Still, no-one moved. They stayed with their backs to the site, as instructed.

Finally, when it was deemed safe, the order was given and, in unison, the crowd turned to see the aftermath of Taranaki.

They didn't need their binoculars and field glasses now. Towering in the sky, pulsating and growing by the minute like a living being, was the great mushroom cloud. And clearly depicted in it, hundreds of feet high, complete in every detail, was the gigantic silhouetted face of an angry bearded man.

They all saw it. Some said later they thought it was the face of a Greek god. 'The nose was Grecian,' they said. Others disagreed. 'No,' they said. 'Oh, no, the face was most definitely Aboriginal.'

For a full ten minutes the face remained in the cloud, and those watching certainly agreed upon one thing. It seemed to be looking down in judgement.

# Chapter Twenty-one

Following the detonation, the members of the press in attendance were transported back to Maralinga for their customary debriefing, after which they were to be taken to the airport. They would be flown directly to Adelaide, where those from interstate or overseas would stay the night before attending the press conference the following day and then returning home.

The forty or so journalists and photographers were ushered into the main conference room in the administration block by military police. Although the MPs were not overly officious, they were nonetheless a reminder of the vigilant security in place as they took up their positions by the room's several entrances. No wayward reporter was tempted to duck through a door for a quick snoop around the nearby offices.

Chairs had been provided, and at one end of the room were tables with jugs of water and paper cups. After a long afternoon standing around in the sun, the men made a beeline for the water, fanning their faces with their hats and loosening their collars and ties. Regardless of discomfort, the mood was relaxed and conversation was rife. There were few newcomers amongst them, most having witnessed the previous detonations, and the general consensus of opinion was that this had been the most spectacular.

'The balloons,' they said. 'And the shock waves . . . And what about that face in the cloud!'

The face in the cloud was a particularly popular subject amongst the photographers, most of whom were convinced they'd caught it to perfection.

'Got every little detail,' Ron Woods boasted to Macca. 'It'll be front-page stuff, mate, a real beauty.'

As it turned out, Ron was wrong, and so were all the others. When the pictures were developed, there was no face. The cloud was just a cloud.

The babble of voices continued and there was the scrape of chairs on wood as they shuffled into their seats. No-one took any notice of the young man in the pinstriped suit and grey fedora who sat with Macca and Ron. But no-one had paid him much attention all day.

'Where's Georgie?' one or two of the old hands had asked Macca, with a querying look at the young man who appeared little more than a youth.

'Georgie couldn't make it,' Macca had muttered, 'so I brought young Les along. He's only a cadet. Not a word, mate, he's travelling on Georgie's ticket.'

The reaction from the several old hands had been 'lucky kid'.

'You don't get a break like this often, young fella,' one had said. 'Make the most of it.' The lad had nodded deferentially and looked down at his shoes without saying a word.

The general conclusion amongst the few who'd noticed the kid had been that although he was respectful enough, he didn't deserve such an opportunity. Why had Macca put himself out on a limb for a kid so shy he was tongue-tied? Pretty-boys like that didn't belong in the business anyway. The old hands ignored him. Why would you bother?

Once she'd passed the initial test, Elizabeth had had few problems. She'd stayed close to Macca and Ron, speaking to no-one, knowing that her voice was the giveaway, and when they were out at Roadside, she'd simply become one of the crowd. She'd been relieved by the ease with which the deception had been carried out. She'd worried that she might have been discovered right from the start.

'Won't they demand identification at the airport?' she'd asked.

'They've already got it,' Georgie had said. 'You're me. Macca hands over the pass, they tick off the three-man team from *The Advertiser* and you're on the plane. It'll be that simple.'

Georgie hadn't minded Elizabeth going in his place. In fact, he'd found the idea hilarious. When he'd been called into P. J.'s office, he hadn't even recognised Liz. He'd given a nod to the kid in the pinstriped suit lounging against the wall with his hands in his pockets, and when P. J. had said 'Liz has got an idea', he still hadn't twigged. And then the kid had spoken and Georgie had been knocked for six. 'What a hoot,' he'd said when they'd told him the plan. 'I can just see the headlines: *Lone Female Reporter Foils the Might of Maralinga Security.*'

P. J. hadn't even cracked a smile. If they could pull off the scam, that was exactly the story he could foresee a little further down the track when the paranoia had lessened. Indeed, they could drum up a whole exposé on the ineffectuality of national security measures if and when the time seemed right. Meanwhile, an inside account of Maralinga and the Taranaki firing written by a journalist of Liz's calibre would be extremely worthwhile. And further down the track, with or without the exposé, they could announce that it had actually been written by a woman. P. J. had seen a wealth of value in Liz's plan.

'You don't mind missing out then, Georgie?' Elizabeth had felt guilty about depriving him of the Taranaki experience.

'Nah. You've seen one atomic explosion, you've seen them all, love,' Georgie had said with a wink. 'Besides, hanging around in the middle of the desert for hours isn't a barrel of laughs. I'd rather be down the pub.' Georgie's principal regret was that he wouldn't be part of the fun.

Ron Woods had also embraced the idea. Like Georgie, Ron was a bit of a renegade and he too had seen the whole thing as a huge joke. The only one with serious misgivings had been Macca. A cautious man by nature, Macca hadn't relished playing a part in the deception one bit. But he'd comforted himself with the knowledge that should they be discovered he could hardly be blamed. He had, after all, simply been carrying out orders.

Now, as they waited for the debriefing to commence, Macca finally allowed himself to relax a little. Things were all pretty much downhill from now on, he thought. It looked as if they'd got away with it. Thank Christ for that.

Elizabeth felt herself tense. An MP guarding one of the doors had stood aside and Nick had appeared. Her main problem now was to escape detection by her lover. She lowered her head, peering from beneath the brim of her fedora, thankful that a number of the others had kept their hats on and that she didn't look conspicuous.

Two men followed Nick into the room. Elizabeth recognised them both in an instant. The first was Sir William Penney. The second was Harold Dartleigh.

She studied Dartleigh. He was a figure with whom she'd been well acquainted over the years, his image regularly appearing in British print media and newsreel footage. He was imposing in the flesh, she thought, although she could see what Nick meant when he spoke of the man's arrogance. Even at a glance, Dartleigh had the air of one born to a life of wealth and privilege.

As the three men walked to the front of the conference room, Elizabeth's eyes followed Harold Dartleigh. His every move, his every nuance were those of a man utterly inviolable, but she refused to be daunted. Regardless of his position, Dartleigh had actions to answer for. And what better platform could she find upon which to raise her questions than right here? MI6 would undoubtedly fob off any approach she attempted through legitimate channels, she was aware of that. Indeed, she'd been aware that Nick had considered her plan virtually useless. But here, surrounded by the press, Dartleigh would be personally caught out. He'd have to give himself away somehow.

The debriefing being a quick formality, the three men did not sit. The provision of chairs for the press, while ostensibly a courtesy following a long afternoon in the sun, served an eminently more practical purpose in reality. It was simpler for the MPs to monitor men who were seated and easier for those conducting the debriefing to make eye contact with everyone present.

As usual Nick opened the proceedings. 'I'll be seeing most of you at the press conference tomorrow, and we want to get you to the airport while it's still light, so I'll hand you straight over to Sir William Penney who's graciously offered to say a few words. Sir William . . .'

'Thank you, Colonel.' The scientist stepped forward. 'As you're no doubt aware, gentlemen, I don't usually attend these debriefings, but this being the final test I'd like to offer my thanks to you all for the courtesy and respect you've displayed.

Quite a number of you have been with us throughout both major series, Buffalo and Antler. Seven tests in all, and I think you'll agree each one of those seven detonations has been a spectacular event to witness . . .'

As Penney addressed the gathering, Elizabeth continued to study Dartleigh, carefully angling her head so that the brim of her hat obscured Nick. Dartleigh was paying no attention whatsoever to William Penney. In fact, he wasn't even feigning interest. He was staring vacantly out the nearest window at the dusty street lined with she-oaks and his mind appeared a million miles away. Elizabeth wondered where.

Harold was thinking of his wife, Lavinia, and his son, Nigel, and even of his daughter, Catherine, whom he didn't really like. But above all, he was thinking of home, of his country estate in Sussex where the air would be crisp and bracing and where the trees would be painted in their glorious autumn hues. Outside in the street he could see the she-oaks. Who had come up with such a name, he wondered. She-oaks? They weren't *oaks*. They didn't deserve to be called oaks. They weren't even trees. They were scaly-trunked, mothy-leaved pretenders. Thank God he was leaving tomorrow, he thought. Thank God he'd soon be home in England in the bosom of his family and this ghastly Australian desert would be no more than an unpleasant memory . . .

'Thank you, Sir William.'

Harold snapped out of his reverie at the sound of Nick Stratton's voice and, realising he was about to be introduced, looked benignly over the gathering. As his eyes roamed the room making friendly contact with all and sundry, he caught the intense gaze of a young man. A very good-looking young man, he noted, one with the androgynous quality of true beauty, and the lad was peering directly at him from beneath the brim of his fedora. Harold held the youth's gaze, expecting him to look away, but the cheeky little blighter didn't. How intriguing, he thought.

He barely heard the colonel's brief introduction, until . . .

'Lord Dartleigh . . .?' Nick prompted. The man appeared not to have been listening.

'Yes, yes, Colonel, thank you.' Harold stepped forward, his arms outstretched in a gesture of bonhomie. 'And now, gentlemen, we come to the true purpose of these debriefings,' he said with a smile, 'and that is of course my customary caution, which some of you may well be able to recite off by heart.'

He glanced again at the young man, whose eyes still hadn't left him. The lad must be a newcomer, he thought, such youthful beauty could never have escaped his notice in the past.

'Yes, yes, I know, it's all in the pamphlet you received upon your arrival . . .' He gave a regretful shrug of apology – Harold was always the show pony in front of a crowd. 'Nevertheless, gentlemen, I'm afraid I am required by law to say the words out loud.'

Having charmed his audience, he usually rattled through the caution, which was dry old stuff. But he didn't today. Today he actually slowed things down in order to observe the young man, who seemed to be intent upon some form of exchange. What was his intention, Harold wondered. No longer was he peering from beneath the brim of his hat; he'd raised his head and was staring in brazen defiance.

'It is a crime, under the British Official Secrets Acts of 1911, 1920 and Part VII of the Australian Crimes Act of 1914, to disclose or publish information obtained in contravention of the said Acts . . .'

As he recited the caution, Harold couldn't help but feel a frisson of excitement. There was something in the boldness of the young man's manner that reminded him just a little of Gideon when they'd first met in Washington. Gideon had dared him in just the same way, and it had meant only one thing.

'In particular I must remind you that newspapers, and indeed journalists, who publish information in contravention of section 3 of the Official Secrets Act are guilty of a crime punishable by fine and imprisonment.'

How very rewarding to be found attractive by one so young, Harold thought. Naturally he would make no response and offer no encouragement, but he wondered whether he might have a brief chat with the lad after the debriefing. He did so admire beauty. Fancy encountering it here, he thought, in this Godforsaken place where even the trees were ugly.

'And that concludes the official caution, gentlemen. I thank you for your patience.'

He smiled graciously at the room at large and the youth in particular and was about to step back so that the colonel could wrap up the debriefing when, to his amazement, the young man rose to his feet. How extraordinary, Harold thought, and he stood his ground waiting to see what the lad had to say.

There was a reaction from some even before she revealed herself.

Oh my God, Nick thought. It's Elizabeth. But he made no move, his eyes darting about seeking who would intervene.

Oh shit, Macca thought, she's about to give the whole game away.

What the hell's she doing, Ron wondered. Christ, she's got guts.

All eyes were upon the young man who seemed to be squaring up to Harold Dartleigh. The MPs were wary. Was the kid about to cause trouble? The old hands were confused. What was the pretty-boy up to?

For one brief moment, there was complete silence. Then Elizabeth took off the fedora.

'My name is Elizabeth Hoffmann,' she said, and the place erupted.

Good heavens above, Harold thought, it's a woman, how very amusing. Someone's idea of a joke, he supposed.

Elizabeth raised her voice above the babble of amazement. 'I have some questions to ask you, Lord Dartleigh.' The babble came to an instant halt and she continued, her focus concentrated solely upon Harold. 'I was engaged to Lieutenant Daniel Gardiner whose death here at Maralinga was reported as accidental . . .'

At the mention of Daniel's name, Harold was instantly on the alert. Young Dan's fiancée, he thought. This was not a joke after all.

'. . . But I know, Lord Dartleigh, that Daniel's death was not the accident it was reported to be . . .'

Harold refused to be shaken. The grieving fiancée compelled to apportion blame, he thought, but he was angry. How dare she do so in such a public manner.

'We are all aware,' he said coldly, 'of the tragic circumstances of your fiancé's death, Miss Hoffmann –'

She cut him short. 'Nor was it a suicide as military records purport!'

'And we sympathise with your pain,' he continued icily, 'but it does not warrant your flagrant disregard for the law. You are in breach of security regulations and you will be charged accordingly.' He gestured to one of the military police who stepped forward.

Elizabeth ignored the threat, raising her voice in accusation. 'I received a letter written by Daniel just before he was killed,' she announced clearly for the benefit of the entire assembly. 'I know the truth, Lord Dartleigh –'

'Take her away,' Harold angrily ordered, and another MP stepped forward. 'I will not tolerate these histrionics. You make

477

a mockery of the law, madam. Get her out of here,' he growled with a wave of his hand.

Those seated near Elizabeth hastily stood to make way for the MPs, who, taking an arm apiece, started escorting her from the room. But Elizabeth wasn't about to go peacefully. She struggled and, as they got her to the door, managed to drag herself free from the grip of one of the policemen. Whirling about she flung a final accusation at Harold Dartleigh.

'I know about you and Gideon Melbray!' she yelled.

Harold froze. Gideon? How could she know about Gideon?

Elizabeth saw the flash of recognition in his eyes and realised she'd hit home.

'Daniel knew too, Dartleigh,' she shouted, bluffing wildly, throwing everything she could at him. 'He wrote and told me –'

'Get this madwoman out of here,' Harold roared.

'I know the truth about both of you!' she screamed. 'I have written proof –'

She gasped as her arm was wrenched behind her back. She tottered on her feet, knees threatening to give way, a fierce pain shooting through her shoulder.

Suddenly the room was in chaos.

Nick, upon seeing Elizabeth so manhandled, automatically launched himself at the policeman who had her in an arm lock. He threw a powerful punch that connected and the man released his hold, staggering back against the wall. Elizabeth fell to her knees. People jumped to their feet and chairs overturned as other MPs sprang into action, wrestling to control the colonel who appeared to have gone insane.

The scuffle didn't last long. Nick made no attempt to resist arrest. He was quickly overpowered and both he and Elizabeth were handcuffed.

Harold Dartleigh took immediate control.

'Lock them up,' he barked. 'I'll interview them in due course. Until then, they're to remain in the cells and no-one is to speak to them.'

As the two were bundled out of the room, he directed his anger at the members of the press. 'A serious breach of security has occurred here today,' he said. 'A full investigation will be held and whoever assisted this woman in breaking the law will be duly brought to justice. In the meantime,' he turned to the MPs who stood awaiting their orders, 'have everyone taken to the airport and returned to Adelaide as planned.'

Harold stormed from the conference room, leaving the press bewildered and Sir William Penney utterly flabbergasted. What on earth had just happened, they all wondered.

As he strode to his office several buildings away, Harold did not dwell upon the woman or how she may have discovered the truth. The simple fact was that she had, which meant he must take immediate action. There were plans to be made.

He popped his head into Ned Hanson's office.

'There's been a bit of a fracas in the conference room,' he said. 'A breach of security regulations. I've had a couple of trouble-makers taken to the cells. One of them's a woman.'

'Good grief –'

'They're not to be spoken to until I've interviewed them. Go and keep an eye on things, there's a good chap. No-one's to come near them until I give the order.'

'Yes, sir.' Ned stood. 'A woman?'

'And leave me the Land Rover keys.'

'Yes, sir.' Ned took the car keys from his pocket and handed them to his superior. 'A woman? How on earth did –'

'On the double, Ned.' Harold wanted to smash his fist in the dullard's face, but he smiled genially. 'Off you go now, there's a good man.'

'Yes, sir, of course, sir.'

As soon as Ned had gone, Harold closed the door, sat down at his desk and telephoned the airport.

'I've received a communiqué from London,' he said, 'they need my immediate return. Have the aircraft and crew standing by and arrange clearance. I'll be leaving tonight instead of tomorrow morning.'

He made another brief phone call, hushed and urgent. And finally he rang Gideon.

'Gideon, old man, would you pop over to my office. Quick smart if you wouldn't mind. Something's cropped up. We need to have a bit of a chat.'

He replaced the receiver, took the Walther .32 from the top drawer of his desk and attached the silencer. Then, nursing the pistol out of sight on his lap, he leaned back in his chair and waited.

He didn't have to wait long. Several minutes later the familiar tap sounded on his office door.

'Come in,' he called, and Gideon appeared.

Harold continued to lounge in his chair, a picture of nonchalance, as Gideon carefully closed the door behind him. Gideon always took great care to ensure the door was firmly latched these days. And so he damn well should, Harold thought with a flash of annoyance. If he'd taken a little more care in the past they wouldn't be in this current predicament. In all fairness though, he couldn't place the entire blame on Gideon's shoulders. They'd both been slack.

'What's up?' Gideon asked as he turned to face Harold.

'Bit of a change in plans, I'm afraid. Take a seat, old man.'

Gideon sat in one of the two wicker chairs opposite the desk. 'What sort of –'

He didn't get any further as, in rapid succession, two bullets thumped into his heart.

Harold lowered the gun. In Gideon's eyes, was a puzzled look. *Why*, he seemed to be asking. *Why?*

'Sorry, old chap, no choice, I'm afraid. Can't take you with me, and you're a liability if I leave you here.'

But the eyes had clouded over. He was talking to a dead man.

Harold moved quickly. He cleared space in the large cupboard behind his desk, then he examined the body. There were two neat holes in the front of Gideon's jacket and, as he'd expected, no exit wounds. Good. No evidence of blood as yet, and if he laid the corpse on its back there would be little seepage. He dragged the body to the cupboard, piled it inside, checked the room for any telltale evidence, and, satisfied that all seemed in order, he closed the cupboard door. He had a flash of déjà vu as he did so. It was not the first time the cupboard had served such a purpose.

He put the Walther in his briefcase, locked both doors to his office, and minutes later he was in the Land Rover heading for the airport.

When he arrived, he was relieved to discover that the aircraft taking the journalists to Adelaide had departed, but irritated to learn that, although his RAF crew was standing by, it would be a further hour before the ground crew finished final checks on the de Havilland.

'We weren't expecting her to take off until tomorrow, you see, sir. She's all fuelled up, but we –'

'Yes, yes, quick as you can, man, quick as you can.'

Harold spent a very tense hour waiting. He had time to think now and he was feeling distinctly uneasy. What if the MPs had disobeyed his orders and spoken to the woman? What if she'd shown them the letter, the written proof that she'd said she had? He comforted himself with the thought that Ned was standing guard. Good old reliable Ned, he thought, loyal to the bitter end.

That was one thing he had to give the chap. Ned would die before he'd allow anyone to disobey the orders of Lord Dartleigh.

Nevertheless, as Harold sat in the small, near-deserted air terminal, his eyes kept flickering to the doors, expecting that any minute a storm of police may arrive.

It was dark by the time they took off, and when they were finally airborne he felt a sense of relief. His ordeal was very far from over, he knew, but being away from Maralinga was a start.

Ned was manfully holding the fort, just as Harold had supposed.

'I'll take the meals in,' he insisted. 'Lord Dartleigh's orders. No communication until he's interviewed them.' He'd said the same thing at least a dozen times by now.

The MPs were good-natured enough. They'd had to talk Ned into allowing the meals in the first place.

'The woman can't be flown back to Adelaide until tomorrow, mate,' Gus Oakley, the sergeant had said. 'They'll both be staying in the cells overnight and they have to be fed.'

Ned had given in, and the coppers had shared a smile. Ned Hanson's devotion to duty was considered a bit of a joke.

A policeman opened the door to the cell where Nick and Elizabeth were being held and Ned appeared with a tray, which he set down on the table.

'When you've eaten you'll be moved to another cell,' he said abruptly to Elizabeth, taking care to avoid eye contact. 'The bunk's being made up, you'll be staying the night.'

Then he left very quickly before either she or Colonel Stratton could get in a reply. To Ned the rules were abundantly clear. The issue of instructions did not qualify as communication; conversation in any form did.

The policeman raised an eyebrow at Nick as he closed the cell door.

'Welcome to army food,' Nick said, surveying the plates of stew and mashed potatoes.'

'It looks fine to me,' Elizabeth replied. 'I'm starving.' She picked up her fork and tucked into her meal. 'Much better than anything I could cook,' she admitted with absolute honesty.

Realising he was hungry, Nick also tucked in and they ate in silence. They'd said everything there was to say. He'd ranted a little to start with.

'You should have told me, Elizabeth!'

'If I had, you would have tried to stop me, wouldn't you?'

'Of course I would. It was a very dangerous thing to –'

'Besides, if I'd involved you in any way, you'd have been an accomplice, which would have landed you in a whole lot of trouble.'

'And I suppose this isn't a whole lot of trouble?' he said dryly, waving a hand at their surrounds.

'I'm sorry, Nick. I'm so sorry.' She felt wretched. 'I didn't know you were going to come charging to my rescue.'

'Nor did I.' He shrugged. 'It just happened somehow.'

'Is this a major dilemma? What will they do to you?'

'Well, decking a member of the military constabulary doesn't win you a promotion, put it that way.'

'But he seemed really nice about it, the sergeant.'

As the two MPs had taken them to the cells, Nick had apologised to the man he'd hit. He knew Gus Oakley well.

'I'm sorry, Sergeant, I don't know what came over me,' he'd said.

Gus had exchanged a knowing look with his mate. It wasn't half obvious there was something going on between Nick Stratton and the good-looking woman. Half his luck, their look had said.

Gus had accepted the apology with equanimity. 'You landed

483

a beauty, Colonel,' he'd replied, gingerly touching the side of his face that was sore, and Nick had apologised again.

When they'd arrived at the holding cell, Gus would have chatted on a little longer – he liked Nick and didn't give a stuff about Harold Dartleigh's orders – but Ned Hanson had turned up.

'Gus isn't the problem, Elizabeth,' Nick said. 'Harold Dartleigh is. Dartleigh will insist they throw the book at me, you can bet your last penny on it.'

The mere mention of Dartleigh's name had been enough to get Elizabeth going. 'Did you see the look in his eyes when I mentioned Gideon Melbray, Nick?'

'No, I was too busy looking at you. So was everyone else.'

'He was caught out. We were right. Gideon Melbray's MI6 too, they're working as a team . . .'

She was off and running again without a shred of proof, he thought. She really was amazing. 'Great,' he said, 'I'm glad we sorted that out.'

His cynicism was wasted on her.

'Which means MI6 killed Danny,' she concluded triumphantly. 'And I tell you what else, Nick. I believe it was Dartleigh himself who did the deed.'

'Because of the look in his eyes, I take it.' There was no mistaking his sarcasm this time.

'Yes,' she said with more than a touch of defiance, 'because of the look in his eyes, because of the way he overreacted, because of his whole manner. The man's entire reaction was one of guilt, surely you must agree.'

What a very female viewpoint, Nick thought. To his mind, Dartleigh's reaction had been absolutely in keeping with that of a man in a position of authority confronted by the gross flouting of top-security regulations. It would have been surprising had

Dartleigh acted in any other manner, he thought. But there didn't seem much point in telling her that.

'Whether I agree or not is incidental,' he said diplomatically. 'You still have to prove your case.'

That had successfully brought the conversation to a close, and now, as they ate their meals in silence, Elizabeth was a little subdued.

'Do you think if we ask him, the sergeant might let me stay here with you?'

'I hardly think so, Elizabeth, and if he did, Ned Hanson would have a heart attack. It might not look it, but this *is* a military prison, you know.'

'Oh. What a pity.'

She sounded forlorn, which for some strange reason gratified him.


Harold spent an anxious hour or so waiting as the de Havilland refuelled in Darwin. Again, he expected the arrival of police with orders for his arrest. He was not so much worried about the discovery of Gideon's body, which he considered safe for a day or so – no-one but he used the cupboard in his office. The woman, however, was a different matter. Had she talked?

But no incident occurred at Darwin airport and the de Havilland took off for its next fuel stop, Singapore. Having left Australia, Harold felt a degree safer, but time continued to be his enemy as they flew through the night. In the morning, when it became known that he'd left Maralinga, they would have to release the woman. He kept a watchful eye on the clock.

After refuelling in Singapore, as the aircraft set off en route for Bombay, Harold's fear became palpable. It would soon be morning, he thought. Any moment now they would radio through to the aircraft. Any moment now, a member of the RAF crew would point a gun at him and place him under arrest.

He lifted his briefcase onto his lap, unlatched it and slipped his hand inside. His fingers encircled the Walther and, as the minutes ticked by, he sat there waiting.

Ned Hanson sought out Harold Dartleigh first thing in the morning to ascertain his further instructions. He'd spent a sleepless night, most of it propped up in an office chair outside the holding cells until the duty officer had persuaded him to go back to his barracks with the absolute assurance that there would be 'no communication with the prisoners throughout the night'.

In the early morning, however, Ned could find no sign of Harold, either at his office or his barracks. Aware that Lord Dartleigh was to fly out that day, he rang the airport to check the time of his departure, although he knew it wasn't scheduled for several hours yet.

'Lord Dartleigh flew out last night,' he was informed.

'What? When?'

'Around 1900 hours,' the controller said. 'A last-minute change of plans. He had an urgent communiqué from London.'

Ned was utterly astounded. Why hadn't he been informed? What was he to do? Where were his orders?

Upon reporting the news to the military police, Ned was fortunately relieved of any further responsibility. The MPs informed Nick Stratton's superior officer, and the brigadier ordered the colonel's immediate release and return to duty. Personally, the brigadier considered the sooner the whole messy business was swept under the carpet the better, although he was exceedingly angry with Nick. He bawled him out in the privacy of his office.

'Assaulting a member of the rank and file – and in public, man! In front of the *press*, what's more. What the deuce possessed you!'

'I'm sorry, sir.'

'Fortunately Sergeant Oakley has no wish to press charges,' the brigadier said, 'which is just as well. This outrageous business of the woman being smuggled into Maralinga must be kept quiet at all costs. You say you're absolutely sure she's no risk?'

'Absolutely sure, sir. I can personally vouch for her, I promise.'

'Yes, yes, I'm quite sure you can.'

The brigadier gave a disapproving snort. Nick had admitted to having an affair with the journalist, which, in his view, was entirely improper. Thank God the Hoffmann woman's credentials were impeccable, he thought.

'Of course, I'm not so sure Lord Dartleigh will see eye to eye with you,' he continued sternly. 'If Dartleigh considers the woman a security risk she'll have to be investigated, in which case you may still have to answer for your untimely outburst, you do realise that?'

'Yes, sir, I do.'

'Now get yourself off to Adelaide. And at the conference, you're to stress to those members of the press who witnessed the fiasco that occurred here yesterday the vital importance of discretion in the interest of national security. I don't care how you do it. Seek them out individually if you must, but this story is not to see the light of day.'

'Yes, sir.'

Elizabeth was returned to Adelaide on the same flight, and Nick was surprised at how calm she was. He'd been surprised by her composure from the moment of their release. There'd been no protestation, no accusation. She hadn't attempted to explain her case to the brigadier or the MPs; she'd simply apologised for the trouble she'd caused. He had to admit that, at the time, he'd been grateful. It had certainly helped his own case.

'All right,' he said when they were safely airborne, 'what's going on?'

'What do you mean?'

'You had the perfect opportunity back there. Why didn't you put your argument to the brigadier?'

'Firstly, he wouldn't have believed me, and secondly, I don't have any proof.'

He looked at her askance. Neither reason seemed to have bothered her in the past.

'But mainly,' she continued, 'because I didn't feel the need.'

'Oh?'

'Dartleigh's doing it all for me, don't you see?' She turned to him, her eyes gleaming with excitement. 'Ned Hanson had no idea he'd gone. Dartleigh disappeared without even telling his own staff. That's the action of a guilty man. There was no communiqué from London. Harold Dartleigh's on the run, Nick. I've frightened him.'

Her excitement was contagious, and so now was her theory. Nick found himself tending to agree with her. Perhaps Dartleigh really was guilty, he thought, but if so, guilty of precisely what?

Harold couldn't believe his luck. They'd left Bombay hours ago and still no crew member had confronted him with the news of his arrest. At one stage he'd dozed off, his hand still resting in the briefcase on his lap. By now he'd been twenty hours without sleep. But he'd snapped wide awake as he'd felt the briefcase move. He'd clasped it tightly to him, his right hand clutching at the Walther inside.

'Sorry, sir,' the crew member had said. 'Didn't mean to disturb you; just thought I'd make you more comfortable.'

'Thank you, Lieutenant,' he'd heard himself say, as cool as a cucumber. 'How very kind of you, thank you.' He'd closed the briefcase and put it on the seat beside him. 'How soon do we arrive in Istanbul?'

'Four hours, sir.'

'Splendid. Radio ahead and book me into the Istanbul Hotel, will you, there's a good chap.'

From that moment on, Harold had started to relax – only a little though, not enough to let down his guard.

They landed in Istanbul, where they were to stay the night, just twenty-four hours after leaving Maralinga. It was shortly before midday and Harold caught a taxi directly to his hotel. The crew members were staying at the nearby RAF base, and everyone was to report to the airport at 0600 hours, one hour before the scheduled take-off for London at 0700.

The following morning, the crew members reported as ordered, but there was no sign of Harold Dartleigh. No-one worried; it was typical of the man's arrogance. But twenty minutes before departure time, when he still hadn't appeared, there was genuine cause for concern. They had a schedule that needed to be maintained. The flight lieutenant contacted the Istanbul Hotel and was informed that Lord Dartleigh had not checked in.

'We have a booking for him,' the desk clerk said, 'but he never arrived.'

Harold Dartleigh had disappeared without a word, leaving behind him a very confused RAF crew unable to explain his absence.

# Chapter Twenty-two

Several days passed and still there was no explanation offered for Harold Dartleigh's mysterious disappearance. Nick's far-reaching connections could come up with nothing, and when Elizabeth contacted Reginald Dempster in London, he too was confronted by a wall of silence.

'MI6 isn't giving out a word on the subject,' he said when he phoned her back. 'A strictly "no comment" response, I'm afraid.'

Always thorough in his investigations, however, Reg was able to offer the interesting news that Harold Dartleigh had not been sighted in his home area of Sussex, nor had he been seen at any of his regular London haunts.

'The chap seems to have vanished.'

Elizabeth, convinced that her bluff had proved successful, was delighted.

'They think I have proof, Nick,' she said, 'proof about the circumstances of Danny's death. They've secreted Dartleigh away somewhere. It's time to stir the pot.'

P. J. was more than happy to give Elizabeth's article front-page prominence. Why not? The subject matter appeared controversial in its suggestion, but the article simply reported the facts and was in no way libellous. Elizabeth's story was an editor's dream.

*MARALINGA MYSTERY*, was the eye-catching headline, and the subtitle beneath a picture of Harold Dartleigh read: *MI6 has questions to answer.*

The article, written by E. J. Hoffmann, who had gained quite a following amongst *The Advertiser*'s readers, stated that Harold Lord Dartleigh, deputy director of MI6, had mysteriously disappeared from the Maralinga atomic test site on 9 October. Lord Dartleigh had left no details of the reason for his abrupt departure, the article said, or of his intended destination. His on-site staff had not been informed, and it appeared no-one knew of his current whereabouts. MI6 was refusing to release any information.

Elizabeth then turned the piece into an indictment of MI6. Surely, she suggested, the British public had the right to demand accountability for the actions of one of its most senior public figures. She wrote of the historical ties between Britain and Australia and the strengthening of the bond the two countries shared through the post-war atomic test project, and closed the article with a direct challenge:

*Australia, too, as the host country for the British nuclear test program, has every right to insist upon answers from MI6. Why has such a key figure in our midst vanished without a trace and without giving any reason for his actions? This journalist, for one, demands an explanation.*

The E. J. Hoffmann article was picked up by other leading newspapers and syndicated throughout the country. Harold Dartleigh's disappearance became a major story in Australia, a fact which was quickly brought to the attention of the relevant authorities in Whitehall, but still there was no response from MI6.

Gideon Melbray's body was discovered three days later. He'd been reported missing by his workmates and barracks roommate for a whole week now, and it had been presumed he'd gone AWOL, although no-one could understand why. The discovery of his decaying body came as a shock to all.

Ned Hanson, who had duplicate keys to Harold Dartleigh's office, had unlocked the doors to allow the cleaners access. A putrid smell had instantly been detected, and the office cleaners had traced its source to the cupboard.

London was notified immediately and MI6 stated it would handle the murder investigation, then, in typical secret service fashion, refused offers of collaboration from all other relevant authorities, both British and Australian. Again no announcement was made and no information offered regarding Harold Dartleigh.

It was Elizabeth's article that eventually proved the catalyst. The editor of one of the more salacious London newspapers whose editor's eagle-eye constantly roamed the world for gossip, noted the Australian interest in Harold Dartleigh. Although Marty Falk considered the content of E. J. Hoffmann's article of no particular value, the disappearance of Lord Dartleigh of Somerston greatly interested him. A peer of the realm always made for good reading, particularly a peer of Dartleigh's stature.

The story appeared on the tabloid's front page exactly two weeks after Harold's disappearance. The headlines were lurid: *HIJINX IN THE PEERAGE! PEER OF THE REALM VANISHES! WIFE AND FAMILY DESERTED.*

Beneath were two photographs of Harold with a different beautiful woman in each, and beneath the photographs was the further headline: *THE BLONDE OR THE BRUNETTE – WHICH IS IT, LORD DARTLEIGH?*

A third and smaller photograph of Lavinia Dartleigh, impeccably groomed and dignified as always, was inset to one side. The actual content of the article was remarkably thin, Marty's principle being that carefully cropped photographs and headlines that insinuated were all that was necessary to provide the readers with what they wanted.

*Aspersions have been cast on the supposedly idyllic marriage of Harold Lord Dartleigh, 6th Baron Dartleigh of Somerston*, the article snidely read. *Apparently His Lordship disappeared a fortnight ago, abandoning his wife, well-known socialite and benefactress Lady Lavinia Dartleigh, without so much as a word. He's not been seen since and his whereabouts are unknown, but rumours abound. One can only presume that in deserting his marriage of over twenty years, Lord Dartleigh's latest affair is a little more serious than his previous peccadilloes.*

Upon reading the article, Lavinia Dartleigh was furious. How dare they portray her as the pathetic deserted wife, she thought. How dare they intimate her husband was a philanderer. *Previous peccadilloes* indeed! Harold had never once strayed throughout their marriage. As if she didn't have enough to contend with, she thought angrily, and she stormed out of the house.

Later that afternoon, upon returning from the local beautician and hairdresser, Lavinia found herself accosted by members of the press who'd travelled down from London. No sooner had she pulled up in the front courtyard and stepped out of her car than reporters and photographers appeared, apparently from nowhere.

They'd actually been waiting for some time, but had kept themselves well hidden for fear she'd drive off upon seeing them. Now they emerged like magic from behind bushes and shrubs and conifers in stone tubs to surround her, camera shutters clicking and questions firing.

As always when sensing a major story, the general press had moved with startling speed. Having been alerted to the fact that Harold Dartleigh had vanished, they'd swooped upon MI6, but had been unable to glean any information whatsoever. 'No comment' had been the terse reply to all queries. The reporters were not to be fobbed off, however. The disappearance of the deputy director of MI6 was big news and the press had every intention of getting the story by whatever means possible, including the harassment of Dartleigh's wife.

'What can you tell us about your husband's disappearance, Lady Dartleigh?'

'Is there another woman involved as rumoured?'

'Has he left the country?'

'Why has there been no statement to the press?'

Alerted by the commotion, the domestic staff appeared on the scene. The housekeeper stepped out onto the porch glowering forbiddingly, the cook and the maid peered through the front windows, and Wilson, the butler, strode into the courtyard waving an imperious hand at the reporters, bent on rescuing his mistress.

But Lavinia did not need rescuing.

'I'll tell you about my husband's disappearance,' she screamed at the top of her voice. 'I'll tell you about the bastard I married!'

The past month had been altogether too much for Lavinia. She'd had enough. She would tell her story and MI6 could go to hell.

The banner headlines shocked the world. Splashed across a photograph of Harold Dartleigh was the single word *TRAITOR*, and in bold black letters beneath the picture: *DEPUTY DIRECT-OR OF MI6 A RUSSIAN SPY.*

The story that followed was brief. As yet, little specific data had been made available to the press.

*The British secret service community is in a state of shock this morn-ing with allegations that Harold Lord Dartleigh, 6th Baron Dartleigh of Somerston and deputy director of MI6, has been identified as a Russian spy. The allegations, made by his wife, Lady Lavinia Dartleigh, came to light when Lord Dartleigh's recent disappearance was investigated by the press.*

*Buckingham Palace, MI6 and New Scotland Yard have all declined to comment on the matter. However, the Palace has informed us that an announcement will be made later today.*

*Lady Dartleigh stated that she has been interviewed and relentlessly harassed by MI6 personnel for the past four weeks. She knew nothing of Lord Dartleigh's activities, she says, and the threat of her title being revoked owing to the treasonous acts committed by her husband has proved the final straw.*

'Hell hath no fury . . .' Harold murmured. He put down the newspaper and gazed out his apartment window at the Moskva River. Naturally Lavinia felt betrayed. Poor dear, he thought. His peerage would most certainly be revoked, and she would so hate being plain Mrs Dartleigh. She'd probably abandon his name altogether and revert to her own highly respectable maiden name in an attempt to avoid any association with the traitorous creature who had been her husband. Harold won-dered if his children would do the same. Yes, he thought, Nigel undoubtedly would. But Catherine, surprisingly enough, might not. Catherine was a rebel who didn't care tuppence for public opinion. That was what had so annoyed him about his daughter, he recalled – her steadfast refusal to conform. So dangerous for a man in his position to have adverse attention directed towards members of his family. But who knows, he now wondered. Perhaps Catherine and her arty friends in Paris were communists. Many of the artistic community were. Perhaps his daughter might even understand.

Harold did not consider himself a traitor at all. He considered himself a soldier in a war against injustice. Far more than a soldier, in fact: he was a leader paving the way for a new world order. There were those born to lead and those born to be led and, like any great movement, communism needed leaders. Harold Dartleigh considered himself the perfect man for the job. He always had.

Harold had embraced communism at Cambridge University, along with Guy Burgess and Donald Maclean and others of his *alma mater* who'd been stimulated by the exchange of ideas and philosophies. The passionate intellectual bonding between young men was heady stuff, particularly to Harold, an only child who'd led an indulged but empty existence. Communism had also served as a form of private rebellion against a father whose apathy and weakness of character he'd despised. Harold had needed a purpose and commitment in his life, and communism had provided both. He'd joined the Party, readily accepting the ideals of those who believed wealth and position should be earned and that people should share equally in the benefits of national prosperity. Given his privileged background, his zeal had surprised some of his fellow Party members.

Harold had never applied the principles of communism directly to himself, however. There'd been no need to. He'd far better served the cause by continuing to live a life of luxury. The power and privilege of his position was not only advantageous to the Party, but, in the eyes of his employer, the Komitet Gosudarstvennoi Bezopasnosti, it provided the perfect camouflage. The KGB was unrelenting in its insistence that its operatives maintain appearances. Even Harold's marriage to Lavinia had been arranged for the purpose of camouflage. He'd become genuinely fond of her, he had to admit, although at the time he would far rather have married Aline, a Lebanese girl he'd fallen desperately in love with while serving at the British embassy in Beirut. But Aline hadn't at all fitted the required image.

Harold had been a first-class spy. He'd delivered high-level documentation and intelligence on all manner of subjects that the British and American governments had believed were top secret, but he was particularly proud of his recruitment of Gideon Melbray to the cause of world communism.

When the two had met in Washington, Harold hadn't been able to believe his luck. Gideon Melbray was perfect material. He spoke four languages, including Russian, as indeed did Harold, and there was the added bonus of his beauty. Their brief mutual infatuation had made the conversion easy.

When Harold had finally been offered the deputy director-ship of MI6, he'd been elated by the power such a position afforded him. He'd been elated too by the recruitment of his comrade-in-arms, Gideon Melbray. His only regret had been the necessity to temper the ardour of the relationship they'd shared in their Washington days. Sexual dalliances were one of the very few luxuries Harold denied himself. A man in his position could not afford to be caught out.

For twenty long years, Harold Dartleigh had served the Party, a passionate and committed communist devoted to the cause in which he truly believed. For twenty long years, he'd also led the life of the seriously wealthy, with country estates, servants at his beck and call and every whim indulged. Harold had always had the best of both worlds.

Not any more, he thought as he gazed out at the majesty of the Moskva River. The view from his rented two-bedroom flat on Kutuzovsky Prospekt was quite spectacular and he knew he should be grateful for the fact. There were many who lived in community blocks with no outlook at all. But the apartment was poky and cold, and already he ached for the beauty of Sussex and the warmth and comfort of his country house. He would miss his baronial estate and his lifestyle and his family. He'd always known they were the price he would possibly have to pay, but he hadn't expected the change to be quite so radical. He'd expected more of a hero's welcome. Indeed, he'd anticipated that, if and when the time came, his arrival in Moscow would be heralded as a triumph for the Comintern; he was, after all, a genuine British aristocrat who had defected to his beloved Mother Russia. Surely the Kremlin propaganda unit would wish to make an example of such devotion. Surely he would be offered a highly respected consultancy position within the KGB.

He now realised, however, that, like Guy Burgess and Donald Maclean, both of whom had defected in 1951, he was to be largely ignored and forgotten. Already he'd been assigned to the Government Translation Unit where he worked long hours in the bowels of a nondescript office building. The life he was destined to lead would be a sad one, surrounded by former fellow spies, expatriates who met in bars along the Bersenevskaya Embankment and talked of 'home', wherever that may have been, whilst assuring each other that their treason was excusable because they were seeking to make a better world.

Harold considered such men pathetic. He should not be subjected to the same treatment. He deserved more; he was better than the others. The KGB had never had a spy of his stature in British society. Well, no, that wasn't altogether true, he had to admit. It was rumoured there were a number in high circles, one with royal connections no less, and there were many who had successfully infiltrated the system at high levels. Kim Philby, for example – he was sure that Philby was working for the cause. He couldn't be absolutely certain, of course – operatives never got to know who was who – but it was comforting to think there were others of his ilk still in place, still carrying on the good fight.

Despite treatment that he considered unfair, Harold's belief in the cause remained unshaken. He could neither dismiss nor regret an indoctrination that spanned over twenty years. To do so would be to deny his reason for living. Besides, he was fully aware of why the KGB had hidden him away. The KGB knew what the world would soon know.

He looked down at the newspaper on the table before him, at the headline that screamed 'Traitor!' This was only the beginning, he thought. Now that Lavinia had let the cat out of the bag, MI6 would be forced to admit the truth, and every gruesome detail would be spewed forth by media all over the world. He'd be labelled 'murderer' as well as 'traitor', a title which, strangely enough, he found far harder to bear.

Harold knew that Gideon's murder was why the Kremlin had not given him a hero's welcome. The KGB understood the necessity for Gideon's termination, but once the world found out – and the world was bound to find out – the Russian government must not appear to sanction such an act. The moment Harold had pulled that trigger he had destined himself to a life of obscurity.

Personally he felt no guilt at all about Gideon's death. Gideon Melbray had been a casualty of war. It had been his duty to kill Gideon rather than risk exposure. He would have killed himself too had it been necessary. He'd had the Walther at the ready for that very purpose.

In his twenty-year service as a spy, Harold regretted nothing. Not the betrayal of his country, not the desertion of his wife and family, not the necessary killing of Gideon Melbray. But there was one act that rested a little upon his conscience, simply because it had resulted from slack behaviour on his part. He'd tried to blame Gideon, who was so often cavalier in his attitude to their work, but he knew that he was equally to blame.

Harold felt guilty about young Dan Gardiner.

He recalled the trip they'd made to Ceduna, how he'd promised the lad he'd make enquiries into Pete Mitchell's death. 'Don't you worry,' he'd said, 'we'll get to the bottom of this. Nothing goes on around Maralinga that I don't know about or can't find out.'

And he had found out. A quick bribe to the fettler had provided the truth. But he'd found out for himself rather than the lad. If by any chance the army had killed Pete Mitchell as young Dan had feared, then Harold had wanted to know why. And that was where the problem had occurred. Once he'd satisfied his own curiosity, he'd forgotten all about his promise to the boy. 'You pop into my office in a few days and I'll let you know what I've come up with,' he'd said. But he'd forgotten that he'd said it. And that had cost young Dan his life.

Harold could not forget the look in the lad's eyes as they'd met his. Try as he might, he'd found that look strangely difficult to dismiss from the recesses of his mind.

Gideon had admitted later that he hadn't latched the door. It must have swung open automatically when young Dan knocked, they'd both agreed, because he would most certainly have knocked. They obviously hadn't heard him, either of them. They'd been caught off guard. It had been midway through the second meal shift, Ned had gone to lunch, the whole building had been virtually deserted, and they hadn't given a second thought to unexpected visitors. None of which was a valid excuse for his own appalling complacency, Harold thought. It wasn't the first time he'd been slack either; he'd allowed Gideon to file reports from his office on a number of occasions. Maralinga had lulled them both into a false sense of security. Stuck out there in the middle of that Godforsaken desert they'd thought they were inviolate. Harold had cursed Gideon for not locking the door, but he'd cursed himself too. They'd both killed the boy.

Gideon had been talking on the telephone, he remembered, and he'd been lounging in the corner of the office listening to the conversation, nodding his approval of each point Gideon made. They'd been looking at each other and neither of them had seen the door swing open. By the time they had, it had been too late. The boy had been standing there in a state of stupefaction.

The scene young Dan had encountered must certainly have amazed him, Harold thought. Gideon had been sitting behind Harold's desk, talking on the scrambler phone that was the exclusive reserve of the deputy director of MI6. And he'd been talking in Russian.

The boy hadn't noticed him lounging in the corner. The boy had had eyes for no-one but Gideon. Harold had to give young Dan top marks for guts: he hadn't turned tail and fled; which had been just as well for them really. Instead, he'd confronted Gideon.

'What the hell do you think you're doing?' he'd demanded, by which time Gideon had been on his feet and already circling the desk.

Harold had given the order to kill. He'd had no alternative. '*Ubeite yego*,' he'd said.

In that instant the boy's eyes had met his. And that was the look Harold could not forget.

In one swift action Gideon had smashed the heel of his right hand upwards with brutal force, spearing Daniel's nose cartilage into the brain. Death had been instantaneous.

They'd hidden the body in the large office cupboard where it had stayed until the workers had left for the day. Gideon had returned in a supply truck that evening – nobody had noticed anything unusual about Gideon Melbray transporting equipment and supplies – and, when it was dark, Harold and Gideon had driven out to the bomb site in separate vehicles and left the corpse there in the Land Rover. The detonation of Breakaway had done the rest.

For close on a year now, Harold hadn't given much thought to young Dan. It was true that on the odd occasion when he had, the look in the boy's eyes, strangely etched in his memory as it was, brought with it a twinge of guilt at the unnecessary waste of a young life. But it had happened and there was no point in dwelling on the fact. Since his defection, however, young Dan had been constantly on his mind, which was hardly surprising. The boy's death had proved his undoing.

Following the knee-jerk reaction to his discovery, Harold's entire concentration had been upon self-preservation. In fleeing Australia he'd had no time to reflect on the finer points of exactly how it was he and Gideon had been detected. Even when he'd arrived in Istanbul to be met by his case controller, he had not felt safe. The process of secreting him across the border into Russia had still been fraught with danger. Throughout his entire flight for freedom, Harold's one and only thought had been that of survival.

But following his arrival in Moscow, he'd had all the time in the world for reflection, as he would have for the rest of his life. It was plainly clear that Daniel Gardiner had not discovered the truth and written of it to his fiancée, as she had so boldly stated at the Maralinga debriefing. How could he possibly have done so? Daniel Gardiner had not known the truth until only seconds before his death.

The look in the boy's eyes would now haunt Harold with more than guilt over the waste of a young life, for the look in the boy's eyes told him that Elizabeth Hoffmann had been bluffing. She'd had no proof at all, he thought. Not that it would have made any difference if she had – the woman had been about to expose him as a spy, and he could have taken no course of action other than the one he'd chosen. But how in God's name had she known, he asked himself yet again. How in God's name had Elizabeth Hoffmann known he was a spy? Harold would go to his grave wondering.

'He actually thought I knew,' Elizabeth said. 'Isn't that amazing? I still can't believe it. He actually thought I knew he was a spy.'

'The perfect bluff,' Nick replied. 'Poor old Dartleigh showed his hand unnecessarily. Excellent poker play, Elizabeth, well done.'

'It would have been the perfect bluff if I'd known what I was doing,' she agreed. 'More like luck, I'd say.'

'More like sheer arse, I'd say.'

They were walking along the beach at Glenelg in their bathing costumes. The mid-November sun was unseasonably warm and, as it was a weekend, a number of sun worshippers were sprawled out on the sand working on their pre-summer tans.

Since the announcement of Harold Dartleigh's defection, the world press had gone mad. The full story had been released, and news of Gideon Melbray's murder had quickly been followed by the revelation that he too had been a spy. Nick and

Elizabeth had discussed the ramifications of the whole intrigue and had agreed that everything pointed to the fact that Harold Dartleigh had killed Daniel, possibly with the assistance of Gideon Melbray. In any event, the two had been in collusion. Both had given witness to Daniel's state of depression, and it had been principally their word that had confirmed the verdict of suicide.

'Supposition again,' Nick had said as they'd sat on her balcony surrounded by newspapers. 'There's no way we can prove any of this, you know.'

'Why would they kill Danny, I wonder? Do you think he found out?'

'Oh, I'd say he did, yes, most certainly. But it's something you'll never know, Elizabeth. Are you content to leave it at that?'

'Yes, I am. As you say, we've no proof, and it's best for the family that Danny's death remains the accident it was reported to be. All I ever wanted was the truth. I'm happy with that.'

Now, as they walked together beside the water's edge, Elizabeth felt a sense of completion.

'It wasn't bluff or luck, Nick,' she said. 'Nor was it, to quote your colourful turn of phrase, "sheer arse". It was Danny. Danny wrote the letter that set the whole thing in motion. It was Danny who exposed Harold Dartleigh and Gideon Melbray as spies.'

'You're right,' he agreed. He was glad for her. She needed to know that Daniel hadn't died in vain. 'Let's sit down, shall we?'

They sat on the sand and looked out at the ocean, both lapsing into silence. Elizabeth's mind was blissfully blank, but Nick was wondering where to from here.

'So what are your plans?' he asked as casually as he could. 'Will you be going back to London?'

She sensed the underlying tension in his query and glanced at him, but he was staring resolutely out to sea, giving away nothing. She wondered if he would ever actually tell her he loved her, but it didn't really matter.

'Good heavens above, no,' she said. 'I'm not leaving Australia until I can swim really well. And that means a lot of lessons – it could take some time.'

He turned to her, but she ignored him and stared out to sea. Two could play at that game.

'Besides,' she added, 'the Cold War can't last forever. Someone's going to have to write an exposé about Maralinga some day. And I intend that someone to be me.'

She spoke lightly, but he knew she was serious. Life was not going to be easy, he thought, but he didn't expect it to be with Elizabeth around.

*1984*

*Matilda and Violet are Kokatha girls. They are cousins
and have grown up together – they are thirteen years old
now. Their families live in Ceduna where the girls go to
school. Tilly and Vi are very best friends. They share
everything they own, although the balance is not really
equal for Tilly has things Vi's family can't afford. Tilly's
father is employed by the state railways and makes more
money than his brother who is a farm labourer.*

*Today is a very exciting day for the girls. Their
mothers and other women of their extended family
group have called a meeting of the clan. Word has
spread far and wide over the past two weeks – the
women will gather at the Yari Miller Hostel in Ceduna
to welcome a new family member. The hostel, designed
to accommodate itinerant workers, is a common meeting place and those who have travelled into town from
Tarcoola and Yalata will stay the night. Twenty or
more women and children are now gathered in the
hostel's central courtyard. There would be a far greater
number if the family's men and youths were in attendance, but such a gathering is considered women's
business. Besides, the men have more important things
to discuss. They are forming a council and gathering
information to be presented to the Royal Commission
next year. The commission is to investigate the damage
caused by the Maralinga experiments.*

*As the women's group waits a number of little boys play raucously around them, but amongst the women themselves, some sitting on benches, others squatting on the ground nursing young ones, there is a feeling of quiet expectation. This is a momentous day for all present, and for a variety of reasons.*

*For Tilly and Vi, this is the day they will meet Delaney Wynton.*

*Delaney Wynton is their idol. They play her albums endlessly on Tilly's cassette player and know the lyrics of every single song off by heart. She is an inspiration to them both, but most particularly to Tilly. Tilly writes songs and can play the guitar, and has determined that she too will be a famous singer one day, just like Delaney Wynton. After all, Delaney Wynton is one of their mob, and if one of their mob can make it, then why shouldn't she? Tilly is very ambitious.*

*The women, too, are impressed by Delaney Wynton's fame, but she symbolises far more than one of their own who has achieved success in a white man's world. Delaney Wynton symbolises triumph over a fearful time in the lives of the Kokatha, and in the lives of the Pitjantjatjara and the Yankuntjatjara and many others who people the lands of the great southern desert. She symbolises triumph over a time when some amongst them were blinded or suffered mysterious illnesses, when men died prematurely, when women were rendered infertile or gave birth to stillborn babies. Many still suffer the consequences of those fearful times, and their stories will be heard at the Royal Commission. But Delaney Wynton, who was born in the very midst of the mayhem, has lived to become a symbol of survival.*

*For the women present, this is the day they will welcome Etta's child, the miracle baby of Maralinga who has traced her family and returned to meet her people.*

*A taxi pulls up outside the hostel where Tilly's and Vi's mothers are waiting to greet Delaney. She has flown from Adelaide and will be staying overnight at the Ceduna Community Hotel, but she has travelled directly from the airport to the gathering.*

*The two women welcome her, Vi's mother with a formal handshake.*

*'Hello, I'm Ada,' she says. 'Welcome to Ceduna.'*

*Tilly's mother is less inhibited. Tilly's mother is the undisputed matriarch of the extended family group and considers it her responsibility to set the ground rules.*

*'I'm Vonnie,' she says. 'Welcome to the family, Delaney.' And she gathers the young woman to her ample bosom in an embrace.*

*It is a wise move, breaking through any awkwardness or self-consciousness Delaney might have felt. She returns the hug warmly.*

*'I'm Del,' she says and she smiles her beautiful smile. Like her mother before her, Delaney is a pretty woman.*

*'Come on inside and meet the mob, Del.'*

*Vonnie picks up Delaney's overnight bag and she and Ada usher the young woman into the courtyard where those gathered wait, respectfully silent.*

*Tilly and Vi stifle a longing to squeal and run to their idol with their cassette covers all ready to be signed; their mothers have warned them to wait their turn. Protocol must be observed. Delaney is to meet the women first, and most particularly the one who is closest to her, the sole remaining member of her direct family. The girls squirm with impatience. They've watched Delaney on* Countdown *and she's even prettier in the flesh than she is on television.*

*Vonnie beckons forward the first person who is to be introduced. Bibi is a shy woman in her early forties, plainly in awe of meeting Delaney and uncomfortable at being the focus of attention.*

*'This is Bibi.' As always, Vonnie gets straight to the point. 'Bibi's your auntie. Etta was her sister.'*

*Delaney Wynton is moved, everyone can see it. 'You are my mother's sister?' she asks. She speaks softly, but her voice is clear and all can hear her.*

*Bibi nods self-consciously, twisting the thin cotton fabric of her frock between her fingers as she looks down at her bare feet. She has travelled all the way from Yalata with her cousin and her cousin's family just for this moment. But now that it's come, she doesn't know what to say.*

*'Say hello to Del,' Vonnie urges heartily. Vonnie can be bossy at times, but usually with the right motives. 'Come on, Bibi, don't be shy, she's your niece.'*

*'Hello, Del,' Bibi whispers obediently.*

*'Hello, Bibi.'*

*Delaney takes her aunt's hands in both of hers and Bibi looks up. Their eyes meet and as Del smiles, Bibi cannot help but respond. She sees her sister in that smile. She'd been twelve years old when Etta had disappeared. Bibi had loved her big sister.*

*As the two women embrace, Vonnie leads a round of applause.*

*The more formal part of the proceedings is quickly over. The senior women amongst the group are introduced one by one, a hug is shared with each, then the younger women gather for more hugs, and then it is the children's turn.*

*Tilly and Vi lead the troop of children that surrounds Delaney. She personally signs the girls' cassette covers To Tilly and Vi, as they request.*

*'Are you sisters?' she asks.*

*'No, we're cousins,' Tilly says, 'and we're best friends.'*

*'Tilly's going to be a famous singer, like you,' Vi adds. 'She writes her own songs too, just like you do.'*

*'Sing us a song, Del,' Tilly says, and the other children take up the chant. 'Sing us a song, Del. Sing us a song.'*

*But Del is apologetic. 'I don't have my guitar,' she says.*

*'I got a guitar.' Tilly disappears to return only moments later with the second-hand guitar her father bought her. 'It's tuned up good.' She hands it to Del.*

*Del strums a few chords. 'Yes, it is,' she agrees.*

*'Sing "Don't Look Back",' Tilly begs, referring to Del's latest hit. Del had sung it just the other night on* Countdown.

*'No, I'll sing a song you haven't heard before,' Del says. 'A song I wrote a long time ago, when I was around your age, Tilly.'*

*She addresses the entire gathering. 'This is a song about family,' she says. 'I knew that one day I would*

510

*find you. I was twelve when I wrote this, and I was thinking of you.'*

*She rests her foot on a bench and prepares to play. The children gather about her, squatting on the ground, hugging their knees, their eyes bright with anticipation.*

*'When I was a little girl growing up in Adelaide,' she says, 'I learned about the stars of the Southern Cross – the five that form the cross and the two that point the way. Seven stars in all. This is my song.'*

*She plays the introduction arpeggio, her fingers expertly picking out each note of a pretty melody. Then she starts to sing:*

'Whenever I'm down, when I'm feeling low
When the world spins too fast and the time goes
   too slow
I wait for the evening stars to appear
And seek out the seven that glitter so clear . . .'

*She sings without artifice, a natural voice, warm and pure.*

'For I know that my family sees those same stars
And all of us wonder where each of us are
And each of us sends all the others our love
As each of us watches those same stars above . . .'

*The gathering is enraptured. The courtyard is hushed. Even the youngest and most raucous of the little boys is silent.*

*Delaney reaches the end of the verse. The tempo of the song builds, and as she embarks upon the chorus she encourages the children to clap along. She no longer plays arpeggio, the chords are strong now, and her voice rises to match their strength.*

'I clap clap my hands, shake the dust from the land
And smile up at the stars as I dance in the sand
For I am a child of the great universe
Who cannot be humbled and will not be cursed . . .'

*The power in her voice is compelling. The song has become defiant. It is a celebration as she sings to the stars.*

'My star family's with me wherever I go
And we dance to the rhythms of long long ago . . .'

*Everyone present has joined in now. They are stamping their feet and clapping to the rhythm, infected by the strength and joy of the song. When finally it comes to its resounding conclusion, there is huge applause.*

*Tilly wants to know why Del's never recorded the song. 'I reckon it's one of your best songs ever,' she says.*

*'No,' Del replies, 'it's a private song, a family song. It's just for us.'*

*'What's it called?'*

*'"The Song of the Seven Stars".'*

*'It'd come in at number one, I'll bet,' Tilly says.*

# Regarding Maralinga

The British army packed up and went home in 1962. An attempt was made to decontaminate the area, but it was ineffectual. Maralinga closed in 1967, and the site was left to fester in the eternal silence of the desert.

During the years that followed, growing concerns about the safety standards observed during the conducting of the nuclear trials and the disposal of radioactive substances and toxic materials began to snowball. By the 1980s, British and Australian servicemen and traditional Aboriginal owners of the land were suffering blindness, sores and illnesses such as cancer. Groups including the Atomic Veterans Association and the Pitjantjatjara Council pressured the government until, in 1984, it agreed to hold a royal commission to investigate the damage that had been caused.

The McClelland Royal Commission into the tests delivered its report in 1985 and found that significant radiation hazards still existed at many of the Maralinga test areas. It recommended another clean-up, which was completed in 2000 at a cost of $108 million.

During the proceedings, local Indigenous people claimed

they were poisoned by the tests. The McClelland Commission could find no evidence of this. However, in 1994, the Australian government paid compensation amounting to $13.5 million to the Maralinga Tjarutja people in settlement of all claims relating to nuclear testing.

The Commission did find that some British and Australian servicemen were purposely exposed to fallout from the blasts. With regard to these health and welfare matters, an Australian Department of Veterans' Affairs study concluded that 'overall the doses received by Australian participants were small . . . Only two per cent of participants received more than the current Australian annual dose limit for occupationally exposed persons (20 mSv).'

However, these findings were contested by the Atomic Ex-Serviceman's Association, which claimed that out of 10,700 personnel who worked in the area over a ten-year period in the 1950s and 1960s there were over 9,000 persons who had died by 2005 and approximately 75–80 per cent of those deaths were from cancer.

On 6 June 2009 (ironically the anniversary of the D-Day Invasion in 1944) approximately 1,000 ex-servicemen from Australia, New Zealand, Fiji and Britain who were involved in nuclear tests during the 1950s finally won the right to sue the British government over health problems they blame on radiation.

It is to be hoped the British High Court decision will force the Australian Federal government to finally recognise health and welfare claims by Australian veterans.

Despite the governments of Australia and the UK paying for two decontamination programs, concerns have been expressed that some areas of the Maralinga test sites are still contaminated.

# Acknowledgements

Love and thanks as always to my husband, Bruce Venables. My thanks also to those family and friends who continue to offer both encouragement and practical assistance: big brother Rob Nunn, Sue Greaves, Susan Mackie-Hookway, Michael Roberts, Colin Julin and my agent, James Laurie. A big thanks to all the hard-working team at Random House, most particularly to Brandon VanOver for his creative support.

For assistance in the research of this book I am indebted to many, but first and foremost my thanks must go to Leon and Dianne Ashton, who, as on-site managers of Maralinga, offered Bruce and me such a warm welcome and gave so generously of their time and knowledge. Thank you also to David Johns, who granted government approval for our visit to the site, and to the Maralinga Tjarutja, who allowed us to travel their lands.

A big thank you to all those wonderfully helpful people I met during my research trip: from Ceduna Library, Julie Sim (and husband Bob, whose hand-drawn map was of inestimable value), Chris Blums and Meralyn Stevens; from Ceduna Aboriginal Arts & Culture Centre, Pam Diment and Sue Andrasic; Allan Lowe from the Ceduna Museum; Tanya and

Andrea from the Maralinga Tjarutja Land Council Office; Patricia Gunter; Des Whitmarsh; the friendly staff at the Ceduna Foreshore Hotel and many others from the highly hospitable township of Ceduna. Thanks also to June Noble and Dick Kimber of Alice Springs.

Among my research sources, I would like to recognise the following:

*Fields of Thunder*, Denys Blakeway and Sue Lloyd-Roberts, Allen & Unwin (Publishers) Ltd, 1985.

*Field of Thunder: the Maralinga Story*, written and researched by Judy Wilks, with Rolf Heimann (Art), Nic Thieberger and Richard Watts (Graphics), Friends of the Earth, 1981.

*Maralinga: Australia's Nuclear Waste Cover-up*, Alan Parkinson, ABC Books, 2007.

*A Political Inconvenience*, Tim Sherratt, Historical Records of Australian Science, 1985.

*Fallout: Hedley Marston and the British Bomb Tests in Australia*, Roger Cross, Wakefield Press, 2001.

*Maralinga's Afterlife*, John Keane, professor of politics, Centre for the Study of Democracy, University of Westminster, London, *The Age* Company Ltd, 2003.

*A Toxic Legacy: British Nuclear Weapons Testing in Australia*, published in *Wayward Governance: Illegality and Its Control in the Public Sector*, P. N. Grabosky, Canberra, Australian Institute of Criminology, 1989.

*I'm the One That Know This Country!: the Story of Jessie Lennon and Coober Pedy*, Aboriginal Studies Press for the Australian Institute of Aboriginal and Torres Strait Islander Studies, 2000.

*The View Across the Bay*, Sue Trewartha, published by Ceduna Community Hotel, 1999.

*Broken Song: T. G. H. Strehlow and Aboriginal Possession*, Barry Hill, Random House Australia Pty Ltd, 2002.